I0576991

Richard H. Wilmer, Florence J. O'Connor

The Heroine of the Confederacy

Truth and Justice

Richard H. Wilmer, Florence J. O'Connor

The Heroine of the Confederacy
Truth and Justice

ISBN/EAN: 9783337195571

Printed in Europe, USA, Canada, Australia, Japan

Cover: Foto ©Andreas Hilbeck / pixelio.de

More available books at **www.hansebooks.com**

THE

HEROINE OF THE CONFEDERACY;

OR,

TRUTH AND JUSTICE.

THE

HEROINE OF THE CONFEDERACY;

OR,

TRUTH AND JUSTICE.

BY

MISS FLORENCE J. O'CONNOR.

"We understand any epoch of the world but ill if we do not examine its romance; there is as much truth in the poetry of life as in its prose."

Preface to the Last Days of Pompeii.

LONDON:

HARRISON, 59, PALL MALL.

1865.

LONDON :
PRINTED BY HARRISON AND SONS, ST. MARTIN'S LANE.

WITH FEELINGS OF

ADMIRATION AND ESTEEM

THIS VOLUME

IS

D E D I C A T E D

TO

T H E   H E R O   O F   B E L M O N T

(Col. Robert H. Barrow),

BY

THE AUTHORESS.

PREFACE.

" Nothing extenuate, nor set down aught in malice."

EVERY reader of history is fully aware that much of the material which guides the opinion of posterity is derived from memoirs, the writers of which little fancied they would ever see publicity, and from private letters, penned in all the confidence of friendship. Necessarily there must be· much in the every-day life of a people which escapes the chronicler, however acute.

The war which is raging between the Federal and Confederate States has been, and I believe still continues to be, a subject of interest throughout the civilized world, and though much has been published by the extensive press of the Federal Union, as well as by correspondence in European journals, there still remains sufficient matter for the employment of the historian, or novelist. I have not presumed to penetrate into explanations which may be unknown for half a century, but I would say that the contents of this work may cast some light on many minor points, which in their own way may be co-relative with weightier evidence. I have followed with faithful and untiring zeal the progress of the strife between North and South, and treasured up in the storehouse of memory every incident worthy of record, from the fall of Fort Sumter up to the present date. Thus, knowing much of the tone of feeling in the various portions of the South, I believe I am justified in drawing inferences of the thoughts, hopes, and aspirations of the interior life of those who dwelt there, and have deemed that I have not inappropriately woven a connected chain (the results of my observations and experience), which I most respectfully present to the public.

THE HEROINE OF THE CONFEDERACY;

OR,

TRUTH AND JUSTICE.

———•———

CHAPTER I.

O, THE SWEET SOUTH.

By W. GILMORE SIMMS.

O, the sweet South! the sunny, sunny South!
Land of true feeling, land for ever mine!
I drink the kisses of her rosy mouth
And my heart swells as with a draught of wine,
She brings me blessings of maternal love;
I have her smile which hallows all my toil;
Her voice persuades, her generous smiles approve,
She sings me from the sky and from the soil!
O, by her lonely pines that wave and sigh!
O, by her myriad flowers that bloom and fade!
By all the thousand beauties of her sky,
And the sweet solace of her forest shade,
   She's mine—she's ever mine—
   Nor will I aught resign
Of what she gives me mortal or divine;
   Will sooner part
   With life, hope, heart—
Will die—before I fly.

O ! love is hers—such love as ever glows
In souls where leap affection's living tide ;
She is all fondness to her friends—to her foes
She glows a thing of passion, strength and pride ;
She feels no tremors when the danger's nigh
But the fight over and the victory won,
How, with strange fondness turns her loving eye
In tearful welcome on each gallant son !
O, by her virtues of the cherished past—
By all her hopes of what the future brings—
I glory that my lot with her is cast,
And my soul flushes and exulting sings—
       She's mine—she's ever mine—
       For her will I resign
All precious things—all placed upon her shrine ;
       Will freely part
       With life, hope, heart—
     Will die—do aught but fly !

AT the time this story begins, there was situated, a few miles below the city of New Orleans, a magnificent chateau, on a large and extensive sugar plantation. In front swept the bold Mississippi, bearing on its bosom the mighty ship freighted with cotton or sugar, or the lighter craft of some Cuban Dago, returning to his island home after his sale of fruits. Ships and vessels of all nations were plying the river, and the hum of voices and song of the sailor were heard at all hours, night and day. In the rear of the building lay, for miles in extent, the cane fields, whose verdure and undulations in the wind resembled a heaving sea of emerald. Here and there were seen the sturdy negroes, as they worked at their daily labour, and in the background their cabins, at whose door, after their tasks were completed, they assembled to dance by the light of the moon or stars, to the sound of the all-inspiring "banjo." All spoke of happiness and repose, as well as of industry. The interior of this Southern home was not the less inviting than its exterior; it was built in a square form, intersected by halls of polished marble, and on either side were beautifully carved doors, entering upon suites of apartments, which an inhabitant of the Orient might feel rich in possessing. Statuettes lined the halls, and filled the niches of doors and windows, while little Dryads were seen peering from the richly wrought leaves of the carved staircase, which led to the upper apartments of the building. Everything bespoke the elegance and refinement of the possessor, to whom the reader will now be introduced.

Seated in the library in an arm-chair was a gentleman of about forty-five years of age. His classic head and face would have been a study for an artist; though advanced in years, his hair was jetty black, and his flashing, dark eyes bespoke him a Creole of the sunny clime, in which we find him. Poring over a book with the intentness of a deep thinker, and with contracted eyebrows, he had sat for hours, until, startled by a soft hand placed on his own, he started and exclaimed:

"This you! my beautiful girl; have you come to arouse me from my dreams of ambition to the realities of my state, or to chide me for spending my time in reading of the heroines of romance, when there are those around me rivalling far in excellence and beauty anything that history affords us?"

"Ah, no; the first I would not rouse you from, for my own soul soars aloft on the wings of ambition, and I feel *that* within me which, I am assured, did circum-

stances afford an opportunity, would give the power to
execute deeds such as only a Joan of Arc could dream of;
as to the latter, I know your preference for the heroines
of the ancient school, and am not willing they should lose
any part of your admiration."

"Possibly, then, my dear girl, you will soon have an
opportunity of displaying the power to which you allude,
and I may yet be so lost in admiration at the adventures
and exploits of my darling ward, as to be disgusted for
ever with the tame heroines of romance."

"Why think you so? Is there aught in the elements
which forebodes a storm? Is the political heaven in a
murky state, and do the Jupiters of our country forge
the thunderbolts of battle?"

"Alas, I fear that ere another month glide away,
the clangor of arms will be heard amongst us, and the
shrill bugle note will call to arms every honest citizen.
And then will come the worst of all wars,—fraternal and
civil conflict."

"My soul, perfectly resigned, my dear guardian, will
go forth to meet it. Too long, too long, indeed, have
those fierce myrmidons of the North been allowed to
make laws for us, to govern us, to teach our youth, and
worst of all, to enter our homes, and bring, concealed
under their sheep's clothing, the wolf's teeth, destined
to gnaw out our very vitals. Yes, my dear guardian,
come what will, I am ready to give my last cent to a
cause so holy as that of our independence. Jealous of
our wealth and happiness, they have sworn to exter-
minate us, as sincerely as we are determined to be exterminated ere they shall rule over us."

"Yes! it is indeed too true," he answered; "we

have brought into our homes, and warmed at our firesides the serpents that, with renewed life, were to turn
and sting us. But we must triumph; our's is the holy
cause. The South will only rise when she is invaded.
It is our determination to act on the defensive; and as
South Carolina has already seceded, our own State will
soon be in rebellion against a government who places
in the Presidental chair a negro president or defender.
Would I were a Titan, to hurl him from where he sits,
together with his adherents."

"Yes, dear guardian, it is the base machination of a
minister who, with a host of satellites, sit at his elbow,
and whisper in his uneducated ears their own well-
matured and fiendish plans. He is controlled by a crew
of abolitionists, whose only grudge against the South
is—slavery. Guardian, I feel that, woman as I am, I
could seize a sword in so just a cause."

Rising from his seat, he took the maiden's hand, and
pressing it to his heart, answered—"My dear Natalie,
you would not be the grand-daughter of General de
Villerie, did you not feel thus; and I have no apprehension that should it at last come to a conflict between
us, that the girls and women of sixty-one will not be
behind those of seventy-six in deeds of daring and
courage; though your Southern blood rises in all its
vigour, I feel that you are yet too much the woman
not to wish for an amicable arrangement of our difficulties."

"Assuredly, you do me but justice in saying so;
though I feel my spirit rise in defiance, my heart would
bleed to think that a day would come when brother
would wield knife against brother, father against son,

son against father, and friend against friend ; but should that hour come you will not see me shrink."

"Well, adieu, Natalie, until my return from the city. I shall be absent to-night and to-morrow—I shall return and bring company with me; be prepared to meet them; and say to Madame Ernestine I shall expect such a welcome for my visitors and self as she can so well prepare, and which will do credit to herself and me."

"Rest assured, all shall be as you desire, and with your permission, and to render your happiness more complete, I will ride over to Valambrosa and bring your fair friend home with me, that she, too, may be here to welcome you on your return. So, *au revoir!*"

"*Au revoir*, my dear girl."

In another moment our hero was seated in his carriage on his way to the city, while his fair companion, mounted on a magnificent steed, with a groom following, dashed gaily down the coast.

The young lady who has thus far interested us was the orphan daughter of Colonel de Villerie, and upon the death of her father was taken to the house of his earliest friend, Judge de Breuil, the subject of our story. He was the only son of an old French Count, and who, with an only sister, his senior by some years, were the sole inheritors of the plantation and grounds which have just been described.

Miss de Villerie, on the death of her father, was brought to their home, and, ever since that event, had been the light of the household. Not very wealthy herself, she was not the less aspiring, and those around her, although possessing greater wealth, felt themselves when near her of less importance. Proud, high spirited, intellectual, and beautiful, she shone as a star of the first magnitude in every assembly, and was the observed of all observers. No relatives, she felt herself entirely alone in the world, but, her good sense and refinement caused her to look with feelings of love on those who had taken to their home the bruised flower and nourished it in their hearts. She was never so happy as when near her guardian and his gentle sister, and their happiness was ever hers. We will now leave her to pursue her ride and turn to other scenes which will be described in the next chapter.

CHAPTER II.

"THE SOUTHERN CROSS AND THE NORTH STAR."

"Lo ! the crowned virgin lifts her silver shield ;
From Alleghanian peaks resounds the strain,
' Let glowing freedom stand once more revealed
Nor bend beneath the tyrant's yoke again.
Better the sickle to the sword should yield ;
War's desolation mar the fertile plain ;
The ripened harvest rot upon the field—
Far better than to wear the despot's chain.'
From shadowy vales, from mountain summits bright
Gleam the sharp lightnings of the Southern sword ;
Bathed in the warm meridional light,
Symbol of faith and token of reward,
Flaming aloft the Southern cross shall rise
While pale Arcturus wanes in Hyperborean skies."

SEATED around a dining-table in the *salle-a-manger* of
one of the most stately and imposing private residences
in Esplanade Street, was an assemblage of the most
intellectual gentlemen of the crescent city. Though
wine flowed freely, as it ever does at a Southern dinner
party, there was no gaiety visible in the countenances
of those who composed the company. The party consisted of four gentlemen. At the head of the table was
seated the host, a man of about fifty years of age,
small in stature, with a face the traits of which displayed

no ordinary intellect; a quick, penetrating eye, that would seem to fathom the very soul, and a voice which could inspire a crowd with whatever feeling the possessor might wish to convey. To his right, was seated one who was, by at least fifteen years, his senior, and whose countenance bespoke more of generosity and philanthropy than that of decided intellect; though it did not lack the expression of intelligence, it rather wore the look of genial kindness. Opposite to this gentleman was placed one who, for many years, had shone as a conspicuous member of the bar, but who had, in the last few years, retired to private life to enjoy the fruits of his labour. He had long been the brilliant orator and statesman, and was again, in the political emergency of his country, called forth from the privacy of his retreat, to lend, once more, his voice and counsel to his country's cause. His countenance was marked by a quick, shrewd, and haughty expression. The fourth party was one whom we have already described, and his visit to the city was for the purpose of meeting and discussing, with the prominent men of the day, the state of national affairs. As the servitors waited on the guests, and poured out wine into goblets of Bohemian glass, the following conversation was carried on :—

"My friends," said the host, "we are assembled to day for the last time, I imagine around a table of the Union; for, ere another month passes away, the tocsin of war will sound in our streets, be echoed in our vales, and re-echoed from the mountain tops of a Southern Confederacy. The hour is at hand when we must strike for our rights ; when a nation consents to relinquish its

independence it must take the consequences of its condition. It must obey the behests of a power to which
it is subject; it must follow the dictates of a master, or
endure the stripes which are the penalty of disobedience.
I ask you, gentlemen, will you calmly submit to servitude? Negotiation might arrest a war; negotiation
might effect a peace. How to come to a negotiation, is
the difficulty. According to our theory, a way is open,
to a common basis, upon which the parties might nego-
tiate, but Northern theory has excluded the very possibility of a basis. It places both the North and the
South on as entirely different planes as Hades and
Elysium. It has left a chasm, between which nothing
but hate can fathom, and nothing but war can pass."

" But," said the gentleman to the left, " if the South
were even to compromise her theory, for the purpose of
meeting the North in negotiation, the expedient would
defeat its own object, for the moment she yielded one
jot of her theory, she would, by her own confession, lose
her national character, and pass out of the pale of diplo-
matic intercourse. On the other hand, the Northern
theory would seem to be essential to the very existence
of the Lincoln government, or it might be said, perhaps,
of any government at all in the North. Nothing, indeed,
at this moment, appears to stand between what there is
of government left in the North and a whole legion of
revolutionary demons, save the pending war with the
South, Lincoln must fight for the life of his government.
He must labour, or seem to labour to crush out rebellion,
restore the Union, or, in other words, to satisfy the
arrogance, the rapacity, and the complex fanaticism of
the dominant party in the North; or, must confront

the certainty of being himself overthrown as the head of the government. War will be the issue, and war to the knife let it be. It may be, that we shall never see the daylight of peace breaking through the clouds and darkness of war, until the last remnant of Federal government has passed away, and the last Bruce or Wallace has slept with their fathers. But be the end as it may, let SECESSION be our guide and watchword, and, until our independence is achieved, let not a voice be silent, but let our determination to be free ring abroad, as did the cry of our forefathers, when, crouching beneath the English lion, they broke the chains which fettered them; and may our efforts be as glorious and successful."

"Yes," replied the individual to the right, "let our watchword be SECESSION and *Independence*, but let it be done peaceably, if possible; if not too late, we may yet arrest the progress of that fatal demon—war, and spare the lives of thousands, ay, millions. We sit calmly, in our council chambers and discuss the liability, possibility, and necessity of war, but we little think of the misery it will entail on those who will be compelled to fight our battles. The clouds are not, as yet, all lowering. I perceive one bright spot in the horizon, and we may yet reach the shade of its protecting shelter, ere the thunderbolts burst over our heads and leave us exposed to the storm of violence which is agitated in the political horizon of both parties. God forbid, that I should live to see this glorious Union dissolved, that my forefathers had fought, bled, and died for, whose flag, waving over all seas commanded the respect of all nations, and whose influence, none could deny. Wherever the American standard floated there might the poor and oppressed of every nation gather beneath its folds. America was the mother of the exile and homeless emigrant, America the mother, the impartial mother, who received, with outstretched arms, her children from every clime. Pause, my kind friends, ere this step is taken. The shades of our forefathers rise up to warn you, to entreat you to pause, ere our mother lies bleeding at your feet, and your matricidal hands are steeped in her blood. Will you look calmly on, and take no effective means to redress such evils ?"

"Shall we, sir," exclaimed the third party, "bend our backs to the lash of insolent would-be masters, and, helot like, receive the chastisement of these Romans— Romans only in cruelty ? Shall we go on in this course and not take effective means to redress such monstrous evils, shall we forfeit self-respect, abase ourselves in the eyes of posterity, or shall the South, thoroughly aroused to the necessities of her case, insist upon war to settle our difficulties ?"

" Sir, do not deem that I wish to see our country humiliated, no sir, I am Southern, as well as you, and I believe I need not refer you to the pages of history to prove my ancestors no cravens. Their names shine on history's page, as brave and honourable, but humane men. I shall not presume, longer to speak of them, it is only to vindicate myself; my birth is Southern, my education is Southern, my family and friends are Southern ; but with these sentiments come stronger feelings still, the feeling of philanthropy, which forbids my desire to see the blood of the human race flowing in streams from the sanguine altars of Moloch, when it might be arrested by those who rule at our seat of government. Yes, I am Union now, Union ever, but the South must have my defence, my assistance, should 'Greek meet Greek.'"

"You speak, Sir, as a Christian and a Southerner," said the host, "but there is no aid that is human, to avert this war. Have we not foreborne until it has ceased to be a virtue; are we not looked upon, already, by other nations as the footstool of a greater power. We are deemed, Sir, but another Ireland or a Poland. A press, which has pretended to be Southern, is found not only to applaud the doings of our enemies, but, also to direct its slanders against those who adopt a patriotic course. What wonder is it, that we should sink in the estimation of other nations. Has not the South neglected to employ her instrumentality in the production of native, vigorous, healthy, loyal institutions; and, has she not, thus far, apart from local politics, depended on foreign nations for her reading? to pause would be for her to manifest a fatal hesitation; and has she not doomed herself to dwell amid the defilements of a detested past, and to famish in arid plains, to feed on Dead Sea apples? but she is now about to break her bonds. She is now standing on the threshold of a glorious, mysterious, and wonderful future. Beneath the rainbow arch of hope that spans the dreadful cloud of war, her gateway lies, her path extends; but she must not hesitate, she must not cast one regretful look upon the doomed cities of the plain, under peril of being petrified upon the spot, to remain a melancholy monument of national suicide."

"To the future we must look," replied the person to

the left, " our past relics of pride and greatness, a patriot would blush to gaze upon."

" But, sir," said the host to the fourth party, "you have not, as yet, given us your opinion ; you sit a silent listener. What are your sentiments ? "

" Mine, sir," said the person addressed, " are those of the South in general, or that of every true Southerner. Lincoln went into the Presidency with the declaration on his lips that the Union could not exist, half-slave and half-free, and, he called to the chief places in his council the Northern politician, who proclaimed an irrepressible conflict between slave labour and free labour, which no constitutional provision and no state measures could withstand. I now state that the only condition for peace which any part of the South will consent to, is that of final separation from the North and acknow-ledgment of complete independence ; that wars to resist and force unwilling millions into connection as subjects with a government they have deliberately denounced, will be a gigantic folly, as well as an enormous sin. Abolition has taught its children to curse the South, to abhor the slaveholder. Could so saving a principle be sedulously inculcated without, at the same time, carry-ing along with it a group of destructive instincts and venomous propensities, that would annihilate all that is beautiful, truthful and good ? Abolition, with its capa-cious mouth, has swallowed up everything. In that one idea, all self-culture, virtue, and intelligence has been neglected. What abolition has sown, that also must it reap. Its manifold crimes against society and mankind have been heinous and unnatural, its retribution must be equally so. The South, when she once shakes the dust off her feet, will never enter the gilded portals of the union again. She is confident in the glorious destiny that awaits her, and feels her mission to be one of extension and conquest, and will stand alone and unaided. It may be years ere the trial is ended, but aught that can be urged to the contrary, is as nothing in the way of her determined will. To-day we know that in every Southern state the cry is 'Secession," and many more suns shall not rise ere the Confederacy will be organised. South Carolina, with all the spirit of its Irish ancestry, has sprung, armed *cap-à-pie*, from the head of the revolutionary Minerva. She shall not go forth alone; but what think you of our navy?"

"Sir, our navy is as nought, in comparison with that of the North. In fact, we possess none; but then we will be acting on the defensive. Our ancient foes possessed all the arts and implements of warfare, but, being the aggressors or invaders, were defeated. Rest assured, they will find us equal to the emergency, and when all our Southern officers shall have left them, they will have little to boast of in a naval point. Then let Secession be the watchword of every true Southerner," exclaimed our host; "and now, gentlemen, we will cease this discussion for the present, and enter the drawing-room, where you will find the ladies, with whom you will, no doubt, be pleased to discuss other topics."

"Union, Sir, is my motto, and will ever be so. Nevertheless, I shall lend my assistance to the South," exclaimed our distinguished and philanthropic friend.

As the folding doors opened, the ladies rose to exchange courtesies with the gentlemen, and, on re-seating

themselves, Madame B—— remarked to Judge de
Breuil, "You have been quite engrossed of late, I
presume, with the politics of the day, as your female
friends have not had the pleasure of seeing you very
often ; and even your charming ward, I hear, is quite
an enthusiast on the subject of secession."

"Yes, Madame, my ward, as well as myself, I
believe, is prepared to rise and don the sword and
buckler in defence of our country ; and, I doubt not,
she could almost lead an army herself against the foe."

"Ah, indeed," exclaimed Madame S——, "is she so
determined and patriotic? If she were not so beautiful, I
should fear her offering herself as a sacrifice on the altar
of her country, something on the Joan of Arc style ;
but from what I know of her, I would say she will be
more prudent, and offer sacrifice on the altar of Hymen."

"She is a noble woman, indeed, and happy the one
who will call her his," exclaimed Mr. R——.

"By the way, Judge," said Madame B——, "we
learn from the best of authority (which, of course, you
know, is Madame Rumour) that your ward is soon to be
led to the altar by the elegant Lieutenant Belden. May
I ask, Sir, if there is any truth in the report."

"As you have received your information, Madame,
from so reliable an authority, my gallantry does not
permit me to contradict a Madame, so I shall have to
refer you to Miss Natalie for particulars."

"Ah, Judge, you are very severe, at all events. I
did not give credit to the rumour, as Lieutenant Belden
is a Northerner by birth, as well as by education, and I
am sure that, with her high principles, she would never
consent to wed one of our enemies. No, we cannot

consent to see our beautiful flower borne from us. She must wed one of her own clime."

"It is unhappily the case," answered Madame S——, "that our Creole young ladies are, most generally, in favour of the blue-eyed, fair-haired sons of the North, and that, *vice versâ*, the Creole gentlemen admire Northern beauty. But should a war take place between us, it will end such relations between them for years to come, and I shall be only too happy to know how soon it may be the case."

The conversation was here arrested by the entrance of the usher, bearing, on a silver waiter, a card, which he delivered to Madame S——. Glancing at the card, she remarked, "Usher the lady in," at the same time, turning to her guests, she said, "Those amongst you who have never met before the elegant Madame N——, of New York, will have the pleasure of seeing her now." As she ceased speaking, there entered a lady, gorgeously attired, of a commanding person, but not, what we of the South would even term handsome.

Madame S—— advanced to meet her, and, after their salutations were over, turned, and in a most graceful manner introduced her to the company.

"I have called to make my parting adieus, Madame S——, and I am happy to find some other of my friends with you, as my time is limited, and I might not have the pleasure of seeing them ere my departure for New York."

"Then do you leave us so early," replied Madame S——, "you have, generally, remained much longer with us, and have often spent a portion of the season at our summer resorts."

" Yes, such had been my intention when I came South, but our difficulties have thrown up a barrier between us and enjoyment. That hissing word, Secession, whose very sound would suggest the proximity of a serpent, is the only thing to be heard in your city, and there is not even the common courtesies of life exhibited towards any save those who utter Southern sentiments."

"I am sorry," replied Madame B——, with a smile, "that your stay should be rendered so unpleasant, but, at the same time, must inform you that you are addressing Southerners who are quite as devoted to that unpleasant word as you are against it, and though to you it may suggest the proximity of a serpent, to us it is only like the brazen serpent which Moses erected for the Israelites. We will only have to look upon it to be healed, and, like the Psylla of ancient times, we are *proof* against the venom of serpents ; were it not so I fear, my dear Madame, your Northern reptiles would . have exterminated us long ago."

"My dear Madame N——," exclaimed Madame S——, "I am sorry that our city is not more agreeable, but I dare say that, during the present state of affairs, a Southern lady in New York would not be any more agreeably situated when listening to words such as union, abolition, &c."

The gentlemen who conversed apart were amused at the conversation, and Judge de Breuil hastened to remark, with all the courtesy of a true Southerner, "Madame N——, you, of all persons, I should say, have the least cause to think harshly of us. I have ever deemed that you had received so many *fêtes,* and met with such flattering attention, during your visits here that we had almost won you to our cause. I trust, however, we shall meet in better and happier times. So, wishing you '*bon voyage*,' I will now bid you farewell." With a graceful bow he left the room, followed by the other gentlemen.

Madame N——, after several bitter vituperations, took leave, and there was not one of the party who regretted her departure. She was one of the Jellaby sort of women, the only difference being that she had wealth to assist her in disseminating her ideas. She was one of that style of wealthy, ill-dressed, ill-bred Northern aristocrats who fill our hotels during the winter, and who, through courtesy, are invited to the homes of our planters, and then return to the North to write of " Legrees " and " Uncle Toms."

CHAPTER III.

" Know ye the land of the cedar and vine,
  Where the flowers ever blossom, the bees ever shine ;
  Where the light wings of zephyr, oppressed with perfume,
  Wax faint o'er the garden of Gull in her bloom ;
  Where the citron and olive are fairest of fruit,
  And the voice of the nightingale never is mute ;
  Where the tints of the earth, and the hues of the sky,
  In colour, though varied, in beauty may vie,
  And the purple of ocean is deepest in dye ? "

THE reader is now about to be introduced to another
scene, one that may be seen at all times during the
winter or spring in our clime. The air in the Southern
States, or those bordering on the gulf, is fresh and
salubrious. It fans the cheek with a fragrance borrowed
from the aroma of deep green fields, which the frosty
hand of winter scarcely changes. The forests stretch
far away and are pictured in dark relief against the
sky. The heavens seem rounded up in their sublime
expanse of deep blue, in which the diamond stars appear
to swing as it were on golden pendulums. As was said
above, the breath of winter does not wither the dark
and rich green leaf of the forests. The flowers are
gorgeous and flaunting while the entire scenery of this
boundless Eden reminds one of a flower garden on an

extensive scale. Music of thousands of birds fill the air, and their variegated plumage, golden green and red, present a brilliancy of appearance which the most fervid imagination can scarcely realize. The mocking-bird swings on the branches of giant trees that seem to sweep their arms against the sky, while the Spanish moss, swaying gracefully to and fro, seems like a morning drapery worn for the ancient owners of the land (who are in this region almost extinct), and re-calls to mind the beautiful lines of the Rev. T. Hemp-stead :—

" There is a little tangled plant that grows,
   Within our Southern clime ;
And in the fanning breezes hangs and flows
   Like flakes of hoary rime.

" The red bird singing 'gainst the tassels grey,
   Presses her flaming breast ;
And tears, with her strong beak, the threads away,
   To weave them round her nest."

All nature seems here to be offering her incense to the great Giver, and here the boundless heart of Southern philanthropy seems flowing over with good will and generous hospitality. The future of the Southern country is as glorious as ever were those of Italy or Greece, and her brightest and best days are but dawning. Her sun is but beginning to cast its early beams around, her noon will awaken the world.

In the midst of such scenery as has just been described was located the home of one who will figure conspicuously in this story. The house was adapted to Southern comfort, being a one-story building with a

verandah running round it, opening on which were
windows descending to the floor. A spacious hall ran
through the centre, on either side of which were
situated parlours, library, and drawing-rooms; the
right wing contained bed rooms and boudoirs, the left
being devoted to the " *salle-a-manger.*"

In the front of the house was a large park, while, in
the rear, a terraced garden displayed to the visitor
flowers of every hue and clime. In the distance might
be seen the negro quarters glorying in brilliant white-
wash, and almost hid beneath the vines which grew in
front of each door-way, and which formed a pleasant
shelter from the rays of the sun at noon-day. To each
cabin was attached a little garden, in which the useful
and ornamental vied with each other. Far away, as the
eye could reach extended the verdant enclosure, by
which fields, house, and cabins were encircled. The
beautiful cherokee rose turning its tendrils, and forming
a fence so dense that not even a bird could penetrate it,
and reminding one of a rich mosaic brooch in a setting
of emerald.

Standing side by side on the steps of the mansion
just described were three ladies. The eldest was about
forty years of age, and from her fair hair, and yet un-
wrinkled brow, you could easily perceive her to be a
daughter of the North. The youngest, from the great
resemblance she bore to the former, might easily be
recognised as her daughter; though her complexion and
features were very like her mother's, she possessed that
dolce-far-niénte air which is only peculiar to native-
born Southerners. Her face was round, childish, and
artless. Her complexion, fair as a lily, with the rose

tints blushing on her cheeks, while her long golden curls swept over her neck and shoulders in wanton disorder.

Her figure was tall and slender; with hands and feet so delicately moulded that they would have served as a study for an artist. She was dressed in a riding-habit of dark-blue cloth, with a cap of blue velvet and black plumes.

Her companion, the very opposite of this, was Miss Natalie, spoken of in the first chapter; she seemed like a very Diana, as, with whip in hand, and attired in a dark green velvet riding-habit, with a cap, the feathers of which floated over her shoulders, she stood awaiting, while the groom brought forth two richly caparisoned horses.

"Adieu, Mrs. Clifton," she said, gaily; "I shall keep your charming Cornie with me until you issue one of your stern mandates for her return, or until, at least, I can send her home under the protection of such an escort as shall prove agreeable to her."

"I trust you will not keep her long; she is the light of Vallambrosa, and her voice, ringing through our halls, dispels somewhat the gloom which weighs upon our hearts, when we permit our thoughts to stray outside the home circle."

"*Chere* mamma," replied the daughter, "I shall soon return to you; and say to papa, if either he or brother will come for me, the day after to-morrow, I shall most willingly return." Kissing her mother, she sprang into her saddle, and joining Miss de Villerie, their horses were heard clattering down the road through the park, and they were soon out of sight. As they rode onwards, the following conversation, commenced by Miss Natalie, took place.

"When I look around and behold our beautiful forests, noble lands, and majestic rivers, I think how blessed we are in this lovely clime; but then, when my thoughts dwell upon what it may become, through the cruelty of an invader, my heart sinks within me. Look, Cornie, and see those sturdy negroes in the field; do they look much like what the fiends of Abolitionism represent? Well clothed and well fed; their songs are rising on the air in anthems of happiness. See, yonder, the smoke rising from their cabins where they rest after their day's labour is done. No care, no fear for the morrow. If sickness prostrate them, they are nursed and cared for; not like the poor *white slave* who toils without ceasing, and then, when illness prevents him from labouring, he is wretched at the thought at having to pay all his hard-earned money for the services of a physician or a nurse. Which is the happier, think you?"

"Ah, my dear Natalie, to us who know the difference, of course, the former state is preferable, but liberty, you know, is sweet. The negro may imagine that to be free comprises all the necessary enjoyments of life; he knows nothing of self-reliance; and, almost in every instance, where freedom has been bestowed he was willing, after a very short time, to seek the home of his master, content to roam no more. Freedom, like many other things, palls upon his senses when he finds that it merely consists of independence, coupled with the necessity of supporting himself. My father, though a large slave-holder, whose very interest is in the South, is of my mother's opinion — that a means might be adopted for their emancipation at some future day, which, if undertaken at the present, would involve the ruin of the whole South."

"I fear, my dear Cornie, that your father has been biased in his judgment by your excellent mother, whose northern principles and education has prejudiced her too much, perhaps, in favour of the land of her nativity, and too much against the land of her adoption. Such an advent will never arrive; God forbid it should. What, think you, would become of this beautiful land? Who would there be to till those large fields whose bosoms teem with the wealth of nations? And who, think you, would work beneath the tropical sun? They alone are fitted for it by nature. If no other feeling than that of interest would prevent my desire of their returning to their own land, the feeling of pity for their condition, which in their own country is so degraded, would banish for ever such an idea. By ancient as well as modern writers we are told of their low state, morally and physically. They worship nought save reptiles, and, if we can believe statements made by men of science, they are, in themselves, only a higher order of serpent. Have you ever read Dr. Cartwright's treatise? if not, I should be pleased were you to do so, as it will elucidate more clearly my remarks. If his statements have any truth in them, or, any of those from whom he quotes, then slavery has been, indeed, a mercy to them."

"Yes, I have read his discourse; but O, Natalie, it would be terrible to entertain such a belief. If I imagined it was so for a moment, I could never consent to live surrounded by them."

"Cornie, it is not in your power or mine to render their condition happier; but we should be content with the thought that God has willed it thus, and that we are carrying out the Divine intentions when we strive, in the manner we do, to ameliorate their unhappy condition. But, Cornie, here we are at home, and here comes the porter to open the gates for us."

"Glad you come, Miss Nat'le, and how ee do, Miss Cornie; I was jist 'bout to go arter you. Masser dune kum home, and de house full ob cumpany, and only waitin for de ladies to make der felishity kumplete."

Ere the old man had finished this compliment the young ladies had rode in and dismounted, and were exchanging salutations with their friends, who had come out to greet them.

"Miss Natalie," said an elegant young gentleman, stepping forward, "I feared we were to be deprived of your society this evening, as the day was waning, and you had not arrived. I accepted your guardian's invitation to Rosale for the express purpose of seeing you, and enjoying a spirited conversation with you.",

"I am most happy to see you, my kind friend; but before proceeding further, permit me to present to you my friend Miss Clifton. Miss Clifton, allow me to introduce you to Mr. La Branche."

"And now, if you will excuse us," said Miss de Villerie, " we will retire and exchange our habits for more fitting attire, and then have the pleasure of rejoining you in a few moments." Bowing low, he left them, and our young friends ascended the staircase to their rooms, where we will leave them until their return to the salon.

CHAPTER IV.

" From life without freedom, say who would not fly ?
For one day of freedom, O ! who would not die ?
Hark ! hark ! 'tis the trumpet ! the call of the brave,
The death-song of tyrants, the dirge of the slave.
Our country lies bleeding—haste, haste to her aid ;
Oñe arm that defends is worth hosts that invade.''

RECLINING on a divan, in the back parlour of Rosale,
was a lady of about fifty years of age ; her face was fair,
and the bloom of earlier days was still visible on her
cheeks. Her hair was silvered over by Time's frosty
fingers, but her dark, clear, and penetrating eyes would
have added a charm to one even younger. She was
attired in a steel coloured silk, while her head was orna-
mented by a rich barbe of pointe d'Alençon, fastened
with pins of jet set in the Etruscan style. She possessed an easy, self-possessed manner, while her voice
had that distinct, but modulated tone of the well-bred
woman. By her side was seated a young gentleman,
to whom the reader has just been introduced in the
former chapter, while his friend, Count Beauharnais,
was in a deep conversation with Judge de Breuil.

" You will, I trust, remain with us some time, Sir.
A person cannot be a judge of a country, its manners,
customs, and institutions in less than, at least, a six

months' sojourn. There have been too many histories, books of travel, and such like, written on only a bird's-eye view of a nation."

"This is my first visit to America," replied the stranger, "and, though I cannot see much in its institutions to admire, still, the courtesy of its people adds a charm to one's tour, and makes one love and respect them for receiving, with such open hospitality, the stranger in a foreign land. They seem to be perfectly unsuspicious, and receive one in a truly democratic style."

"You are, possibly, mistaken in your judgment, Sir, of us, and draw your conclusions from our Northern friends, or rather, our enemies now. They are more enthusiastic than we, and receive, with out-stretched arms, any one who may present themselves bearing letters with any stamp of nobility or marque; but we of the South must be very well assured of a person's claim on society, ere he is introduced into our home circle. You do not find our Southerners making beasts of burden of themselves to draw the chariot of one even royally descended, much less that of a danseuse or prima donna, as was, and is, the case still, in the North. No, Sir, though we do not lay claim to any coat of arms, save those of nature's noblemen, every man in the South feels himself a *free*-man, and that is more than I believe your kings, queens, or princes can say. Merit, with us, is the only nobility we acknowledge. You are well received, Sir, both North and South, not for the fact that you bring letters of undeniable marque, but for the reason that your family is not unknown to us. We are quiet, unostentatious, but sincere people."

" Yes, the difference of manner is very observable to a traveller," said the gentleman ; " but, to one who can linger but a short time in the country, the manners of the Northerners prove more agreeable. They seem to be warm-hearted and unsuspecting; and, if it be but ephemeral, it is like the ray which gilds the mountain-top, though it melts not the snow upon its summit, nevertheless, lends a charm, while it lasts——"

" And to complete the metaphor, I will add," said Judge de Breuil, " that, like the mist which floats around the mountain peak, obscuring, for a while, the snow on its summit, that reserve we bear towards strangers when we prove their worth, vanishes as imperceptibly as does the mist. Should you remain with us for any time, I trust you will leave us with the impression that, if not so democratic, we are, at least, more sincere, than the people of the North."

The young ladies entering, the gentlemen rose to receive them, and, Albert La Branche introduced his friend, Count Beauharnais, to Miss de Villerie, when the latter introduced her friend to the Count. Salutations being over, the party seated themselves, and Albert la Branche, turning to Miss de Villerie, said—

" Madame de Breuil," (which she was termed, in courtesy to her age,) " and myself have just been listening to a long discussion on the manners of North and South, between your guardian and my friend. I am sure the North will find a warm advocate in you, *n'est ce pas.*"

" Though I am no friend to the North, I am not, yet, so prejudiced in my opinions but to confess that there are many, very many great intellects and shining lights amongst them, and some, too, that we might be proud to denominate Southern. Yet one who will claim the politics of the North can never be very dear to me."

"Miss Clifton, may I ask your opinion on this all-engrossing subject?" said Albert la Branche.

"My opinion is of very little weight," she replied; "but having relatives North, my views are, probably, not unprejudiced. I love the Union, and, regret that aught should have ever occurred to render its dissolution necessary. We lived so happily together, all like one large and happy family, that I must say that I dread the hour which shall see us sundered; but my friend, Miss de Villerie prays for the separation as ardently as I do the contrary."

"Ay, verily," said Miss de Villerie, "we will put it to the test.

> ' And say, as stern Elijah said of old,
> The strife now stands upon a fair award,
> If Israel's Lord be God, then serve the Lord:
> If he be silent, faith is all a whim,
> Then Baal is the God, and worship Him.'"

"South Carolina, Mississippi, Alabama, Florida, Georgia, and Texas, have already seceded, and, to-day, we look for the returns of Louisiana," said Judge de Breuil.

"Having so many friends at the North," said Miss Clifton to Miss de Villerie, "I should imagine that you would feel some pang at the impassable gulf which Secession will inevitably cast between you. Are there none whom you wish to retain as friends?"

"Not one, I would sever my very heart strings, if I

thought they bound me to an individual of Northern principles. What! to kiss the rod that smites me. Never! No, never! I trust to-day will bring the news of our separation from our detested enemies."

"I was not aware the ladies of the South were politicians," said Count Beauharnais, "but I perceive that Miss de Villerie is quite a strong one. I had imagined it was only the ladies of the North who ever expressed themselves on politics, and had supposed, that, into the sacred precincts of a Southern symposium such subjects were never introduced nor debated."

"I am well aware, Sir," said Miss de Villerie, "the *very* exalted opinion most nations have of us. They imagine us to be entirely devoid of the fundamental principles of an education, with only a slight knowledge of accomplishments; that we do nothing; are, in fact, incapable of thinking for ourselves, and, worse than all this, they imagine that we dream our lives away in quite an Oriental style, and sip our *café* or *eau sucré*, quite *à la Turque*. We are indebted to our fair sisters of the North for this very flattering portrait. In future, we shall paint and draw our own, even should we be considered somewhat egotistic for so doing."

"They should employ you then to paint for all, Miss de Villerie. I think a better artist could not be found, but one so ardent and sincere as yourself on political subjects, would not be the less so in matters of love, friendship, or any feeling of the human heart. I do not think for an instant that you would cease to love one because his principles did not coincide with your own, or that you would yield up, on the altar of dis-

sension, the affection of years' standing, or the claims of
an old friend."

"Then, Sir, you do not judge me rightly; not
because another's principles do not in everything agree
with mine, but for the reason that those who affirm that
the North is just in her course to the South, and that
Lincoln is right in his determination to force her to
remain in the Union, and by so doing to oppress us in
the manner we have already submitted to. But hark!
heard you that sound? Yes, there it is again. I am
sure we have seceded, yes, again and again."

"Miss Clifton," said the gentleman, "do you not
rejoice with us."

"No, no, I can never exult with you over this. To
you the sound may be sweet, to me it is almost a death-
knell, tolling the dirge of all I love. How very sad
the booming of those cannon strikes to my heart."

"Boom on," said Miss de Villerie; "to me it is
sweeter than the music of the spheres. Count Beauharnais, behold Miss Clifton, she is positively weeping."

"I am not weeping, my dear friend," said Miss
Clifton, as she hastily brushed a tear away, which
trembled on her eye-lid; "but tears will start involun-
tarily when I behold the once triumphant flag of our
country each day losing a bright star, and that too of the
first magnitude. What to you brings joy, to me brings
sorrow." As she ceased speaking, she rested her arm
on a corner of the table, and bowing her beautiful head,
whose golden curls swept over her, she gazed out into
the dark, until you would have supposed, from her attitude, that she was holding converse with unseen spirits,
and from the expression of her deep blue eyes, that she

could read, on the defaced records before her, the future of her unhappy land.

Count Beauharnais seated himself by the side of Miss de Villerie, while Albert la Branche seemed rapt in an admiring gaze of Miss Clifton. He at length approached, and, seating himself by her side, said, "Miss Clifton, you seem to be quite abstracted; will you allow me to ask what may be the subject of your meditations?"

"Certainly. I was just thinking that when we shall cease to exist on earth, will our troubles end for ever, or is there still another and yet another world, where the good and evil passions of man shall strive for the mastery. If we are all, as Plutarch supposed us to be, each possessed of a good and evil genius, or, as the moderns have it, a good and bad angel, is it not a pity that the Evil One's counsel most generally predominates?"

"It is, indeed, to be regretted," added he, "that such is the case. We are all born, or supposed to be, in the state of original sin, and our inclinations tend more in the direction of evil than of good. From the time of our first parents' trespass to the present moment it has been the same. There seems to be more pleasure in doing evil than good. Unless we have been fortunate enough to have been morally educated, man's passions, when not governed by sentiments of morality, are apt to lead him astray, and when once he does lose sight of his good angel or genius, they seldom meet again on this side of the grave."

"Yes, it is too true," she replied, "that when the angel guardian takes leave of some poor wanderer, in this

vale of sorrow, or rather, when some misguided youth
turns his back upon his monitor, or closes his ear to
his low but kindly whisperings, he nevertheless still
follows on. Ever ready, should repentance come, to
administer counsel, and to plead his cause with the
King of Kings ; it is seldom he is recalled, unless the
dying struggle of some poor erring one summons him
to his bedside at the eleventh hour, to offer some atonement to an offended Deity. There, even at that moment,
the gentle guide is standing, his wings drooping over
the couch of the dying sinner, until the last sigh is
breathed forth when his earthly mission is ended ; then,
pluming his flight for heaven, he records the deeds of
one whose footsteps he followed here below. It is a
beautiful idea, that when all desert us, that there are
two who sympathise with us, our Heavenly Father, and
our good angel."

"You cannot, certainly, Miss Clifton, have ever
known such sorrow as would have caused you to seek
sympathy from any source, celestial or terrestial."

"Sorrows of my own I have never experienced, but
sorrow for others' woes I have. I feel an interest in
every one's joys and griefs. The poorest wayfarer on
life's high road is one of God's creatures, and, as such,
is entitled to my consideration. Oh ! how I have sighed
for some fair Arcadia, where all might live in peace and
tranquillity, where no storms should arise to destroy the
calm of life ! "

"You desire, then, to inhabit some fair Utopia,
where all would be perfect. I would say to you, then,
dream on, fair dreamer, for this state of affairs can never
be while the human race exists. Sir Thomas Moore

wrote his work under the inspiration of some fair spirit of another sphere. The idea is sublimely beautiful, but would require creatures of a different species as inhabitants, totally unallied to the human race." The servants entering, placed before each of the guests small tables of rosewood, others served the tea in cups of Sèvres china, while cakes were passed around in baskets of silver. The conversation now became general, when, tea being over, and the tables removed, the young ladies were called upon for music. Mr. la Branche arose, and, throwing open the piano, requested the ladies to sing a *duette.*

" As we can sing with more ease standing," said Miss de Villerie, "it would be better if Madame de Breuil would play the accompaniment for us."

" Will you be so kind, Madame de Breuil, as to play for us?" said Miss Clifton.

" *Avec plaisir,*" said Madame de Breuil, and, rising she was escorted to the instrument by Mr. la Branche.

" *A votre service,* mademoiselle."

" What would you like to hear—something from Norma, or La Juif?"

" The former, Miss de Villerie, as it is well adapted to your style," said Count Beauharnais. " I think you will do Norma justice, while Miss Clifton, will make a fine, imploring Adalgisa."

Soon music filled the room, and the exquisite voices of our fair friends rose and fell in rich bursts of melody through the halls, while the moments flew on unheeded, as song after song was sung, and piece after piece executed. Madame de Breuil played with a masterly touch, as did also the young ladies.

D 2

"Miss Clifton, you will, please, play and sing something *toute seule*," said Judge de Breuil, "something soft and sweet?"

"*Certainement;* but I shall ask Miss de Villiere to sing the first, and I will sing the second."

"Guardian only desires to hear you, Miss Clifton; I shall not break the magic of the spell your voice will throw around him by any discordant notes of mine."

"Miss de Villerie, 1 should be delighted to have you sing with Miss Clifton, if she requires a voice to sustain her, but I am more anxious to hear it unaccompanied."

"Thus, you see, my dear Miss Clifton, I am formally dispensed with."

"Allow me to turn your music," said Mr. la Branche; "what will you sing?"

"Your favourite, if you wish."

"Then sing your own, and that will be mine," he answered, bending over her. She softly and tremblingly struck the chords, and sang, in her most touching tones, "Ave Sanctissima." Her voice rose and fell like the sighing of a lost spirit, and the "ora pro nobis" died away in lingering cadence. When she ceased, there was not a sound; silence reigned supreme. All seemed too rapt in the dying echoes to feel that she no longer sang, and ere they were aroused, our fair cantatrice had left the piano, and sought a seat in a retired part of the room."

Miss de Villerie was the first who broke the enchantment. Smilingly pointing to her guardian, who sat as though fearful to move, lest he should lose a note of the melody, she said, turning to Miss Clifton, "Behold thy work, fair syren."

"Thanks, many thanks, my dear Miss Clifton," said Judge de Breuil. "Your voice has lost none of its pathos since I last heard you. When I listen to such music as yours, I do not doubt of the power of Orpheus."

Madame de Breuil, rising and bowing to the gentlemen, withdrew, followed by the young ladies ; they retiring to their rooms to spend a gay hour in discussing the events of the day, and then to sacrifice to the gods *Somnus* and *Morpheus*, while the gentlemen retired to the library to enjoy a cigar. As we have no disposition to know what *they* have to say, we will follow the young ladies, and, for your pleasure, reader, become eavesdropper on this occasion, and will relate, as accurately as possible, their conversation.

On entering the room, Miss de Villerie remarked—

"Now, my dear Cornie, we shall discuss the gentlemen, as, no doubt, they will take the liberty of doing with us. How are you pleased with our young scion of nobility and my old friend Albert la Branche."

"They are both so agreeable I can scarcely make a distinction."

"Ah ! it is useless to ask you for a decided opinion upon any subject. You are too grand a diplomat. I think Albert would be more candid, from what I was able to discover this evening. Cornie dear, you opened the artillery of your charms upon him, and he surrendered at once."

"Natalie *chere*, you are cruel. If I were desirous to make use of the *lex talionis*, I do not think you would have much the advantage, but I shall be merciful. May I ask what you think of Count Beauharnais?"

"Most assuredly. What do I think—let me see. Rather a handsome Frenchman, air, *tres distingué*, very much more modest and retiring than most of his country-men ; not remarkably intelligent, but quite graceful in his manners, with a radicated sense of his position and aristocratic connections, with a very capacious heart, and your humble servant, if I judge aright, occupying the largest chamber in it this evening. To-morrow I shall abdicate (being the best policy, where a French-man's love is concerned) in favour of a more fortunate rival. Is this sufficient, or shall I be still more candid ?"

"*Ma cheré* Natalie," you have been over candid, I assure you, but, as you are such an excellent delineator of character, draw a slight portrait, if you please, of Mr. la Branche."

"Yes. Albert la Branche, an elegant, high-bred, high-souled Creole, partaking in disposition and tem-perament of the tropical nature of the clime of which he is a native. Fiery and impetuous, generous and the soul of honour, devoted to friends, implacable to enemies, loving with all the ardour of a sincere nature : and now that I have finished the picture, I will give it to you to treasure in your heart of hearts."

"Thank you for the gift, but I am scarce worthy of such a keepsake ; but, Natalie, *vraiment et entre nous*, have you never loved any one, or do you, and have you ever treated your admirers as cavalierly as I have ob-served you to do on all occasions. Is there none who has ever made an impression."

"*Tres bien pour vous*, my fair inquisitor, you have donned the priestly robes, and are prepared to hear and absolve, I suppose. Well, you deserve to have your penitent make a clean breast of it, and now listen : the citadel of my heart was stormed and taken possession of the first winter of my *début* in society. The victorious general was one whom you have never seen, though he is not unknown to fame. He is a native of the far-off north, but I know he entertains no such ignoble sentiments as those by whom he is surrounded. I feel assured, when the war-cry rings from hill and dale, we will find him foremost in our defence. I know that he will never become the oppressor of the South."

"*Ah, ma chere* Natalie, think you that he will yield for ever his claim upon home, friends, and kindred to become the champion of a cause in which he can have no interest, save that of his love for the daughter of a clime where everything in it is opposed to him and his except that one fair being. I am no logician, my dear Natalie, such is my opinion, and you will find your idol dust; if so, be not disappointed. He may love you ardently (and who is there, knowing you, that would not ?) but, Natalie, he will never, no never, desert the cause he will espouse for any love, be it *human* or *divine*."

"Then hear me, Cornie, the moment he becomes my country's foe he can no longer be anything more to me than any other invader of our homes and firesides, though I love him as I can never love other than my God, I would cast him from me, and the gulf of oblivion should for ever roll over every reminiscence of the past. I would offer my love, my burning, my first, last, and only love, as a sacrifice on the altar of my country. But this can never be, he is too noble ever to become an oppressor."

" I trust, for your sake, dear Natalie, that he may be all you would wish him, but should 'a change come o'er the spirit of your dream' you will remember, often, what I have said to-night."

Miss de Villerie, sounding a bell, a nice-looking mulatto girl answered the summons. "Cornie, Victorine is at your service, I shall not retire just at present, when you feel disposed to do so, act *sans ceremonie*."

"I shall do so forthwith, and leave you alone in your boudoir, for I am anxious to seek my couch to revel in the land of dreams, while I leave you to think on the past and dream over the future. Bon soir," she whispered, bending over Miss de Villerie until her curls, like a veil of golden mist, enshrouded both. " *Dans votre orisons souvenez vous de moi,*" and then turning to the maid she said, " Vien Victorine." Alone in her boudoir Miss de Villerie sat till long after· midnight. As the damask curtains fell on the retreating form of Miss Clifton, our heroine threw herself at the feet of the statue of the blessed Virgin which reposed on an altar in the room, which served both as oratory and boudoir; long and fervently she prayed, her dark hair falling over her shoulders in artless confusion, and her large and dark eyes raised to Heaven, while her hands were clasped in an agony of despair. Her words were wild and stormy, and ran thus :—

"Oh, God! who hearest thy suppliant, I beseech thee, if possible, to let this bitter, bitter cup pass from me ; but, like thy Son, I too say, ' Thy will, not mine, be done.' Dark and dreadful presentiments fill my soul, but He, to whom there is nothing in Heaven or on earth impossible, shield me from all ill and dash not to earth my brightest hopes. The darkest day of my life, but the brightest for my country, I see now dawning. Far into the future my soul's eyes have pierced, and I see the glorious land of my nativity shining forth from the clouds which have so long environed her, and growing brighter and still brighter as ages roll away, until, comet-like, her splendour blazes forth, and comet-like will dazzle all the world. Yes, Thou who rulest the heavens and earth, and who giveth victory to the just, art with us, Thy strong arm shall divide the sea of blood which will flow between the North and South. Thou wilt pass thy chosen people through its depths, and Thine arm shall be withdrawn and, like Pharoah and his hosts, our enemies will perish in the surging waves which shall pass over the last remnant of them. God of my forefathers, thou hast given me the gift to foretell the fate of our blindfolded enemies, and though, Cassandra-like, I should trumpet it forth, it would meet with a Cassandra-like reception. Not until the fire and the sword should have devastated and swept all before them would my words find belief. The hour is fast approaching in which shall sound the clarion note of war; oh! in that hour remember the father, the mother, the sister, the brother. In that hour, oh, God! the father shall go forth from his family, mayhap never again on earth to behold them. The son shall go forth in the might of right, and his young blood shall flow upon the battle field, and his last sigh escape to Thy throne from his gory bed of death. In that hour, beloved Saviour of mankind, as in this, I pray thee to have mercy. I pray, not alone for those who are near and dear, but alike for the humblest of thy creatures, who shall march forth to vanquish the invader. I pray Thee, oh, God! to spare the inhabitant of the humblest cot in our valleys, the dweller in the rude hamlets of our mountains as well as the occupants of stately mansions. I, oh, Lord! am but a creature of a day, formed but to die, but not eternally. I am thy victim, do with me as thou wilt. If my young life would serve as a holocaust on the altar of my country, thou knowest, who readeth all hearts, how gladly I would yield it up an offering to thee and to my own beautiful sunny South and native land! Like the daughter of Jephtha, I would go forth to meet the victorious general and bless the hand that smote me. Thou, blessed Mother, whose arms seem stretched forth to receive me, intercede with thy dear Son in behalf of my country and of me. Sainted Mother, look down upon thy child and hear me. Mother of sorrows, mother of Divine Grace, beg of thy dear Son the boon, that when storms and strifes of nations shall cease, all who fight bravely under His banner, friends and enemies, shall enter hand in hand (terrestrial pains and sorrows alike forgotten) together into Heaven. Jesus, Mary, and Joseph, I retire to dream that I am with you."

CHAPTER V.

"Tune your harps,
Ye Angels, to that sound ; and thou, my heart,
Make room to entertain my flowing joy !"

"Sweet notes ! they tell of former peace,
Of all that look'd so rapturous then ;—
Now wither'd, lost—Oh ! pray thee, cease,
I cannot hear those sounds again !"

MORNING found our party assembled around the break-
fast-table discussing over their chocolate and café, the
morning journals, which contained the news of the
seceding of the State. The gentlemen were exultant
while Madame de Breuil uttered her sentiments in
favour of the act with her usual quiet dignity. Miss
de Villerie's eyes sparkled with enthusiasm and all
were joyous, save Miss Clifton. She was true to the
union.

"The city, I presume, will make a demonstration
to-night in the way of an illumination," said Judge de
Breuil.

"Without doubt," said Albert la Branche, "and
Judge, Count Beauharnais, and myself will be pleased
to accompany you in your drive to the city this morning,
as we are anxious to see and hear all we can."

" My dear guardian, Miss Clifton and myself will also go this morning, as Madame de Breuil wishes to illuminate, we are to send out the necessary materials; and, if you have not forgotten, my *fête* to celebrate secession comes off as soon as possible. Miss Clifton and myself will spend the day in the city, giving the necessary orders and superintending the purchases."

" Then I perceive, Miss de Villerie, that you are determined your sentiments on political subjects shall be blazoned forth ? " said Count Beauharnais.

" Most assuredly, Sir; I trust no one will deem me other than I am, a loyal Southern woman."

" Ladies and gentlemen, the equipages await you," said a servant.

The ladies retiring, in a moment returned attired in carriage costume, and rejoined the gentlemen, who were waiting to assist them to their carriages.

" Miss de Villerie," said Count Beauharnais, as he placed her in the phaeton, " I shall long have cause to remember my pleasant visit to Rosale, can I hope the remembrance of it will be at all agreeable to you ? "

" Why should it be otherwise ? " she answered, slightly colouring; "it affords me much pleasure to receive and welcome to my home all my friends, and as such I cannot but denominate any one to whom my old and well-beloved friend Mr. la Branche may introduce me, and will certainly be remembered by me with pleasure."

" Then adieu for the present, Miss de Villerie," and springing into the carriage he sat awaiting his friend, Albert la Branche.

The latter, as he was taking leave of Miss Clifton

said, "May I hope to be permitted to call on you at your own home, and cultivate an acquaintance with one whom I am desirous to know more of?"

"If a farther knowledge of myself is pleasing to you, I shall be happy to see you at Vallambrosa."

"Then, with a hope of meeting at an early day, I bid you good morning." Bowing low to Miss de Villerie, he rejoined his friend, and they were soon driving rapidly up the coast towards the city.

Madame de Breuil, with her housekeeper and maids, sat all day twining wreaths and triumphal garlands; arches of evergreen were made, and doors, windows, and gates were festooned, while japonicas and other flowers were suspended from pillar to pillar, which were entwined with evergreens. Evening came, and brought with it our young ladies.

"Oh! how perfectly charming, Madame de Breuil," said the young ladies, in the same breath; "we have seen nothing throughout the whole city to compare with it; you may feel assured that your residence will be far more beautifully illuminated than any."

"I think my design very pretty, as did your parents, who drove over this morning," said Madame de Breuil. "By the way, they desired me to say to you, that your brother would be over this evening, and that, if you chose, you could go home with him; though she did not leave it to your choice until, at my earnest solicitation, that if you wished to remain longer with Natalie, you could do so. I trust you will consent to remain with us and assist in issuing invitations for our *fête*."

"I know that mamma is anxious to have me with her; notwithstanding, I shall remain with *chere* Natalie until everything is arranged for her entertainment. Will mamma illuminate, Madame de Breuil?"

"Your father wished her to do so, but your mother, I believe, objected. Your brother will be here this evening, and will join with us in our demonstrations. He, I believe, is not of your sentiments."

" Yes, my brother is a Unionist; but he has always said he would fight for the land of his nativity."

"Ah ! Cornie *chere*, your brother knows the just side, *mais allons*, there are many things to be arranged before night, and we have yet our toilettes to make, and let them be quite becoming, as my dear guardian seldom comes home alone."

Night came, and saw the mansion one blaze of light —halls, doors, windows, and gates shone forth in all the brightness that two thousand wax tapers could throw upon the scene, while in every tree hung coloured lamps, and through the garlands entwining the pillars light shone forth and was reflected far out into the river. In the centre of the house, and over the door-way, on a ground of cerulean-coloured silk, shone lights representing the constellation of the Southern cross, and the emblem of the State embroidered in silver—the pelican and her young; while, in rainbow colours of light, shone the motto, "We live and die for those we love;" on the archway of the gate blazed the word "Secession," while the sparkling waters of the fountains throughout the grounds added their tinkling sound to the loveliness of the scene as they fell into their marble basins. All beauty and light without, while revelry and harmony reigned within.

"You cannot conceive, Mr. Clifton, what a strong

Unionist your little sister is. I firmly believe that when the Union ship is beheld a sinking wreck, she will be found clinging to the mast."

"My sister is devoted to the cause, I know, as much so, possibly, as any strong-minded woman of the North; but, like many others, her birth was cast upon an evil time. She is no politician; she is guileless in the world and all that pertains thereto. You have drawn, Miss de Villerie, a very good portrait of my sister. Whatever cause she espouses, she will cling to it with tenacity, and where she loves, it will be with devotion."

"Miss Clifton, if you have no objection, we would like to hear 'La Marseillaise,'" said Judge de Breuil. "Shall I open the piano?"

"Yes, if Miss de Villerie will lend her voice to mine. and my brother and yourself consent to sing the chorus. Madame de Breuil, will you be so kind as to accompany us?"

The latter was escorted to her seat by Beverly Clifton, and soon that soul-stirring air rang out and rolled in swelling numbers through the spacious halls. As the song ended, there were heard approaching voices, and the servant, entering, announced Colonel Leland, Madame Bienvenu, Hon. P. S——, and Madame S——.

"Rather late visitors," said Colonel Leland, as Judge de Brieul advanced to meet them; "but we were attracted by the beauty of your illumination, together with the singing, and we at once drove in to see and admire. We rode all round the city to-night, but they have nothing there to equal the beauty of this scene."

"I am delighted to see you, and thank you for the compliment, and am glad, as you have just arrived in time for supper. I see Victor coming to announce it."

Bowing low, the servitor advanced, saying, "Supper waits." He remained standing to usher them in. The guests entered, and partook of a delightful repast, of which oysters, soft shell crab, mayonaise, with champagne and old burgundy, formed the principal.

"Miss de Villerie," said the Hon. P. S——, "did you design this illumination? If so, it speaks well for your taste."

"I designed it," she answered, "but it was arranged by Madame de Breuil."

"How are you, my charming friend?" said Colonel Leland to Miss Clifton; "I am surprised to find you here this evening, and lending countenance to such a demonstration. Public Opinion deems yourself and family Unionists."

"I was not aware, Sir, that 'Public Opinion' ever did us so great an honour as to think at all of us; but I am pleased, that when it did, it thought correctly, as is but seldom the case with that well-known *busy-body*. My family are Unionists, Colonel Leland, but they are, notwithstanding, Southerners."

"The rockets are ascending, ladies and gentlemen," said Judge de Breuil; "will you walk out on the balcony, to have a fine view?"

" Oh! how transcendently beautiful," exclaimed the whole party, as one after another they flew up into the air and exploded, sending out their meteor-like lights.

"You have yet to behold the most charming sight," said Madame de Breuil; "but," she added, "I believe we will have the whole city with us," as carriage after carriage stopped in front, depositing their occupants at the gate, which entering, they sauntered through the grounds in admiring wonder.

"*Bon soir*, ladies and gentlemen," said Albert la Branche and Count Beauharnais, as they sprang up the steps on to the balcony, where our party were standing. "We could not resist the temptation of driving out to have a view of this scene."

"I assure you, Miss de Villerie," said Count Beauharnais, "such a scene of enchantment would do credit to the taste of a Madame de Pompadour, and vies with any scene, I think, ever given at 'La Petite Versailles.'"

"There is nothing that taste or art could suggest, Count Beauharnais," she answered, "but is worthy of the cause, for which this is but a feeble demonstration."

"Miss Clifton, I had not hoped for so great a pleasure as again meeting you here, and the enjoyment of this evening will be greatly enhanced by your presence," said Mr. la Branche.

"Thank you, Sir, for your kind sentiment. But, hark! what is this?" The company all rose, as a most magnificent band was heard in the distance. Nearer and yet nearer it approached, until immediately in front of the mansion were seen several beautiful sailing-boats. In the front were seated the musicians. The masts were wreathed with flowers, while lights, varied as the rainbow, threw a charm over the whole, far too beautiful for the power of description. Resting upon their oars immediately in front of the mansion, the band discoursed the most delicious strains, to the delight and amazement of the guests.

"How soon does your *fête* come off, Miss de Villerie?" said Albert la Branche. "If this is the prelude, I am sure it will be a most magnificent affair; and, by the bye, I must not omit telling you of some distinguished arrivals in our city. There is at Madame G——'s a most charming young lady. She is from Cuba, and spends a few months in our city. I trust Miss Clifton and yourself will call on her, and show her some attention while she remains amongst us. Her name is Senorita Inez Montijo. The other distinguished arrival is Lord Ethelred, a Scotch nobleman, whom, if you will permit, I will take pleasure in introducing to you."

"My *fête* will come off as soon as I can issue invitations, and as I do not think I shall be able to call on Senorita Montijo, I shall remember to drop her a card, nor shall I forget your other distinguished acquaintance."

"I do not think, Miss de Villerie," said Count Beauharnais, "that you will be able to forget him when once you have seen him, for he possesses the peculiar tact of saying or doing something that generally makes an impression."

"I should not judge that you were very much prepossessed in his favour," said Miss de Villerie, smiling.

"I cannot say that I am. He seems to possess that barbarian style of manners only fitted to the highlands of his own country. A *lord* he may be, and with right and title too, but a gentleman never."

"You should not judge so harshly," she answered; "you know there are many rough diamonds."

"Certainly there are, Mademoiselle, but we do not

wear them in the rough. They are left with the lapidary until such time as there is sufficient polish on them."

"The lapidary, in this instance, Count Beauharnais, to whom this gem may have been entrusted, may have been unskilful. We are told that there is but one in the world at present to whom jewels of rare value can be entrusted, and this is, I believe, Coster, of Amsterdam, and I do not think a Scotchman would consent to a polish from a ' Hollandais.' "

"I shall not argue the subject further, but will await your opinion of the gentleman, and if it does not agree with mine, then Miss de Villerie will deceive me very much in the estimation I have formed of her judgment. However, to change the subject, would you like to promenade over the grounds?"

"Yes; I have had but a contracted view of the whole scene this evening, and will walk out as far as the levee, and take a glance at the scene. Miss Clifton," she said, "will yourself and Mr. la Branche join us in a promenade to the margin of the river? The view, I imagine, is quite pretty from thence."

"Most willingly," they replied; and soon their voices were lost in the distance, and their forms amidst the mazy labyrinths of the shrubbery. While they pursue their walk we will return to the other guests.

"Who is that *distingué* looking gentleman with your ward, Judge de Breuil?" inquired Madame Bienvenu. "He appears to be a foreigner."

"It is Count Beauharnais. He has been here but a few weeks, having, as is the case generally with all visitors to America, paid his respects to the North first.

E 2

He is quite an elegant man, and one of no ordinary intellect, but, like most foreigners, sees nothing to admire in our country. Ever comparing its buildings, its manufactures, its commerce, and institutions to those of the ancient world, forgetting that our nation is but in its infancy, and that, Hercules-like, it can now strangle in its infant grasp the monsters that would seek its destruction."

"Yes," said Colonel Leland, "it is but too true that there are but very few who can look upon our country as it was, and as it is. To think, but yesterday, in comparison with other nations, this vast country was but a boundless wilderness, and that too where foot of white never trod; where the Indian war-whoop rang through hill and dale; and that nothing larger ever floated on the surface of those broad lakes and rivers than the birch canoe of the savage. Behold it now! Palatial steamers ply our waters; and see yonder forest of masts, and then think of what we were and are. America, independent of the whole world, bears within her maternal bosom the teeming wealth of the globe. The seed of the old Puritan stock, dashed upon Plymouth rock from the Mayflower, has spread its poisoning influence throughout our lovely land, and choked up and withered that purest of all seed, the seed of brotherly love. The latter can never blossom again; there is one part of the nation where it has not taken root. The proper method shall be taken to prevent it from doing so."

The young ladies returning to the house, the guests took leave, and as the gates closed upon the last stroller through the grounds, the band struck up the beautiful

air of "Farewell, farewell to thee, Araby's daughter,"
and soon the fairy boats were out of sight.

Our heroine and Miss Clifton were up early the next
morning, and after breakfast commenced their preparations for the *fête*. The first thing to be done was to
issue cards of invitation, and the two young ladies
spent a greater portion of the morning in this employment, while Madame de Breuil went from room to room
superintending the arrangements. Victor was employed
with his corps of assistants, and Mannassier in the con-
fectionery department.

"Victorine," said Miss de Villerie, "tell John I wish
him to deliver these cards."

The servant withdrew, and soon returned, accompanied by John, who bore a large, silver card basket.
Miss de Villerie arranged the tickets in the basket, and,
with an injunction to return as soon as possible, sent
him on his way.

"Young ladies," said Victorine, "Madame de Breuil
wishes to see you, in the library."

"Come, Cornie, we must now assist in the upholstery
of the arrangements."

Upon entering, Madame de Breuil said to them,

"I merely wished to ask you if it would not be well
to partition the library into separate apartments, with
hangings of damask, for card tables. The drawing-
room being hung with green and gold, I thought I
would make the partitioning for the library of crimson."

"Where will you have the dancing, Madame de
Breuil; not, surely, in either front or back parlour, it
would ruin the elegant hangings?"

"The devotees of Terpsichore will have the drawing-rooms devoted to them, while the salons will be devoted to those who feel disposed to be merely 'lookers on in Verona.'"

"But, my dear young ladies, if you expect to receive your guests at the appointed time, you must assist yourself, and Miss Clifton can order the arrangement of these hangings with much more taste than I. How unfortunate that Siebrecht could not come; possibly he may be here to-morrow."

The hours wore on, and night fell upon the scene, when our heroine, fatigued by the labours of the day, sauntered forth to breathe the air, unattended. The moon shone bright and beautiful upon the earth, and robed each object in silver sheen. A little star trembled beside the moon, and now and then a dark cloud would roll over and obscure both moon and star.

"Pale trembler!" said our heroine, "I, like thee, follow at a distance, in thought, a planet still more lovely, for it is the image and likeness of Him who created thee. Sail on in thy unwavering course, thou beautiful moon! The little star is still beside thee. Dark clouds enshroud, but when they vanish, your little star is still seen following on. So when the clouds of misfortune shall have lowered around or enveloped thee, dearest, in thy far-off home, I shall be found beside thee, and when they pass away your little star will still be seen lingering near thee. Where art thou now? Does the same orb which shines so calm upon me, look on thee, too? Is it in joy or in sorrow? Oh! why is it not given us to know the future, or does God withhold it for the best?"

Here a rustling of the branches in the orange grove

startled her. Turning, she beheld an old negress gathering the leaves of the trees.

"Good evenin, Miss Natlie, I 'spect yu in lub, as I see yu here at dis late time ob night, meandrizin trou de grove, seemin so sperrit like, and lookin so butiful."

"I might ask the same question of you, Cynthia; you are not wont to come out of your cabin at so late an hour. Are you a worshipper of your namesake, or the stars? I was not aware that Africans worshipped them; supposed the Chaldeans were the only worshippers at that shrine."

"Yu see, Miss Nat'lee, I've cum out to gather some leaves and yarbs to make tea for my granchild, Jake s little son, what's named Nub; he's orful bad fever, and his modder knows nuthin bout practis medcin."

"I have understood, Aunt Cynthia, that medicine is not your only profession. I have heard that you are a foreteller of events, and that the stars, that to others are but soulless and speechless, to you are as the Delphian oracle."

"Ef you mean I'se a fortin teller by that long name, Miss Natlee, I must just tell yu, honey, that the bressed Lord sometimes spires me wid a knowledge of de future."

"Ah, if that is the case, you will not, I feel assured refuse to draw aside the veil of the future, and read the inscription within. Come, Cynthia, in simple words, tell my fortune."

"Ah, my dear chile, I'se sorry you axed me, but I'll tell ee de plain truf, I'se read your life, chile, not by de stars, nor de moon, but, chile, by your sweet, proud lookin face long 'go. Your'e not gwine to be happy

and 'fliction soon'll kum. Not many days 'll pass afore
that lubly high head ob your'n 'll be bowed in sorrer,
and den, Miss Nat'le, you wont care no more for lumi-
nashuns, parties, nor nuthin. Sum body way far off
yonder lubs you mitey well, Miss Nat'le, but he's gwine
to disappoint you; not kase he's ontrue, but kase, Miss
Nat'le, he's gwine to have his own 'pinion, and dat
wont coinslide wid yourn. But you'll not die ob grief,
Miss Nat'le, for you know de bressed Savior says as how
he 'fits de back to de burden.' Yu'll be like de eagle,
Miss Nat'le, yu'll soar bove it all ; and now good night
and 'scuse me if I'se ben too forrard in telling you
what's to kum."

"Good night, Cynthia, and many, very many thanks
for your information. You are not, at least,

'The Sybil who weaves
Sweet hopes for the future from memory's leaves.'"

Retracing her steps, she was soon within the portals of
the mansion, and finding all had retired, sought her
room, where we will leave her, and proceed to the next
chapter.

CHAPTER VI.

"There is a festival, where knights and dames,
And aught that wealth or lofty lineage claims,
Appear—a high-born and a welcome guest
To Otho's hall came Lara, with the rest.
The long carousal shakes the illumined hall,
Well speeds alike the banquet and the ball ;
And the gay dance of bounding beauty's train
Links grace and harmony in happiest chain :
Blest are the early hearts and gentle hands
That mingle there in well-according bands ;
It is a sight the careful brow might smooth
And make age smile and dream itself to youth
And youth forget such hour was past on earth,
So springs the exulting bosom to that mirth !"

"Lo ! all the elements of love are here—
The burning blush, the smile, the sigh, the tear."

MORNING dawned clear and cold, but found all the inmates of Rosale astir, each anxious to see the last or finishing touch given to the arrangements for the evening festivities. Siebrecht, with his corps of assistants, had arrived, and was arranging, with his usual taste, the hangings of the apartments. Victor and Mannassier were controllers of pantry and cuisine; and when evening with its purple tints fell upon the scene, it found all complete.

"Victorine," said Miss de Villerie, as she sat before
her elegant toilette mirror, "I trust you will exert your
utmost skill this evening, to render me as beautiful as
possible, as I presume this will be our last *fête* this season,
and, mayhaps, for years to come."

"Yes, mademoiselle, but it is impossible to contribute
a ray to the sun."

"Ah, Victorine, I permit not flattery, and now do
your duty in silence."

Her toilette complete, Miss de Villerie descended to
the parlour, where she sat with her guardian and
Madame de Breuil, awaiting the guests. Before their
arrival, however, we will spend a few moments in a
description of her attire, commencing with her coiffure,
which was arranged in a most becoming style. Her
glossy black hair was braided on either side of her
face in a massive, triple plait, while the back was
caught up in loops with a diamond comb. In the left
front plait, glittered a diamond star, while a chain of
the same jewels, but of larger size, crossed her hair just
a little above the forehead, and fell in a glittering festoon
of light on the right side, and was connected with the
comb in the back. She was attired in a rich crimson
rep silk, with two deep flounces of rich Chantilly lace.
Her corsage was *tres décolté*, displaying her beautiful
neck and shoulders to advantage, while her *bouquet de
corsage* was composed of flashing diamonds. Her ear-
rings, necklace, and bracelets were composed of the
same, while in her hand she held a fan, which was
literally covered with the same jewels, and which would
have been envied by a Sultana.

Madame de Breuil was dressed in a rich black silk

velvet, while her white, and yet well-rounded neck, shoulders and arms were covered by a guipure spencer. Her only ornaments were a lace barb of guipure fastened on the side of her still glossy hair by diamond pins, while her spencer was caught in front by a brooch of the same jewels. Judge de Breuil, with his usual taste, was habited in a suit of black cloth, while a white vest and kid gloves completed his simple toilet. It was now the hour of ten, and the gates, thrown wide open, admitted the carriages with their elegantly attired and fashionable occupants. Soon the parlours began to fill with as *distingué* looking a crowd as ever assembled in the halls of fashion. The lights of the chandeliers were softened by the lambent rays of six hundred wax tapers, and the blue and gold hangings and furniture of the front parlour, as also the white and gold of the back, shone like the starry vault of heaven, while the swaying crowd seemed like the galaxy. There was quite a stir in the assembly as Monsieur G——, Madame G·——, and Senorita Montijo were announced, and, though we have heard much of Spanish beauty, Senorita Montijo rivalled all that was ever seen or heard of. She was of the medium height, of a dark olive complexion, and black hair, with large and flashing dark eyes. She was dressed in a heavy satin of pale straw colour, with over-skirt of rich white blonde. Her hair was richly braided with pearls, and gems of the same kind adorned her ears, neck, and arms. Her corsage, formed in the Spanish style, of satin and blonde, was fastened with a *ceinture* of pearls. She had the tread of a queen, and in her countenance was perceived the dignity and bearing of one who sprang from a noble race. She had all the grace of an Andalusian, with the perfect features of a Castilian. As she passed through the rooms, escorted by Monsieur G——, she was followed by crowds of admiring beholders.

Soon music rose with a voluptuous swell, and soon the dance began.

Albert la Branche led out the graceful Miss Clarendon, while Lord Ethelred sought the hand of the bewitching widow Bienvenu, who, though not beautiful, possessed that *esprit* which never failed to draw around her a gay and brilliant crowd of admirers. Judge de Breuil, with Madame S——, was the *vis-à-vis* of Colonel Leland and the beautiful Senorita Montijo, while Mademoiselle de Villerie's hand was sought by Count Beauharnais. Many stars of lesser magnitude sparkled in this festive throng, but, amidst all, none shone with so much splendour as the Cuban beauty and Mademoiselle de Villerie. They reigned supreme, and seemed to rival each other in graceful display, as both seemed to possesss the very poetry of motion. Miss Montijo, as she glided through the mazes of the dance with her floating veil and drapery, seemed a very Venus, with the foam of the sea still resting on her; while Miss de Villerie, with her regal, queenly, brilliant diamonds and flashing eyes, seemed a very Juno.

"Ye Gods," said Lord Ethelred, as Miss de Villerie passed him, "I must say it would be a difficult matter for a Paris to decide this evening to whom the apple should be awarded. I must candidly confess that, in all the assemblies in which I have been, either in Europe or America, I have never seen two more beautiful ladies. In fact, I have noticed that the Creoles of New Orleans

in beauty can vie with any nation of the earth, not ex-
cepting the fair Circassians, and in taste of dress excel
even the Parisians."

"I thank you for the just compliment you pay my
countrywomen," said Albert la Branche, "and they
would not be the less grateful could they know your
flattering opinion; however, Senorita Montijo is a Cuban,
but not the less entitled to your praise of her truly transcendent beauty.

"She is indeed beautiful," replied Lord Ethelred, "but
I rather prefer that lofty style of Miss de Villerie; her
face is classically perfect and highly intellectual, while
her eyes speak volumes. I would imagine her equal to
any sacrifice when her pride was aroused."

"Miss de Villerie is, most certainly, the undisputed
belle, I shall not say of our city, but of our State; she
is not unknown either in a literary point of view, and
bids fair, in poesy, to be the Landon of America, while
her prose equals that of De Staël."

"She is, then," said Lord Ethelred, "a *blue* belle."

"Yes," said Albert la Branche, laughing, "and I
believe gentlemen of your nationality are partial to
bluebells."

"I am, indeed," said he, "and should be proud of
such a lovely specimen of that class."

"You will excuse me, Sir," said Albert la Branche,
"while I speak to some friends, who, I see, have just
arrived."

As he spoke, he bowed to Lord Ethelred, and the
latter, joining a party of ladies, was soon engaged in
brilliant repartee, while Albert la Branche hastened forward to greet Miss Clifton, who had just entered with

her brother; and now all eyes were turned upon brother and sister. Beverly Clifton was about medium height, being slightly but well formed. His head was covered with wavy, golden hair, which fell over his fair and highly intellectual forehead in the most careless manner, while his large, full, blue eyes with their darkly-fringed lashes, Grecian nose, and well-formed mouth, completed as perfect and handsome a face as is ever beheld. We have already described the sister, but we will now endeavour to pourtray her as she stood at the present moment. Attired in white glacé silk, with an over-skirt of puffed illusion intermingled throughout, with rich blonde and small bouquets of white moss-roses and gauze ribbon confining the puffs here and there. She wore no jewels, her only ornament being a natural white moss-rose bud fastened on the left side of her hair, and confining her golden ringlets in their place. If Miss de Villerie and Senorita Montijo were the Juno and Venus of the occasion, Miss Clifton was certainly the personi- fication of the lovely and retiring Psyche.

Albert la Branche paid his devoirs to sister and brother, and was presently seen promenading the superb apartments with Miss Clifton leaning on his arm, while Beverly Clifton was observed bowing low at the shrine of the Senorita, to whom Judge de Breuil had intro- duced him.

" This is, I presume, your first visit to our city," said Mr. Clifton, " as I have not had the pleasure of meeting you before."

" Yes," she replied, with her rich accent, "but I grieve to say it. Had I known of its many attractions, I think I would, ere this, have been an old friend. As it is, I do not feel as if this were but a first visit. I seem to think that I have seen each object, and met each face in some familiar scene. It may have been in dreams, but I have encountered many here to-night that are strangers only in the etiquette of the word."

"They may truly deem themselves fortunate who bear in their face an impress of your dreams, for I imagine you regard them with more favour than the unfortunate individual whose only recommendation is his introduction."

"By no means; yet it is pleasant to feel that we are surrounded by scenes and persons that are seemingly old acquaintances; and yet it may be my feelings arise from the fact that Louisiana, at an early day, was under Spanish government. How strange it is, the many changes the government of this state has undergone. First under the French government, then under the Spanish, again the French, lastly the United States, and soon, I presume, to be under that of the Confederacy. How does the latter, Mr. Clifton, accord with your sentiments?"

"I feel it were useless to express my opinion, as it has now gone too far for aught that one of Union principles could do or say to arrest the great issue, which is war. My family are Unionists, and regret to see the bright stars of the old spangled banner disappearing from the cerulean sky on which they shone so brightly for so many years. It may be only their sidereal day. I trust if so the sun, which rose so gloomily, may have a refulgent setting. The South is mine by birthright, the Union mine by heritage from forefathers, who fought, bled, and died in her defence."

As he ceased speaking, Madame de Breuil advanced towards them, leaning on the arm of the Hon. P. S——, and said, in her most engaging manner, "Mr. Clifton, I trust you have not been entertaining our fair guest with treasonable sentiments. Methinks I heard the words 'Union' and 'star-spangled banner.' You are aware, I presume, that these are ostracised from all patriotic assemblies."

"Most assuredly, Madame, and lest I should meet with the same fate, I shall henceforth be more guarded in my use of the condemned expressions; however, I know that you, Madame de Breuil, would refuse to deposit a shell against me."

"I will promise you my support, I assure you, but on condition that you will never more offend. And now let us go and take a view of the card tables and their occupants, as I do not think you have yet even glanced at the rooms devoted to the graces." As they entered the room Miss Montijo's eyes became riveted on the face of one of the card players, a lady, seemingly but in the prime of womanly beauty, though, on close inspection, she was no less than forty-five years of age. She was above the medium height, of a rich brunette complexion, dark brown hair, and large, penetrating, hazel eyes. Dressed in a robe of crimson velvet, with a scarf of black blonde, richly embroidered in gold, thrown over her magnificent neck and shoulders, which the art of none but a Creole would dream of covering. She sat with one arm resting on the table, gazing steadily on the cards which the rest of the party had thrown down.

"What magnificent lady is that?" said Senorita Montijo to her companion. "She is my very idea of an Oriental beauty." As she spoke, Beverly Clifton turned in the direction to which he saw her looking, and replied,

"Is it possible that you have not seen before the superbly handsome Madame D——, of our city? She is the wit, and undisputed married belle. You perceive how completely absorbed she is in the game before her. She is accounted an unexcelled card-player, and report says she almost nightly at her palatial home either wins or loses a fortune."

"I was under the impression, Mr. Clifton, that my country alone permitted the fair sex to indulge in such amusements. I had imagined it to be something unknown in America for a lady to bet on cards."

"With the American portion of the community it is not tolerated, and it is only so amongst those Creoles who adhere to the customs of their French ancestors, and have clung with tenacity to a fashion which the very idea of its being Parisian is enough to make it legal in the upper circles. But let us on to other scenes, Miss Montijo. The band has ceased, and I hear a magnificent voice in strains of song. Will you go with me in pursuit?"

Leaving Madame de Breuil surrounded by a coterie of octogenarians, of whom she was the divinity, they advanced towards the chamber from whence the singing proceeded. Miss Clarendon stood at one side of the piano, a very beautiful and attractive girl, while Miss Clifton stood on the other, and the melody of their voices soon drew a crowd around them.

"What an enchanting voice Miss Clifton possesses," said Lord Ethelred. "Her voice is perfect supplication

F

and tenderness. I never listened to a sweeter in my life. Though Miss Clarendon's is more the superb style, I do not like it as well. The latter would urge one to deeds of daring, while the former would soothe one to acts of gentleness. The one the lark, soaring aloft, while the other is the plaintive dove. But see," he added, "here is the Philomel," as Miss de Villerie was seen advancing with a party of ladies and gentlemen towards the piano.

"Come, Miss de Villerie, give us some music," said Madame Bienvenu, who anticipated the wishes of Lord Ethelred.

"To afford pleasure to my friends, I consent," said Miss de Villerie, and, seating herself, she sang, with a soul-subduing tone, the beautiful solo "Viens," from Charles VI.

As she ended she was called upon again and again, and politeness only caused her to relinquish the seat to others, for had she yielded to the solicitations of her friends she would have done so at the expense of her courtesy. Miss Montijo was now called upon to play, and seating herself at the harp, she struck the chords with all the wildness and mastery of a Welsh bard, and sang in thrilling tones, "The Moorish Lament." Her large and liquid eyes seemed to swim in revenge, and her voice rose and fell like the sighing of a storm spirit on ocean's rock-bound coast. Her style was lofty and grand, and her every note thrilled to the very soul. When she ceased the band struck up a march, and the doors being thrown open, the guests entered the *salle-a-manger*, where was spread a banquet that the most fastidious disciple of Epicurus could not find the least cause to complain of. Wine flowed, and wit sparkled from fluent tongues, and the hours rolled on in revelry. Miss Clifton and Albert la Branche had separated themselves from the festive throng, and sought the inviting beauties of the conservatory, which opened from the parlours, and which was now illuminated, displaying the various exotics and gaily-plumaged birds in their golden wire cages. There in the depths of artificial groves, cataracts, and fountains, one might easily forget their identity, and imagine themselves in the midst of a South American forest, or standing amidst the deep and fertile valleys of Switzerland, as here and there a miniature *châlet* peeped forth from an artistic opening in the shrubbery. In one part might the sad notes of the arapengo and alma-perdido be heard, and in another, and not far distant, the tinkling of a sheep bell, reminding one of Alpine glaciers, and the grazing of flocks at their vernal base. Arriving at a fountain at the lower end of the conservatory, Miss Clifton and her companion seated themselves. The tableau was beautiful. By the side of this fountain, in whose waters their forms were pictured, they sat while Time's flying hand pointed to the "wee small hours." Shaded by the leaves of a graceful palm, and gazing abstractedly at the nereids and dolphins which sported in the basin of the fount, sat Albert la Branche and Cornie Clifton, seemingly in all the boyishness and girlishness of a Paul and Virginia.

"Miss Clifton," said Albert la Branche, as he took within his own her yielding hand, "I trust the impetuosity of my nature will be sufficient apology for what I am about to say to you, and this, I find, is quite as appropriate a place as any other for the avowal of my feelings. I need scarce utter the words, for you must have known that, from the moment we met, I loved you with all the ardour, depth, and sincerity of one who, though possessing a susceptible heart, never knew the meaning of the word *love* until he met you. Yes, though I have knelt at many shrines, it was done with the same feeling as one who bows at the altar of the idol his ancestors worshipped, with the conviction that there was a *true* God, not formed from things of earth. I, like this idolator, have found my idols dust, but in you have found the true divinity, at whose shrine I shall only offer heart-incense, pure as ever rose in clouds from the altars of Baal, or the *true* God. Speak, Miss Clifton; tell me that I may hope to win your love, and that I am not wholly indifferent to you."

As he ceased speaking, she raised her eyes to his, and said, as the blushes suffused her neck and face, "Mr. la Branche, is it possible you can love, or *desire* the love of one whose feelings and sentiments are so diametrically opposed to your's?"

"What matters it to me," he said, "what your sentiments in regard to other things or objects, so that I possess your love? If we love each other there will be no difference of opinion. Parthenia gives to Ingomar the only true definition of this divine feeling—

> ' Two souls with but a single thought,
> Two hearts that beat as one.' "

"Then," she replied archly, "this implies a yielding up of one or the other's nature, which yields? I presume, however, chemically speaking, the weaker substance is dissolved by the stronger fluid *n'es ce pas ?*"

"Miss Clifton, there is nothing weak in love, be it human or divine. It was the latter that caused a God to immolate himself for ungrateful men. It was the former which caused Coriolanus to forego a victory. It was the latter which left us records and footprints of saints and martyrs. It was the former that gave strength to a queen to suck the poison from the wound of her husband, caused by an envenomed dart. It is by the latter we hope for our salvation. Yes, Miss Clifton, it is only those who can boldly face suffering, and are prepared to make sacrifices, who can love. I feel assured, too, that your sentiments on this subject coincide with mine."

"Vraiment," she said, "you are a most excellent expounder of the code of Cupid; he has an able advocate."

"Ah, Miss Clifton," he answered, "I perceive that you are disposed to trifle with me, or that my homage has been offered to one who cares not for it, or who possibly gives me to understand by evasions that she would spare me the pain of a rejection."

"Do not, Mr. la Branche, I entreat you, judge me so lightly, nor think for a moment I would trifle with any one's feelings, particularly one who has honoured me with such sentiments as you have expressed. No, be assured that your kind regard for me is not unappreciated, and believe me when I say that I am grateful for the partiality which has sought me out from amongst so many fairer and worthier ladies, and which has placed me, too, in the enviable position of being chosen by one whom it might be deemed a privilege to be permitted to love." She stopped soon as this sentence was uttered, and the blood which had died away, now returned in gushing tides, surging over neck and face, and Albert la Branche rapturously and respectfully placed her hand to his lips, and then pressing it to his heart, said,—

"Bless you, Miss Clifton, for those words, though they do me more than justice. I knew I was not mistaken in your true womanly heart, and though if you could not love me, even I should deem myself happy and honoured in being possessed of your friendship. I know that our acquaintance is brief, almost too much so in the estimation of the world, for the liberty which I have taken in giving utterance to words and feelings which are but the outpourings of a heart burning with all the intensity of a first, pure, and devoted love. I had dreamed I loved before, the reality convinces me, Miss Clifton, years of acquaintance could never make me more wholly yours than I am at this moment. If you doubt, then let years of devotion prove it. Exile me, if you will, I would deem centuries of toil as little, compared to any ray of hope that you would in the end be mine. May I look forward to that moment, say, dearest Miss Clifton, shall I be allowed to hope?"

"Mr. la Branche, I am unskilled in the world's arts, and in its deceptions. I have never, like many others, been able to don the habit of hypocrisy to suit a purpose, and then lay it aside at will, like an unpleasant garment. I know, however, that if a woman wishes to be loved, she must conceal her sentiments from the object of it. This may be a true philosophy, but it is only suited to the Stoics. I, like yourself, am a Southerner by birth, though a current of Northern blood flows in my veins, and has somewhat tempered the burning, and lava-like tides, which would otherwise consume me, as it does many. I, however, am not sufficiently philosophic (if it can be so termed), to school my heart to falsehood, and be it for weal or woe, I most unhesitatingly place my hand in yours, and say to you, beside the waters of this fount, in whose crystal purity I trust is symbolised our hearts, that I love you fondly and devotedly, and let the world, in its cold sense of propriety, deem me what it will for so readily confessing it; I would not wish to know you longer, or better, if time or a greater knowledge could dispel the affection I have for you now."

"Generous and devoted girl," said Albert la Branche, throwing his arms around her, and drawing her close to his heart, " you shall never have cause to regret the confidence you have reposed in me. Yes, love and trust me, darling, and you will find me not unworthy ; and may the love which you here confessed this evening, joined to my own, grow deeper, stronger as time passes away, and may it, when your golden locks and my raven hair are changed to argentine threads, may it be still as now, each loving and beloved. Dearest in your love, I possess strength to arm me for the combat, and a shield, which shall be my safeguard from all evil. And now, beloved, let me have once more your sweet assurance (ere we are intruded on), that I am loved, and that you promise to be mine ?"

" Yes, dearest Albert, I love thee, and thee only, now and *eternally*."

"May this then seal the compact which angels now record," he said, bending over, and kissing her fair cheek, "and may your assurances be as often, ay, more often renewed than that rainbow covenant, which reminds us of God's mercy to men."

They arose from their rustic seat just as the merry voice of Madame Bienvenu broke upon their ears, saying in the most bewitching tones, " Here are the truants ! Come, you must give an account of yourselves, and tell us how you dared to absent yourselves from the presence of our noble company, thus displaying your preference for the solitude of the forest to the splendours and gaieties of a palace."

" Your Majesty being surrounded by so many cour-tiers, should not envy your less fair *dame d'honneur*, the attendance of one of her truest, faithful, and most liege subjects," answered Miss Clifton, in the same ironical tone; " but see," she continued, " your court approaches ; gay ladies and their attendant cavaliers, and Misses de Villerie and Montijo being alone likely to dethrone you by their seeming conspiracies amongst the nobles of your realm."

" *Ma chere*," so long as the *vrai* nobility are loyal (alluding to Lord Ethelred), I shall not even fear a dethrouement a misfortune, as you are aware that royalty seldom succeeds in pleasing the rabble. *Mais allons*, Lord Ethelred, I have many beauties in Rosale to point out to you." Bowing they passed on, and soon our young friends were surrounded by the crowd, who now filled the conservatory, and when each and every one seemed delighted to rove. The band discoursed sweet strains, which fell upon the ear harmoniously in this lovely spot, and served to drown in melody the tones of lovers, as they breathed forth their love tales. But the brightest scenes must fade, and so, too, our brilliant pageant, as one by one the guests left the festive chambers, and bade "adieu" to their hospitable entertainers. There still lingered one "when lights had fled and garlands were dead," and *he* alone had not "departed." Reader, can you divine who it is? Not to keep you longer in suspense, it was Albert la Branche, *the accepted.* When the crowd had dispersed, the lovers had returned to the conservatory, and now he stood with his arm around her slender form, seemingly loth to part from his chosen and beautiful *fiancée.* But footsteps are approaching, and he must leave. Dipping his fingers into the waters of the fountain, he said (as he sprinkled the water drops upon her head), "I baptise thee, my own dear Cornie, in a new faith, that of trust in the one you have chosen as your guide through life, and in that of the noble cause I have espoused, and may it be pure as these crystal drops which I sprinkle upon your golden curls ; and may it wash away for ever every Union sentiment now existing in the bosom of my lovely, beloved, and affianced bride, and may this parting kiss be the seal on these lips to close for evermore the eloquent pleadings, which in a *just* cause might win a world." Thus, with a kiss, they parted, and leaving her, he hastened to pay his respects to the family, and then left a happy and a *proud* man.

Miss Clifton stood still beside the fountain where he had left her, and truly she looked the "spirit of the fount, as with her eyes dreamily gazing into the waters, she seemed not of earth, but of a holier sphere." The lights were fast paling as she arose to seek her chamber, there to "think on the past, and dream o'er the future." We will follow her, and listen to her soliloquy. Seating herself, she rested her arm upon the marble slab of a table near her, and clasping her hands in an attitude of prayer, murmured, " Engaged! and to one I have so lately known, but yet so *dearly* love. Oh, happiness inexpressible! Yes, my own dear Albert, how gladly I would forsake all else save thee, to follow whithersoever thou should'st go. I said I was thine. and thine only. Oh, how cold, how chillingly cold are these words to my burning love for thee! How truly does that minstrel of Erin—Moore, express my love for thee when he says,—

> " Imagine something, purer far,
>   More free from stain of clay,
> Than friendship, love, or passion are,
>   Yet human still as they.
> And if thy lips, for love like this
>   No mortal word can frame,
> Go ask of angels what it is,
>   And call it by that name."

" Yes, dearest Albert. Go ask of angels what it is, and call it by that name!" We will now drop the curtain upon this scene and soliloquize ourselves. " Beautiful dreamer on Life's tempestuous sea, no clouds of sorrow appear above the horizon of your hopes, and no winds ever ruffle the surface of your sunny sea. Beautiful mariner, keep close to shore! Gentle gales will at first arise to tempt thee farther into the treacherous depths. The sails which bear your little bark on so gallantly now will soon be furled, or lowered by the storms and billows amidst which you will fearlessly venture. See you not already in the distance the boiling, eddying waves advancing slowly and threateningly? No, you are dreaming, my ocean-bird! But see you not the stormy petrel as it dances on the foam-crested waves? No, thy little shallop floats on merrily with no fear of breakers a-head. Dream on, it is meet that it should be so. Soon enough the veil of the future will be raised, and too soon, alas! your little boat will sink beneath the whirling maelstrom of trouble. It is afar off, but like the Arabs of the desert, I am accustomed to the indications of the simoons' scorching blast, and just as plainly in the distance I see thy bark overwhelmed, and thy white arms clinging to the wreck, thy wild eyes raised to Heaven, and thy failing voice crying as he of old, 'Save Lord, or I perish.' Yes, sail on, beautiful dreamer, but keep close to shore."

CHAPTER VII.

"I stake may fame (and I had fame),—my breath—
(The least of all, for its last hours are nigh)
My heart—my hope—my soul—upon this cast !
Such as I am, I offer me to you
And to your chiefs, accept me or reject me,
A Prince who fain would be a citizen
Or nothing, and who has left his throne to be so."

"Poor human love ! when did its current run
Without a rock, a fall, beneath the sun ?
When wind through daisied meads and singing bowers,
Without a dragon lurking in the flowers ? "

A MONTH has passed by since the events recorded in the last chapter, and Time in his onward march has wrought many changes. Nought was now heard in the streets of the city save the measured tread of the regular soldier, or the less perfect of the raw recruit or volunteer. Business houses were closed, and but few gatherings were observed on the pavement of our once busy thoroughfare, Carondelet. Revolution, together with no cotton going to market, has wrought this change, and the haughty merchant, princes of Carondelet, bowed low in reverence to its once humble, rival, Camp, which now with its banks, brokers' offices, insurance houses, publishing and printing offices, draw vast crowds to its once less frequented resorts. Camp was decidedly *the* street, and daily were seen thousands flocking to the doors of the few, *very* few banks that still discounted. Hurrying home from the North came parties having property and assets in the city, in order to save their interest from sequestration, leaving their families in the North, where they have been citizens for many years. Pale and anxious these individuals passed one by, so occupied with their schemes of outwitting the Government, and making transfer of property that they brushed past unheeding all save self. These despicable beings, who sucked the blood, and ground the bone and sinew of our wealthy planters, as the last act could only turn traitor to a country that had bestowed affluence and position on the sons and daughters, children and great grand children of Yankee school-masters and school-mistresses, as well as milliners, shopkeepers, and pork-dealers. Ingrates, that they were, their hour was fast approaching. Camp Street, as before remarked, was now *the* street, and this morning thousands thronged its broad pavements to witness the *entrée* of General D. E. Twiggs who was just returned from Texas, after having delivered into the hands of the Confederates the United States garrison. Every door, window, and balcony was lined with welcoming spectators. Soon the swell of music rose upon the air and fell upon the ear of the expectant multitude, telling that the "chieftain advanced." Now the chariots came in view which bore the honourable escort, which consisted of the first gentlemen of the different seceded States then in the city. Next came the veteran himself in a

splendid landau drawn by four beautiful white steeds.
Bowing and smiling to the ladies who were enthusi-
astically waving their handkerchiefs and strewing his
way with flowers, he passed slowly on, and every now and
then the vast assembly of people rent the air with accla-
mations as he "bent his eminent top to their low ranks."
On he passed, and the vast crowd of people rolled on in
waves also, until, arriving at his mansion, he entered
and was lost to view. Night came and still they
sought to do him honour, and when the serenade roused
him up at the close of his day of weary travel, but of
pleasant reminiscences, his heart bounded with gratitude to think he was still remembered, and advancing
into the corridor bade his domestics throw wide the
portals and admit those who sought to do him homage, and to prepare a banquet worthy of his name.
(The author need not dwell upon this subject, for
others who were also witnesses of the honours conferred on him, and the high appointment which was
soon after bestowed will recognise the sentiments of the
people, and the patriotic devotion which prompted
them). It was far into midnight when the crowd once
more reluctantly withdrew, and the shouts of "Hurrah
for Jeff. Davis, Gen. Twiggs, and the Southern Confederacy," broke upon the still air and died away in the
glooming. But a patriot's act had called forth these
huzzahs, and in the soul, heart, and voice of every man,
woman, and fair maiden, did it echo and re-echo again
and again. Yes, the hour had dawned for Southern
liberty, and to her standard flocked the great and
lowly, and one amongst the first to place his sword at
the feet of the Southern Bellona was the hero just

named; he had served too to an honourable old age in the service of the United States, but when his native soil was threatened he, like a true son of a noble mother, espoused her cause and rallied to his standard his faithful adherents. Sublime is the picture, "When all deserts thee I shall still be with thee," and such were his sentiments now in the hour of his country's need. He was not however alone, and every day found the desks in the senatorial chambers at Washington deserted one by one, until none but the republican or Abolition party remained, and our hopes grew bright and strong. The North at this hour was losing the radiance that had made her appear as the light of a new universe, and in her political, moral, and martial firmament her stars were beginning to pale, while in the Southern canopy of Heaven beamed forth new and brighter constellations. The storm of hatred had not as yet swept over the earth (true some blood had flown), but it was brewing, and the elements looked dark and forbidding. Did it find us unprepared to meet the issue? *The end will prove.* Dark clouds and rolling thunders, presage, ruin, but after they are passed come brighter days with smiling sunny skies. Dear reader, I am not an historian, nor do I wish to venture on historic soil. My work is only intended to pourtray a few (to some perhaps interesting) events that will be probably lost sight of by more worthy "gray goose quills" than mine, but which are not the less *true* or valuable. Oh no! I assure you I have a great horror of the female politician, the literary lady who affects the Madame de Staël, or Roland. Let her appear in what guise she may, wife, mother, or *maid*, she is dangerous in *any* form and sure to be the *mother of mischief!* So now, kind reader, I will transport you to other and more agreeable scenes.

We will now return to our fair heroine with whom we parted so unceremoniously on the night of the *fête*, on this bright spring morning, and find her seated in a grotto, whose rocky sides are thickly covered and over-hung with jessamine and honeysuckle. She holds in her hand a book entitled "Woman's Faith," and so intent is she gazing on its pages that she hears not the footfall which approaches. The intruder speaks, when slightly starting, she arises to her feet as Count Beau-harnais says—

"Miss de Villerie will, I trust, pardon this intrusion on her privacy of so warm a friend as Eugene Beau-harnais will prove himself."

"You are pardoned, Count," she answered, with a slight blush; "but may I ask who gave you the clue to this Rosamond bower? it is not many, I assure you, who ever enter here—this is my *sanctum sanctorum.* Tell me, I pray you, who directed your footsteps to this spot?"

"Most willingly," he responded. "Being told you had gone forth to promenade in the grounds, and not caring to sit in the parlour to await your coming, I thought I would stroll through the groves of this arcadia likewise. So, sauntering through interminable labyrinths of flowers, vines, and trees, I came at last upon this grotto which, in its appearance, reminded me of Calypso's, and I thought I would enter—and, behold! —and lo! a divinity! And now, Miss de Villerie, I have but one word more to say, and that is, that I promise to act towards you with more gratitude than Ulysses or Telemachus, provided you are as generous towards me in your invitation to prolong my stay."

She smilingly remarked, "I do not think, Count, that you stand in need of the consolations of either of those classic heroes, as you have not as yet apprised me of your misfortunes, nor on what coast you suffered shipwreck—as the latter will only entitle you to my protection."

"Then, fair *mortel ou déesse*, I claim it, for I have long since been wrecked on the *coral reefs*, and I now throw myself upon your mercy, as you alone have the power to render me insensible to my sufferings."

"Then, *allons* to the mansion, where I shall take pleasure in receiving you, and where my *jeune nymphes* await your pleasure."

"No, Miss de Villerie, let it be here, where nature vying with art may render me eloquent to express my sentiments to you. We will now lay aside trifling, and speak sincerely. Sit down, Miss de Villerie, I have much to say. I will not speak to you of love in the hackneyed strains that is always used, but I will tell you simply *that I love you*—have loved you from the moment we first met—and that now I desire a candid response from you."

As she essayed to speak, he said—"Hear me through, Miss de Villerie, and then answer sincerely, and, as I know you to be a *true* woman, considerately. I came this morning to lay at your feet my heart and hand, as also to ask if the love which burns within my own breast has met with a reciprocal feeling in yours; and to say that, should you not entertain feelings of love

G

for me, such as would prompt you to accept my proposal at this moment, I would say, Miss de Villerie, that if you can but esteem me, and still will permit me to love you, I shall hope to win you at last. If, on the other hand, you love me, as I have been vain enough to hope, will you consent to wed now, and leave with me a country that is soon (I may say already) to be the theatre of a civil war, which will end in the ruin of every one? Yes, Miss de Villerie, I prophesy for your country a lengthy contest, then consent to be mine, and fly with me to *la belle France*, where mid its scenes of splendor you are fitted by birth and nature to adorn, you will forget the woes of your native land, and with my devoted love to guard and cherish you, you will cease to regret the honoured, loved, but distant guardians of your child- hood's days. And now, Miss de Villerie, I await your answer."

She had in vain essayed to speak, and now as he ceased she arose from her sitting posture and stood erect, leaning her arm upon a jutting rock, and regard- ing him with a sad, regretful look, she said—" Count Beauharnais, you will confess that it is your own fault that you have gone thus far in making an avowal of feelings that I can never—no, never, reciprocate. If I had ever given you to understand, by word or action, that such feelings were known or would be reciprocated, then, I assure you, it was done without any such inten- tions on my part. But were it otherwise, and that I loved you, Count, you know little of my nature when you would make such a proposal as your last. Think you, would I leave my country when the invaders' foot- steps are polluting its soil, and when their assassin hands are raised to strike at the heart of each and every countryman of mine, to revel in the halls of fashion and nobility? Count Beauharnais, you little know me. Could I, suppose you, leave the graves of my father and mother behind me, and know that they were being trodden upon by our ruthless enemies, and I, too, far away? Could I leave either the honoured, dearly-beloved guardians of my childhood, girlhood — ay, womanhood, to brave the storm alone, who had sheltered me from the tempests which usually beset an orphan's life. *No, never*, Count Beauharnais! My God, my country, and her people first—these are termed *celestial* affections. Love of *man last*, which is terrestrial. One who is untrue to the three former, would never be true to the latter. So, now, my dear friend, you will perceive that if the first of your proposal were possible, the latter were *impossible*. And now I trust that I have answered you as fully, as concisely, and considerately as you could desire, trusting that my candour has not forfeited your esteem."

"My esteem, Miss de Villerie? No; nor what is more, my love, which you still possess, and which is but increased by the utterance of these noble sentiments. I shall not be long in your city, Miss de Villerie, and I trust that I still shall be permitted the pleasure of your society, as, notwithstanding all you have said, I hope to win you yet. Yes, I will hope on—hope ever, for you will never meet with love so true as mine; and when ocean's waste is between us, remember that I shall need but one word of recall and I shall be with you. Your friendship, Miss de Villerie, I accept for the present; all aspirants to honours must serve an apprenticeship."

Saying this, he took her hand, knelt before her, and
pressing it to his heart, impressed a burning kiss upon
it, and then rising, said—"Come, let us home; I have
no desire to remain longer here." As he led her forth,
he plucked an ivy leaf, and said—"Permit me, Miss de
Villerie, to fasten this in your hair." She bent her head
gracefully, and as he secured it with her golden pins in
her raven tresses, he continued—"I am like the ivy you
will find—should adversity overtake you, I will cling
the closer to you." He walked beside her for some
time in silence; at last, glancing at the book she now
held closed in her hands, he said—"May I ask of what
subject your book treats that you were so engrossed with
when I entered this morning?"

"I was reading and pondering on the inconsistency
of this author, who evidently advocates abolitionism,
and Protestantism, yet in her writings has been culpable
of many errors, inconsistencies, and, without malice, I
can say, untruths, some of which I will read you. First,
the writer is evidently a rank Protestant, and can find
nothing in the *Catholic religion* to censure, but launches
forth into a very pathetic strain of moralizing, which
she puts into the mouth of her hero, referring to N. O.,
says, 'Here no temple-spires frown upon the gay
votary of pleasure, but beneath the very shadow of the
old cathedral, and under the unreproving eye of those
who minister at her altars, I may pursue pleasure in her
wildest revels, to her hidden and most secret retreats.'
In this the author has displayed such malevolence of
spirit, as well as gross and astounding *ignorance*, that,
though controvertible in every point, the very idea of
combatting the arguments of such a benighted indi-

vidual, worries me; for though we would be willing to instruct a child, we would hesitate to begin the task with one who had grown up to manhood, or woman-hood, with such a foundation for their guide, and with false views on every subject, gathered from those with as small a share of enlightenment as themselves. So it is in this case. To plant the seed of a good fruit is pleasant enough, but to uproot the bad, is not so agree-able a task. But, notwithstanding, our ministers do not reprove us for sinning; her hero comes to the conclu-sion that in our church (the Catholic) alone are found the 'self-sacrificing angels of earth.' Hear what she says. 'I know, rejoined Blanche, that few of our sex have won for themselves the golden opinions of the world, by acts of disinterested and self-denying benevo-lence, but there are some who, though their names are not blazoned upon this world's scroll of fame, will find that they are written in the book of life for the unseen and blessed charities which from their hands have fallen like the dew upon the poor and deserted children of humanity. How often by the bed-side of wretched want, and pining poverty, are seen those *Sisters of Charity* providing for the necessitous, even to the most menial offices, or soothing the last hours of the sick and the dying, when others of our sex, blessed with the most ample means by the Father of us all, look with stolid indifference, and unconcern, upon the saddest picture presented by the wretchedness of our fallen race! The world looks upon these, I know, as a part of a great orginery prepared by the Roman Catholic church, but such acts could spring from no sectarian feeling, and no more belong to that church than does

the magnificent old Gothic architecture, the living,
breathing pictures of the Madonna, and the crucifixion,
or the *ora pro nobis*, whose mellow, rich, solemn tones
are so deeply entrancing.' 'My dear Mademoiselle
Blanche,' continued Miss de Villerie, 'this is just so
much wholesale robbery on your part. Will you tell
me who it is that recognises the crucifix as the emblem
of salvation, or who it is who has preserved from the
wreck of time the ' life-breathing portraits of the
Madonna,' as also who the composer of this chant, whose
solemn tones seem so deeply to entrance you? These
were all in existence ere your Luthers, Amsdorfs,
or Melancthons were dreamed of, and generations ere
their presumptuous separation from the mother church.
Ye have wandered forth like the prodigal, and would
now willingly gather to yourselves the crumbs which
have fallen from our groaning board. Return, kind
friends, like that prodigal, and we will share our
treasures with you, even to the 'fatted calf.' But permit
me to read you again another of her *very consistent*
speeches. After anathematising slavery and slave-
owners, she says, in reference to some slaves who were
emancipated, and sent north, in response to the following
question. 'How are the negroes,' said Burns, 'treated
by their white neighbours?' 'I am sorry to say,'
replied Eaton (who, by the way, is a Methodist minister,
and, as something quite *rare* in this instance, *one* of
that sect tells the truth), 'with no little degree of dis-
favour. Even those are loudest in their denunciations
of slavery, are the least *tolerant* of the dark skins of
these children of Africa.' And further on, a Northerner
by birth expresses these sentiments. 'I regret to

admit,' said Burns, 'that there is strange contradictions in the conduct of those who reside in the free States, upon the subject of the rights of the coloured race. They exclaim, with holy horror, against the sins of slavery, and yet their prejudice against colour is vastly greater than it is at the South. And in some of the free States they have carried it to the extent of passing laws forbidding free persons of colour to reside within the limits. This is the philanthropy they boast so much of, and this is the consistency you will ever find amongst them. I can truly exclaim, 'Consistency, thou art a jewel!'"

"From the style, Miss de Villerie, in which it is written, I should judge the author to be a female, and you know a good writer amongst your sex is seldom met with, and still more rare the *jewel, consistency.*" He said this with an arch look, and was about to speak again, but she stopped him with the imperative command of, "Not one word more, Count. Not one word more will I listen to, after this flattering compliment paid our sex. Not writers indeed! Is it not well known that the Greek poetess Corrinna took the prize *five* times over Pindar; and that in a later day a woman's pen caused one of the greatest Generals the world ever knew, afterwards an Emperor, viz., Napoleon, to tremble and grow pale. So much did he fear the world-renowned De Stael that he even ordered her to quit his dominions. I could quote *many*, but *you* are too well aware of those *facts* to make it necessary."

They had now reached the door of the drawing-room, and Judge de Breuil, advancing to meet them, said, as he handed Miss de Villerie a letter, "My dear

Miss de Villerie, I was about to go in pursuit of you, as I imagined you would be pleased to peruse the letter. The Count and myself will excuse you while you retire to learn the contents." Saying this, Judge de Breuil drew the Count's arm within his own, and they entered the library, where we will leave them to smoke their Havanna cigars if they like, while we follow Miss de Villerie. What has caused the blood to rush in crimson tides to our heroine's neck and brow? Glancing at the superscription, she had clasped the letter to her wildly-beating heart, and with hurried steps had sought her chamber, and there, turning the key in the lock to prevent intrusion, she kissed the seal, and there opened the missive. Reader, as her eye glances over the page, what causes her cheek to pale, and the tear-drops to dim those lustrous eyes? Can you not divine it? The next chapter will unfold all.

CHAPTER VIII.

"A change came o'er the spirit of my dream."

MISS DE VILLERIE sat for hours gazing upon the letter she held in her hand, while the large tears coursed slowly down her cheeks.

"Can I be dreaming?" she murmured. "Oh! is it not some dreadful illusion, or is it indeed true that he whom I have loved so fondly can be other than he once seemed to me? And yet I thought him noble, and would have yielded up my life for his happiness; but now, when he sees my country on the eve of a revolution, which may end in the ruin of her people, he ingloriously consents to wield his sword in defence of a Union which long since ceased to be just. Oh, Clarence, Clarence, recall what you have said. No, no, I can *never, never* wed the enemy of my country and her people." But, kind reader, I will not hold you longer in suspense, and will lay before you the letter which called forth those remarks :—

"My beloved Natalie,

"Long ere this reaches you, possibly the blockade of your Southern ports by our Government (or rather

mine) may render a response to this by mail impossible.
In the event of such being the case, you will please
send your reply to our mutual friend E. G. A——, and
he will promptly deliver it. And now, my own dear
Natalie, I will lay before you the exact position of
affairs in regard to us both, and I know that as usual,
with your good sense, sound judgment, and loving
heart, you will triumph over and defeat every obstacle
and objection that may come between yourself and the
fulfilment of my own, and I trust *your* wishes, and consent to be mine without further delay. The dissolution
so long looked forward to, by some with sorrow, by
others with joy, has at last arrived, and our country
(though we of the North still mention it as *one*, we
must inwardly confess that *in feeling* it can never be so
again) is divided, and civil war now frowns upon us in
its most fearful panoply. Natalie, my own dear, be
mine, ere rivers of blood shall flow between and separate
us, mayhap for ever. I have espoused the cause of my
native land, and am now clothed *cap-à-pie* in the armour
of faith, right, and justice, to go forth to quell this
unholy rebellion. Beloved, there are none to whom
you owe obedience. Though early ties will cling around
your memory, and mayhaps cost you many struggles,
fling them aside, darling, and trust in one whom you so
fondly promised to love. Trust in me, and give me
that right which you long since promised, to protect
you, and I shall feel strengthened for the contest which
approaches. Give me but the *right* to claim you, Natalie,
and I will soon be with you. Remember, dearest, that
let your decision be as it may, I will *never* surrender my
right to your hand, and though you disclaim me for

ever (for I have presumed from your letters that your heart is with the cause of the South, and I have feared that possibly your love has changed for one whose politics differed from yours, and that I have forfeited your love, your undivided love, which I once felt was mine), I will *never, no, never* resign you. One word, dearest, will bring me to you; *less* may separate us for all eternity. Be it in this world, or in the next, you can never be other than mine. Fly with me, my Natalie, from a land that will soon be deluged in blood, and its now verdant and cultivated fields and gardens be laid waste and desolate. Yes, fly with me to a clime where there are those who await to shower all the blessings of peace, love, affection, and heart-worship upon you. I await your decision, my truly, dearly beloved *fiancée.*

"CLARENCE BELDEN."

"This, then, oh Clarence, is the alternative—you leave me! I cannot give thee up. Oh, why dost thou play the tyrant in this trying hour? But I must yield one or the other, and though it sever my very heart-strings, I will resign him for aye. Yes, now while love, pride, and honour struggle for the mastery, I will write *my last* (O God! that it should be so) to one whom it is the sacrifice of all my earthly happiness to resign, but whom it were now dishonour to love." Sounding a bell, she said to Victorine, who answered the summons, "My escretoire, and let none enter my apartments, and say to all calls for me to day, 'Not at home.'"

"Oui, Mademoiselle, but the gentleman below,

Count Beauharnais, just desired me to say to you that he wished to say adieu *en personne*."

"Say to him that I am indisposed, but will be pleased to see him on his next visit to Rosale, which I hope will be soon."

The maid disappeared, and in a few moments returned, bearing the escretoire, as also a large crimson poppy, which she presented to her mistress, saying, "Count Beauharnais desired me to present to you this flower, which he said he himself had culled on the *parterre*, and the card attached." Taking up the card, she glanced at it, and seeing the word "Consolation," remarked, "Nothing could indeed be more appropriate. I do indeed need consolation, but there is none save One who can afford it me. Noble-hearted as you are, Count Beauharnais, I could never love you, though perhaps on the altar of a less true idol my heart's best gifts have been offered up, and now the idol has proved but common clay, and those God-like attributes where are they? Ay, echo answers, 'Where are they?'" Seizing her pen, she wrote the following reply :—

"Rosale Plantation, Louisiana.

"To Clarence Belden, Esq.,

"As you yourself have adopted the means of eternal separation, you will not nor can you be surprised at the manner in which I herein address you. The step you have taken will for ever efface from my heart, ay, even *memory*, all reminiscences of the past, and though I loved you with tenfold the strength of my nature, I would sever with my own hand the last heart-string that bound me by even one thought to the enemy of my country, my home, and fireside. I need not tell you now of my trust in you, and how I had fondly imagined that you would be among the first to resign in the service of a Government which equals in its oppression of the South only England's tyranny over Ireland, and Russia over Poland. I need not say to you how I had trusted in your bravery and chivalry, and, lastly, I need not say (for you must know it) that by your last act you proved to me that my idol was only formed from common dust or gilded *loam*, and the last stroke of your pen transferred my *beau ideal* into all and everything but that which is noble, elevated, and sincere, and how, when Clarence Belden donned his sword and buckler and armed himself *cap-à-pie* for the contest, that the first thrust of the glistening steel entered Natalie de Villerie's heart. Oh, no! this were all unnecessary. It may be some consolation to you to feel that when the 'deluge of blood,' of which you speak with such unconcern, shall have inundated our country, and our 'verdant fields are laid waste' that its sanguine floods will sweep over the graves of every man, woman, or child of our own sunny land, and that when the avarice of our Northern foes shall drain these fields which you say are to be laid waste, and with the natural consequence of a sanguinary deluge to be submerged in blood; when they shall drain them I repeat, to plant, and in time to reap their ill-gotten harvests, they will find, perhaps, the dragon's teeth which they sowed with such diligence as the fruits of their labour. Yes, the blockade will soon be established at all our Southern ports, which is intended to starve us into submission, but rest assured we have not been idle. Our mountains,

lakes, hills, valleys, and rivers contain within their bosom
an ample supply for the wants of our people, and even
should it last so long as to exhaust these resources,
we of the South have faith enough in the right of our
cause to believe that He who suffered not the Israelites,
his chosen people, to perish, will send to us that
which was vouchsafed to them—the manna. Rest
assured we are prepared for all emergencies, and even ·
our women, in devotion to their country's cause, will
stand unparralleled in history. Each and every Southern woman's cry is 'Give us but a crust of bread
and a cup of water from the running brook, but *give*,
oh, give us liberty.' The truth of what the poet has
said in the following lines is but well exemplified in the
unanimity of the sentiment which pervades all ranks
and condition of my sex :—

> 'The love that bids the patriot rise to guard his country's rest,
> With deeper mightier fulness thrills in woman's gentle breast.'

"Yes, like the Spartan mothers of old, our women
say to their husbands, sons, fathers, and lovers, ' Come
with your shield, or on it.' What would under other
circumstances have been death for me to do, under the
present I do without one pang of regret, not even one
lingering thought of the *past*. After this letter shall
have received its address from my pen and be des-
patched to you, the waters of oblivion will roll over
every souvenir of the past, and efface even your name
from a heart where once I had thought it as deeply
written as Queen Mary said of Calais, it would be
engraven on my heart. And now farewell. Let no
thought of me when you go forth in your armour of

'Truth, Right, and Justice' add weakness to your arm; be assured you will find your equal in every man and a foeman worthy of your steel in the humblest Southerner. Then defend yourself, at least what you do *do well* and *bravely*. Believe me in all sincerity unchanging in my resolution,

"NATALIE DE VILLERIE."

The struggle was now over when Miss de Villerie laid down her pen; she was calm, but it was the calmness of a martyr who lays down his life for his faith, but whose *flesh* only writhes on the rack of torture, the soul being elevated far above the ephemeral joys of this world. Her nature was one that loved deeply and with all the intensity of those who can love but once. To Clarence Belden the first pure gushing love of her youth and womanhood was given, and now that he had failed to be all that she had deemed him she had no further faith in men. Alas, how sad it is to think how mere gilding can seem so like genuine gold! Rising from her seat Miss de Villerie paced the apartment slowly and thoughtfully, murmuring sadly, "Yes, I have given thee up Clarence Belden, but like Marino Falerio who condemned his son to banishment, the sentence I have pronounced will kill me. Oh! how false the words 'without one pang of regret,' and yet they are true, for it is not *one pang*, but *ten thousand*, and my poor heart is breaking 'neath its weight of *pride* and *honour*. Did not the rich blood of an ancient honoured line pour its strong tides through my veins, I would fly to thee and thy promised love; *but never!* rather let this heart of mine suffer until it cease to beat than dishonour the

ancient house from whence I have sprung by an alliance
with the foe of home, friends, and country. My father,
dost thou watch over thy child from thy far off home in
heaven? If so strengthen me in this bitter hour.
Must I say farewell to him I love (yes, oh God, more
than words can tell) *for ever?* Must all the pleasant
happy days be effaced from memory by the waves of
that river Lethe which to some afford joy, to others grief.
Away ye phantoms of evil which surround me with your
flapping wings, and who seek to destroy my peace for
all eternity. Away, I say, to the dark shades from
whence ye sprang." Throwing herself upon a couch,
she fell asleep, with her dark hair falling around her she
slept a fevered sleep. Madame de Breuil entering, and
seeing her thus, gently drew the letter from her hand,
which she held close pressed to her heart. She then
summoned Victorine, and ordered her to bring ice-water
and lavender. She gently bathed the brow, temples,
and neck of the unhappy girl, and bending over her
with all a mother's tenderness kissed her fevered cheeks,
while a hot tear stole down her own and dropped upon
the burning cheek of Miss de Villerie, who starting
from her uneasy slumber, and seeing Madame de Breuil
raised her head from the pillow and said wildly, "Yes,
yes, he is gone for ever, and past recall, and like Mary
Queen of Scots I have signed an abdication to all happiness. Oh God! why have I loved so fondly?" Burying
her face in the lap of Madame de Breuil, who understood
all, she wept convulsively, and tried to speak. At last,
obtaining the mastery over herself, she said, "All
was as I feared, Clarence Belden has espoused the
Northern cause, and thus has sealed my fate and

his own! You thought I slept when you entered. Oh no! It was only a delicious dream of that long ago, dreams of that sad but still happy time—when the few shadows that fell around my path in life was like the green spots in the desert where the traveller halts to rest awhile, and feels the cool refreshing influence of repose. Oh, I saw him as when I had first met him, in the moment when he first taught my young heart the delight, the ecstacy of loving and being loved; and when he had breathed into my spirit bright and sunny hopes as well as celestial aspirations—making the world, this life itself, a Heaven of bliss and unalloyed felicity! Oh, as I dreamed, there stole over my senses that perfect sense of repose which children of earth rarely feel, and to which I doubt the famed cup of Haskesch could add one drop to. This sensation thrilled my whole being, and I felt borne upon the wings of angels far past earth and clouds, ay, further, and yet further still into the realm of eternal light. Then such strains of music burst upon my ear, that it seemed as though the melody was produced by the rushing of angels' pinions, as they swept past each other in their worship before the throne of the Eternal. But slowly died away the mellifluous cadences—and slowly, one by one, Heaven, its angels— bright wings and golden throne—fled from my view, and earth again appeared to me as I slowly passed through aether descending. When, lo! as I approached nearer, there stood an angel on a beautiful green knoll, who beckoned me towards him. Unconsciously I was borne to the spot; and seating myself at the feet of the angel (methought his wings o'er-shadowed the whole hill and valley in front of me), I glanced beneath at the base, beyond the valley, there rolled a river of blood, and beyond it nought save desolation; while on the side on which I sat with the angel, smiled verdant plains, clear and sparkling streams, with charming cottages beside sylvan lakes, and at my feet grazed flocks and herds, and all seemed busy, active life. On this sanguine river floated a gilded steamer, out of whose pipes flew birds instead of smoke. To the opposite side there flew the vulture, raven, crow, and petrel, and the side on which I sat with the angel, flew over the dove and gay plumaged songsters, until all the vale rang with their song.

After I had beheld the sight, the angel plumed his wings for flight, and saying, "Thou hast chosen well," vanished into the thin grey air; and thus, methought, there fell upon my face a holy dew, which dropped from his wings as he ascended; but alas! dear, dear friend, I awoke to find it but a dream, but yet you have endeavoured to make up for the dew of Heaven by the refreshing dew of friendship, which your kind hands were administering when I awoke. Would thou were a Joseph to interpret my dream or vision. Oh! why is it, that it should be thus; that he, whom of all others I idolized, should now prove unworthy, but still dear, ever dear to me. Why, oh! why, did I rely so implicitly in him? I, whom the world has termed cold, and even austere, am stricken like a fragile blossom by the first gale on life's shores. Oh, my country, my people, though I love you much, this sacrifice, for me, is greater than Jephtha. Yes, for he promised to offer the first he should meet; but alas, I have offered myself upon the altar of patriotism. Oh, my God! accept this heart—

this life-offering, as a willing, but, oh, it is a bitter holocaust. Slowly she sank upon her couch, and with her white hands crossed upon her breast, she once more sank to repose.

She had asked for his letter, and it now rested on her heart. One large tear trembled on her eyelid, coursing its way down her fevered cheek, fell upon her bosom, and rested like a diamond on polished marble. She slept calmly, peacefully, and when morning dawned it found her serene as a spring day.

No one could have told how hard the struggle had been who saw her as she greeted Judge de Breuil, as he entered the breakfast apartment on the morning after her reception of Clarence Belden's letter. No, not the keenest observer could trace, in the smiling face, and proud manner, a single mark of grief or self-sacrifice. Little do the smiling valleys, green and fertile sides of the volcano, with here and there a hamlet at its base, bespeak the convulsion which oftens rocks the earth to its centre, and devastates the land. So with Miss de Villerie, the convulsion had passed, and the lava which flowed from the fire of love out of the crater of passion, had now cooled, and she appeared like the exterior of the volcano, smiling and unconscious of the still slumbering sparks within. Breakfast was eaten in silence, and though not a word was spoken on the subject to Judge de Breuil, he had guessed all. As they arose from table, he said to Miss de Villerie, " at your leisure I would see you in the library."

" Then let it be now, dear guardian, as my leisure is ever at your pleasure."

On entering the library, Judge de Breuil seated Miss

H 2

de Villerie in a chair, and drawing one beside it, seated himself, and thus began :—

"My dear ward, I would speak to you this morning, not as your guardian, but as your father, which part I have acted, to the best of my ability, since the demise of my highly esteemed and much valued friend, your father. I shall ask of you no recital of what I have already my suspicions, though none but the anxiety of one who loves you with parental devotion could have discovered it. I would not lacerate your heart by requesting any particulars of a subject which, as a woman, you would feel a delicacy in discussing, even with me; but thus much I would say, my beloved ward, that, if Clarence Belden has possessed your heart until this moment, permit him to retain it, and do not blast your hopes of earthly happiness by resigning him. No, let no such love of patriotism destroy your felicity. You are now of age, and your own mistress, still though we (my sister and self) would regret to see the moment in which you parted from us arrive, yet if you can be happier with him who has won your heart's worship than with us, we both would resign you to love and joy, though it must be confessed we would feel a pang in yielding you to one whom I learn is now our declared enemy, and thus placing a barrier between the intercourse of love and friendship, which, if your lot had been cast amongst us would exist. Nevertheless, by following the dictates of heart and conscience, you will never forfeit the love of those whom long years of acquaintance have endeared you to; rest assured dear Natalie, that because you should give us up for a newer, but less tried love, we should not love you the less, or would the name of Mrs. C. Belden should ever be less esteemed, nay worshipped, in our hearts and homes than that of Natalie de Villerie. Your property which the laws of the Confederacy, under such circumstances, would not yield to you, I have taken the precaution to save, and secure to you, and to the amount your father left you, I will add fifty thousand dollars, as your marriage portion; thus you perceive, I have shielded you from all the obstacles which generally make the road to true love so unsmooth ; and now, my dearly-loved Natalie, choose as you will, and rest assured if it be the ' better part' it shall not be taken from thee."

Miss de Villerie had sat with her face averted during this conversation, and now she knelt before him, from which position he in vain endeavoured to raise her, as, sinking low at his feet, she rested her head upon his knees, and clasped his hands close within her own, in vain she essayed to speak, when a torrent of tears coming to her relief, she said, " Oh, my guardian, my own dear father, how could you speak thus? Leave you, oh no, never. Leave you to go to the love and home of one who is now and for evermore your enemy, and that of all that is true to me. Oh, my own kind, my own dearly-beloved guardian, how could you deem me such an ingrate. Yes, Clarence Belden, I have loved deeply, fondly, ay, almost madly, but it is passed now. The power he held was a tyrant's, and now I am free. Yes, free, but like a bird in the serpent's power, my heart yet clings to reminiscences of the soon to be for ever buried past, and sighs for the love-illumined paths through which I once roamed when under his fond eye. But think you, oh think you, I would accept bliss at

such a price? No; to happiness I have breathed a
long, a sad adieu, and on the shrine of God and my
country I have laid my bleeding, but trembling, lacerated heart. Yes, dear, dear guardian, I have cast the
die, and crossed the Rubicon, and am now passing on to
victory, sadly, but gloriously. No more shall love's
spells weave their thralls around me; never again shall
my bosom inhale the consuming air of passion, save love
for tried and faithful friends, such as you, my dear
father, by your care have proved to me. Yes, dear
guardian, I shall choose the better part, and where my
girlhood days have passed in blissful repose, here will
Natalie remain, and when once more tranquillity of mind
asserts its sway, you shall see no tears bedewing these
now dimmed eyes, but you shall see me the happy, gay,
almost thoughtless, being I was when first your kind
hands, and those of your sister, commenced the training
of this crooked vine. Yes, your home shall not be sad-
dened by any sorrows of mine. Yes, oh yes, these bitter,
bitter tears in which my eyes now swim, shall cease to
flow, and I shall never look beyond the threshold of home
again for love and happiness, save far above to that
One whose love shall never change, and in whose
guidance I shall ever trust through life. Yes, my
guardian, with thee have I lived, with thee will I die.
The storms that may ruffle the waves of thy existence
shall break over mine also, and the billows which may
engulf thee shall also roll over me. The friends who
are thine shall be mine also; the stars which beam o'er
thy pathway shall shine on mine; the breeze which fans
thy cheek shall sweep o'er mine; the flowers which
waft their fragrance to you on the summer air will bear

my prayers for you as incense to the throne of God; and, lastly, that God who shall be thine shall be mine, and the grave that closes over you shall also clasp me in its cold embrace. And now tell me, oh tell me, have I chosen well, my father, or do you doubt that I love you, and all the bright joys of a life which was spent with thee, and which shall continue? Clarence Belden was all to me once, but now the spell is broken, and here alone in my childhood's home will I seek love such as will survive the ephemeral joys of earth. Keep the dowry which you so generously offer to bestow, or lay it as an offering on our country's altar, and take all else, but leave me, oh leave me, your love, which is far more preferable than gold can ever be." Arising, she caught his hand, pressed it to her heart, and imprinting a kiss upon it, turned to leave, when gently arresting the movement, he drew her to his bosom, saying, "My daughter, you have indeed chosen well and nobly, and may you find in the affection of those around you compensation for the love you have so heroically resigned. *You have won the victory over self*, and proved yourself by far a greater general than those who have won their laurels upon a gory field. Your father, who, perhaps, at this moment is witnessing your noble self-sacrifice, smiles a benison on thee from his far off heavenly home. Time, the great assuager of grief, will dry those tears, and you will again love as truly and ardently as you have loved your misguided Clarence."

"Never, oh never, my guardian. I have—I have loved Clarence, and though on earth the irrevocable will of Fate is such that we have been separated, I shall at last be his in that land to which we are all hastening,

where no cold terrestrial ideas enter; and though I
renounce him for ever here, yet beyond, far beyond,
'the foes that threaten, and the friends that weep,' we
shall be one. Though, like the flowers, my love dies
for awhile, it shall bloom again in the clime where
spring is eternal. Though the world may deem me
stern and cold, and though Clarence should think me
false-hearted, I reck but little, we shall at last meet to
part no more. Then speak not of other love for me.
No, never shall other love come between mine and
thine, my dearly-beloved Clarence. My country now,
my Heaven hereafter."

"Then be it so, my child; and may no clouds darken
the vision of the celestial joy which you have so beautifully pictured, but may every gale waft you nearer
that port in which your hopes are centered, and may all
your aspirations of unalloyed bliss be fulfilled; and now
dry those tears and come with me for a drive to the city"

"If it were to any other I should plead an excuse,
but to you, my beloved guardian, whose will is law, I
shall say I go with pleasure."

Leaving the room, she hastened to her apartment,
and soon after Judge de Breuil, who stood on the
verandah, whip in hand, awaiting her, handed her into
the phaeton, and they were soon seen dashing up the
coast. The morning breeze, as it was borne from the
Gulf, fanned our heroine's still flushed cheeks, but soon
they paled, and returned to their usual healthy, but
peach-like, tinge. They drove briskly, and though Miss
de Villerie was far from happy, you would say she was
perfectly so, could you have seen how entirely she seemed
to forget self, as she gaily talked with her guardian.

"I received this morning," said Judge de Breuil, "a card from Count Beauharnais, who leaves to-morrow for Europe, and wishes to know if a visit from him this evening would be agreeable; I, therefore, thought we would take him home with us ; what say you?"

"I shall be pleased indeed to say farewell *en personne*, and regret exceedingly the loss to our circle of friends, to which Count Beauharnais has been such an acquisition. He combines in himself the true gentleman and the man of the world, and forms a rare exception to the latter class in retaining purity of heart and mind, though in constant intercourse with the world's most varied scenes. Though wealthy and noble, he is unassuming, and humble—he is a true descendant of his illustrious house, though he is quite as modest, if not much more than one of our republican-born creoles."

"He certainly possesses a fine eulogist in my fair ward, and, I fear, if he were heretofore not proud, and heard your eulogism, he could no longer boast humility as one of his characteristics."

"Well, I assure you, I admire Count Beauharnais, and seek not to disguise my sentiments, and must candidly confess that if my heart had not been smitten ere I met the Count, it would most undoubtedly have surrendered itself to him. There are none even among my oldest acquaintances who claims a higher place in my regard and esteem than does Count Beauharnais."

"A countess's tiara would well become my ward, and I shall be delighted to see one sparkle upon her brow. What sayeth Natalie?"

"'Tis not in glittering gems that truth, love, and

nobleness are found; oh, no, my dear guardian! nor
would Count Beauharnais stand less in my estimation
dispossessed of rank, wealth, and coronet. No, place a
man like him in a rude hut, amid the wilds of our own
native forests, and he would be distinguished from the
common herd *by soul.*"

They had now reached the suburbs of the city, and
the morning sun gilded spires and domes, and its
radiance fell alike on the elegant mansions of the rich
and the less pretentious abodes of the poor. Market
carts were returning from the city, and their owners
were chatting gaily as they drove to their humble
homes, while the light bark of the fisherman glided over
the waves, as, with sails unfurled, he swept down the
stream to his home on the gulf coast. Singing gaily,
these rude children of nature passed on their way, and
our heroine contrasted her happiness, her hopes with
these, as thus she mused in silence. "Ah, were it not
well for us if the gilded visions of joy, bliss, and content-
ment which our vain imaginations picture forth, should
ignis fatuus like evade us as we pursue; and that we
might descend to the tomb still trusting that the far-off
morrow would realise the hopes of to-day. Their anticipation of each honour and aspiration are as great,
according to their sphere, as mine; but how far short
when we have tasted the cup of reality, from that of the
sparkling fount of imagination. There is the same
difference as that between the appearance of the ocean
which, to the observer, is deep blue, but when put into
a glass, proves that only to the eye it appears thus."
They rode on in silence, occupied solely in thinking and
gazing at the different sights which now crowded on

their view. All was busy animated life, the Rue Royal was crowded with persons of every age and sex, and Canal-street's broad pavement thronged with the beauty of this gay city, while the drum and fife of the W. A. were playing a martial air, to the time of which the young volunteers stepped. Dashing officers rode by on prancing chargers, and all was as a holiday. Our heroine bowed low as she passed down the Rue Rampart to a couple who were promenading, and whom she recognised as Lord Ethelred and Madame Bienvenu, the sprightly lady returned it, and passed on, seemingly engaged in a deep political discussion which, doubtless, had more to do with Scotland's being the most agreeable place in the world for one to reside, than the States of America at this period, and of which he might doubtless convince his fair companion, who it seems he had almost won to his opinion and politics, and who bade fair to be Lady Ethelred. Our heroine had now arrived at the residence of Colonel G——, and, ringing the bell, Judge de Breuil left her at her friends' to spend the morning, while he returned to town to meet his gentlemen acquaintances. Miss de Villerie was ushered into the parlor, and was very soon in the warm embraces of her friends, of whom there were many.

"Oh! my dear Miss de Villerie, you cannot imagine the happiness it affords me," said Madame D——, "to receive you once more in my home, you have scarcely afforded your friends a view of you since spring, and I have understood that your kind friend, Madame de Breuil, could not even prevail on you to come from your recluse's cell. I trust, my dear it does not originate from the same cause that permitted a certain disease to

prey like a worm in the bud on a certain young lady's
cheeks ? "

"I assure you I have not denied myself the pleasure
of my friends' society for any such reason as your
remark might suggest, but in spring-time my custom is
to seek the society of more inanimate natures than the
human kind.   I spend a great deal of time enjoying the
unfolding of the buds, and with my botany in hand I
spend hours in wandering among these gentle harbin-
gers of spring, thus I feel more pleasure in receiving my
friends' visits than in returning them, as I know you will
agree with me in saying that it is much more pleasant
to be the dispenser of hospitalities than the recipient."

"I quite agree with you in its being a great pleasure
to dispense them, but I assure you I find an equal
pleasure in the reception, and trust on being convinced
of the latter.   My dear Miss de Villerie, you will make
your visits much more frequent, and thus afford me an
opportunity to dispense the honours of hostess much
oftener.   And now I intend to engage your fair hands
in our service for some weeks to come, and I know if
your love for your friends does not draw you from
seclusion your well-known patriotism will.   We are
engaged in making up clothes, uniforms, for the volunteer companies, and have formed societies to this purpose, of which my friends have appointed me president,
Miss Bienvenu as vice-president, and yourself, *sans
votre permission*, secretary, knowing that you were
anxious to further the cause, *et maintenant*.   What
say you ? "

"That I accept with pleasure.   And now tell me, if
you please, when begin my duties ? "

"We shall hold our first meetings in the parlour of the 'St. Charles,' until we arrange a suitable place for assembling to sew. Madame Bienvenu was here this morning, and said that it would be much better for us to meet alternately at the houses of those who are disposed to join us, and appoint, and obtain some place or room where those persons who are employed and paid to sew for the soldiers can work. The companies are rapidly forming throughout the State, and it is only just that we should do all we can to aid the glorious cause of independence. 'Miss Clarendon, montrez Mademoiselle, the bannerets which you have made.'"

That young lady arose and brought forth the bannerets of silk, which were made for the regiments, and, as she presented them to Miss de Villerie, said, "To you we have left the design for the grand banner which we propose presenting to the regiment next week, who leave on the 15th; and I was requested in the name of the ladies of our mutual acquaintance to beg that you would also consent to present it."

"I thank you, and my friends, for their generous partiality in selecting me for so distinguished an honour among so many entitled to that distinction, and will most willingly accept, if but to manifest that I shall not only thus prove my loyalty to our cause, but the gratitude I owe them for their kind preference. So trusting to meet you again soon, I beg leave ladies to wish you good morning, as Judge de Breuil awaits me without." Taking an affectionate leave of her hostess our heroine was soon on her way home.

CHAPTER IX.

Is it for this the Spanish maid, aroused,
Hangs on the willow her unstrung guitar,
And, all unsex'd, the anlace has espoused,
Sung the loud song, and dared the deed of war?
And she, whom once the semblance of a scar
Appalled, an owlet's 'larum chill'd with dread,
Now views the column—scattering bay'net jar,
The falchion flash, and o'er the yet warm dead
Stalks with Minerva's step where Mars might quake to tread.

" Yet others rapt, in pleasure seem,
    And taste of all that I forsake;
Oh! may they still of transport dream,
    And ne'er at least like me awake!"

" One should our interests and our passions be
    My friend must hate the man that injures me."

" Who dares think one thing, and another tell,
    My heart detests him as the gates of hell!"

THE immense concourse of ladies which filled the
saloons of the " St. Charles " on the morning of the
—— testified the sentiments which prevailed, and
unanimity of heart-felt interest in the noble cause,
they each and every one espoused. The morning too
seemed to smile on the efforts of these patriotic women,
who left their homes and children to look after the
comfort of their noble volunteers. On foot and in

carriages came the daughters of the South, all and every one but too anxious to be first to place their name amongst those most willing to serve their country, but it would be a difficult problem to solve, as at one and the same moment arrived, the pedestrian and the more opulent, who rolled to the doors in their carriages. The meeting was soon called to order by Madame ——, and after some two hours, the regulations being formed and the places of meeting being decided upon, the assembly adjourned, *sine die*, but not until they had appointed a place of rendezvous for those in the paid employ of the committee.

A spacious room at the corner of Canal and Camp Streets was the place decided upon for the seamstresses of the committee, and Madame L—— was appointed to the charge of this department, while Mesdames Gardame and Millendon were authorized to receive all donations for the society. Mesdames L——, F——, T——, R——, were chosen to present subscription lists, and to Misses de Villerie and Clarendon were given the charge of the flag department, with the request of the committee that Miss de Villerie should design the same. The forethought of the ladies seemed to embrace everything which might contribute to the wants of a soldier, and to the comfort of a camp life. One was appointed to receive lint bandages, and jellies, for the wants of the sick soldiers, while others were to receive shirts, drawers, and socks, for the comfort of those who were well.

As the President of the Committee parted from Miss de Villerie, she said, "I trust you will have your *drapeau* in readiness for the sabbath, as we wish you to present it to the battalion."

"I shall not fail to do so," said Miss de Villerie, "as the fair hands of Misses Clifton and Clarendon, as also Madame Bienvenu have volunteered to assist me in the work of love."

"*Certainement,*" these ladies responded, while Madame Bienvenu continued, " I assure you it will be a pleasure to set the stitches in a flag which shall wave triumphant over our foe, and it will be more agreeable still to think that as many foes as there are stitches shall fall on the spot over which it shall ever wave victorious."

" Ah, *ma chère amie,* you seem to be sanguinary, but I am happy to think though you wish our enemies annihilated, that you do not display that blood-thirsty feeling after all which has immortalized the Chicago young lady, who, it is well known, said 'that if the South did secede, and war ensued, she would have what she most of all things wished as an ornament, viz., a necklace of the eyeballs of Southern men,' which her *beau,* or lover, has promised to bring her."

" *Mon Dieu!* what fiendish cruelty. I think a woman who could give birth to such an idea worthy of the most cruel death that could be inflicted, and after death to undergo eternal punishment," said Madame Bienvenu. "Oh, no," she went on, "though I trust our foes may be defeated, and suffer for their wrongs and insults, yet such punishment, or the idea of it, could not originate in the mind of either a woman or man, but only a fiend incarnate; and all I have to say for this young lady is that if she had existed in the time of our Saviour, he might have been called upon to dispossess her of a fiend, as none but one possessed could ever dream of such a thing ; or had she lived at that time she would possibly have whispered

something into the ear of Herod which would have suggested a more agonising death, if, indeed, there could be
one more terrible, for our Saviour. Yes, I will pay her
the compliment that in cruelty she surpasses the most
refined ideas of the Jews or Romans."

"I agree with you," said Miss de Villerie. "No
woman can ever entertain such feelings. Woman's
heart has but two feelings which are natural, namely,
love and pity. Revenge is not part of a true woman's
nature, and hatred has no part in her breast. When
her foe lies bleeding, her resentment is gone, be the
wound literal or allegorical, and she flies to render all
the assistance in her power, and to pour into his gaping
wounds the balm of Gilead. Such is woman, the ministering angel in adversity, the sage counsellor in prosperity. But, come, let us go; time flies, and we forget
our banner is to wave on Tuesday next over the heads
of our brave battalion."

The ladies were soon in their carriages and on their
way to Rosale, where they had soon arrived, and
were busying themselves cutting and sewing long strips
of red and white, and embroidering white stars upon
the blue ground.

"*Ma chère* Natalie," said Miss Clifton, looking up
from her embroidery, "I am told the Count has left us
for his native shore. How could you let him leave,
when you might have retained him?"

"Yes, Count Beauharnais has left us, and it would
have afforded me pleasure to have had him remain; but
I do not imagine that I could have influenced his
actions."

"Ah, *ma chère* Natalie, *soyez sincère,* you cannot deny

but what you held him enthralled, and that it must have been a strong power that dispelled his hopes. There are not many who would be willing to let a coronet slip so easily from their grasp. Do you know," she remarked in a low tone, "that report says you rejected Clarence Belden to marry Count Beauharnais."

As she said this she glanced up, and became silent, when she saw the agonized expression of Miss de Villerie, who first crimsoned, and then paled, but sustaining her courage she left the room in a few minutes, but was quickly followed by Miss Clifton, who said, throwing her arms around the convulsed form of Miss de Villerie, "Forgive, oh forgive me, Natalie; indeed, indeed, I did not intend to wound you. You know I did not," she weepingly cried. "Oh, how could I have been so thoughtless! Tell me, oh tell me you forgive me, my own dear friend, whom for worlds I would not wound in thought, word, or deed."

"My darling Cornie, forgive? you were forgiven ere you asked. What is there to forgive? Nought can come between thee and me, my darling, but pardon me if I caused you one moment's anxiety by an emotion that I cannot resist. But, oh! Cornie, never until this moment have I breathed to other than my cherished guardian one word of that which has separated us for ever. I——, Clarence, and myself. Yes, Cornie, it was as you predicted, Clarence espoused the cause of his native State, and thus we are sundered from each other, as far apart as the North and South pole. But, oh, Cornie, if it should be as you say, that the world with its foolish, heartless babbling, shall say as you have said, and that it reaches Clarence, he may think that it is indeed for rank and unbounded wealth I have cast from me the holy ties of long, long years, but time shall prove how fondly I was his until he declared himself my country's foe. Yes, I was and am his, and though we meet no more here, Cornie, I shall be his in heaven."

"Oh speak not thus, Natalie, my friend of friends, you will meet again to be happy, I trust, when war's stern voice shall cease to be heard within our pleasant homes, and when once again you will be the brilliant, gay Natalie of yore. Hope for the brightest, whatever betide."

"No bright sun shall ever rise to me again, Cornie; I have sacrificed my happiness on my country's altar, and never again shall bliss on earth be mine; but pardon this weakness, my dear Cornie, I did not mean to betray it and thus distress you. Come, I shall summon courage to bear the next shock, and now let us descend to our friends." They were soon within the room where the ladies were employed, and seating themselves they commenced the embroidery of the stars.

"I assure you, Miss de Villerie, you deserve to have conferred on you L'étoile de Légion d'Honneur, you have embroidered these so beautifully," said Madame Bienvenu, as she glanced over the shoulder of Miss de Villerie and caught sight of the beautiful golden stars which seemed to sparkle as in the firmament on their rich azure ground-work.

"Thank you for your graceful compliment, Madame Bienvenu, but as I have no aspirations for any insignia of favour that Royalty can bestow, I shall feel perfectly happy in the legion of brave soldiers that shall stand beneath these stars, and fight for not *me*, but all the fair sex, and whose life-blood will flow to protect their standard."

"Oh, I am well aware of your very independent and truly American spirit, but feel surprised that you should have no ambition to win the smiles of royalty. I am sure, had I conferred a less compliment on our friend, Madame L——, of world-wide reputation, she would scarcely have thanked me. Nothing less than a *royal compliment* would be noticed by her."

"Yes, I am quite well aware of our friend's weakness, and have felt amused at her conversation in regard to the nobility with whom she mingled during her brief sojourn abroad. I have often been surprised that a lady who had held a position in her own country could have ever so far forgotten the *nobility of self* as to pay the court to rank which she did."

"It is not at all strange to me," said Madame Bienvenu, "anxious to shine in a sphere herself, to which she was a stranger, she deemed it more politic (which it certainly was) to serve than to act as her predecessors had done, she stooped therefore to curry favour where an *American lady* would not more than condescend. The glare and tinsel of court, accompanied with its show of pomp and ceremony, had she been a true American would have been in ridiculous contrast with our simple and unpretending ceremonies at the "White House," where all alike receive the smile and greeting of our President; but she is evidently one of the kind who would pass carelessly by the humble violets of life, which are covered in their modest simplicity with their green leaves, emitting their fragrance unseen, to revel in the rank odours of a sunflower, which would more flatteringly turn its broad coarse disk towards her, as its *height* would command her respect. But she is no representative of an American lady. No, an American lady would make these scions of princely races feel how much greater to be an American, each free and independent, than be the footstool of hereditary greatness. I am astonished that she should have been as well received even, as it is generally the case, that those whom we seek to please most, we generally succeed least with."

"I am not at all surprised, Madame Bienvenu, as after a twenty-five years' diplomacy with foreign countries, through the medium of every sprig of nobility that appeared on our shores, and the entertaining at her home of every traveller of note, she was certainly entitled to some notice; it would be more than rude had those whom she entertained, and for whom she strained every nerve to serve, as well as the strain of her purse-strings, treated her otherwise than courteously."

"But why is she so silent now?" said Miss Clifton; "she who is always the first in the public arena; what can be the cause of her silence at this time? Surely, *now*, she were excusable for *appearing* where before she might have been censured for even *speaking*."

"Ah, my dear young lady," said Madame de V——, "her politics are like Talleyrand's. 'Show me the victorious banner, and I'll tell you on which side I am.'"

So said he, and so says our female diplomatist. She would not endanger her popularity by such an imprudent step as to side with either, but like our Saviour

and King James, I say, "Those not with us are against
us."

"So say I," said Miss C——, "but you will find
many, like Madame L——. It is not every one who is
possessed of that innate independence to act without
regard of consequences, and according to dictates of
conscience. Yes, rest assured it is policy, and this alone,
that keeps this modern Countess of Blessington so quiet.
Her voice has been raised on all other subjects, why not
on this? Policy! It must indeed be a stern policy
which should dictate to a woman silence in such a
cause."

"I would breathe my sentiments, and speak them
boldly in the face of friend and foe," said Miss de Villerie.
"In a moment such as this, one should recognise no
claim save their country's; friendship, affection, esteem,
and love should be banished far from our breasts, if it is
to make cravens of us in our hour of trial. Let the tie
of our country's love first be strengthened, and afterwards let us find room in our hearts for other. Maledictions rest upon the head of those Tarpeias who
would sell their country's fair fame for golden favours of
the enemy, and may the fate of Rome's recreant daughter be that of all lukewarm persons, who, by their conduct display the traitor or the craven. Too many of
the kind have dwelt in our midst, and it is necessary
that our land should be rid of these moles, who plot in
the dark, and undermine with their subterranean machinery the foundation of our most glorious institutions.
Now is the time to judge friend from foe; now is the
time the pruning knife should be placed at the root, to
eradicate the budding imperfections of the glorious

Confederate tree, whose branches shall o'ershadow the earth, and whose blossoms shall be '*defiance*,'—whose fruit '*victory*.'"

"*Bravo, ma chère* Mademoiselle," said Judge S——, who had entered unperceived, and stood silently admiring the eloquence of Miss de Villerie; "Bravo! Such an advocate in our cause is sufficient guarantee of success."

"Welcome to Rosale, thrice welcome, Judge S——," said Miss de Villerie, advancing towards her guest, "and permit me to assure you I am not alone in my sentiments, as each of my fair lady friends here expressed themselves with quite as much spirit, but I was only fortunate in being heard."

"By no means, Miss de Villerie; to you we most unhesitatingly and unanimously accord the palm of patriotism, and to you alone there seems to be given an inspired voice in advocating your sentiments," said Madame Bienvenu, "but we, though unable to express ourselves in the same glowing terms and speech, nevertheless feel the justice and truth of all you say. You know, Judge, it is not all who share the gift bestowed on Isaiah.

"Ah, my dear Madame, I would still suppose, from my knowledge of the ladies, and from their powers of oratory, that, like Elijah's mantle, it was cast upon them as an inheritance, ere he left this terrestial sphere, his power of persuasion was certainly transmitted *to one*, whose lips I have myself seen glow as though touched by living coals, whatever cause she espoused."

"I thank you," said Miss de Villerie, "in the name of my sex, for this graceful compliment; and now I presume, Judge, we ladies are indebted for this visit to the complimentary rumour which has been spread abroad relative to our handiwork, and the design of the flag, which was originated within these walls, and in the fertile brains of the ladies whom you see present."

"I will admit, fair lady, that such is the object of my visit, and I feared I would be compelled to return without gratifying my very laudable curiosity, as your porter informed me our sex were entirely excluded from these meetings; but on informing him of my septegenarian claims to entrance to these sacred precincts, and assuring him that I possessed no attractions to distract the demoiselles from their occupation, I was permitted to enter on my own responsibility. I think had I remained silent, I could have proven conclusively there were no Freemasons in your society, as you all seemed so intent on your own affairs, that I think I could have made my exit undiscovered, had not Miss de Villerie's oratory drawn forth the exclamation which betrayed my presence."

" Then," said Miss Clifton, " we are indebted to Miss de Villerie, for had you remained longer, we know not what *dénouement* might have been made, and it is well there were no traitorous sentiments expressed, or you might have brought us before the grand jury for these Roland assemblies."

"On the contrary, dear Miss Clifton, I should doubtless, by force of logic, be converted to your principles, and joined your meetings."

"Judge," said Miss Clarendon, "I think you more complimentary than sincere with our sex."

"Ah, my fair sceptic, what proof can I give of my honesty? I fear, however, as you are all sceptical, I shall be even compelled to acknowledge more gallantry than one of my age is entitled to, to rid myself of your accusation of insincerity. But come, *ma chère*, bring forth this gonfalon, and I will pass sentence on its worth, and rest assured you shall have my ideas upon it in all candour, if I do not give them on your sex sufficiently so."

Miss de Villerie now advanced, bearing the flag, and firmly planting the silver staff on the floor (whose silver tip was surmounted with gold), the broad and streaming banner almost fell to the floor, in its heavy silken folds. A blue union, with seven golden stars of the first magnitude surrounding a silver embroidered magnolia tree, whose branches overshadowed emblems of the different agricultural products of the state, while a pelican d'argent rested with outstretched wings upon the topmost limb, and underneath the tree, by the margin of a lake, were discovered the female pelican feeding her young, while far above both tree and pelican were seen the stars of the OLD UNION, growing " beautifully less" in the dim horizon, as they were eclipsed by the brilliancy of the mystic seven. The whole surrounded by this motto, " We live and die for those we love." Three horizontal stripes, red, white, and red. The first red and white extending from the union to the end of the flag, and the lower red stripe continuing the whole length of the flag, occupying the entire space below the union. The stripes all of equal width, while bordering the whole was a rich golden fringe.

" Now, Judge, tell us what you think of our ensign," said Miss de Villerie, " as all the ladies are present to receive your opinion? I fear from your countenance, however, that you do not like our design, if so, suggest an improvement, and we will be most happy to act upon it."

"My face, Miss de Villerie, is but a poor mirror of my thoughts, if such a sentiment is expressed. I most assuredly admire your skill and taste; nothing could be more beautiful, and the warrior surmounting the staff with his sword drawn is the most apt device that could be imagined. The pelican, about to plume its wings for flight, while beneath repose his mate and young, is emblematic of those who now leave their homes and children under the protecting shadow of the Confederacy, and go forth to win laurels on the gory field. It is both apt and beautiful, and too great praise, Miss de Villerie, cannot be awarded to yourself and your noble companions. It is certainly the most beautiful of all the state standards that I have seen. I am only sorry that these Alpine hairs are too numerous on my brow, or I should be proud to form one of those who will fight beneath its folds, but I trust my son will do honour to his father's name, and to that of his country and state."

"Ah!" said Miss de Villerie, "no doubt of that. We have not forgotten his father's claim to our lasting gratitude for his noble actions, which called forth the benedictions of our people in the war of 1812, with our more ancient foes, and the strong arm who helped to send those British curs howling from our shores 'Like father like son,' so may it prove, as I have no doubt it will in the present case."

"Thank you, Miss de Villerie, for your graceful compliment. Your memory is no less praiseworthy than your taste and genius, but I fear, if Madame Bienvenu's friend were here he would not relish the latter part of your remark, eh, Madame?"

"I cannot be prude enough to affect not to comprehend you, Judge, and if it is to Lord Ethelred you refer, I will answer for him that he is too loyal a supporter of the remnant of the Bruce and Wallace spirit which exists in his native land, to care for a thrust aimed at the breast of the ferocious and blood-thirsty Taurus, whose horns are ever ready to pierce the hearts of the weak and unguarded, and whose portentous bellowings proclaim his deeds of oppression and iniquity. Be assured he is now standing off in his rich clover pasture chewing the cud of speculation, and looking at our proceedings with dull, sleepy eyes, but interested and avaricious heart. Whatever your sentiments are towards our transatlantic cousins, or however bitter they may be, they are not more so, be assured, than are Lord Ethelred's. There are hearts ready to tear in pieces the first gladiator who shall enter the arena, and I assure you they need no bait to encourage them."

"I am really indebted to you, Madame Bienvenu," said Miss O'Gara, "for your expressions in regard to my foes, for I believe I claim it as an hereditary privilege to detest a nation who left my ancestors penniless, and who, because they could not change their religion with as much ease as Harry the Eighth could his wives, and Luther his principles, were disinherited and cast out from their ancestral homes to wander, some to Spain, and others to America, to seek asylum wherever they could from oppression."

"Ladies, ye are stanch friends, but unrelenting foes, and though I accord with you in your sentiments, they are nevertheless *très amere*."

"Yes, they are bitter, Judge, I own, but not compared to the gall which constitutes the life-blood of those Anglo-Saxon barbarians."

"It is true, indeed, Madame, that their blood seems to be of gall, and not such as course in rich generous streams through the hearts of other nations. And now, ladies, I will say *bon soir*, as I feel I have already trespassed too far on your time and courtesy. To-morrow, I presume, I shall again have the pleasure of seeing you, when we shall meet to present to our noble volunteers this standard, which your fair hands have executed. *Au revoir*." As he said these words, Judge S—— bowed most gracefully to the ladies and withdrew.

"Well, ladies," said Miss Clifton, "we have finished, and now it remains for Miss de Villerie to grace our labour, and her own exquisite taste, by presenting this banner."

"Which I shall not fail to do on the morrow, in the name of my sex," responded our heroine.

"Miss de Villerie, we will now say adieu, with affectionate remembrances to Madame de Breuil, and the Judge, whom we trust to see to-morrow."

"Adieu, *mes chères amies*," said Miss de Villerie, and soon the last carriage had rolled out of the grounds, when Miss de Villerie sought her chamber to seek repose, and prepare for the approaching ceremony, which was but five hours off. Aurora's roseate hands were just unfolding her tissue-like veil to display more fully the visage of the gentle goddess, whose most gracious smiles were bestowed upon her votaries. In donning her robes of green, gold, and azure, she seemed to hasten to the scene to which the vast concourse seemed advancing.

It was but seven o'clock and all the youth and beauty of the city of New Orleans were out, some in carriages, others on foot, but all hastening to the cathedral of St. Louis, where already the deep tones of the organ were swelling through the arches of the magnificent building.

Enter with us reader, with gentle tread, and let us witness the ceremony. This way, for the aisles are already filled with the richly-dressed soldiers of the battalion, and their magnificently attired officers, while every pew and niche is crowded, almost to suffocation, with the *élite* and beauty of the Crescent City. How gorgeous and picturesque is the effect the whole scene presents. The glowing rays of the bright morning sunbeams stealing in through the beautifully-stained windows, mingling with the red light of the innumerable wax tapers, tinging the rich draperies of the altar and its glittering vessels of gold and silver, with a party-coloured light, the stalwart forms of the stern soldiers, clad in their rich uniforms of varied tints, the men like bronzed statues with their dark eyes and beards, and stern and handsome forms; the women fairer somewhat, but wearing an heroic expression on their lovely faces; the array of priests, with their venerable bishop in his purple robes, and the procession of youths in their dresses of crimson silk and white lace, added to a scene which surpasses the powers of description to pourtray; while rich and odoriferous incense rose and filled the vast cathedral, and cast a hazy veil over the scene, both deep and impressive, which obscured some-

what the rich frescoes of the ceiling, but added a more
solemn air to the ceremony.   At length the bishop
advanced in front of the congregation, when Miss de Villerie came forward with her procession of ladies, and knelt
before the altar during the consecration of the banner;
when, rising as the last words of the benediction were
given, she placed her hand upon the staff of the flag
which was supported by Gen. ——, and in a few graceful and impressive words presented it in the name of the
ladies of New Orleans.   As the last words died on her
lips there rose upon the ear a strain so rich, so inspiring,
from the hundred *chanteurs* in the choir, as is seldom
heard on earth, and nowhere equalled unless in Rome
(who yet retains a moiety of her ancient grandeur).
Slow and sad it rose at first, but gradually quickening,
the anthem pealed through the vaulted cathedral, and
as the battalion marched out, each face expressed a determination to die beneath the magnificent standard rather
than yield to the foe, and every soldier seemed to feel
inspired with a divine courage as reverently they left
the house of God, and to the sound of their own band
proceeded to the steamer which was to bear them to
the scene which would soon, they anticipated, be one of
deadly strife.

The steamer has moved off from the wharf amidst
the loud huzzas of the multitude and the signalling of
friends—the last farewell to many, perhaps, had been
spoken, and some have "parted for years, and it may
be for ever;" and now the pearly tears are coursing
down the cheeks of many a fair girl who had restrained
them for "his sake," or lest a betrayal of her own weakness should unnerve him for the coming conflict.

Farewell, brave soldiers! your wives, your children, your homes and firesides, ye have looked upon, perchance, for the last time on earth. Blush not for the rising tear which dims your vision of the loved object you are parting from, for long ere ye meet again, if ever, the grass will have sprung over the breasts of many a loved one whose eye shone bright at parting, but whose quivering lip bespoke the suppressed grief within.

God bless ye, noble men, ye are leaving homes of luxury and ease for the hard and trying scenes of camp life. Your beds of down will be exchanged for hard earth, and your only canopy often will be the spangled firmament. But ye are happy in the thought that ye will bequeath to posterity names whose glory shall vie with those of Greece or Rome, whose untarnished lustre shall shine on history's page when the poor form of clay shall be mouldering into dust, and whose memory will breathe inspiration into the breasts of the youth of future ages. Then blessings on ye, noble soldiers, where'er ye go.

Among the last carriages that homeward turned from the wharf were the magnificent equipages of Judge de Breuil and Colonel Clifton. In that of the former were seated Miss Clifton, Miss de Villerie, and Colonel Clifton, while in the latter were seen Madame Bienvenu, Madame de Breuil, and Judge de Breuil. As the carriages slowly turned, Miss Clifton leaned forward to catch one other parting glimpse of her brother, who stood upon the deck of the steamer, in his appearance reminding one forcibly of a description of one of Ossian's heroes. " In peace thou art a gale of spring, in war the mountain storm." His golden hair shone like a halo round his classic face, and in beauty he seemed a very Adonis.

"Farewell, my brother, my darling brother," sobbed Miss Clifton, while her slight form seem convulsed with grief, "you have left us, I feel, for ever. I shall never again hear thy loved voice, never again wait to welcome thee at twilight's hour, when night seemed only to draw her veil around where thou wert not. For, oh! my brother, I lived, I breathed in the sunshine of your bright, noble, happy face, and now all is darkness in our home. Has not indeed our day-star sped? Alas! yes, for it is only night where thou art not Oh, my dear brother, my own dear brother, we have parted to meet no more on earth. I feel thou art lost to my earthly vision for aye; but Beverly, far from the pains and ills of life, in that starry world beyond the clouds, and beyond the tomb; 'in that mansion of whose beauty' eye hath not seen, ear hath not heard, nor hath it entered into the heart of man to conceive, there, my brother, there shall we meet once more, and thou shalt know me as thy own dear sister. Yes, there I shall find thee, like St. John, resting on the bosom of thy God. Yes, Beverly, farewell until that last meeting."

Miss de Villerie, whose own heart was aching, and down whose pale cheeks the tears coursed, gently stole her arm around Miss Clifton, and said, "Do not weep thus, my friend. I feel it is sad to part, and trying it must be with your only brother; but remember it is not all who enter the field of battle that are slain. Your brother is brave, and has proved it ere to-day; then trust that he will return as formerly."

"Oh, dear Natalie, it is for this I fear. I know him

to be brave. No, bravery is not the word. He is more than brave; he is Mars himself; and knowing this, I fear for him the more, simple victory will not content him; it must be a complete triumph, or death."

"My daughter," said Colonel Clifton, who had up to this moment sat silent, almost choking with emotion, "your brother will return to us ere long, and your tears will be changed to joyful exultations. He will, I feel, win laurels for himself and family. At all events, my daughter, he has offered himself as a victim to his country's god; and though he is my only son, I have freely sent him forth to fight for his native land, and should Almighty God see proper to take him hence, in the flower of his age, and thus bereave me, I shall only bow this grey head of mine in resignation to the Divine fiat, who thus chasteneth me. Then, my daughter, be hopeful, be cheerful; it is time sufficient to prepare for the shower when the sky becomes clouded."

Thus he sought to cheer her, though his own heart was sore and heavy. It was all in vain; her tears flowed, and would have washed to view a bed of diamonds had they fallen on the mine, so bitter was her woe. She was no picture of Niobe, she was Niobe herself.

"I imagine," said Miss de Villerie, "that a speedy contest is at hand in Virginia, and I daily anticipate the news of a great battle."

"Yes," said Colonel Clifton, "our armies are approaching each other rapidly, and the cry with our foes seems to be 'On to Richmond.'"

"Affairs are indeed portentous at present, and I think this war will not be a very short one. Nor would I have

K

it a brief struggle, unless it should result in complete independence. I would rather, if I were a man, share the fate of William Tell and his brave companions, and flee to the mountain fastnesses, to make my home with the beasts of the forests and birds of the air, than consent to any measure that did not establish perfect separation and freedom, if it takes years to accomplish, —let us in the end be free, and separate."

"Yes, this is the only compromise that ever can, or ought to be made," said Colonel Clifton, "but it is one that never will be, only at the point of the bayonet, and much blood. Yes, rivers will flow ere this."

They were now arrived at Judge de Breuil's, and Miss de Villerie politely requested Colonel Clifton and his daughter to remain to dinner. They respectfully declined, and entered their own carriage that had just arrived with the other party, and drove home. Madame Bienvenu dined with Miss de Villerie, and returned to the city in the evening, where she made one of a most brilliant *soirée* at Madame D——'s, as she had no one in particular for whom to grieve amongst the departed battalion, she was the gayest of the gay, being as usual accompanied by her (now *fiancée*) Lord Ethelred. She shone the star of the evening, and many were the envious glances cast upon her by the young ladies, and the young (old) ladies whom Lord Ethelred had found favour with, but for one smile of the widow he would have yielded all other marks of favour. Report said she was soon to be Lady Ethelred (a pretty name, is it not?)—I do not know. Time, who proves all things, will tell, and who, with his usual good sense, reveals nought until the proper moment.

CHAPTER X.

" By the hope within us springing,
  Herald of to-morrow's strife ;
By that sun, whose light is bringing
  Chains or freedom, death or life—
Oh ! remember life can be
No charm for him who lives not free !
  Like the day-star in the wave,
  Sinks a hero in his grave."

THE voice of mourning is already heard within our
Southern homes. List to the swelling wails that arise
from our midst. Hark ! 'tis the sobs of a mother, wife,
and friends, for one of Louisiana's fairest, brightest, and
most gifted sons. The brilliant orator, and the brave
warrior, were never better illustrated than in the person
of C. D. Drew, since the days of Pericles, but, unlike his
ancient prototype, he did not live to see his country's
enemies vanquished, but died nobly in defence of his
native land. Gifted and brave, his voice was one of the
first raised for secession, and he willingly went forth to
contend against the foe with his valiant little band.
Affable, kind, and noble in demeanour, together with a
person which Apollo might have envied, he won all
hearts to himself, and we felt as we gazed upon the

placard which met the eye at every corner, and in
gleaming letters proclaimed a company forming called
the "Drew Avengers," that it was not love of country
alone that called it forth, but undying love for the brave
young Creole, who was first among the Crescent City
youth to offer up his life, and to die at the foot of the
altar erected to patriotism. Yes, his young life's blood
has consecrated the soil of Virginia. From every drop
shall spring a warrior, armed *cap-à-pie*, to revenge him;
and solemnly did that little band bear their valorous
leader from the spot on which he fell, and dire and dread
was the oath they swore on the shrine of Nemesis. And
now they are preparing to bear him to his native city,
to do honour to his remains; and now the corpse is
lying in solemn state in the parlour of the City Hall,
where the young, the old, the great, the lowly, are
wending their way to do him reverence, and to gaze
upon those features which death even, with all its
horrors, has not deformed. Come with us now to the
home of this chieftain, which not many months ago he
was the light and soul of. I will introduce you "but
one day previous" to the arrival of his body. Seated in
her parlour, surrounded by her friends, was the wife of
him of whom we write, and in her arms she clasped a
beautiful child. Her friends, who were all cognisant of
her husband's death, gazed upon mother and child with
admiration, mingled with pity, but none could summon
courage to broach the dreadful subject to her, for her
heart seemed light, and to her friends she had never
seemed happier, or more beautiful, than on this sad
morning. In vain they essayed to introduce the subject, and though they discussed many things, that which

was nearest to the heart seemed farthest, and most difficult for expression, and the tears were welling to many eyes.

At last Mrs. Drew, observing their grave looks, remarked, " I know not why you are all looking so sad this morning. As for me, I have never felt happier in my life ; that is," she added gaily, "in the absence of Charles."

At length her brother-in-law entered, and said to her, " I have sad news for you, Mollie ; but you must meet it with fortitude. Mollie, Charles is dead. He was killed, and they are bearing his body home ; but look upon it with strength, and God will help you."

She gazed at him incredulously, and then laughed, saying, " Ah, my dear brother, you cannot deceive me ; you think me credulous enough to believe anything, but I know this is not true." Then seeming in a moment to realize the truth of what he had told her, from the countenances of those around her, she gave one piercing scream, and fell fainting in the arms of her brother. Language is inadequate to describe the grief of the desolate wife. Her life seemed only to return to display more plainly before her her heavy loss, and convulsion succeeded convulsion until nature seemed exhausted, and she lay calm in her desolation and grief, like a beautiful ruin over which the moonlight throws its charm, adding a ten-fold beauty to this lonely one. Madly she pressed her child to her bosom, and wildly she called upon its father's name, but, alas! he was deaf to her entreaties, till both babe and mother wept themselves to sleep, while the angel of sorrow enshrouded them with his wings. Stricken wife, fatherless babe, and heart-broken mother and friends, ye are but types of the many whose tears shall flow ere the fierce Mars shall be appeased. It is not one hecatomb, but many, that shall be slain, and may the presentiment of death, which must, and could alone have dictated the following letter of him of whom I write, nerve your arms to write likewise, when writing to those ye love, that your country, and wife too, may claim you alike. "Come what may, my dear, I belong to my country, and you know you belong to me." But read for yourselves, a letter teeming with loyalty and noble affection:—

"Richmond, Va.
"June 18th, 1861.

"Dear Mollie,

"I wrote to you a long letter yesterday, and as if Providence wished to encourage me in writing to my own dear Mollie, I received almost at the same time a long, most welcome, and long-wished-for letter from you. It makes my heart beat with emotions of noble patriotism when I read the burning words of inspiration that flow from your pen. In fact, I have read a few passages of your letter to my fellow-soldiers, and every one ardently wished that he had such a brave and noble-hearted wife. The days of political differences and party are gone, and only one spirit animates us all. The invaders are at our gates, and they MUST be repelled. You have doubtless before this read of the glorious victory achieved by our troops a few days ago at Bethel Church. I have seen and conversed with eye-witnesses of the battle. The Yankees ran away like whipped curs, leaving for over five miles, all their muskets, canteens, knapsacks, etc.,

on the ground. It was a perfect rout, a complete defeat.
The moral effect produced by that exploit on the part
of our troops is not easily to be estimated. The Southern
Volunteers are all awake, and 'eager for the fray,' and
Richmond looks like a 'Champ de Mars,' so many soldiers
are seen around it. You hear nothing here but the
sound of the drums, the piercing notes of the fife, and
rumbling of heavy waggons, loaded with war baggage.
Troops move every day and every hour. To tell you
the truth, my dear, we also have to move; the orders
have just been received by me from the Adjutant-General,
and the camp is now in a stir, preparing to move army
and baggage. We are ordered from this place to York-
town, within eight miles of the enemy's line, and with
most glorious prospects of an early and good brush.
When there, we shall be under command of Colonel
Magruder, who succeeded so well in the *debût* at Bethel
Church. The boys are delighted with the prospect
before them, and we are all in the highest glee. May
the God of battles smile upon us. Cheer up, my dear wife;
I have brave hearts and strong arms to sustain and cheer
me on, and I feel confident of the result; many a
noble son of Louisiana may fall by my side, and I may
be the first to bite the dust, but rest assured that they
or I will always be worthy of the esteem and respect of
our countrymen, and endeavour to deserve well of our
country. When I reach Norfolk I shall write again, and
give you full particulars. Rest assured until you hear
from me, or until the telegraph gives you bad news of
our expedition. Come what may, my dear, I belong to
my country, and you belong to me ; one in all, all in one,
we owe our duty and our lives to both. Were you as

good and brave a man as you are a true and noble
woman, I know I would have you by my side, fighting
with all your might the base and miserable invaders.
Excuse me, dearest, for the digression. To-morrow we
leave for the seat of war. What to-morrow will bring
forth I know not, but through prosperity or adversity,
opulence or poverty, security or danger, I am still your
own Charles.

"Tell father I am ashamed to promise to write, for
he may know I shall break my promise. Kiss one and
all for me at home; press our sweet little one to your
heart, and tell her to love and cherish you, for the sake
of her papa.

"Your own CHARLES."

This epistle needs no comment. To the heart of
every patriot, husband, and father, it speaks in thrilling
language, and long after peace shall smile upon us, that
page on which this touching letter is inserted, shall be
turned to and read, while tears shall bedew the lines
which were traced by him, whose form is mouldering to
dust, but who still exists in the hearts of his people.
This brief letter was traced by the patriot husband and
father; it is these who speak, and not the orator, statesman, or warrior. Of his own, and to his own was it
written, and flowed from his pen with all the ease with
which the silent stream courses onward to the great
river, for it flowed from his heart. Here is display of
no rhetorical and pompous language, which so often is
traced by the pen, but so seldom emanates from the heart.
In his lone and distant camp he wrote to her, who was
the choice of his youth, and whom he was never again

to behold, and to her he poured forth his last thoughts. Two objects of love seemed to possess his entire being, and like a Christian who, standing on the confines of eternity, is offered on the one hand a terrestrial kingdom, where he shall rule as king, and on the other a celestial and eternal inheritance, where he shall be subject of none save God; who, with the faith of a Christian yields his earthly for heavenly bliss, and closes his eyes to all, save his implicit trust in the Divine assurance, so he closed his eyes on the alluring joys of home, and followed where duty led, confident in the noble sense of honour and justice. For his native land he resigned these, and to-day it proves that it is not ungrateful nor unmindful of the sacrifice and wrongs.

From early dawn the whole city seemed astir, and now it was approaching the hour for his burial. Up and down the streets rode officers, while sentinels were placed at the corners of all the principal thoroughfares, and with their pointed bayonets repelled the mass, which otherwise would have blockaded the way of the procession, but which, thus driven back, stood on either side of the pavement, like the moving, rolling waves of the ocean, while the space between reminded one forcibly of the passage of the Red Sea. Every balcony, window, doorway, or niche was crowded with anxious spectators, who came from far and near to gaze for the last time upon the youthful hero's mortal remains. Eulogies fell from every lip and voice, as every one proclaimed the departed's merit. But silence, like a spell, falls upon the crowd. Every voice seems hushed, and not a breath seems to float upon the air, for the procession is seen in the distance advancing, and the dirge-note and solemn beat of the muffled drum break upon the ear. Slowly it advances, headed by the band, whose instruments were draped in mourning; then came a company of cavalry, followed by several other companies of foot and horse, with furled and draped standards; then came carriages bearing the bishop and clergy, the former, as also the latter, arrayed in their robes, next to which (surrounded by a small number of his company, who had arrived from Virginia, as the escort of his remains) came the corpse, enclosed in a magnificent coffin of rosewood, and resting on gun carriages (while, by its side, walked an African groom, leading his splendid charger, elegantly caparisoned). A magnificent pall of black velvet drooping below, while bannerets and floating streamers waved from each festoon, above which were flowers of rich fragance, as also on every portion of the carriage, and breathed their sweet incense around him. Then followed all the other military companies—cavalry, artillery, and foot; while the procession wound up by carriages bearing private citizens, with the students of the Jesuit College, and the orphan boys brought up the rear, with their juvenile musicians, who played a sad, sweet requiem.

Slowly and reverentially wended the cortege through the principal streets; when at last, arriving at the St. Louis Cemetery, the body was borne to its last resting-place, and there an eloquent oration was delivered over the remains ; and thus, the last religious rites having been paid, they slowly lowered him to rest, while the banner of the Confederacy enfolded him in its embrace. Sadly rose the requiem on the air, as the magnificent procession turned to leave ; and fast fell the tear-drops which sprang from many hearts, as the cannon and guns were fired, and they cast a last glance on the spot which contained the body only, from which the spirit had winged its flight to that "better land." Bitter the regrets for that young oak cut down in all its strength and beauty, but sweeter the memories of its twilight shadow.

The last lingerer had left the cemetery, and when night opened her dusk eyes upon the scene, it found him "alone in his glory." There shall that body slumber on, in its silent repose, until those last dread words shall break the cerements of the tomb, "Arise, ye dead," &c; when man shall don his mortal robes again, and appear in the presence of his God. Then, with the humblest subject in that vale, shall stand the Cæsars, the Hannibals, the Neros, and Caligulas; their smiles or frowns then none shall heed, and in the presence of the "King of kings" shall these tyrants tremble as their lowliest subjects.

The tyranny of a royal decree alone caused men like the above to receive homage at their death, and a royal sepulchre after; but no such compulsory means drew forth the homage to the patriot whose obsequies I have just described. Love and honour were the sole dictators, and these suggested to a grateful nation the magnificent tribute to a warrior's memory, in which none were forced to act a part that did not coincide with their sense of justice or his merit. Happy he who can descend to the grave thus, the beloved of a nation, and receiving on his tomb a nation's homage, in offerings of love and tears. These are richer tributes than the sparkling mines of Golconda or Peru could yield; the former shall live till ages roll away, and after be a proof of his worth and deeds, who receive them before the un-yielding Judge on high; but the latter shall crumble and pass away with earth and all its ephemeral trea-sures. Then let tears and love alone be our offering, which shall come welling up from the heart's pure crystal fountain. Farewell, valiant chieftain, with our *tears*, and *not marble*, will we erect to you a monu-ment, which the dust and mould of time cannot cover or efface—farewell.

On an evening in the latter part of the month of July, there were assembled at Valambrosa (the residence of Colonel Clifton) a party, some of whom the reader has met before, and others to whom he will be introduced. A sultry July air rendered in-doors unpleasant, and sauntering under the piazzas and in the gardens, the guests sought refuge from the ardent heat. The elders of the party confined themselves to the house, while the younger people sought the borders of the lake, where, seated on the verdant turf, they whiled the hours away; moored in the recess of some drooping willows, was a small fairy-like boat, which seemed to invite to a row on the lake, and which espying, Albert la Branche (who formed one of the party, and who was now an old and expected visitor at Valambrosa) said, "Ladies, the water appears inviting, this evening, what say you to a row? As none seemed inclined to go on the lake, I must content myself on the side, though beyond in that dark grove, is nestling that little hut, with its glimmer-ing light reflected in the water, it looks enchanting."

"Well, come then, Mr. la Branche, since you are so anxious to explore my extensive realm," said Miss

Clifton ; " come, Miss de Villerie will join us in a row, if only to prove the truth of Campbell's lines—

" 'Tis distance lends enchantment to the view."

"Come," she said, " wind this horn, and our Charon will appear."

He took the shell, and winding a long note on the horn, there emerged from the hut beyond the lake, a very old, but noble-looking negro, who advanced, and seated himself in the bottom of the boat, and with two or three heavy strokes of the oar, which sent the waters scintillating all around him, he reached the spot to which he was summoned.

Albert la Branche placed the young ladies in the boat, and then seating himself, the old ferryman plied the oars ; soon they were in motion.

"Adieu, fair ladies," said Mr. la Branche; "I am sorry you had not the necessary coin to pay your ferriage, and as this is a ferryman who admits of no gallantry in paying each others' fare, I shall be forced to leave you to wander on the shores, as you lacked the proper coin, which in this case was consent."

"Fear not for us," said a merry voice, " from the number that crosses, I think we shall have a much merrier time on the shores ; at least, we have, I think, the stronger party, and though victory is not always in strength, there is sometimes success in numbers, particularly odd numbers." But, come, let us follow the water party.

Arriving at the opposite shore, they left the skiff, and walked towards the hut.

" Come let us take a peep at the mansion of this

Plutonian subject. Why! quite a picture for an artist, is it not? All the implements for fishing, hunting, and visitors, too," said he, advancing to the back part of the room; he stood at a door leading out under a shed, formed by large branches of the palmetto, spread over long poles; seated there were two persons, obscured entirely by the shade.

"Come, give us an air on this instrument," said Albert la Branche, as he handed a banjo to one of the persons. "Come, play the ladies a welcome to your shores; which is the best performer, Ike or Joe?"

Turning rudely around, they demanded, in a gruff voice, "For whom do you take us, Sir?"

"Well, from your insolence, the place, and circumstances," answered Albert la Branche, boldly, "I should take you for what I presume you are—ruffians; and nothing would prevent my chastising you on the spot but the presence of these ladies, whom I shall at once convey home, and then return and attend to your case, to learn the particulars of why you are here in this place, in the negro cabin of one of Colonel Clifton's slaves, and within the precincts of that gentleman's domain."

Miss Clifton and Miss de Villerie, who had stepped back appalled at the first sight of these intruders, now became alarmed, and the former, trembling violently, entered the hut, and placing her hand on the arm of Mr. la Branche, said—

"Albert, for heaven's sake forbear, if not for your own, for my sake! You know not these men, nor their intention. Come, let us go. Oh! would that we had not come."

Thus entreated, he turned to leave, at the same time he said—"If your design is not malicious in being here this evening, I shall expect to find you on my return, when I shall be pleased to hear you prove your inno-cence, if, on the contrary, you are absent, it shall prove your guilt."

"Ha, ha, ha, ha!" roared this pair of worthies. "Well, you talk pretty fine, young gent. I would like to know if you can fight as well; I think I will try you at a round or two; but let somebody tell us which must have kum out to protect t'other, for I'm darned if I can tell, that black-eyed girl seems to have none of the 'white feather' about her, but I cannot say as much for you, young man; it's a pity you couldn't exchange sex."

Albert la Branche, as well as the young ladies, had now reached the boat, and a deaf ear was turned to this last insulting speech. They were rowed swiftly to the other shore, and springing on to the bank, Albert la Branche assisted his companions out of the boat.

The party whom they had left beside the lake had returned, and they now hurried on towards the house.

"What a singular and alarming rencontre," said Miss de Villerie. "I little presumed we should meet in Charon's hut abolition spies, for such they certainly appear to be, for not even the meanest Southern white man could be found who would presume to enter a gentleman's domain and visit his slaves, as we found those to-night."

"Most assuredly they are spies," said Albert la Branche; "insurrectionary ones, and they must certainly be looked after, and if they remain (which I feel assured they will not), we will administer to them some useful lessons; and now, young ladies, I will say good evening, as I go to speak with Colonel Clifton, and to communicate this strange affair."

"*Ma chère Natalie*," said Miss Clifton, "excuse me for a few moments, and if you feel like retiring, act *sans cérémonie*," and, gliding from Miss de Villerie's side, she placed her arm in that of Albert la Branche, and said— "Come, dearest Albert, and promise me that you will not return to that dreadful place to-night. Oh! that grove beyond the lake with its twinkling light, which we so admired, now that I look back upon it after the terrors of that interview, seems like some dismal marsh, while its light appears the *ignis fatuus* which leads us on to deceive us—do not return, Albert; let those men go their way in peace, they cannot injure us, our slaves are faithful, and you, dear Albert, are involving yourself in a difficulty for us and our safety; for my sake, Albert, let this go no further."

"Retire to your chamber, my darling, and fear not for my safety. I think, however, the occurrence of this evening has unstrung your nerves."

Placing his hand upon her head, he bent down and kissed her polished brow, and then disappeared through the library door, where Colonel Clifton sat reading by the light of a silver lamp, which was suspended from the ceiling by richly wrought silver chains, which radiated to the four corners of the room.

Hearing footsteps, Colonel Clifton raised his eyes, and then recognizing his visitor, he arose and placed a chair with all the urbanity of a gentleman of the "old school." Time's icy touch had left its mark upon his hair and brow, and though the noble features still remained, the traces of sorrow lingered in the deep furrows.

"I trust you will pardon the unceremoniousness of this visit when I relate to you its object."

"Most assuredly, my young friend; no apologies are necessary; and now proceed."

Albert la Branche at once entered upon the subject, and related the particulars of the adventure, and then said, "Colonel, I await your advice, for I wish to do nothing rash, or without consulting you."

Colonel Clifton arose from his seat, and rang a bell, which was answered by his valet. "Louis, say to the overseer that I wish to see him immediately." Then seating himself, he said, "It is very evident these men have evil designs, and their true object is tampering with slaves. They must at once be sought for and punished, though as far as my negroes are concerned, I have no fear. These men have been lurking around for some time. I have heard of their being seen at the quarters of several of my neighbours. As to an insurrectionary movement on the part of our slaves, I have not the least apprehension, yet the interference of these men may give rise to a great deal of trouble, which by the immediate execution of one or two of such vile wretches, would be put an end to." The overseer now entering, Colonel Clifton, said, "Valois, have you any knowledge of the two white men who have been visiting the plantations of our neighbours, among the negro cabins, and who were found this evening in the hut of Charon across the lake?"

"No, Sir; none in the least. I have been told there were a couple of low white men loitering about

L

here, but had no idea, Sir, they would dare to enter your grounds. But, Sir, how came they in Charon's hut? I cannot think him capable of receiving them there without permission from you, or myself."

"I know not, Valois; and now you will at once investigate this matter, and leave no means untried to find these men, and bring them to justice. Ring for the drivers, and proceed at once to Charon's cabin, to which place Mr. la Branche offers to accompany you. As for myself, I am too old to be of any service. I would be more hindrance than help."

"Come, Valois," said Mr. la Branche, "we will not cross the lake; we will go round it, and enter Charon's cabin by the back way."

Leaving the house, Mr. la Branche, the overseer, and a few trusty slaves, pursued their way in perfect silence towards the cabin. Not a sound was heard save their footsteps. All was hushed, and the light which had glimmered from the window of the hut early in the evening was now extinguished, and the door half closed. The party entered and found it deserted, save by the old man, who lay in unconscious slumber on a cot. Rousing the old negro, Valois demanded in stern tones of Charon his knowledge of his visitors. The old man appeared stupefied at first, but was soon brought to his senses by the voice of Mr. la Branche, who asked him to say at once by whose permission those men were in his cabin.

"Massa, 'bout sun-down I was sittin by de lake fishin, when de first ting I kn'wd, dem two men kum up behind me, and gan talkin to me. Dey fust ax'd me how many niggers in dis plantation, and den they ax'd how long I'd been here, and if I would'nt like to be free. I told em I was just as free as dey was, and if dat was all de business dey had wide me, dey had better tend to dare own consarns. Dey just larfed at me, and said as how I was a poor nited critter, and if I'd just foller dem dey'd lead me to liberty. Well, Massa, dey sot and talked and convarsed together ontil I got up to go to my hut, and den dey followed me in, and said dat dey'd just go wid me and take a peep at Southern nigger filigity. So dere dey sot until night, and when de horn blow'd I tought dey'd hab perliteness to leave, but dey said dey'd just sit outside until I kum back, for dey had someting ob importance to tell me. I told um I did not know what time I'd kum back, and dey'd better not wait, but dey staid arter all my hintin dat der room was better den der company."

" Yes, Charon, this is all very well, and finely told, but why is it, you did not inform the young ladies and myself of those visitors, as we crossed the lake ? "

" Well, you see, massa, I tought dey'd be gone, and I was just stonished as you, to find 'um still outside my back door—like eve-droppers ; ob course, when dey said dey'd sit outside, I tought, of course dey meent de front door, like white folks, and as I didn't see 'um dare, cluded dey was gone."

" And if they had been," said Mr. la Branche, " I presume you would have said nothing of their visit, nor of what they said."

" No, massa, kase dare won't no harm done."

" Well, see here, old man," said Valois, "your master placed you here because he trusted you, but let me find you again harbouring such characters, and your age will be no protection for you, but like the youngest slave you shall receive chastisement. Shall we proceed in our search, Mr. la Branche?"

Albert consenting, the party started, but Valois turning round said, "Charon, which way did your visitors go?"

"Don't know, massa; dey'd gone when I kum back from t'other side de lake."

Pursuing their way around the lake, they entered cautiously, stables and carriage-houses, and every possible place that could serve for a hiding-place, but all to no purpose. They had entered the boat to return across the lake, when, just as they were well seated, a shot came whizzing by Albert la Branche, and struck the overseer, wounding him but slightly. Pushing back to shore, they sprang out, and made towards the vicinity from whence the report of the pistol came, but all in vain, they were nowhere to be found; and, uneasy in mind, they again returned, with a full determination to scour the whole country when daylight dawned.

They reported their adventure to Colonel Clifton, but made no mention to any other members of the family, who were, ere this, sleeping, unconscious of the vicinity of foes. But those arch-fiends were still abroad; and when four o'clock dawned, it found the occupants of Valambrosa gazing in the distance on the rising lurid flames of their burning sugar-mill, with its two thousand hogsheads of sugar destroyed in its ruin. There were scenes, some of what may be termed the petty deeds of our enemies; and though they were diligently sought after, they managed to escape justice, but we shall see how long they shall do so.

"Gaze upon the ruins, my dear friend," said Miss de Villerie to Miss Clifton, "and then say if you think me too bitter in my hatred to our foes. Is it not a diabolical fanaticism that prompts such deeds towards our own kind, and what policy is there that can palliate such acts? How base must be the creatures (for I cannot call them men), who would stoop to such vile methods to carry out party revenge and prejudices. This is but the prelude, I fear, to more terrible scenes. These are the acts of men who visit our shores with a psalm-book in one hand, while in the other, the torch and assassin's knife are concealed only by the voluminous folds of their cloak of sanctity. What can you say for them now, my friend?"

"Alas! *ma chère* Natalie, I know not what to say. I would fain have both North and South amicably united, but I feel this hope is at an end for ever. We who had lived so long together, like one family, whose laws had been the admiration of all nations for their Cretan simplicity, than which none were more rigorous and equitable, are now torn asunder, never to be re-united, for there is no strife so deadly as brotherly or family contentions."

"Let us trust that it may be so once again, dear, dear friend; let us hope, let us pray, that a veil may be cast over our eyes to their iniquities, and that repentance and atonement on their part, may lead us to forget their transgressions. Yes, let us build a fairy structure upon this hope, and let us try to forgive the trespasses of others, that our own may be forgiven, as our Heavenly Father has said, and if this, at last, prove but a *dorée chateau en Espagne*, will it not, at least, be better to have looked on the bright side of this dark phantom ? "

" Oh! *ma chère* Natalie, why is it that all cannot live happy on this broad, broad earth? God has lavished an abundance on man.   Let us take but a moment's view of the map of our own hemisphere.   See the vast extent of land left, and remaining uninhabited, and there are but few spots upon its broad surface but what would yield the labourer an hundred-fold.   Then, why is it that they dispute for boundary? and why is it that such trifles in themselves foment such terrible disturbances, and involve us in misery and bloodshed?   As for me (you will, with all your great ideas of politics, which I do not comprehend, laugh at my pacific measures) I believe in an amicable settlement, such as Abraham made with Lot, viz., 'If thou will take the left hand, then I will go to the right; or if thou depart to the right hand, then I will go to the left.'"

" I cannot but admire your sentiments, but this was in the patriarchal ages, as the world grew wiser (though *en verité* the contrary), all such gentle noble impulses of the human heart ceased. Ambition, with its thousand poisonous attributes, usurped the throne, where benignity and generosity once sat enthroned. As you say, trifles in themselves have caused the present state of affairs, which, a bubble at first, growing little by little, now threatens to submerge us by its turbulent foaming waves. Why is it, you ask, such trifles become of such magnitude?   I will answer you.   That our political Neptunes first raise with their speculative and designing tridents the first bubble which the firebrand journalists inflate to a most prodigious and overwhelming size, and then when they threaten to engulf all save themselves, and those who encourage them in their murderous schemes, will accept of no quarter, nor listen to any appeals for mercy. See far away, eastward, westward, are hurrying the sombre clouds, where armed bands are gathering, and soon will be wafted on the air the sounds of deathly combat; even at this moment methinks I hear the din of battle. Yes, now even, our noble soldiers may be yielding up their lives on the field of battle, beneath their country's flag. In Virginia, whose soil has boasted so many noble heroes in our struggle for independence, and is made sacred by the nativity of a Washington, and from whence there never sprang a traitor (save one, and he dotage and imbecility will excuse)—in Virginia, I say, will soon be heard the battle-cry, and our Southern youth shall doubly hallow with their young life-blood every spot of ground defiled by the footsteps of these Vandals, or drive them to their own rude haunts. Yes, the smoking ruins which we gaze upon, my dear Cornie, is among the least of the injuries that we have and shall receive from our enemies."

"Then, let it never be our part to reciprocate at least such deeds as these. Let us thank God, dearest Natalie, that we are not the aggressors in this terrible and unrighteous strife. Let our men fight boldly and valiantly on the field, but let no such base deeds as this disgrace our annals. When peace smiles once again upon us, and the sun of glory is sinking to its western rest, let its last rays be refulgent, and beautiful on the lovely horizon, which shall glow with its opal dyes. I am not like you, *chère* Natalie, I cannot wish evil to any of the human race. God has placed us all here for some wise purpose, and let He who doeth all things well, judge,—not an humble creature like myself."

"Yes, Cornie, my darling friend, you possess ideas beautiful in themselves, but not fit for this progressive age of ours. I am not like you, 'tis true. I perceive the fountain from which you were nurtured flowed in gentle and less gushing streams than that from which I imbibed my sentiments. Yes, I feel it surging through my veins at times in its mad career, and it seems as if, in its force and impetuosity, it would bear rocks, trees, and every obstacle before it. But see, great Sol is soaring high in mid heaven, and his burnished chariot throws almost too bright a reflection around. We will not linger to receive any further indications of his royal presence. *Allons*."

CHAPTER XI.

Like clouds of the night the Northmen come,
  O'er the valley of Almhion lowering ;
While onward moved, in the light of its foam,
  That banner of Erin, towering.
With the mingling shock
Rung cliffs and rock,
While rank on rank, the invaders die :
  And the shout that last,
  O'er the dying pass'd,
Was " Victory ! victory !"—the Finion's cry.

" 'Tis a cruelty,
  To load a falling man."

VICTORY is ours!   Let us proclaim it far and wide, until
hills and dales re-echo the sound, and all honor, fame, and
praise to the great general whose wonderful Napoleonic
genius has thus, with desperate, overwhelming odds
against him, achieved so glorious and brilliant a victory—
a victory unrivalled in the annals of America, North or
South, not only for its magnitude, but its effulgence.
Louisiana may well be proud of her great son, and
Beauregard's is the name which shall shine brightest on
history's page amongst the many brave heroes of the
day, among whom shone conspicuous Bee, Kershaw,
Johnston, Bartow, Smith, Hampton, Sloan, and others,

whose names will live on the records of our country.
From the great general himself to the lowest private,
all, all fought valiantly, nobly, and only as Southerners
alone know how to fight. To all we are indebted
to-day, but I feel that from rank to rank I can hear
each voice assenting that upon the brow of Beauregard
alone must rest the triumphal wreath of laurel. Yes, to
him who has so signally defeated and humbled the
enemy on several occasions, award we the palm. Under
him Fort Sumpter fell, and now the great battle which
so long was maturing in his brain has been fought, and
the foe was routed, pursued, scattered, captured, and
slain, and had he been provided with troops to-day
Washington would have been in our possession. But as
it is, another fearful and sanguinary battle must be
fought, and we may not fear the result if a proper force
be placed in the hands of Beauregard. Blood must
still flow, and aching hearts there still must be, but
who will fear the issue who place their trust in God
and Beauregard? Let us look when he first took
his position at Manasses. Gloomy indeed was it, and
nothing but the terror of his genius could have restrained
the enemy from crushing him. With a mere handful
of troops, within one day's march of the enemy, boldly
he made his stand in the very face of an overwhelming
force. With weak forces badly provided, his fertile
brains had to achieve all. With unwearied energy he
bent his mind to the task, and planned the campaign
according to his condition, and the means furnished
him. The whole field was drawn and marked out
according to his plans. Batteries rose up everywhere ;
time was gained ; and the enemy stood oft appalled,

making preparations, while he carried on arrangements
for their glorious achievement. Then all honour, fame,
and praise to our noble general. In every home to-night
ascends his name from the shrine where the pure in
heart lay their offerings, and " God bless thee," Beauregard, is breathed by the fresh and rosy lips of beauty,
no less fervently than by the wrinkled lips of age.

But come with us, reader, to the interior of Southern
homes, and listen to the well-merited eulogiums of our
chieftain.

"Let us indeed congratulate ourselves," said Judge
S—— to Colonel F——, as he hurriedly glanced over
the columns of the morning journal, " upon this brilliant
victory, for truly it is the most stupendous battle ever
fought upon the western hemisphere; with a hundred
thousand men upon the field, and fifty thousand men
actively engaged in the contest, with all the most
approved, fiendish, and murderous appliances of modern
warfare, with all the deadly rancorous hate that low
fanaticism and foiled avarice could engender on the one
side, and all the burning hate that bitter scorn, and
outraged honour, and trampled right could arouse on
the other, has been fought between the Northerns and
Southerns, planned and *won* by our great Beauregard.
He taught them, to use the language of the London
' Times,' ' that Southerners are not to be walked over
like a partridge manor, and that they have some military heads amongst them.' Yes, their cry of ' On to
Richmond' is changed to one of wailing, and their
floating banners, under which they marched, are either
in the hands of the Southerners, or trampled in the
dust, and the grand army of the Potomac is dispersed

like chaff before the wind. As an army they are completely annihilated. Gallantly have the invaders been
repelled, and have not Generals Beauregard and John-
stone well sustained their reputation for valour? Has
not Beauregard won the greatest battle since that of
Waterloo, and has he not established a claim to ample,
to perfect confidence? To what now amounts the
vain **boastings** of the North that an 'exhibition of
Federal power would soon **crush** the rebellion, and
bring back **the revolted** states to the old Union?' They
said that the contest would be easy and brief if the
old Government would use force; but to manifest that
strength, which it possessed, would cause a change in
all the seceded states, and that the greater number
would be found loyal to Lincoln. In all and every
thing they have asserted and done, they have been
woefully deceived and frustrated."

"Yes, 'tis true," said Colonel F——, "they are now
beginning to feel, and we to understand, the sage
remark of Solon—'It would have been easier for us to
repress the advances of tyranny and have prevented its
establishment, but now that it is established and grown
to some height it will be more glorious to demolish it;'
and most valiantly have our brave soldiers acted upon
his words. Yes, our Beauregard has won a name than
which there are none brighter. With Beauregard in
the field and Jef. Davis in the presidential chair, supported by such men as Stephens, &c., we may look
forward to nought but success. Yes, we now have a
form of government, not an experiment of statesmen,
but one which has proved to be the best ever inaugurated at the time, pruned of those errors, and improved

by the addenda that were pointed out by the experience
of nearly a century's test, and weeded and brought to
still greater perfection by Jef. Davis, our modern Pub-
licola. Now let those of the North, whose extravagant
conceits led them to believe in our weakness, feel our
strength, and whose proud boastings and vain exultations unhorsed them at Bull Run and Manasses. Our
foes' early victories in Western Virginia and in Missouri,
seemed to sustain the complacent theories of sanguine
Unionists, and they predicted a speedy annihilation of
the 'rebel mob' (which term the London 'Times'
gracefully applies to both armies), but now their tone is
changed to loud lamentations, and the predictions of
Webster and Seward are now about to be realised, 'that
the great controlling power on this continent would
ultimately be in the Mississippi valley.' Yes, looking to
our portion of America, we view the Confederate States
as the model republic of the world, possessed of every
element of greatness and prosperity that can exist in a
mundane Government. We are a strictly agricultural
people, and will never cultivate commerce and manufactures further than our own necessities require, hence
we have common interest and aim. We have one and
the same social system, that from its peculiar nature
unites us in feeling against surrounding powers, and
cultivates that manly independence, boldness, and love
of liberty which have ever distinguished the Southerner.
We have a common heritage in the achievement of our
freedom from political vassalage, and the laurels won
and blood shed by our volunteers fighting side by
side against the Northern foe, fully equal to that which
almost alone caused Southern men to cling sorrowfully,

yet tenaciously, to a Union that had become for them
an engine of injustice and oppression. We have a compact and united territory, a common object, and a
common destiny, and though we cannot say with the
mother of Bresidas, should our Beauregard fall 'that
Lacedæmon could boast of many better men he,' yet
there are other brave chieftains in our Confederacy who
could lead us on to victory."

Such were the sentiments and such the praise
awarded to the chieftain whose triumph was complete
over the invader. Yes, in their admiration and love of
their general, the Southerners had been almost idolaters,
and in every house was found an image of the hero,
and in every heart was enshrined his deeds of chivalry;
but come with us to Valambrosa, where, reader, you
shall peruse the letter which Albert la Branche has
placed in the hands of Miss Clifton, from her brother,
who fought upon the renowned field of Manasses.

"My dear Sister,
    "The great battle which was so long looked forward
to, is fought, and the grand army, with its streaming
flags and glistening bayonets, is now a defeated and dispersed rabble. We are in possession of the field, and I
have seized the first few moments of repose since the
battle, to give you a brief account of our glorious victory.
    "The scene opened on a quiet Sabbath morning,
but the red light of the sun had not more than dawned
upon the rich tableaux of landscape, forest, and armed
men, when the whole was obscured by the dense smoke
of battle. A fierce and terrible conflict was kept up on

both sides, and the storm of battle seemed only to animate and add strength to the weakest arm. Heavy losses were sustained on both sides, and our shattered columns fell back more than once, under the enemy's terrific fire, but at last our retreat was arrested, and animated with heroic courage, we again dashed into the thickest of the battle, and we renewed the dreadful work of carnage. At this moment fell several of our most brilliant officers. The enemy bore hotly down upon us, and many brave hearts felt their hopes expiring, when Generals Beauregard and Johnson appeared, and by their presence re-animated our flickering spirits. General Beauregard rode through the ranks with words of encouragement, and urged his soldiers to the noble resolution of victory or death, to which they responded with cheers of 'Long live our noble General Beauregard.'

"Now the fortune of the day seemed to change, and the enemy, who at one time deemed themselves victorious, began to fall back precipitately, and the last charge made by General Beauregard sent them flying over the field, where, panic-stricken, they fled towards Bull's Run. The rout now became general, and our soldiers pursued the flying enemy for miles, but want of a cavalry force arrested the pursuit. No language can describe the mad, the wild, insane flight of these cowardly bravadoes. In this disgraceful flight, hundreds of the wounded were crushed to death, and sights of thrilling agony met the eye everywhere. For ten miles the road over which the ruthless Vandal had marched with gay, floating, and unstained banners, and with confidence of ability to defeat the rebel, was strewed with the remains of the retreating foe, which in one day had all the magnificence of months' labour demolished and strewed upon the earth. We have won a glorious victory, and though many are the bright names which will be enshrined in the hearts of the nation, Beauregard must ever stand first, while those of Johnston, Early, Bee, Withers, Stuart, Kirby, Smith, and others will be none the less dear, while to those nameless heroes who fought so valorously, and who fell upon the gory field, is due a nation's gratitude. The victory is ours, but dearly it was won, by the blood of some of our best and bravest, and though the universal joy is great, the inward sorrow is not less so, and no loud bursts of triumph or enthusiasm escaped from the conquerors; no, it is a solemn, glorious achievement, and it is *felt*, not *spoken*. We cannot forget the noble **dead**, and rejoicings would be ill-timed. But alas! the scenes I witnessed when riding over the field on the morning after the battle, are almost too painful for description. There lay dead and dying around our path, and our officers were going amongst them, doing all they could to relieve them.

"Observing an elegant-looking man lying in great agony, I went towards him, and turning upon me a look of intense agony, he said 'Water!' I had none, but taking out a small bottle of brandy, I offered it to him, and placing it to his lips he swallowed some, which seemed to revive him. Being in great pain, Colonel F—— (who accompanied me, and who seems to be possessed of more valour than heart), said, 'What brought you here to fight us? This is the fate that awaits all our foes.'

"He turned his reproachful dying eyes upon him, and said, 'Is this the place for such language?'

"I felt my face crimson at the just rebuke, and wished myself out of the company of such a heartless, soulless being. To our enemies in the field, and with arms in their hands, or compassing our injury in any respect, we cannot be too terrible. May Heaven guide every shot, and strengthen every blow aimed at such, and may every spy and traitor be brought to a just punishment. May every battle-field be a Manasses, save in its martyrs, and may many Bethels witness as in the ancient days and of late, the presence of the Divine favour. But an enemy at our feet is no longer the target of a brave man's wrath; the captive who asks for quarter, and he whose wounds appeal to our humanity, no magnanimous man will embitter the lot of such with rudeness or unkindness. It is a very safe thing, no doubt, to reproach a helpless man. It is very easy to deliver lectures to him who is on his back, groaning under wounds. Alas! how true is the proverb, 'It is only the ass who spurs at the dead lion.' But, thank God, we have few such men, and no generous spirit will (except from great inconsiderateness) thus violate the teachings and the instincts of chivalry. We next passed to one who was lying under a tree. His appearance and dress indicated high social position. By his side lay a beautiful sword, and a handkerchief was thrown over his face. I removed the covering, and I thought I had never beheld a more beautiful face. Calm he lay in death, with his dark locks falling over his high pale forehead, and his hands clasping a small book. Desiring to know something more of the person,

N

I withdrew the book from the hands which clasped it so fondly to his breast, and on opening, perceived it was a small and very elegantly bound bible, while in the front was a photograph of a most beautiful woman, seemingly too young for a mother of one of his years (who was about twenty), but whose strong resemblance to the deceased led me to presume it was his mother or sister. In a beautiful hand was written on the fly-leaf, "To my son, A—— T——, from his devoted mother." "My son, remember thy Creator in the days of thy youth." Sadly I turned from him after placing in his hand the cherished *souvenir*, and as I gazed down upon that inanimate form, I felt that the grave should bury every error, cover every defect, extinguish all resentment. From its tranquil mould should spring none but fond regards and tender memories. Who can gaze upon the grave of even an enemy and not feel a throb of compunction that he should ever have battled with the poor handful of earth that is lying before him?

"Many other heart-rending scenes met my view, and I must confess that I was not so callous as not to be affected by the sight. I turned away, overwhelmed with feelings of sorrow and regret. Yes, my dear sister, though bred in a military school, I lack one trait of the soldier, that is, to be stony-hearted, and for this it requires a man should not only be bred but born a soldier. I can never become insensible to the miseries of others. But I must draw my letter to a close, as doubtless the newspapers will give you a much better account of it than I can in so brief a space, and all I can say is to repeat that all fought bravely. South Carolina's, Tennessee's, and Alabama's sons reaped laurels, and the hardy freemen of the Virginia mountains, who know nothing of the scientific rule of warfare, deserve a more lofty eulogy than could emanate from my pen, and which doubtless they will receive. The Mississipians, who fought with a reckless daring 'Seize-him-Towser'-ferocity came in for their share of the glory of the day, and their renowned 'Bowie-Knife Fighters' will long be remembered by those who witnessed what dreadful slaughter followed wherever they made their way.

"These men, throwing away their muskets, met the Yankees hand to hand. The knives, with which they fought, were from 15 to 20 inches long, and were attached to a lasso some 4 feet in length, fastened round the wrist. They would plunge their knives by throwing them in harpoon fashion through and through the bodies of their antagonists, and then, with the ferocity of a tiger, jerk them out again, and repeat the experiment until they themselves were slain. As for Louisiana, it is unnecessary to say what her soldiers have accomplished; all the troops sent from that noble state are gallant specimens of soldiers, and well and nobly has Louisiana acted her part in this war ; and still her brave sons flock to the standard of their country. She can boast some of the best soldiers in the field, and she has furnished *the* Beauregard.

"I am proud of my native State, and of my brave regiment, to whom possibly the journals may do more justice than I could. Victorious we have been, and are, and will continue to be, and say to Albert la Branche that while such laurels are to be won, he should be in the arena.

M 2

"And now, farewell, while the sun of victory shines upon us, we must not forget to be wary, for our ambushed and couchant foe is ready to spring upon us in its first eclipse. We must therefore be watchful and ready.

"Affectionately your brother,

"B. CLIFTON."

"Yes," said Albert la Branche, "it is indeed time I were in the field, and I am heartily tired of a delay which prevents my being placed in some active position, where I can prove to my country my devotion to its cause. I feel a contempt for myself, and yet it is not my fault, for I have in vain desired a command, which would at once place me in active service. Yes, I must at once quit this life of inaction, and if not win laurels for myself, win them for my country. Yes," he said, and I feel that you will be the first to bid ' Go where glory, waits thee.' "

"Indeed, Albert, I wish to see you win laurels, but I cannot say that I am Spartan sufficient to be the first who bids you go. I cannot say that I wish it even; it is only such natures as Miss de Villerie's who can make such sacrifices, I am not equal to them."

"My dear Cornie, then be mine, and go with me, and though you cannot be beside me on the field, you will be near to cheer me in my hours of leisure. Come, darling, be mine, and let us be united now."

She turned pale, and said, " Oh, Albert, you know not what you ask, or how I have dreaded this hour. My mother will never consent to our union, though she has never said it. I feel that she will not yield to our wishes. My mother is, as you no doubt have often heard, a Northerner, and to that cause she clings. My brother resigned his commission in the army, against her will; he espoused the Southern cause against her will, and is now fighting against her will. I have heard her often say that she would never form a tie of any kind with a Southerner. Though my father is a Southerner, she will not yield to his wish to go into the army, and thus we are a disunited, unhappy family. I feel it is but natural for my mother to cling to her people, but oh! why render us all miserable? To my dear brother she had ceased to speak, and refused to bestow her blessing on him the morning he left. I know that she will never consent to our union."

"Do not despair, my darling, I shall speak to your mother on the subject; but should she refuse, then, Cornie, what is your intention?"

She leaned her head on his shoulder, and placing her hand in his, looked up into his face and said, "Oh, dear Albert, what alternative remains?'

"To be mine, darling, at all hazards."

"Oh, tempt me not, I feel that happiness could not follow such an union."

"Then, dearest, we will not anticipate her refusal. Give me but your consent to ask her, and this evening shall decide our fate. Be it as you will, then; I will seek an interview at once."

Rising he summoned a servant, and said, "Say to Mrs. Clifton that I should be pleased to see her for a few moments."

"Oh, Albert, I dread the result of this meeting," and saying this she went out as Mrs. Clifton entered.

Our hero was by no means bashful, but as Mrs. Clifton

appeared, his courage faltered. Rising and placing a
chair for her, he at once entered upon the subject :

"My dear Madam, my devoted attentions to your
daughter have doubtless ere this arrested your attention,
and given you some idea of the purport of this interview, which is simply this, to demand in marriage the
hand of her whom I love, and have loved since the
moment of our first meeting. I have the assurance that
this affection is reciprocal, and have sought this interview with your daughter's consent; and now, dear
Madam, with your knowledge of my character, social
position, etc., I await your answer, and trust you will
view this matter favourably, so that at any moment
I may leave with my command."

"Colonel la Branche," said Mrs. Clifton, and as she
spoke she drew herself up to her full height, rising, and
standing before him, "it is needless to state that I feel
you are fully aware of my political views, and that I am
not a Southerner, in birth, education, or feeling, in
nought, sir, save my place of residence. I have no
sympathy with the cause of the South whatever, and
let my husband's and children's feelings be what they
may, I can never be other than I was born—a loyal
Unionist; nor can I ever consent that my child should
wed any save a friend of that glorious banner under
which they, as well as their mother, first drew breath ;
nor can child or friend of mine ever receive my benison
who shall raise an arm against the standard of our
forefathers. These are my sentiments, Colonel la
Branche, and furthermore I will add that if I could be
base enough to yield her up to an enemy of the Union,
I would not wish to confide her to one who is more

worthy of her, and who is every way more estimable than Colonel la Branche, but whose misguided zeal in an unrighteous cause has placed a barrier to a union which, under other circumstances, might be the acmé of any mother's fondest ambition. Colonel la Branche, it is needless to prolong this interview; you have my irrevocable response, and I will have the honour to bid you good evening."

She walked out of the room, and Albert la Branche, not wishing to convey in person the answer of Mrs. Clifton, took out a card, and wrote upon it a few words, which, after summoning the servant, he desired to be delivered to Miss Clifton, and then, leaving the house, he was soon on the road to the city.

Miss Clifton was immediately requested to attend her mother, when upon entering, she threw herself into her mother's arms, saying, "Mother, dear mother, do not, oh! do not blight my happiness for all eternity; recall what you have said, and bestow your blessing on us both; let not your devotion to the land of your birth destroy for ever the peace of all the loved and loving inmates of our once happy home, and in blessing us may not your benediction be wafted to your darling son and my dear brother, whom you permitted to leave, perhaps for ever, without one kind adieu. Oh, my mother, you who are so noble, so beautiful, can you, oh! will you, suffer the felicity of our home to be banished for aye, by the refusal of your gentle smiles, which of yore cast a halo over all, and everything upon which they fell. Mother, darling mother, restore the sunshine upon our household, which has so long been eclipsed by the clouds of disunion which exist amongst us."

Mrs. Clifton gently raised her daughter, and, clasping her arms around her, kissed her pale brow, and stroked her sunny ringlets as she said—" My daughter, the cause which was strong enough to sustain me in parting with one of my idols will sustain me in this trying hour. Darling, ask life, or anything of your mother, and all she has will be bestowed freely on you, but to prove recreant to the Union —that Union which my forefathers bled for and assisted in forming—I will never, my child, never ; and, my child, let us proceed to the termination of this sad interview, which is now necessary, but which, by your consent and submission to my will, need never be renewed again.   Then, my daughter, promise me faithfully that you will never again suffer Colonel la Branche to approach you, and that by word, verbal or written, you will not encourage his addresses. Avoid him as you would a mortal enemy, and should you meet him, remember, it would be the roseleaf on the surface of my already brimming cup if you were ever to disobey my last injunction ; and were I dead, darling, remember that from the portals of the tomb my voice would still proclaim the existence of that immeasurable abyss which must for ever separate yourself and Colonel la Branche "

"Oh, mother! mother !" shrieked the wretched girl, "this will kill me—unsay it, mother dearest, or your poor already blighted blossom must perish by the same dreadful fiat that separates Albert la Branche and myself."

" Courage, Cornie, courage ; you will, I trust, soon overcome ·this unworthy affection and be yet happy in the love of one whose addresses your mother can sanction; and now, dearest, give me your promise that you will act in accordance with my wishes."

As she said this, Mrs. Clifton fondly imprinted a kiss upon her daughter's marble brow.

Summoning all her courage as for a mighty effort, Miss Clifton said, " My mother, you who gave me life and being, have the right, I presume, to take it from me when you will; I obey you, but when all that is mortal is laid in the grave of your daughter, think then in that hour, dear mother, that you could have bid me live for love and thee, and that though Cornie Clifton may have loved deeply, fondly—ay, wildly, her duty of obedience to an earthly parent, according to the laws of God, triumphed over all other feelings, and in this thought, dear mother, you may find a solace for your grief for though a stern parent, I know you love your child." Raising her mother's hand, she kissed it and pressed it to her heart, then silently left the room and proceeded towards her father's study to imprint the wonted kiss upon his brow, and receive his nightly benediction, which he never failed to accord her.

Oh! how wildly, tumultuously, palpitated poor Cornie's heart as she hesitatingly drew near the door! with what keen anguish did she stop to press her hands upon her bosom, endeavouring to arrest its wild throbbings! She leaned, oh! how painfully, against the door before entering, but an almost preternatural fortitude seizing her at this moment, as it often does at the crisis of the most trying ordeals, she regained her composure, and tapping gently at the door, she entered. She drew an ottoman beside him, and taking one hand in hers, she threw the other arm round his neck, and drawing his head down, the sunny curls of eighteen summers mingled their hues with the silver locks of sixty winters.

"My dear father, will nothing dissipate the sombre shadow which darkens your otherwise glorious brow? Can your own Cornie do aught to dispel the gloom which seems to surround her dear, dear father?"

"No, darling, the shadow is on our hearthstone, and the reflection falls here;" and pressing one hand to his heart, he bowed his head upon the other, and a large tear-drop fell upon his daughter's hair and rested there like a diamond upon golden sands; "but," he continued, "let not this gloom take possession of your buoyant soul; and now, darling, forget my too inconsiderate speech and everything, my beloved, only how I ever, and shall ever, study your happiness." Pressing a kiss, warm and fervent, on her brow, and resting his hands upon her head as she knelt to receive his blessing, he spoke his gentle "good night." Raising her he led her to the door, and as she passed out he repeated his benisons upon his lovely child.

Miss Clifton sped to her chamber. She cast herself upon a couch, and the pent-up stream of grief then burst its bonds, and threatened to destroy the channel through which it flowed. She rose from the couch, and wildly throwing herself upon her knees, she called on God to strengthen her in this her bitter woe. She gave vent to low and passionate wailings, and incoherent words of agony. Alas! it was sad, sad indeed, to think that one of her years, who was but just verging on the bloom of womanhood, and when the world should be expanding before her as a lovely garden full of roses and lilies—Oh, it was sad indeed, that one

like her should experience such bitter, bitter desolation ; and yet, poor Cornie, thy cup was but half filled
at this hour. To her father, whose cup was already
brimming, she could not flee, and thus she sought for
days to conceal the canker gnawing at her heart. But,
alas! nature at last sank under this ineffectual effort,
and as she lay upon her bed of grief, her pallid face in
vain appealing to her mother, who watched and nursed
her kindly, but sternly repelled every approach to that
subject which alone occupied the thoughts of the suf-
ferer as she lay before her. Not that Mrs. Clifton was a
hard-hearted woman, but she had schooled herself for
this trial, and her resolve was irrevocable. Next to
her God and husband, she loved her country, and
though she married a Southern planter, her soul ab-
horred the system of slavery, and ever her thoughts
returned to the green fields of her New England home,
where free labour tilled the soil and garnered the grain ;
and though her children were born and bred in the
South, her deep-rooted principles could never be eradi-
cated. In her early wedded days she had often sought,
for her husband's sake (whom she deeply and ardently
loved), to mould her ideas to suit his tastes, but alas!
in vain, the teachings, the inculcations, and prejudices of childhood and youth triumphed over the experience of maturer years, and at the age of forty, when
her home should have been the harbour of repose for
herself and all she loved from the storms of life, she had
made it the maelstrome of affliction, to which she beheld
every loved object approaching, and calmly she sat to
see them drawn into its eddying depths. Oh, woman,
what a fearful responsibility is yours! Yours is the

high and holy mission to plant the seed, and rear the tender flower. If thorns or thistles enter, thine is the hand to pluck them from amidst your blossoms. If they wither, bear evil fruit, or perish, thine is the fault. Nourish them kindly, and if thou see'st the worm at the roots, or in the heart, fear not to strike and kill, though in doing so the blossom or root should even perish, but so long as one green, unblighted branch remains, you will, with tender care, be able to produce roses of richest fragrance and lovely dye; but should but one decayed remain, if not lopped off, 'twill soon spread to other and fairer parts of your cherished plant, until all becomes diseased, and dies. Yes, woman's is the proud mission. To her is given the charge of man, in childhood, youth, and age; and though she be allowed no voice in the council of a nation (as the "woman's right" society would desire), does not her voice ring loud and clear in the Senate Chamber, in the pulpit, on the battle-field, and through the press, by the medium of husbands, fathers, sons, and brothers? Yes, ah, yes, and be the voice of man raised where, or when it will, for good or evil, rest assured it is his mother's teachings. We crave no greater freedom. *Man owes to God and woman his existence, his principles, and his education.* From the cradle to the grave she is by his side as his ministering angel, no less needed in the tottering steps of childhood than in those of old age. Women, fair countrywomen, women of every nation, would you seek a nobler sphere? No, ten thousand times no; it were selfish indeed to desire all the glory of life, when we possess the greater portion, for man is but the medium of woman's ideas and projects, and *she plans* while *he achieves.* Thus, alike in the cottage and the palace—woman rules her lord; and beautifully has Longfellow expressed this unseen, silent influence, "As the bow unto the cord is, so the man unto the woman." These should be congenial in all sentiments, and without this unison of feeling no felicity can accrue from marriage.   In Mrs. Clifton was exemplified the truth of this.   Clinging to false ideas, which neither reason nor time could subvert, she gazed coldly upon the ruin of her fast fleeting happiness, ready and willing to sacrifice all she held dear to that false idol who sat enthroned in her heart, and whose name is *Fanaticism.*

"My daughter," said Mrs. Clifton, "Miss de Villerie will soon be here; but as she has been so much engaged recently since the battle of Manasses in her various patriotic pursuits, I fear it will be trespassing on her kindness to invite her to be the companion of an invalid."

"Oh no, dearest mother, I feel assured she will consider it no importunate demand to come to me.   Oh! mother, you know not her generous nature; but, list, she comes, dearest mother.   I hear her tread."

Throwing open the door of the chamber, the servant ushered Madame de Breuil and Miss de Villerie into the presence of mother and daughter, and the two young friends were soon clasped in a warm embrace, while tears welled from Miss de Villerie's eyes, as she gazed on the pale face of her sad friend.

"Oh, Cornie, darling, why did you not inform me earlier of your illness, and I should have ere this wooed you from this close chamber," and again she pressed her friend to her bosom, while Cornie drooped her radiant head upon Natalie's breast, and wept.

Mrs. Clifton and Madame de Breuil soon withdrew, and Miss de Villerie directing the servant to draw the couch towards the western oriel, she said, as she placed the cushions gently, and laid her friend's frail form upon them, "Come, *chère* Cornie, unburden your griefs to me, if you will, and here, while gazing out upon rich flowers, birds, lake, and bower, take courage and remember, yon brilliant orb, which is just descending, sets only to rise brighter on the morrow."

CHAPTER XII.

"Weeping for thee, my love, through the long day,
  Lonely and wearily life wears away.
  Weeping for thee, my love, through the long night,
  No rest in darkness, no joy in light!
  Nought left but memory, whose dreary tread
  Sounds through this ruin'd heart, where all lies dead—
  Wakening the echoes of joy long fled!"

WITH hand clasped in hand, those two friends whiled
the evening hours away; and between sobs and bitter
tears did Miss Clifton unfold to Miss de Villerie her
woes, and ended with these words—"Oh, dearest Natalie,
you who seem to be above the weakness of the flesh,
impart to me, in this trying moment, somewhat of
your lofty fortitude; endow me with a portion of your
philosophic nature to face this blasting simoon of
affliction which threatens to destroy both me and mine.
Oh, Natalie, would that, like you, I could give up, for
the sake of duty, what you relinquished so nobly for
country; but, Natalie, within me rages a fearful storm,
and, amid the muffled din, Albert's voice appeals to me
not to desert him; then counsel, aid, and guide me,
dearest friend, in the true path, be it for weal or woe,"
and throwing herself on the bosom of Miss de Villerie,
Miss Clifton wept bitterly.

Miss de Villerie's own bosom was torn and rent with convulsive sobs, and though she endeavoured to soothe her friend by sisterly caresses, it seemed as though her own heart was bursting beneath its weight of agony ; language seemed a mockery, as a source to convey consolation ; but the wildest storms must cease, and, casting herself back on her couch, Miss Clifton closed her eyes, while the last tears from grief's fountain were seen welling to her eyes, slowly overflowing their fringed margins, and coursing down her wan cheeks.

Miss de Villerie gazed upon her friend, and there seemed an inward struggle of contending feelings, which appeared visible in her actions. She slowly drew forth from the folds of her dress a note, and placing it in the hands of Miss Clifton, said, " Cornie, darling, forgive me if, ere this, I have not gladdened your heart by the sight and perusal of this missive, which Albert la Branche entrusted me with for you. Read it, and may its contents be more soothing than my poor expressions of condolence ; and forgive me if I withheld it ; I feared to interfere, dear Cornie, in matters between mother and daughter, but your grief has reopened the wounds in my own heart, which bleeds for you, my sweet friend, from every pore. God grant you grace to bear your sorrows like a Christian and as a woman, and rest assured, that He who permitteth not a sparrow to fall to the ground without His will, will at last dry your tears."

Miss Clifton seized the note, and tremblingly broke the seal, then kissing it, she was about to read it, when she hesitatingly laid it down beside her, as she said,

"Oh, I fear to read it; I fear that Albert's pride has abandoned me to my fate, and that my mother has separated us for ever. Oh, Natchi, my friend, my heart sinks within me, when I think of the possible contents of this note, but I will read it, and learn to bear my sorrows." Once more pressing it to her lips, she tore it open, and her eyes glanced quickly over the page.

"Beloved one, fear not, though, at present, our sky be clouded, the sunshine of a glorious love shall yet beam upon us in all its splendour. Yes, dearest, ere this reaches you, you will have, I presume, heard all from your mother's lips relative to our interview, whose issue was as you feared. But fear not, trust as implicitly in my love, as I do in yours, and all will end, darling, as we desire. Love and trust me as you ever have, and I fear not that any earthly power shall part us. Yes, for the moment we are parted, and heartless as it may seem to you, I have pledged my honour to your mother, that all communication between us, either verbal or written, shall cease, until she shall herself desire its renewal. I have hope, darling, and like Pandora's box, the lid of my heart has closed upon it, and there the bright spirit rests securely. Honour on my part, duty on yours, will prevent our meeting; but the future, dearest, is before us, and but a silver veil intervenes, through which I view, with the soul's eye, a happy, peaceful vision beyond. To our mutual friend I entrust this missive, and I ask for no response, save what she will bear me verbally. I ask not to win you, darling, otherwise than nobly—

N

and now farewell. Love and trust me, Cornie, and leave *the rest with* **God**.

"Your own,

"ALBERT la BRANCHE."

"Oh, Albert, if I loved you before, I worship you now; yes, I will 'love and trust thee,' and endeavour to buoy up my fainting spirit until the happy hour wherein we shall meet to part no more. But, oh, Natchi, never, never will my mother yield to our wishes. No, she would rather clothe me in my burial robes than bridal. Tell him, oh, say to him, my friend, that he cannot doubt my love, nor its depth. Say to him that I will love on, even though it may be hopeless; tell him his bright spirit has done well to fold her wings and rest in the chamber of his generous soul; had she appeared to me, she could have found no dwelling-place. 'Tis well he gave it admittance, for, indeed, we know not when the angel is at the door.

"Yes, Albert, cherish your fair spirit of light, for mine is one of darkness; but tell him not, Natalie, that this is so, tell him only that I am happy, very happy, in all and everything, but the knowledge that we are to meet no more renders me miserable. Oh, strange inconsistency! Happy and unhappy too. What shall I say, dearest Natalie? tell me, you who seem to scorn the weakness of a feeling which has overpowered me, tell me how to veil my words, that no foolish or inconsiderate expressions of mine shall add to his grief. Render him insensible to mine, if possible, but oh! assure him of my love, which no time nor circumstances shall ever change."

She had raised herself from the couch as she proceeded, and as she said the last words, she threw herself back upon the pillow and wept silently. Gently
Miss de Villerie smoothed her golden hair, and kindly
she soothed her sad spirit.

"Cornie," said Miss de Villerie, "have you appealed
to your father in regard to this affair?"

"Oh, no, *chère* Natalie, I would not for worlds broach
the subject to him; already his poor heart is bowed
down with woe, and I would suffer my own to break
rather than add one pang to his; besides, Natalie, it
would be a source of strife in our already unhappy home.
My father would consent, while my mother would pronounce maledictions on me, more fearful to me than
death, for oh! what child can be happy in the knowledge that she has disobeyed a parent, one who has
cherished her from infancy, through thoughtless girlhood, to perilous womanhood? Oh no, my friend, though
I love Albert dearly and well, I could not leave my
home to follow him, with the knowledge that I left that
home blighted and desolate, nor would he wish me to
do so. No, he would scorn me, and justly too. A faithless daughter will be a faithless wife, and never will such
a union be productive of good. This is all we can do
to repay a parent for their care,—to marry in accordance
with their desires, if at the altar we can feel we are not
perjuring ourselves, but should we feel that by acting
in accordance with our parents' wishes, we are acting
contrary with those of God, we should obey our Heavenly
Parent's dictates, and never marry if we cannot feel
that in doing so we obey the voice of our terrestial and
celestial guardians."

"But may not your father prevail on your mother to sanction the union?"

"No, never, though she loves my father devotedly, she would not yield in this. I know her well, and she would not give up her prejudices for either love or reason. No, Natalie, to God and time I trust for happiness; but I have a strange presentiment, which seems to warn me of evil."

"Banish it then, darling, it is only your sad state of mind which conjures up these phantoms. In a few weeks more your mother will relent, and then, my dear friend, you will once again be joyous and glad. Come, dearest, rest your head upon my bosom, and gaze upon this gorgeous sunset. See, it seems to bid farewell to earth lingeringly, and to cast upon it its most lovely dyes and warmest embraces, though it passes from us to light another sphere; so with you, dearest, your sun of sorrow is but setting for a joyful dawning. You, Cornie, are unlike me; your gentle Christian spirit can school itself to resignation, through the Divine influence of religion, while I act simply from the sentiments of duty and honour. I feel that I am not one of the chosen, and yet at times, when all my senses seem slumbering, when I feel as it were dead to the world, there steals over my soul that sublime feeling of repose, which elevates me, and seems to bear me on its wings to the feet of Jesus, where oft I have lingered in meditation for hours. Oh, Cornie, in those moments I feel I have given up for ever the world and all its vanities; that all, all is but a day-dream, compared to the glories of eternity. But soon the dream is dispelled, and then the weary round of every-day life again commences, until in some sad

moment my gentle guardian returns, and seeks to lead
me to the only true Fountain of peace. Oh, my friend,
in those moments how ardently I have prayed to die!
How gladly would I leave this earth, and all its loved
objects, to dwell for ever with Him! With you it is
never thus. You, my friend, seem ever ready to plume
your wings for heaven, and to feel none of those
relapses of conscience which must prove fatal in the
end to the soul. At the feet of Jesus, Mary, and Joseph
I have indeed poured forth my sorrow, and have risen
from thence much happier. Alas! I have felt that though
they loved me, I was not their favoured child. Some
natures, like gentle streams, wind slowly on, and empty
into the great river of life, and flow silently into the
great ocean of eternity, without one single obstruction,
while others course madly onward, bearing all before
them, and hurl their seething waves into the vast waters.
Such a nature as the latter is mine. Oh, Cornie, darling,
what would I not give to possess your gentle spirit, to
feel that, like you, I could 'wrap the drapery of my
couch around me, and lie down to pleasant dreams!'"

"Dearest Natalie, your partiality does me more than
justice. It is true that I have ever sought for bliss in
the holy teachings of the Church. Nurtured in her
bosom I am indeed her child, and alike in sorrow and in
joy my spirit turns ever to her, and in her ear is poured
forth the wail of affliction or the glad tones of exulta-
tion. To the shrine of Jesus I ever go, dearest Natalie,
and in the arms of Jesus, Mary, and Joseph, I trust to
breathe my latest sigh."

"Yes, bliss is thine, Cornie, in your lovely faith you
possess the alchymist's power, not to turn earth to gold

but to tinge all objects with its golden halo. Would it were mine to believe implicitly in all which the Church has taught and now teaches, but ever the tempter Incredulity whispers 'believe not,' and in doubt I turn from all that gives to religion its charm, and yet I still pursue this Protean shadow which treacherously melts from my grasp and leaves my mental as well as physical faculties prostrated."-

"Ah, dearest Natalie, if you are the true and sincere lover and follower of Jesus, the more doubts and conflicts with Satan here would but more surely lead you to that more bright immortal existence hereafter. Beyond the dark and dying struggle man will be for ever and completely free. The grave is the spot where he will lay down his weaknesses, his desires, sorrows, and sins, that he may rise to a new and bright existence in the realms of everlasting day. This glorious hope of finally being 'made alive in Christ' is the only true and inexhaustible fountain of happiness on earth. Turn to it, darling friend, drink deep of its waters; it is accessible to all. All who taste of its sparkling waters are substantially free and equal. We are all journeying to the celestial world, where happiness unalloyed will be our portion, where the ties of love and friendship are indissoluble, whose bright and enduring realities will never be dimmed by the clouds of sin or affliction."

"You, Cornie, are one of the few who were born in the knowledge of Christ, and who seem to possess that mystic comprehension of the great (and to me incomprehensible) works of the Unknown. I admire the works of the Great Being, while you seem *to understand their uses.*"

"Ah, Natalie, God has given all the heart to love him if not the spirit to know him. Surely you, possessed of so glorious an intellect, do not feel your comprehension fail on this subject alone?"

"Yes, Cornie, religion alone to me is a mystery which I fain would solve; I believe in a God, I believe in the apostolical succession, and many other sublime articles of our faith, but, oh! Cornie, there are many, very many, pious doctrines that have been handed down by tradition at which I am perplexed and doubting. My religion is that of the heart alone, I know none other. If to belong to a church be to believe *all* it teaches, then I must say I am of no particular creed, though bowing at the altar of Catholicism."

Thus sped the evening hours, and Miss de Villerie sought in such converse to soothe the mind of her unhappy friend, and when she arose to leave she was repaid in the quiet and peaceful expression of her friend's angelic face as she whispered, "Yes, dearest friend, tell him I am happy, that if I were not previously, your visit has made me so."

Madame de Breuil and Mrs. Clifton entered, and the former bidding an affectionate adieu to Miss Clifton, said, "My dear, we trust to see you soon at Rosale, and also we hope for your assistance, as we are getting up tableaux for the benefit of the soldiers, and we are anxious you should take part in them."

A servant entering, handed to Miss Clifton a letter.

"Stay, my dear friends, and learn the news. This is from Beverley, and bears the postmark 'Columbia.' Be seated, pray, and list to the tidings."

Coldly Mrs. Clifton rose, and excusing herself, left
the room, while Miss Clifton, too feeble to read, placed
the letter in Miss de Villerie's hand, who proceeded at
once to read :—

"Darling Sister,

    "Since my letter of the 15th ult., there has been
fought a great battle, and our arms have won a brilliant
victory. Ere dawn on the morning of the 7th inst.,
General Polk was informed that the enemy was under
command of General Grant, and were prepared for an
attack at the small village of Belmont, on the Missouri
shore. General Pillow was ordered to cross at once
with four of his regiments, to the assistance of Colonel
Yappen, who was stationed at Belmont. No sooner
had our men got into position than the conflict opened.
We were, as usual, greatly outnumbered, and there
were sufficient of the enemy to have completely vanquished us, had their valour been equal to their hate.
Again and again, were attempts made by the enemy's
infantry to flank both wings of our army, but the attempts on the right were defeated by the galling fire
kept up by the 13th Arkansas and 9th Tennessee, commanded by the brave Colonel Russell, brigade commander. That on the left proved ineffectual through
the gallant conduct of Major Beltzhoover, whose bat-
tery belched forth destructive fire. Firm and unbroken
stood these wings for hours, but at last the centre,
being greatly exposed, began to falter, as Colonels Ball,
Wright, and Beltzhoover, almost at the same moment,
reported themselves out of ammunition. The enemy's
force now boldly advancing into the open field, General

Pillow ordered the line to use the bayonet. The charge was valiantly made by our men, and soon the enemy sought the forest, but unbroken and steadily, not a line being broken, keeping up all the while a heavy firing, and being supported by a large reserve, which soon sent us retreating before them. We now desponded of victory, and General Pillow ordered the whole line to fall back to the river bank. In this movement the line lost all order, and they reached the river bank more like a dispersed and panic-stricken mob. However, the loyal hearts took courage with the hope of reinforcements, and at the very moment when Pillow reached the river, hopeless, and, as he himself believed, defeated, there arrived fresh troops under command of Colonel Marks, which were ordered over to the assistance of General Pillow by General Polk.

" Arriving at the scene of strife, and seeing his men mowed down like chaff, Colonel Marks ordered his men to retreat, saying, ' Boys, we shall all be cut to pieces,' when Lieutenant-Colonel Barrow rode up and exclaimed, ' No, no, never. We can at least cut our way to the river, and come on, my brave boys, *if we have to die, I can teach you how as well as any one else,*' and seizing the command from Colonel Marks, who seemed paralysed with fear, and waving his sword, he dashed into the thickest of the strife. To this bold and courageous act are we indebted for the great victory of Belmont ; the flank movement which gained the day, and turned the tide of battle in our favour, was made upon this able officer's own judgment and responsibility. Too much eulogy cannot be awarded him, and in after days, as now, he must ever be regarded as the HERO OF BEL-

MONT. On history's page this action will scintillate with an undying brilliancy. This was a moment that tried men's souls, and he was found equal to the emergency; one of the veterans of Florida and Mexico lost his laurels on the field of Belmont, while they were transferred from his brow to that of the modern Caractacus. But, the foe vanquished, he modestly placed himself under the command of his senior, though less worthy, officer. Modest and retiring, he seems to seek no fame save the shedding of his blood for his country, and when the din and struggle of battle were over, and he sought his tent once more, there arose along the lines a deafening shout of joy and admiration for the brave ' Hero of Belmont,' as the soldiers have styled him. By his kind and generous deeds this officer has endeared himself to the rough soldier, as well as the more refined officer. Suffice it to say, that his conduct was worthy of more praise than my poor pen can award him, and in the hearts of those who fought under him on that day will ever live the name of this gallant man. This is one of the few cases which have proven that it does not require a military education to form the warrior. The effect of this movement was the dismay and flight of the enemy, who were soon seen pressing to reach their boats. General Polk ordered the pursuit, and the remnant of the Federal army retreated in their boats, and they steamed through an avenue of fire, (which was formed by the sharpshooters,) and up the river for more than a mile.

" The dead and wounded lay everywhere, and when we sought the battle-ground to gaze upon the dead, our eyes rested upon the noble form of the elegant and brave Major Edward Butler, who had fallen in the first charge of his regiment, the 11th La. He was borne to the headquarters of General Polk, and there breathed his last. 'Tell my father, mother, and sisters, that I died as a soldier should die, and as became a Butler to die,' he said to General Polk. Peace to his slumbers! A warrior's wreath, and a warrior's grave are his! Many brave men fell, but there were none more gallant than he. A gentleman in every sense, he won the esteem and admiration of all, and there were but few exceptions, save where his evident superiority excited their envy. As for myself, dear Sister, it will suffice you to learn that I escaped uninjured, though I was everywhere surrounded by the missiles of destruction. Oh! my dear Sister, you cannot conceive the horrors of this war. Mercy seems to have fled from us for ever, and war, in all its dread significance, we have surely. Yet it is but just we should show no mercy, but it is only on the field of battle that we neither grant nor ask for quarter. While I have seen these Yankee soldiers thrust their swords through our wounded and sick men, ay, even in the agonies of death. The vindictiveness of these Yankee hirelings know no bounds, and indeed we must prepare for the worst, for long and bloody will be the contest. Craven-hearted indeed must be the man styling himself Northerner, who would consent to remain one moment under such a Government. The tender mercies of the wicked are cruel. The ravages and devastations of Attilla the Hun, the fanatical rage of Omar, the Turks' oppression, the Sepoys' revenge, have been humane and charitable compared with the conduct of these hyenas.

We can now have some conception of how terrible the malignities of our foes would be, were their capacity for evil in proportion to their malignity, which exceeds anything ever known or heard of. But the arch-fiend is chained in darkness, and thus powerless; so it is with human beings. In the goodness of Providence those who surrender themselves to the dark passions of their nature are doomed to blindness and impotence.

"When we look at the results that have been achieved by the South, in spite of the incalculable disadvantages growing out of the fact that we have been cut off from the commerce of the world, and forced to depend almost solely upon our undeveloped and otherwise limited resources, I confess that I am astonished at the might and prowess of an infant nation that has thus grappled successfully with a powerful antagonist whose gigantic strength, humanly speaking, should have crushed us long ago. Hence no wonder that the sages of the North laughed to scorn the first premonitions made by the South to establish and defend herself as a distinct Government among the nations of the earth. They saw our weakness, more than we did ourselves, for we were in a degree blinded by that mysterious 'Divinity which shapes our ends, rough hew them as we may.' Seventy-five thousand men were thought, at first, amply sufficient to put down the rebellion, and at that time it did seem to be a formidable army, especially when panoplied so magnificently, and marching under the *prestige* of a flag that had never been known to trail in the dust of defeat. But time has proved the insufficiency of this army, and then *five hundred thousand* were added to them. Strange to say, this also proved too small to overcome the 'little rebellion' which had been sneered at as a 'ninety days affair,' at which no one should be alarmed. They still call for more troops, and soon they will be sent in millions instead of thousands. Thus far the victory has been ours. We have foiled and defeated the enemy in almost every engagement. The sympathies of the European world have been stirred in our behalf, and tributes of praise are being showered upon us from every direction. In view of these facts, the future possesses nothing in reserve to discourage us. The finger of Providence has traced in the events of the past sufficient to indicate that we are yet to *be free*. Our situation in Kentucky is one of weakness at present, though the occupation of a portion of it is of great and imminent necessity for our own benefit, and for her own. By menacing Cincinnati and the Northern shore of the Ohio, we can effectually checkmate all further raids into Western Virginia or Missouri, and, at the same time, remove the fear of trouble in East Tenessee; Kentucky is decidedly Southern, and the assumed powerful position on the part of the Union party was, from the first, a mere farce. It was but a hypocritical scheme, conceived by her designing and disappointed politicians of the stamp of those who would 'rather reign in hell than serve in Heaven,' such men as Magoffin, Wickliffe, Holt, and others to betray their State into the hands of the abolition oligarchy. But we have all the military talent of the State with us, Buckner, Smith, Williams, Marshall, Breckenridge, Hanson, and others who have seen service, and who are prepared to marshal their hosts around our standard. All are with us save the Tory,

Rousseau, who is too dastardly to be a Southern, and too little souled to be a great man. But enough, the once proud and lofty State of Kentucky has been doubly obscured and humiliated. She was refused even the ignoble privilege of wearing the gilded chain of prosperous servitude, which her demagogue statesmen sought to enchain her with. She is in the midst of a civil warfare, so cruel and sanguinary, that by the side of its prodigious horrors, the cruel troubles in other States appear cold and tame. The unrelenting system of persecution of Secessionists has begun, domiciliary visits are being made, and midnight arrests incessantly repay these *mild* neutral people for their servility and baseness. It is hard that it should 'rain on the just and unjust alike.' Farewell, dear sister. To father and mother remember me affectionately, and to our kind friends at Rosale; I know not when you will hear from me again, as I anticipate a transfer to Fort Donelson. In the meantime rest assured of my safety, and of my unchanging love."

"What glorious news, dearest Cornie! This should be all-sufficient to cause you to rouse yourself and assist us in our work of love. Say to Beverley when you next write that I trust every battle-field may be a Belmont for the Federals, and may he live to be the historian."

"Ah! my dear friend, you cannot conceive the dark forebodings that rise within me and before me, whenever I think of my darling brother. I know not what to think, but I feel that 'his hour is at hand,' and when I think, too, that he will perhaps die far, far from either friends or relatives, it almost phrensies me."

"You should not, my dear girl, encourage such gloomy fancies," said Madame de Breuil, "I trust I shall see you soon at our home, and this delightful weather, methinks, should alone be sufficient to call you forth from your chamber. We are revelling in all the delights of a most lovely Indian summer, and the gossamer floats around each object, reminding one forcibly of beauty in tears. A dashing ride, *sur le bord du Mississippi*, would dissipate your sombre *pensées*."

"Miss Clarendon and Natalie, together with the Judge, had a most charming ride on the coast, and were joined by Madame Bienvenu and Lord St. Leonard, who it is said will soon bear our bewitching friend to his Caledonian home. Madame Charlotte Levy, report says, has received the order for her *trousseau*, and I have understood that she is to be married in the morning, and start at once for Europe. I rallied her somewhat a few days ago, and I must say she did not deny the charge. We must all be on the *qui vive* for a card. So adieu, and banish from your mind those gloomy reflections, and be yourself once again. *Allons*, Natalie."

Miss de Villerie clasped her arms around her friend, and gently pressed her to her breast, whilst she kissed her pale cheeks, whispering softly, "Be of good cheer, *chère* Cornie, to every cloud there is a silver lining."

Madame de Breuil and Miss de Villerie, after having sought Mrs. Clifton in her boudoir, made their adieus, and seating themselves in their equipage, were rapidly driven home. On entering the house, Madame de Breuil and Miss de Villerie were agreeably surprised to find the drawing-rooms filled with guests from the

city, whom the bracing air of a November morning called
forth, "to drive dull care away."

"Ah, *chère* Natalie, we are glad to welcome you to
our circle. Give us an idea for killing time. Here are
we, assembled in council to decide upon the most humane
means of disposing of this gray haired veteran, and be
it resolved that he is to meet with an agreeable and
gentle death. Let us crown him with garlands, then,
and let some fair 'Undine' be the executioner of this
most unkind Sir Huldibrand."

"Ladies," said Judge de Breuil, "if this is to be dra-
matised, I shall not object to Sir Huldibrand's *rôle.* Such
a death were ecstasy indeed. I fear, however, I shall
not find an Undine to perform the part. By the way,
speaking on the subject of the drama, ladies, reminds
me of our tableaux; I presume you are all prepared to
enact your parts?"

"Assuredly," they all cried, "but what are we to do?
Cornie Clifton is an invalid, and if she is unable to lend
her graceful person to the scene, half the beauty will
be lost."

"Ladies. I have just returned from Colonel Clifton's,
and I have hopes of the appearance of that young lady
on the occasion of our tableaux. She has been quite ill,
but a few days in the society of her companions will
restore her to health and animation. But, ladies, while
we discuss these matters, we forget the 'urn is hissing
on the board.' We will enter the *salle-à-manger* if you
like."

Just at this moment the porter ushered in Monsieur
la Branche.

The company remained standing, while Judge de Breuil and Madame de Breuil received their guests, and then entering the hall, the scarlet curtains embiazoned with gold, which separated the various chambers, were suddenly parted in the centre, and caught up with golden tassels in festoons, displaying beyond it another superb apartment, with the lengthy and hospitable board glittering with plate and crystal, while epergnes of flowers were placed in the most enchanting manner around. Judge de Breuil, drawing off his glove, presented his hand to Madame Bienvenue, and led her to a seat, while Lord St. Leonard escorted Madame de Breuil. Oscar McAlva presented his hand to Miss Clarendon, and the other gentlemen doing likewise, the ladies were soon all seated. At the further end of the table sat Miss de Villerie, and by her side Monsieur la Branche.

Madame Bienvenue, as usual, was the life of the company. Toast after toast was proposed and drank, and Madame Bienvenue spoke of so many things and in that charming and peculiar manner (which to a pretty woman is invaluable, and which gives an interest even to trifles), that the Judge almost forgot his resolve of remaining a bachelor, and almost vowed to become a benedict, casting such liquid, love-lit glances at her, that Lord St. Leonard's hostile expression aroused him to a sense of honour and recollection of the state of affairs. Amidst this scene, Miss de Villerie and Albert la Branche sat almost oblivious of the gaiety around them, and when all rose from the table and returned to the drawing-room, they were still in close converse, until courtesy admonished Miss de Villerie to seek the presence of the guests, who had ordered their carriages, and were leaving.

The ladies were speedily enveloped in their wrappings, and Judge de Breuil handed them to their carriages.

CHAPTER XIII.

"But lighter thought, and lighter song,
  Now woos the coming hours along;
  For, mark, where smooth the herbage lies,
    Yon gay pavilion, curtain'd deep
  With silken folds, through which bright eyes,
    From time to time, are seen to peep;
  While, twinkling lights, that to and fro
  Beneath those veils, like meteors go—
    Tell of some spells at work, and keep
  Young fancies chain'd in mute suspense,
  Watching what next may shine from thence.
  Nor long the pause; by hands unseen
    That mystic curtain backward drew,
  And all, that late but shone between,
    In half-caught gleams now burst to view."

CARRIAGE after carriage rolled along the streets on the evening of the ——————— and the front of the Opera House was brilliantly illuminated, while crowds of elegantly attired ladies, and their attendant cavaliers, entered the grand portal, and seated themselves in their respective seats, or boxes. All seemed in anxious expectation, and as the curtain rose, a tableau of such marvellous beauty met the gaze, that the hum of voices ceased, and not a breath so faint as to waft the down from the dandelion could be heard or perceived in that vast assembly.

The scene was that of " Miriam, the Prophetess, ex-

ulting over the defeat of Pharoah and his host." On a
cliff overlooking the sea, as it were, stood Miss de Villerie, attired in a dark crimson kirtle, trimmed with
silver, while her rich black velvet boddice, *bien décolte*,
displayed her magnificent form, rounded and beautiful
as ever—a gem of the Orient. Her hair in glossy, jetty
braids, hung over her shoulders, and her arms were encircled with jewels of every hue and description. From
a crescent of flashing diamonds on her brow, fell a veil
of silver tissue to her waist, and with her hands she held
high above her head a cymbal, while her glowing
cheeks, sparkling eyes, and parted lips, whose coral
borders displayed the glistening ivory with which
her mouth was adorned,—spoke but too plainly the
triumph of her heart. In the background were seen
a band of Jewish maidens with their timbrels, in the
act of beginning their dance of victory. A minute
only, and the curtain dropped, to rise again upon the
same scene, amidst thunders of applause. There indeed she stood a very Miriam, for but a short while
before had not "the horse and his rider" been overthrown
when pursuing her own people? Yes, in triumph
she stood, darkly, grandly beautiful, and when the curtain fell upon the scene it was amidst a deafening burst
of delighted voices. " *Magnifique!*" " *Superbe!*" were
heard on every side, and the picture spoke volumes to
the sanguine. A few moments elapsed, and then the
curtain arose upon a scene so enchantingly beautiful
that language cannot even convey an idea. In a light
shallop, whose silken sails were unfurled, stood Albert
la Branche. The waves were about to envelop the
frail shell, in which he stood like a minor Neptune, and

he was in the act of casting anchor. Far off on the shore stood Miss Clifton, despair pictured in every feature, her hands clasped, and eyes raised to Heaven. Her fleecy robe fell around her form like a cloud of ether, and her golden ringlets vied with the rays of morn, which threw their mild beams over the scene. " *Charmante!*" exclaimed one and all, and the curtain once again fell, to rise upon very many other scenes of beauty and interest. As the crowd arose to leave, music burst upon the ear, and died away in gentle cadences as the audience dispersed. On the morrow it was found that several thousand dollars were added to the account realised by the various exertions of the ladies, and this was the fruit of this amateur display of the elegance, grace, and beauty of *la belle Creole.* Many a night when the poor soldier slept on the cold damp earth, with "scarce a sentinel star in the sky above," would the fair images of these devoted women cheer the darkness and solitude around him. And is it not indeed gratifying to them who have left home and all its joys for the tented field to know and feel that they are not forgotten? Is it not a solace for them to think that their friends' only pleasure and amusement consists in some endeavour of the kind to supply their wants? In such acts have our women displayed their devotion to the poor soldier. Each day and hour witnessed fresh proofs of their devotion, and when next the fair ladies of the Crescent City met it was to propose a fair, to provide clothing for the soldiers. The Hotel St. Louis was chosen for the display of all goods or articles sent for the use of the country, and there night after night were the fairest of the fair seen at their tables, selling to the patriotic, or promenading the rooms, in order to purchase something to aid the soldiers. Here was displayed self-sacrifice, and Miss de Villerie was the first (amongst many) to go forward and place her jewels upon the altar of her country. She cast it into the general purse, and her $100,000 set of jewellery served to clothe many a poor man, whose home was in the camp. Momentarily the committee of the bazaar were receiving donations. Ladies sent to be sold, as an offering to their country, their carriages and horses, preferring to walk rather than to see their soldiers deprived of comforts. The most *rare* and costly works of art were here purchased, and one seemed to vie with the other in bestowing their most valuable articles on those who were defending their homes and firesides. Diamonds, pearls, cameos, mosaics, and gems of all kinds were sold here in profusion, all the willing sacrifices of the patriotic.

On the closing night of the bazaar, Miss de Villerie was seen promenading with her friend Miss Clifton. They were followed through the room by a train of admirers and Miss de Villerie was as usual the centre of attraction.

Colonel E—— approached her and said, "Miss de Villerie, what would I not give to possess that bunch of flowers in your belt? I would give worlds for a spray even."

"You shall have them, then, entire, but I shall not expect even one world for them. Are you willing, Colonel, to give my price?"

"Most certainly, Miss de Villerie," he said, "anything I will give that I possess."

"Gentlemen and ladies," said Miss de Villerie, "witness this sale. I resign herewith all right and title to the bunch of roses and geraniums which I hold in my hand for the sum of $10,000, which amount I bestow upon the institution for the benefit of the soldiers of our State."

"Bravo!" they all exclaimed, as, bowing low, she presented him the flowers.

Whether he liked it or not we cannot say, but he bowed and accepted them.

"Step this way, Colonel," said Miss de Villerie, "here is the office, and if you have no objection I will just take your note or order for the amount, as we expect to close with this evening's work."

With seeming goodwill he entered, and gave an order for the amount. As she came out she laughingly remarked—

"I trust you will not think you have paid *too dear for your whistle.*"

"Miss de Villerie," he answered, "I would not think twice the amount too much to give for a leaf even that you had handled."

"As gallant as ever, Colonel; you prove to me that the days of chivalry are not gone by."

"Thank you," Miss de Villerie, "and permit me to reciprocate by saying that you have proven that all the rare, noble, self-sacrificing women did not end with the revolution."

Miss Clifton promenaded the room with the Hon. P—— S——, and though she was seemingly gay, there was a pensive look about her which but added to her marvellous beauty. Many other lovely girls, as well as aged dames, sauntered through the apartments with their attendant cavaliers, and all was life and animation. A splendid supper ended this affair; and when a few days afterwards it was known that by this effort there were $300,000 realised, it thrilled the heart of many an honest soldier.

The Mobilians were also desirous to prove their ardour in this cause, and soon a few of the sister city were doing all in their power to rival the patriotism of "Les belles Creoles."

I must not forget, however, to mention one of the *noblest* of all the efforts of the Southern people, viz., " *The Free Market.*" Too much cannot be said in favour of this institution and its benevolent conductors. To this institution many a brave soldier is indebted for the gratuitous support of his little family, and on every Tuesday and Saturday did this mother of the people bestow with generous hand her gifts of food and clothing to her needy children. Contributions flowed in from all quarters, and the surplus store of every home of affluence or ease was sent to this place, to be disposed of as the committee thought best. All here were treated impartially, and all alike received their allowance of whatever the market afforded. Steamers from the Belize and the upper portion of the Mississippi river, as high up as Memphis, each day arrived laden with meal, corn, sugar, rice, potatoes, molasses, and vegetables, as well also as delicacies for the invalids. Even the confectioners of the city contributed their mite, and many an infant sucked its first piece of candy from the hand of this thoughtful mother. No mendicants were seen in the streets, and Plenty seemed to shower her gifts upon one and all.

In the country or interior of the state (I speak especially of Louisiana) this feeling was alike displayed. In the different parishes various methods of assistance were adopted, and in West Feliciana the most generous provision was made for the destitute. The wife of each soldier was allowed $25 per month for her support, and $5 for each child, until it amounted to $50, when it ceased. She also was provided from the Free Market of the village of Bayou Sara, and by the neighbouring planters, with everything she required in the way of provision.

To give an idea of how these fair dames lived in the absence of their lords upon the field, I will just state here a remark which was made in the presence of a friend (by a poor woman of the village, whose husband was not a model father), and which was told to me, as I knew the woman. She said—"As for me, I never have lived so well in my life as since my husband left me, and for the sake of my children, *not self*, I hope they may keep him where he is, for they have more use for him than I have." This remark did not proceed from want of affection, but from a mother's love for her children. Never were the poor happier, never did Want hang her head so low. In every home in the land Plenty *smiled*, though Bellona *frowned*. True, sadness was in the heart of many, but Hope, bright-winged Hope, stood by all her children in this moment of struggle. Each and every one looked to the *glorious future*, and each mother saw her son a hero, crowned with unfading bay-wreaths. Fear entered no hearts, and though the strong fleet of the enemy frowned in the gulf, they had not dared to venture near the forts.

Shells were sent into Forts Jackson and Phillip, and were rained upon the defenders by thousands. And what had this effected? Nothing. Still our forts sent their fiery response to the invaders, and held them at bay. True, they succeeded in burning the soldier's quarters and all their clothing, yet it mattered not so as they held the fort.

News daily reached the city of the enemy's advance, but the evening edition would generally contradict the morning's statements. The morning journal would exclaim "They come! they come!" the evening's "They fly, they fly!" Newsmongers were abroad, of all descriptions and every variety of reports was afloat. However, things were approaching a crisis. For nearly four months New Orleans had been threatened, and at Shiloh the forces on both sides were soon to be engaged in another terrible combat. But still the cry was "*New Orleans cannot fall, nor shall not.*" The nearer the enemy approached, louder grew the voice of the people in proclaiming it *impregnable.* All was hope and valour.

About this time Miss Clifton was plunged in the deepest grief, as also her family. A hastily written note of a friend had informed the family of the death of Beverley Clifton, whom he said was killed in a skirmish. It said no more, giving no particulars whatever. Miss Clifton bowed once more her lovely head in sorrow, and when summoned to her mother's apartment, it was to hear that mother rave madly for her loved and lost son, and to implore her pardon for the days of misery she had caused her.

"Ah my daughter," she exclaimed, "it is too late now to say how I worshipped my beautiful son; it is too late now to say what agony was mine, when I turned from him, and would not say farewell. It is too late, my darling to shed the bitter tear when he is gone from my gaze for ever. Too late! too late! I have darkened my home, but, dearest, light shall shine for thee yet. False views, false prejudices, and false pride have made me what I am, a curse to my family and self. Oh, dearest, it was not heart, but judgment which erred, and God has stricken me, but *justly*. Have I lost your love, too, as well as all things besides? Have you become estranged, my own *noble* one?"

"Ah, mamma, you pain me even by such a suspicion. Could I cease to love my mother? No, dearest mamma, it is you who have grown cold. You know not how I have longed to cast myself in your arms, and tell you how all our hearts were broken by your coldness."

"My child, you shall no longer yearn for my love, or that of any other; and now, darling, leave me to my own bitter grief, and say to your ever kind father, that I wish to speak with him when he shall be disengaged."

Kissing her mother, she turned towards the door, and there encountered her father. "Mamma desires to see you," she said, as she kissed him, and passed on.

"Ah, dearest husband, can you forgive me for my long and cruel coldness towards you, and my loved and stricken family? I loved you, my own dear husband, through all the changes that have occurred, and though you knew it not, my poor heart has been yearning to unite once more with my family. But, dearest, can I ever be forgiven for my conduct? Oh, dearest, I am lone and sad. Will you love me now that I have blighted our home, and our loved one is gone, to return no more? O God! can it be that I shall never see my beloved Beverley again? Can it be that birds and blossoms return to us, but that *he* is gone from our gaze for ever? Oh, my husband, *can* I be forgiven? tell me, oh, tell me!"

"Calm yourself, Julia, my dear wife, and try to forget this unhappy circumstance in our lives. I will love you, dearest, ever, and had never ceased to love you; in the grave of our child let us bury all reminiscences of the past, and let the first blade of verdure which shall spring from his grave be but to thee a souvenir of how ardently he loved you. Let us, my dear, look to the future for our happiness, for is it not always better than to a mingled past of bitterness and regrets? Calm yourself, my wife, we have yet left our lovely Cornie, whose waning cheek methinks grows paler day by day at the thoughts of this estrangement."

"Again my husband, I must implore your pardon. *I am* the cause of her pale cheek and downcast eye. Has she never told you why? Oh! my children. I have sent one away from me to die amongst strangers, and without the mother's parting kiss; the other I have doomed to worse than death—the separation from her beloved. Has she not told you how I sent him from her, and forbade her ever again to see him? Has she not, my husband, told you it was her mother who was the executioner of all her brightest hopes? Oh! my God, forgive me. I have almost, Medea-like, sacrificed my children to my hatred of those I should have loved. Oh! I shall go mad. My beautiful boy gone! gone! and for aye!"

Exhausted, she threw herself upon the pillow, and wept, as though her heart would break.

As Colonel Clifton smoothed her temples, and endeavoured to calm her, she said, " My husband, it is not *too* late to atone somewhat for the past. Send for Albert la Branche without delay, and let me reward the obedience, the self-sacrificing love of my child, by yielding her up to one who is every way worthy of her. Send for him, dearest, and ere the sun sinks in the west I will see my darling happy. Her poor mother never again can be so. Do not wait to write for him, send at once." As he started to summon the servant, she said, kneeling at his feet, and clasping his knees, " Say before you go that you pardon and love me still."

He clasped her yet beautiful form to his breast as he answered, " Love you, Julia ? no, dearest, I do not, it is *adoration* I feel for you; and, though I may be weak to confess it, never, even on the nuptial eve, did I love you better than now. We have both grown older since then, and both have felt the icy touch of time upon heart as well as brow, but I trust that we can both say, with *sincerity*, that we have never ceased to love one another. My darling, you are weak and nervous, lie down and rest yourself."

He gently placed her upon the couch, and drawing aside the curtains, he said, " Look out, dearest, upon the scene, and permit the evening air to fan your cheek. Spring is with us again in all her beauty, and promises much. I have never seen richer verdure, nor brighter skies; let them be to us a presage of the future, dearest." She sobbed herself to sleep as a stricken child.

When evening's shadows cast their lengthened forms around, a different scene was witnessed in the boudoir of Mrs. Clifton. She still reclined upon the cushions of her couch, and by her side sat Colonel Clifton, holding her beautiful hand. At the foot of the couch sat our friend Albert la Branche, whose face wore the expression of chastened joy.

Mrs. Clifton said, "Mr. la Branche, I have sent for you in this moment of sorrow and affliction, when my poor heart is breaking, and filled with repentance for the injustice of my conduct towards my son and my gentle daughter. Towards one it is *too* late to repine; but yet there is one gentle, tender flower that I do not wish to crush for ever. Say, Monsieur la Branche, if my daughter still possesses your love, unchanged by my harsh measures?"

"Ah, my dear Mrs. Clifton, how can you ask me this? Can you deem me so fickle, so inconstant, as to cease to love her who is to me *all* that makes life dear? Love your daughter? Yes, Madame, now and ever!"

"Thank you, Monsieur la Branche, for your fidelity to one who is every way worthy of it. Zaïdé," she said, as a servant appeared that she had summoned, "say to your mistress that I wish to see her."

In a few moments the door opened which entered from the garden, and Miss Clifton appeared in the apartment. She was clad in a white India muslin, trimmed with Valencienne, without other ornaments. She held in her hand a bouquet of star-jasmine, and in her belt was a bunch of star-myrtle. She entered rather quickly, and was about presenting her flowers to her mother, when she observed Monsieur la Branche, who rose to greet her. She staggered, dropped her flowers, and said, wildly, "What can this mean? Albert here, and at such a time! Father, mother, Albert, tell me quickly what this means!"

"My daughter, come hither. This but means that you must be restored to happiness, and that your father and myself now yield you to one worthy of you. Come, Albert la Branche, and take her hand; she is *yours*, now and eternally. That is right, Albert, press her *close* to your heart, she is worthy the best spot even in your noble breast. Weeping, Cornie, darling? I thought to make you happy."

"Come, Albert, kneel with me, and ask *our* parents' blessing. Mamma, I am indeed happy, a heart too full for utterance; but bless you, dear mamma, for this, and dear, kind papa, for your never-failing kindness and devotion to your child."

As Albert folded his arms around her they bent their heads, and Mr. and Mrs. Clifton joined their hands and blessed them.

"And now, my children, go forth and breathe the air. The last tints of evening are gilding the earth, and my soul longs to pour forth in quiet its song of praise to the Great Giver. The twilight of repose will soon be here, and while you, my children, wander forth to gaze upon the flower and the tree, I will öffer to the Deity orisons for you. But, Cornie, dearest, where are your jasmines? Pick them up, love, and let us each keep one as a souvenir of your betrothal."

She gave to her mother and father the jasmine, but to Albert she gave a sprig of myrtle. And now we will

leave them alone in this, their hour of joy. We will not
speak of the words of endearment which were spoken
by both. We will only say that two purer or truer
hearts never beat than those re-united on that lovely eve
of spring.

The scene must change again. I will ask you,
reader, to accompany me to the family chapel of the
Cliftons.

It is noon, the dazzling sun streams in golden
floods through the windows of the chapel, which is
richly decorated for the nuptials of Miss Clifton.
Elaborate drapery of gold and silver festoons the
walls, partially concealing shrines of precious metal,
on which images of the Saviour, Virgin, and saints
shine, blazing in jewels of " purest ray serene."

The altar, before which the Rev. Bishop O——
now stands, with his numerous attendants, is a perfect scene of light and beauty, with its varied hues
and gorgeous ornaments. The few friends who are
assembled to witness the ceremony stand anxiously
awaiting the party. At length sounds sweep along
the corridor; the folding doors at the lower end of
the chapel are flung open; the bridal party enter, and
slowly pass up the centre aisle to the front of the altar,
where all kneel.

Miss Clifton's beauty is heightened by her expression of countenance, which, as her floating veil falls
apart, reveals her face, which seems to shadow
forth the soul within, and which appears to affect
the most indifferent spectator with a species of awe
and veneration. In spiritual beauty she kneels beside
one, whom in a few minutes will be to her, her all

in life. A breathless silence reigns until, in clear silvery tones, comes the response, " I will," to the " Wilt thou accept this man as thy wedded lord—to love, honour, and obey? " A moment more, and Cornie Clifton and Albert la Branche are receiving the congratulations of their friends as man and wife.

Slowly the guests departed, and the last to leave was Miss de Villerie, after again and again clasping her friend to her heart, and kissing her fair cheek. It was over ; Miss Clifton left the chapel, followed by the train of bridesmaids, to don her travelling robes for departure, as Colonel la Branche had been ordered with his regiment to Corinth.

Already our fair bride and bridegroom are on their way, and as they are borne onward to their new home let us bid them " God speed."

They are now far upon their way, and night has fallen, calmly but softly upon the scene. Oh, who that looks upon the radiant arch above, filled with its glowing beauties, of what are said to be each and every one another, and yet another world, can imagine, without a feeling of pain and sorrow, the great mass of human passion and intense suffering which one little corner of the globe contains? Who that feels this presence of infinity, speaking as it does in the awful stillness of spiritual gloom, can return in thought to earthly things without a repulsive shudder at the misdeeds of man?

The hour was fast dawning for one more struggle, which promised success to our arms, and the steamers and trains which daily left the city, bore food and clothing to the noble undaunted soldiers that stood

awaiting the contest. As usual, our foes not only
armed themselves with steel, but hoped to find their
" pen as mighty as the sword" in promulgating falsehoods like the following (probably the effusion of the
" elegant Madame N——, of N—— Y——, or some
other of her style); I will place it before the reader,
who is welcome to his own opinion.

"A TERRIBLE PICTURE.

" We find in the 'Cincinnati Gazette' some extracts,
purporting to come from the 'London Chronicle,'
descriptive of the horrors of slavery in this country,
and the cruelties and atrocities practised by slaveholders. For the amusement of our readers we cull
the following :—

" 'No country on the globe produces a blackguardism,
a cowardice, or treachery so consummate as that of
the negro-driving States in the new Southern Confederacy. It is not enough for the auctioneers of
African flesh and blood that they can torture their
stripped victims, and commit assassination with impunity; it is not enough that they are privileged
to flay or burn alive their breathing chattels; they
must stalk into the Senate House armed with instruments of murder; they must conspire to establish a
reign of terror by means of a cut-throat policy. They
must plot to take the life of their new President, while
the Republic is charioting him to her sacred throne.
These malignant wretches, impish and paltry beyond
conception in their ideas of political revenge, endeavouring to blow up Abraham Lincoln with an infernal
machine on his journey from Cincinnati; and scheming

to originate a railroad accident by which hundreds
of lives might have been lost, in order to gratify their
jealousy of a man who has triumphed over the most
dangerous cabal in the commonwealth. The worst
element in the position of the Union is this position
of the South, which has derived from the Spaniards
its barbarous vanity; from the Huron and Mohawk, its
savage indifference to suffering; and from the mongrels
of the Gulf its loathsome habit of combining the
manners of the bull-ring with the morals of the bordello.
President Lincoln is called upon to deal with this
seditious, turbulent, and homicidal population. It is
to his credit that he has not yet been provoked into
repaying their menaces in such coin as may be minted
at arsenals and issued at the cannon's mouth.

" 'The South attempts to treat the North as it
treats its own black vassals, who, like the serfs of
Sparta, are scourged to death at the altar of the
only God that the cotton planter worships. And how
is the policy exemplified? Ever since Mr. Lincoln's
ascent to the Presidential chair, the cruelties of the
slave-owners have been multiplied and intensified,
because it is feared that, unless a system of terror
be established, the hereditary bondsmen will make
weapons of their chains, and crush oppression itself
under the heel of revolted slavery. *Not in Algiers,
when the Deys were at the summit of their execrable power;
not in Rome, when the poor captive girl, after being flagi-
tiously abused, was flung into a fish pond; not in Russia,
when the executioner cuts out the tongue of his knouted victim,
have horrors more terrible been recorded, than have been
testified to unwilling witnesses since the triumph of Mr.*

Lincoln. The over-worked, underfed, miserably clad, and wretchedly-lodged slaves, have been compelled, as a means of repressing their intelligence, to work in iron collars, to sleep in the stocks, to drag heavy chains at their feet, to wear yokes, bells, and copper horns; to stand naked, while their masters or mistresses brand them infamously; to have their teeth drawn, to have red pepper rubbed into their excoriated flesh, to be bathed in turpentine, to be thrust into sacks with mad cats, to have their fingers amputated, to be shaved, and to be whipped from neck to heel with red-hot irons. It is of no avail to deny this impeachment. Congress itself, which contains a majority of slave-owners, admits the truth. The American journals teem with advertisements of slaves, whose bodies are marked indelibly with the traces of torture. *Cases are frequently tried in the law courts of the Union, of masters who have not only flogged their black girls to death, but have deliberately carved the flesh from their bones; and since the panic caused by Mr. Lincoln's election, these abominations have been redoubled.'"*

The "Cincinnati Gazette," which ought to have known how stupendous are the falsehoods in the above, not only publishes them without any denial, but calls special attention to the way in which the "London Chronicle" "denounces the brutality" of Southern slaveholders. We wonder if it ever occurred to those pious people who grieve so much over the cruelties practised upon slaves, that interest alone, to say nothing of humanity, would prevent any such treatment of slaves, worth from fifteen hundred to two thousand dollars a-piece, as is above recorded? We suppose not.

The "London Chronicle" got its information, no doubt, from some roving Abolition liar like Redpath, and eagerly swallowed the story. The great Arrowsmith hoax of the London "Times" was a tame and spiritless affair compared to the above.

It must indeed be a credulous community in which such vile misrepresentations can find belief, and the persons who can give it a second thought must be bereft of their senses.

A few mornings after the above appeared, Colonel Clifton, who had been glancing over the morning journal, remarked, "Doubtless these are the same individuals who burnt our mill," and read the following:—"A lady, the wife of a planter, living some few miles from a village, was seated upon her balcony late one summer's evening; her husband being absent, she sat awaiting his return. A horseman rode up to the front gate, and, dismounting, entered the house, saying, 'Madam, it is growing late, and I should like to remain here to-night.' She arose and said, 'I should be happy, Sir, to entertain you, but cannot receive you, as my husband is absent, and there are none here but myself and servants; but,' she continued, 'the village is only a short distance, and you will there be able to procure lodging.' He turned from her with a dark scowl, and went out. Mounting his horse he rode off. Fearing all was not going to pass off so smoothly, the lady entered her room, and, taking her revolver from the bureau, she returned to her position. Just as it grew quite dark the same individual stopped in front of the house, and came into the balcony, saying, 'Madame, I have returned to stay here to-night, and will do so, whether you like it or not,' at the same time walking towards her room door, which opened upon the balcony. She quickly arose, and, placing herself in the doorway, said, 'If you dare to enter here I will shoot you, so do not attempt it;' at the same time she drew a revolver. He attempted to brush past her, and to take it from her, when she fired. He fell, mortally wounded, across the threshold. She then called her servants, and said to the man, who was in the agonies of death, 'If you have any friends, say who they are, and I will send for them. You forced me to do this, but now I will do what I can for you.' He answered, faintly, 'Madame, you are a brave and noble woman. I cannot blame you, nor shall you or yours be harmed. In the village of which you spoke is my accomplice. Send there and have him arrested. He drives a small waggon, seemingly a pedlar, but it has a false floor, and underneath are fire-arms, with which we had intended to arm the slaves of the whole country for an insurrection. May God forgive me, but I hope it is not too late for repentance.' As the last words escaped his lips his spirit went forth to its Creator. The lady dispatched a servant to the village with an account of the affair. The other party was arrested, and his simple little waggon proved as formidable as an iron-clad. He was taken out to see the remains of his companion, and he was then hung in the negro quarters, as also the dead body of his associate."

"They met with a just reward," said Colonel Clifton as he cast the paper aside; "but I trust that God will have mercy upon their souls."

A brave woman, and may all our women prove as heroic on such occasions. These are fearful times, and none should be unprepared; times in which the most trifling accounts are exaggerated. The misrepresentation of the article entitled "A Terrible Picture" proves the bitterness of our Abolition friends, but the following piece of irony gives a faithful and just idea of the falseness of such an article :—

" HYFALUTYN.

" A Tale of the Sunny South.

" Written Expressly for the 'New York Literary Humbug.'

" By Sillyvanus Corncob, Junior.

" At a Fabulous Expense !

" And Secured according to Every Act of Congress passed since 1814 !

" Illustrated with Twenty-four Superb and Original Engravings."*

" 'Twas sunrise in Louisiana! The King of Day ever rises in that luxurious land amid a panoply of gorgeous clouds, whose intermingling tints of pink and blue contrast beautifully with the pale green blossoms of the ever-blooming magnolia bush."

" A narrow horse-path wound through a dense wood, along the bank of the Mississippi, upon whose bosom floated two monster steamboats, while a large ship was sailing majestically up the stream."

" Fish were swimming about promiscuously, and a

* The expense being great, we do not insert them in this work.

turtle was lazily sunning himself on the bank; while eagles, wild turkeys, and snipe flew in towering circles or darted through the air."

"Occasionally a drove of wild horses would leap from the dense cane brakes, and, after slaking their thirst in the river, prance back to their retreat."

"But see! who comes yonder? 'Tis a man of tall stature, noble mien, high forehead, classic countenance, and a complexion clear, but black as ebony. Across his shoulder is hung a stick, upon which hangs a bundle of unwashed linen."

"Seating himself upon the bank, he carefully takes a lyre from his vest pocket, and sings, in a clear, soprano voice, the following sublime and touching ode to liberty."

"(On account of a disagreement with our poet in regard to terms, we are obliged to omit this sublime ode.)

"'Ah!' said Francisco Rodriguez (for such was the coloured gentleman's name), 'now can I say with England's monarch, "Richard is himself again!" Listen, ye free winds that blow from the land of the sainted Fremont, and thou, too, unshackled Mississippi, listen to my tale of woe; and had you only a head, I could, in the language of my favourite poet, Shakespeare, "make each of your particular hairs to stand on end, like quills upon the fretful porcupine." Yester eve I was brutally mutilated by my tyrannical master. See! here is proof;" saying which, he took from his parcel a small package, which, being opened, showed a large molar tooth, with a decayed cavity."

" ' Oh ! were Celestina only here to sympathise with me in my affliction, I could die content.' "

" At this moment, a wild, piercing shriek was heard, and a being, fair as an angel, and graceful as a gazelle, leaped from a neighbouring precipice, with a bottle of the real, old, original, genuine Dr. Jacob Townsend's Sarsaparilla in her hand (only two dollars per bottle, for sale at the Manufactory, No. 614, Nassau Street, New York, and by all *respectable* druggists throughout the United States), and alighted in the arms of her faithful and long-lost Francisco."

" N.B.—The scene that followed was of a nature so affecting, that the author's tears have blotted it entirely out on the MSS. After recovering from her swoon, Celestina applied a magnificently embroidered pocket-handkerchief to her dewy eyes."

" 'Cheer up, my own, my beloved Francisco. We will yet be living in a magnificent mansion in Upper Canada.' "

" ' There I will enliven you with songs of love on the gentle guitar, or the sweet piano. You can then get a false set of teeth inserted, each one of which will be finer than that of which you were so inhumanly deprived. Oh! we will live in an earthly paradise, my own Francisco!' "

" 'Never, my love," gloomily responded the noble black man, ' we can never escape the bloodhounds that are already on our track. Hark! I hear them even now!' "

"Celestina fainted, while four hundred swarthy planters, with moustaches a foot and a half long, armed with two rifles and a shot-gun each, mounted on horses, and followed by a pack of bloodhounds, came in sight.

"'Die, villains! die like dogs!' exclaimed one of the planters.

"Rodriguez clasped one arm about his charming bride, while he shook his other fist at the planters, who immediately dodged behind the trees. The hounds intimidated by the glance of the desperate man's eye, skulked off; and Francisco would have escaped had not one of the planters treacherously picked up a cotton bale, and flinging it at the devoted pair, dashed them to the ground."

"At this, the hounds leaped upon them, and chawed them up, stick, sarsaparilla, extracted tooth, and all, in three minutes and a half by the watch."

"The last words of Francisco Rodriguez were, 'Fred Douglas! T'other Douglas! Seward! Greeley! Giddings! Hurrah for the New York Literary Humbug!'"

"'The only thing saved was a small piece of paper, in one of Francisco's boots; and although all of the leather was greedily devoured, the hounds found this document too tough to swallow. It read as follows:—

"' *Prophecy.*—Douglas will be the next President of the United States; while the New York Literary Humbug, and the real, old, original, genuine, Dr. Jacob Townsend's Sarsaparilla, will be taken by every family in this country.'"

"*** Country editors who will publish a two column prospectus of the N. Y. Literary Humbug, will be entitled to one year's subscription, and six second-hand postage stamps."

Mrs. Clifton remained silent, she had yielded only in her affections, but she could not yet condemn the North. In her inmost heart-cells smouldered still the ashes of the sacrifice she had made to the memory of her son, whose light would never fade. But now she ceased to either speak or think of all such subjects as politics, and calmly she seemed to submit to the chastisement which a Father's hand inflicted. An earnest desire to contribute towards the happiness of those around her, seemed to take possession of her; with an entire disregard of self, the quiet serene smile told of the change within, and of the strength her spirit had gained in its upward flight, and longing for that world where she knew her son now dwelt. The poignant anguish had passed, but the memory of her love for him still lingered.

Some weeks had passed since the events related above, and Mrs. Clifton was seated in the boudoir of her absent daughter. She was clad in deep mourning, and grief was written on her beautiful features. She was glancing over a letter, which we will place before you, reader, as it is from Mrs. la Branche to her mother:—

"Camp Moore, La.

"Dear Parents,

"I have just arrived here, and Albert has this moment left me to join several of his friends, who have

already sent their cards (the petals of the magnolia
leaf, which are here used as such), and who seem
anxious to congratulate him upon his nuptials. While
he is entertaining his friends, I will endeavour to give
you an account of my trip, and what the prospects of
comfort are. On entering the cars at New Orleans, I
met several of my friends, who told me they were
destined for the same journey, and all being in excellent
spirits, and in a mood to enjoy the trip, we anticipated
a pleasant time. The spring morning, with its fresh
gladness, its glowing beauties of earth and sky, and
delicious atmosphere, added to the beauty and joyful-
ness of the scene. For miles on our way we went
through fields inlaid with a perfect mosaic of gold,
white, red, violet, and green, formed by the myriad
flowers with which the gentle goddess crowns herself.
Here and there hedges of the Cherokee rose, and osage,
orange, the impenetrable defence of the cotton fields.
In the various trees all shades of green were displayed,
from the most delicate tinges of the early foliage to the
deeper shades of winter-green, or olive. The borders of
streams and rivulets in our course were gemmed with
smiling flowers, and the wild violet peeped forth from
its vernal couch, seeking a share of the praise which the
more gay and flaunting beauties of the field and wood
received as their just homage.

" Many cottages appeared to us as we flew past in
our steam carriage, and here and there a princely looking
residence would burst upon our view, and ere we had time
to gaze upon it, or consider its style of architecture, it
would disappear from view, and each moment the scene
changed, like some phantasmagoria beneath the in-

fluence of light and shade. On we flew at rapid rate, and though, dear parents, I was, and am happy, my thoughts would return to you, and linger around 'the loved ones at home.' As I sat gazing out upon the clouds of smoke, or mist, as they rose and floated over the extensive fields, seemingly like the spirits of departed ones ascending to heaven, leaving behind them their earthly vestments, I thought of one who has left us for ever, and of his to be for ever vacant place beside our family hearthstone. Forgive me if I have pained you by referring to this, but I could not write *home* without giving a thought to him. It was but a few hours ere we arrived at this place, and though it is not the point for which we started, Albert thought it best we should stop here to rest for a day or so, and, besides, we both have many friends here.

" This, you are aware, is what its name implies, and hundreds of soldiers surround the village. Constantly troops are arriving and departing from this point, and you cannot conceive how picturesque the scene which presents itself to the eye, as one views the panorama-like tableau. The two hotels (or, to give them their proper names, inns) are the chief buildings in the place, and one stands on either side of the railroad, and when-ever the cars arrive, a stream of individuals pour into the open doors of the road mansion. A negro generally appears at this moment on the gallery of each, and rings a bell in the most scientific manner, which the tired, and generally famished, travellers hail as the sweetest of music.

" The hotel to the right as you arrive from the New Orleans train is kept by a gentleman, and the one to the left by a widow lady. In the latter I am now domiciled. You will be surprised, dear mother and father, when I tell you that here we are not put to the trouble of making dinner toilette, and that I find my travelling attire more than stylish enough for the rustic mode of apparel which I perceive here. Albert has returned to escort me to the *table d'hôte*, and I will not close until we return from dinner.

"Oh, dear parents, you cannot imagine what a truly Lacedemonian meal I have just partaken of! One, indeed, must be patriotic to subsist on such fare. Albert, however, ate without comment, and says it is all that a true soldier requires. I tried, for Albert's sake, to eat something, but I hope to cultivate a taste for the 'black broth.' I am sure I can do anything for my Albert's sake. Come what may, I am prepared to meet want, and even beggary, with him.

"And now, my dear parents, both Albert and myself join in love to you, and earnestly request your prayers for us both. and we have to thank you for our happiness, and may God for ever bless you, is the earnest prayer of your

"Devoted child,

"To Mrs. Clifton,   "C. la BRANCHE.
     "Vallambrosa Plantation,
          "New Orleans, La."

Thus she wrote in this child-like and confiding spirit. She carried the guilelessness, the innocence, the freshness of the child into the deeper feeling of woman's clinging tenderness. None of the evil passions had ever found entrance into that pure heart, and her very soul was stainless as an infant's. Her mother read and re-read the pages, breathing a sad and seemingly joyous strain.

"May you, indeed, be happy, my angel-child," said Mrs. Clifton; "you have truly suffered, only, however, to prove your true nobleness of character. My God," she continued, "I am, I feel, unworthy; but spare, oh! spare me this, one of my treasures. What dark presentiment is this I feel? Oh! God, have pity on my already torn, crushed, and bleeding heart, and spare my child, my last, my only one."

Mrs. Clifton bowed low her head upon her hands, and sobbed convulsively. A presentiment of ill seemed to take possession of her, which she could not dissipate, and anxiously she awaited the letters which occasionally the morning's postman placed in the servant's hands for her. The journals were now filled with exciting news of the approaching contest, which the next chapter will reveal.

CHAPTER XIV.

"Forget not our wounded companions, who stood
  In the day of distress by our side ;
While the moss of the valley grew red with their blood,
  They stirr'd not, but conquer'd and died.
That sun which now blesses our arms with his light,
  Saw them fall upon Ossory's plain ;—
Oh ! let him not blush, when he leaves us to-night,
  To find that they fell there in vain."

THE spring has again appeared, and ere we raise the
curtain upon the principal events of '62, we will just
glance over a few incidents worthy of note in the
closing pages of last year's records.   From the first gun
fired at Fort Sumpter to the last boom of the cannon at
Belmont in that same year, the "Rebels" were, with
slight exceptions, the victors.   Many martyrs were
added to the list upon which the noble Jackson's name
must ever be the first, and many were they who met
with the fate of the ruffian Ellsworth, when daring to
seize upon "Southern trophies."   A monument was
proposed to the Hero of Alexandria, and a grateful
people contributed towards the wants of his bereaved
family.   But the wild storm of despotism which has
swept over the sunny South has left no traces of even
the tombs of those whose obscure position should have

rendered them sacred. Churches and cemeteries alike were spoiled by the invader, and for this reason the idea of erecting monuments to the memory of the martyred dead is abandoned for the present. The battles of Bethel, Rich Mountain, Bull Run, Manasses, Carthage, Oak Hill, Lexington, Leesburg, and Belmont, had been fought, and, with the exception of the second named, they were all brilliant Southern victories. Among the heroes whose names should be engraven on all hearts are Generals Garnett and Bee, as also Colonels Bartow and Fisher, who fell nobly upon the battle-field. General Bee must ever be remembered, not only for his valour, but his having bestowed upon noble General Jackson the suggestive name of "Stonewall," and by which he is, and will ever be, most generally known (Thomas F. Jackson). But the last month of the year '61 (December) will long be remembered as that in which the outrage of the Federal vessel, the San Jacinto (Commander Wilkes), to the British flag, in the seizure of the Confederate Commissioners, James M. Mason, of Virginia, and Hon. John Slidell, of Louisiana, and their Secretaries, Messrs. Eustis and M'Farland, who were passengers on board H.M.S.S. The Trent, commanded by Captain Mann. The day after she had sailed from Havannah she was intercepted by the Federal steam-frigate above named, and brought-to by a shotted gun, and then boarded by an armed crew; when the persons of the Messrs. Slidell, Mason, Eustis, and M'Farland were demanded, but these gentlemen refusing to leave it, except at the instance of physical force (and claiming British protection), were informed by Lieutenant Fairfax that he was ready to use it. The

Q

Commander of the Trent made many protests against such a piratical seizure of Ambassadors under a neutral flag; but all of no avail, and the Trent, being an unarmed vessel, could make no resistance. The Commissioners, with their Secretaries, were taking leave of their friends, and the Hon. John Slidell had gone into his state-room to take leave of his family, when Miss Slidell stationed herself in the doorway, to prevent intrusion on the leave-taking of her parents. At this moment Lieutenant Fairfax appeared, and wished to force an entrance into the room, at the door of which Miss Slidell was posted as sentinel (an office which she proved herself worthy of), when that young lady remarked, "You cannot, nor shall not, enter, Sir!" Telling her to stand aside, and endeavouring to force her from her position, the noble girl resented the affront by boxing his ears, thus recalling to mind the action of Cleopatra, who slapped Seleucus, and proving to us that "the most beautiful are most brave." Had it not been, however, for the interference of the British officers on board, Miss Slidell would probably have felt the effects of her rashness, as the chivalrous Lieutenant ordered his men to bayonet her upon the spot. Then numberless cheers for the fair Rebel and modern Cleopatra, and may such examples not be lost upon every Southern woman when called upon in such emergencies. This act, instead of crushing the hopes of our people, brought only renewed confidence in the almost worn.out expectations of "foreign intervention," and these ideal dreams were proven vain, when, at the demand of the English Government, the persons of the "Trent arrest" affair were delivered up and sent on their way. The ludicrous statements of Seward, in his letter to Earl Russell, that "the safety of the Union did not require the detention of the captured persons, and that an effectual check had been put to the existing 'insurrection,' and that its waning proportions made it no longer a subject of serious consideration," were shown to be false, and yet it contained an element of truth. Our people, elated with their success in arms, had felt confident that "foreign intervention" would speedily arrive, and that "King Cotton" would soon wave his sceptre triumphant. But at the close of this year it was evident how useless, how worse than vain, our hopes of any aid, save God's and right. The Southern people, no longer buoyed up with such expectations, nerved themselves, and prepared for a long and bloody contest, to conquer or to die, and felt that the battle-field alone would decide their fate. Our sick and wounded at this period were deprived of many articles necessary for their comfort, and the blockade now commenced to be felt. Diseases of all kinds were daily making their inroads into the army of the Potomac and Western Virginia, as also among the troops at Chute Mountains and the Kenawha Valley. The dampness, exposure, changeable climate, cold, and rain, want of tents, suitable food and clothing, were producing their effects, and the many nameless graves which surround the numerous camping grounds on the borders of our rivers, in our sombre forests, and in the wilds of our mountains, tell of those "unnoticed heroes" whose last days were passed in sacrificing on the altar of their country their love of home and friends. They shall not be forgotten! The nameless brave do not sleep unremembered, and beauty's tears flow silently for them when the announcement of each battle tells us that the brave have fallen.   At this date in our history the folds of the Anaconda seemed tightening around the brave armies of the Confederacy, and a ruthless foe seemed to gloat in anticipation of their ruin ; but they were disappointed, and found our noble soldiers undismayed, and prepared to gird up their loins deliberately, and determinedly to drive the Abolition hordes from our borders.   The prospects of hunger, cold, and heat did not make them shrink ; the wealthy planter and his sons went forth, as freely yielding up the comforts of luxurious homes as the day-labourer did his humble but happy abode.   The issue will prove how a just God repaid them for this self-sacrifice, and that time and suffering but proved them worthy of the success which they felt awaited them.

CHAPTER XV.

" This battle fares like to the morning's war,
When dying clouds contend with growing light ;
What time the shepherd, blowing of his nails,
Can neither call it perfect day, or night."

" Farewell !—God knows, when we shall meet again.
I have a faint cold fear thrills through my veins,
That almost freezes up the heat of life."

" Oh ! fair as the sea-flower close to the growing,
How light was thy heart, till love's witchery came,
Like the wind of the south o'er a summer lute blowing,
And hush'd all its music, and wither'd its frame !

" And still when the merry date-season is burning,
And calls to the palm-groves the young and the old,
The happiest there, from this **pastime** returning
At sunset, will weep when **thy story** is told."

THE morning of the 6th of April, 1862, opened upon a
scene that will long be remembered ; and, for thrilling
incident in the history of the Southern Confederacy,
must ever beam upon its pages in letters of flame.   For
some time this engagement had been looked forward to
with eagerness as to its result, and it was with a shout
of joy the forces under command of Generals Hardie,
Bragg, Beauregard, and Johnston were informed that
the hour had arrived for the attack.

The evening previous to the battle of Shiloh, there had been considerable skirmishing, and early on the morning of the 6th, General Hardie made an advance upon the enemy's camp, who were completely taken by surprise, and, some in demi-toilette, and others cooking their breakfasts, were instantly compelled to cease all operations, and form themselves into line of battle, to meet our forces who were now advancing from every direction.

The spirits of the Confederates were high and buoyant, and the trumpet-notes rang merrily through hill and dale, while the rattle of the infantry drums sounded sharply from the wooded glens, and the bayonets flashed in the morning light, with the Confederate standard waving proudly above them.

As the "rebel" columns advanced towards the foe, many a love-lit eye looked its last upon the beautiful scenery which met its view at every step. Charming the varied scene of hill and dell, rock, lakes, and streams, with now and then the gray gables of the farm-houses peeping forth from the groves of stately trees that screened them from the travellers' sight on the high-road. The wild rose and honeysuckle perfumed the air, as arching over the road they twined their luxurious tendrils with some sister plant, thus forming a triumphal archway, under which, on that morning, some passed to death, but most to victory. Argentine streams wound among the forests, and upon the grassy banks grazed herds of cattle.

As the army passed on, it was cheered in its progress by the encouraging voices that rang out from the cottages by the road side, and each vowed to perish in

defending this beautiful land. All nature was beautiful
—the mists were rolling away from the sun-lit earth,
and the odour of spring blossoms floated upon the fresh
morning air. Nature seemed to wear her brightest and
most resplendent robes, in honour of those whose eyes
might close upon her beauties for ever; and the boom
of the cannon which now pealed across the sky, told
that the strife had commenced. Smoke curled in shell-
like ridges along the hill sides, and soon the bloody
conflict was at its height.

From six o'clock the battle was deadly; and though
each fought with desperation, the brave and disciplined
Federal troops could not resist the valour of the Confederates, who dashed upon the advancing foe like
angry waves, and meeting with resistance, were only
forced back to return with renewed strength and fury;
like chaff before the wind, they fell and strewed the
earth, while their broken ranks rallied behind trees or
underwood, only to meet the same fate afterwards.

Awfully sublime grew the scene. Shells bursting
into flame, and scattering their meteor-lights high in
air, while the sharp crack of their report startled the
dwellers of the wood, as they burst far beyond the
scene of action; peals of musketry rose upon the ear,
while dead and dying strewed the ground. Examples
of reckless daring met the view, and into the very
mouth of gaping fire would the "rebel" soldiers dash
with mad determination. Officers and soldiers alike
won laurels of unfading glory; and, as clouds of smoke
rolled away, the form of some brave fellow would be
seen mangled beneath the feet of his comrades.

Among the first who fell was the commander-in-chief, General Albert Sidney Johnston, who was wounded in the calf of the right leg, and soon after reeling in his saddle, fell from his horse, and in a few moments expired. The knowledge of his fall was kept from the army until the day was secured; and there, amid the cheers of a victorious army, and the roar of artillery, the noble all-lamented hero breathed his last.

Among others whose names deserve more than a passing notice, were General Gladden, of South Carolina; George M. Johnston (Provisional Governor of Kentucky); as also Colonels Adams, of Louisiana; Kitt Williams, of Tennessee; and Blythe, of Mississippi. Among the lesser grade, the slain were too numerous to mention; but as the noble Captain J. T. Wheat was so well known, and so well-beloved in Louisiana, it is only just to mention him.

Native of Virginia, he entered the army the moment the first threat of subjugation came from the North. He had the honour of being secretary of the Louisiana Convention, His brother Robert, noted as Cuban Filibuster, was wounded at Manasses, but recovered and entered again upon duty, and was soon after killed. He was associated also with Walker in the expedition to Nicaragua.

The Confederate victory was complete. The entire encampment of the enemy was taken possession of by them, and they found the fruits of their day's labour immense; an abundance of forage and munitions of war, as also a great amount of clothing, fine blankets, and numerous tents, repaid them for the latter which they had thrown away in their wearisome march.

Sunday night General Beauregard established his

head-quarters at the rude log-church of Shiloh, and the troops were ordered to sleep upon their arms, but the time had now come for feasting upon the spoils, and all night long soldiers and citizens were seen robbing and plundering. Disgraceful as this is to an army, there may be an excuse for such conduct on the side of the Confederates, as they, being deprived for so long a time of even the necessaries of life, they could but hail with gladness the moment such prizes were within reach. Before we condemn, let us not boast of strength to conquer temptation such as our hearts have never felt; it is only those who are exposed to the heat of the furnace, that can judge of its intense heat.

Monday morning found the enemy reinforced, and the Confederates much demoralised by their night of feasting and revelry; notwithstanding they bared their bosoms to the strife and fought valorously, until Beauregard ordered a retreat, which was executed with steadiness. General Breakinridge, who had been ordered to cover the retreat, stood guard and vigil, with his little band prepared, if necessary, like Leonidas at the pass of Thermopylæ, to hold the enemy in check, if it required the sacrifice of his last man. The enemy, already sorely chastised, did not pursue, but Breakinridge and his noble heroes are not deserving of the less praise. Beauregard retired to Corinth, intending to make that place the strategic point of his campaign. But let us return to the field of battle, which presented a frightful scene of slaughter. The whole earth was strewn with ghastly corpses, and the dying who had fallen among horses, muskets, swords, drums, and haversacks; many of whom were in agony, moaning and entreating for

water, or begging that some kind hand would kill them
outright, and thus end their pain. Many had died
whose wounds were slight, from exposure and want of
attention. The calmness of the descending dew revived
some, while to others it sent a chill, as they struggled
in the cold embraces of Death. Alas! a sad and strange
sight is that of a battle field—all those who were, ere
yesterday, strangers to each other, now lying side by side
on their sanguine couch, and taking their eternal sleep
together. A scene of horror from which the coldest
turns with a shudder, while gazing upon the distorted
visages and discoloured features of the dead, over
which insects were creeping, and from which there now
rose a miasma foul and sickening. With morning came
many women, the mothers, wives, sisters, and friends of
the soldiers, to search among the slain for the beloved
ones, gone to return no more, and their shrieks, sobs,
and wild cries, mingled with the moans of the dying,
sent a pang to the heart of the observer, and deeply
did the arrow of sympathy enter the soul for those who
died alone and uncared for. There they wandered over
that field of carnage, some with dishevelled hair, blood-
shot eyes, and blanched cheeks, searching out from the
already decaying mass of human beings, the loved and
brave. Oh! the sight was heartrending. Apart from
the rest of the bodies lay the form of a young man,
beautiful even in death, and over which a young and
lovely woman was bending. Her face was of an ashen
hue, and her eyes were tearless, but in them a wild stare,
as she cast them upon the body before her. She seized
the arm of the dead man, and endeavoured to place it
around her neck, but, alas, its stiffened state rendered

it impossible, then kissing its hands, she madly cast herself on the body, and pressed her lips to the cold forehead.

"Albert, Albert," she murmured, "ask of God to take me too."

The most callous-hearted wept at this scene of desolation, and seeing her endeavour to re-enfold him to her heart, her friends approached, and as they essayed to draw her from the scene, by pleadings and gentle force, she fell fainting upon the body, and was borne from the spot in the arms of her friends.

Reader, do you recognise the characters? They are Albert and Cornie, and soon the curtain must drop for ever upon two whom I feel you have followed with some interest this far. Yes, Albert la Branche was in the thickest of the glorious strife, and fell upon the last day. He had taken a fond farewell of his bride that morning, confident in his promise of returning as soon as the conflict was passed, and had kissed her at the cottage door of the rustic abode in which they had taken up their quarters. Anxiously she had watched and awaited the couriers, as they almost momentarily dashed by, and when Monday passed and no hastily-scribbled line told her of his safety, unheeding the counsel of her friends, she flew to the battle-field, and now the reader, if he will, may witness her last hours.

Sadly her friends bore her to her couch, and weepingly they pressed around her inanimate form, that they might assist in restoring her to consciousness. Thus she lay for hours, seemingly dead, with her icy gaze rivetted upon them. No sound escaped her lips, but at length her breast heaved with heavy sighs, and the tears stole quietly down her checks from that now unsealed fountain in her heart. Tenderly they watched her, and silently she thanked them, while now and then she pressed their hands to her heart, or smiled upon them in her almost seraphic beauty. But the canker worm was at her heart, and momentarily they saw her fading away. Her parents were summoned, and they came and stood beside her, and that mother, now crushed and broken-hearted, no longer raved, but bowed to the Divine will, which seemed not to feel satisfied with the already brimming chalice which she had drained to the dregs. There lay that fragile flower—the blessed, the loved, and cherished; she was passing " to that bourne from whence no traveller returns," and to that land "where never sounds farewell." She gazed lingeringly upon the departing sun, and watched the shadows of the vine-lines, which drooped in festoons from the doors and windows of the room she occupied, and when the last gleam of sunlight departed, with it her spirit fled, to shed its light and radiance on another world. Her delicate hands were clasped upon her breast, and her check shone with a hue unlike that of death. The dark and troubled waves were stilled; the lamp had gone out, and her soul had gone forth to meet the kindred spirit that stood awaiting it. The harps of heaven were hushed, and darkness spread her pall over the scene.

Wrapt in gloom sat the pale watchers by the dead— father and mother. They shed no tears, for they felt their darling was now in her proper sphere—an angel in heaven as she had been on earth. But while these events were passing, other scenes were being enacted in the various portions of the Confederacy, which cast an additional lustre upon the Confederate arms. The commencement of the year '62 was disastrous to the Southern cause, and though many battles were fought, few were termed victorious. Many of our brave men had fallen upon the various battle-fields, and in particular Virginia's soil was crimsoned with the blood of her heroes. Tennessee had felt the foot of the invader, and Nashville was occupied by the enemy. Her citizens turned out of doors, and her most palatial residences possessed by the hordes of hirelings that composed the Federal army.

Not content with confiscating property, the vilest insults were offered to the families of those brave men whom duty to their country left their families unprotected and exposed to their tender mercies. Arrests were daily made, and a repetition of the Washington style of espionage was instituted. Mrs. Greenhow and family's treatment was but tame in comparison with that of many others, and the most sacred privileges of the female sex were wrested from them, and private correspondence of every nature was laid open to the world. No family was deemed secure from intrusion at any hour, night nor day, and though the ladies feared the brutality of those in command, they ever displayed a defiant spirit when face to face with their jailors. Many fled their homes to return no more, and the mansions that a few weeks before blazed with light, and in whose halls echoed happy voices, were now dark and desolate, and the floors soiled with the dust shaken from the feet of the blood-thirsty invaders. Those who remained, however, spurned all attempts at recognition, or effort of social intercourse with the Yankees. Those

who had been sufficiently deluded to imagine that a
union sentiment existed in Nashville saw how false the
impression, when naught met their gaze but scowls, and
muttered imprecations from the men, and the most unpitying scorn and intense hatred of the women. No
condescension on the part of the inhabitants was manifested, and the insulting foe was soon taught that
" stone walls do not a prison make," so that the mind
be free.

The enemy was harassed in every manner, and the
dashing and intrepid cavalier, Captain John H. Morgan*
(since Colonel), was every day performing deeds of
valour which, for strategy and boldness, rivalled all the
daring exploits of the time. Heroic acts and chivalrous
conduct (when the history of this period shall be
written) will place his name far before that of the
heroes of the olden time, and when, in after days, we
shall place the goblet to our lips, we shall exclaim, with
Byron—

> " Wer't the last drop in the well,
>   As I gasped upon the brink,
> Ere my fainting spirits fell,
>   'Tis to thee that I would drink."

Other men have added to their name a list of deeds
by which they will be remembered when the present
generation have passed from earth for ever. One has
passed from amongst us, but when the grandsires shall
sit around the blazing fire on winter eves, with their
young about their knees, the name of General Ben
M'Cullock will be breathed forth, and tales of his

---

* Afterwards promoted to a General, and since killed.

wondrous adventures related. His name was long known, and already historically, when the war broke out, and Texas looked to him as one of her strongest pillars of defence. On the field of San Jacinto and Mexico he had won unfading laurels, and in later days he was known as the "Texas Ranger." This noble man joined his fortunes with those of the Confederacy, and was killed at the battle of Elk Horn; standing on a slight elevation, he was marked by one of the sharp-shooters of the enemy from his conspicuous dress, which was a black velvet suit, patent leather high-top boots, and on his head a light-coloured broad-brimmed hat. His death was regarded as a national calamity, and General Van Dorn, in his official report, declared that no successes could repair the loss of the gallant dead who had fallen on the well-fought field.

In this engagement General McIntosh also fell, shot through the heart; but in hastily reviewing those events I will not forget to pay a just tribute to the gallant veteran, Major-General Price, and his brave troops, who had won glory on other fields than Elk Horn. A more gallant commander than General Price the Confederate army could not boast of, and not only for his bravery and military skill was he remembered, but for his noble heart and tender sentiments. On many occasions this hardy warrior gave evidence of his humane feelings, but particularly on his retreat at the battle of Elk Horn, and I can give no better idea of it than quoting the exact words of the historian:—"In the progress of the re-treat," writes an officer, " every few hundred yards we would overtake some wounded soldier. As soon as he saw the old General he would cry out, 'General, I am

wounded!' Instantly some vehicle was ordered to stop,
and the poor soldier's wants cared for. Again and again
it occurred, until our conveyances were covered with
the wounded. Another one cried out, 'General, I am
wounded!' The General's head dropped upon his
breast, and his eyes, bedimmed with tears, were thrown
up, and he looked in front, but could see no place to put
his poor soldier. He discovered something on wheels in
front, and commanded—'Halt, and put this wounded
soldier up; by G—d, I will save my wounded, if I lose
the whole army!'" This explains why the old man's
poor soldiers love him so well. But even he is not
without his enemies, nor his brave soldiers, and it has
been frequently asked, "Who are Price's men?" and, to
quote in compliment to Missouri's soldiers, we reply,
"These veteran soldiers never falter in battle. They
are never whipped! They do not seek sick furloughs.
They do not straggle. When batteries are to be taken,
they take them! When an enemy is to be routed, they
charge him with a shout of defiance. They have met
the foe on fifty battle-fields! They may be killed, but
they cannot be conquered! These are 'Price's men!'"
General Price had under his command troops from
Arkansas, Mississippi, Texas, Louisiana, and Tennessee,
as well as those of Missouri; and when, after the battle
of Shiloh, it was resolved to consolidate the armies of
Price and Van Dorn with that of Beauregard, the call
was responded to with the most self-sacrificing spirit by
the Missourians and Arkansans. Their devotion to the
cause of their country was manifested in the most
patriotic manner, when, turning their back upon their
homes, they crossed the Mississippi to fight for other

portions of the broad land, feeling that ultimately they would rescue their own State from the detested control of the enemy. General Price's address to his army, though properly belonging to history, I cannot resist introducing here, teeming, as it does, with beauty, patriotism, and flow of soul, which seems to have gushed forth from his honest, manly heart in unfettered language, like one of the mighty streams of his native State :—

"Head Quarters Missouri State Guard,
            "Des Moines Arkansas, April 3rd, 1862.
"Soldiers of the State Guard!

"I command you no longer. I have this day resigned the commission which your patient endurance, your devoted patriotism, and your dauntless bravery have made so honourable. I have done this that I may the better serve you, our State, and our country; that I may the sooner lead you back to the fertile prairies, the rich woodlands, and the majestic streams of our beloved Missouri; that I may the more certainly restore you to your once happy homes and to the loved ones there.

"Five thousand of those who have fought side by side with us under the grizzly bears of Missouri have followed me into the Confederate camp. They appeal to you, as I do, by all the tender memories of the past, not to leave us now, but to go with us wherever the path of duty may lead, till we shall have conquered a peace, and won our independence by brilliant deeds upon new fields of battle.

"Soldiers of the State Guard! veterans of six

R

pitched battles, and nearly twenty skirmishes! conquerors in them all! your country, with its 'ruined hearths and shrines,' calls upon you to rally once more in her defence, and rescue her for ever from the terrible thraldom which threatens her. I know that she will not call in vain. The insolent and barbarous hordes which have dared to invade our soil, and to desecrate our homes, have just met with a signal overthrow beyond the Mississippi. Now is the time to end this unhappy war. If every man will but do his duty, his own roof will shelter him in peace from the storms of the coming winter.

"Let not history record that the men who bore with patience the privations of Cowskin Prairie, who endured uncomplainingly the burning heats of a Missouri summer, and the frosts and snows of a Missouri winter; that the men who met the enemy at Carthage, Oak Hills, at Fort Scott, at Lexington, and in numberless lesser battle-fields in Missouri, and met them but to conquer; that the men who fought so bravely and so well at Elk Horn; that the unpaid soldiery of Missouri were, after so many victories, and after so much suffering, unequal to the great task of achieving an independence of their magnificent State.

"Soldiers! I go but to mark a pathway to our homes. Follow me!

"STERLING PRICE."

CHAPTER XVI.

"But hark! that heavy sound breaks in once more,
　　As if the clouds its echo would repeat;
　　And nearer, clearer, deadlier than before!
Arm! Arm!—it is—it is—the cannon's opening roar!

"Ah! then and there was hurrying to and fro,
　　And gathering tears, and tremblings of distress,
　　And cheeks all pale, which but an hour ago
Blush'd at the praise of their own loveliness,
　　And there were sudden partings, such as press
The life from out young hearts, and choking sighs
　　Which ne'er might be repeated; who could guess
If ever more should meet those mutual eyes,
Since upon night so sweet such awful morn could rise!

"And there was mounting in hot haste: the steed,
　　The mustering squadron, and the clattering car,
　　Went pouring forward with impetuous speed,
And swiftly forming in the ranks of war;
　　And the deep thunder peal on peal afar;
And, near, the beat of the alarming drum
　　Roused up the soldier ere the morning star;
While throng'd the citizens, with terror dumb,
Or whispering with white lips, 'The foe!—they come!—they come!'"

THE morning of the 24th of April, '62 dawned upon the most important event of the times. An event that will long be remembered, and one that cast gloom over the whole Confederacy.

New Orleans had long been considered an impregnable point, and the inhabitants had considered themselves perfectly secure in their defences of coast and river. Vast sums had been expended on the river batteries, and the city itself was supposed to be occupied by a large and well-disciplined force under command of General Lovell, and in its harbour was a fleet consisting of twelve gun-boats, one iron-clad steamer, and the famous ram "Manasses." The outer line of defences were Forts Jackson and St. Phillip, some sixty miles below the city, and General Duncan, who was said to be the best artillerist in the Confederate service, was in command.

The bombardment of these forts by the Federal fleet, had continued some time without much damage, and though 25,000 thirteen-inch shells had been thrown within the forts, the Federals only succeeded in dismounting some guns, and killing five men and wounding ten.

On the 23rd the news from the forts was encouraging, but on the morning of the 24th the Federal fleet steamed up the stream to the forts, and opened fire upon them and the gun-boats. Soon the strife became furious, and in one hour several of the attacking ships sailed past the forts. Owing to the night-signals being the same as those of the Confederates, the vessels were not discovered until abreast of the batteries.

The conflict now became deadly, and the forts belched forth fire from all the guns that could be brought to bear; but it was too late to produce much impression, and the "Hartford," commanded by Commander Farragut, led the van, and the Federal fleet pushed on through the storm of shot and shell. On the other hand, the Confederate fleet, which consisted of only seventeen vessels in all, eight of which only were armed, disputed with desperation the pass, and fought against overwhelming odds, until they were driven on shore. These vessels were scuttled or burned by their own commanders. The "Manasses" was run ashore and sunk, and the famous "Louisiana," the great iron-clad, could not be brought into action, as her machinery was not in good working order. Fifty-two killed and wounded, were the total loss of this contest; amongst the latter was Commander McIntosh, desperately wounded. In the fiercest of the strife, he and Commander Mitchell stood on the deck of the "Louisiana."

Valiantly that little fleet withstood the attack, and towards the close of the action, and just as the "Doubloon" appeared in view, the "Iroon" was about overhauling her, when the "Governor Moore," commanded by Captain Beverley Kennon, darted upon the "Iroon," and ran into her three times. The Federal vessel managed to escape, and was again about capturing the "Governor Moore," when the "Quitman" ran into her amid-ship, and sunk her, thus allowing General Lovell to make his escape. But Captain Kennon, the last to yield, sped down the river into the midst of the Mammoth fleet—dashing hither and thither, attacking first one and then another of his monstrous antagonists. Being ordered repeatedly to haul down his flag, which floated defiantly in the face of the foe, he would answer, "Come and take it down, if you can."

"Haul down that flag," repeated the Federal commander.

"Never!" replied Captain Kennon, as he answered with a volley of shot.

Again came the command, "Haul down that flag, or I'll fire into you!"

"Fire!" he added, with a strong objurgation, at the same time firing away his last round of ammunition, and, seeing that he would be captured, he sprang to the bow of the vessel, and drawing his sword from the scabbard, broke it across his knee, exclaiming "I will never surrender this to a d—ned Yankee." Then, perceiving the Federals about to board the vessel, he drew his pistol, and aiming at one, fired, and the splash which followed the report, told of the precision of the aim.

The wounded lay thick upon the deck of the "Governor Moore," and though Captain Kennon felt that he no longer possessed the means of fighting the foe, he determined not to yield, and seizing a torch, set fire to the vessel and then sprang into the river, hoping to swim to shore, but was captured after some resistance, being only slightly wounded. Refusing to take the oath of parole, he was sent on board the "Cayuga," which vessel bore him to Fort Warren, where he remained some three months, and then, being exchanged, arrived shortly afterwards in Richmond, and once more proffered his services to the Confederacy. He may well be styled the HERO OF FORT JACKSON, and his valorous conduct elicited compliment even from his enemies. The Northern journals teemed with accounts of his gallant behaviour, and articles headed "Honour to whom honour is due," "Give the Devil his due," etc., were devoted to anecdotes of his chivalrous deeds.

When all the other vessels of the Confederate fleet had
lowered their flags at the command of the invader, or
by force, one alone remained floating defiant alike of
threat or force, and when Captain Kennon was sent to
Fort Warren, it was on the criminal charge of having
kept the standard raised when the rest of the fleet had
surrendered. The officers of the Federal navy recognised in this hero their friend of former days, and
Captain Kennon did not sever the ties of sixteen years'
companionship with many of those without regret. But
a Virginian by birth, he sprang from a race of heroes,
and his father will long be remembered as the gallant
Commodore Kennon who was blown up on board the
"Princeton" several years since. He left two sons, one
the subject of this sketch, and the other, Captain Dan-
bridge Kennon, who with his brave cousin, the gallant
J. E. B. Stewart, fought and won laurels from the
commencement of hostilities. Allied to the families of
George Washington (through the Custis's), the Lee's,
and Butler's, we are not surprised at Captain Kennon's
deeds of valour. The "Governor Moore" being the
last antagonist, the Federals had nothing further to
fear from the fleet, and slowly they passed on towards
the city. The citizens of New Orleans, startled from
their slumber of repose and by the tolling of the alarm
bells, supposed that the foe had passed the forts, and
were approaching the city. The entire city was thrown
into a state of commotion, and the whole of its inhabitants rushed into the streets, each enquiring the
meaning of the excitement, and when they were told of
their danger they could not believe it, until General
Lovell arrived, at 2 P. M., from the forts. The river forts

had not fallen, but two of the enemy's gun-boats actually threatened the city and the works at Chalmette; five 32-pounders on one side of the river and nine on the other, still remained intact. The civil authorities of New Orleans entreated the Confederate commander to retire from the city, as it was feared a bombardment would be the result if he did not. General Lovell ordered his troops to Camp Moore, a distance of some seventy miles above New Orleans. Farragut made a formal demand for the surrender of the command, which General Lovell refused, and told the officers who bore the message that he would attack any troops that might land. General Lovell held an interview with Mayor Monroe and offered to hold the city as long as there was a man left. But this sacrifice of life was deemed unnecessary, as the few raw and poorly armed infantry could do nothing against the fleet, and the whole force then in the city amounted to only 2,800 men. Language can give no idea of the scene which followed the order for evacuation. Through an avenue of grief and woe indescribable, the Confederate soldiers passed on the way to the trains which were to bear them from their homes, and all they held dear. Slowly they passed on through the different streets, and hushed and awful was the tread of their feet, like their now muffled hopes. Stern was their look, and they scarce dared a glance of adieu to the fair who bade them "God speed" through their tears and sobs. No drums sounded, not a note was heard, but the beating of many hearts was in unison with the dirge-like sounds of mourning which were wafted on the winds of Heaven to the ear of the brave little band, who were forced to see their beautiful city polluted by the footsteps of the invader.

Lovely in their sorrow even, stood the women of New Orleans, waving farewell to the heroes, and some in their desolation reminded one of the daughters of Zion hanging their harps on the willows by the waters of Babylon. Some stood calm as statues, with clasped hands and tearless eyes, while others wept convulsively, and some again gazed upon the scene with heaving bosoms and kindling eyes. The latter were predominant, and by their manner convinced the parting fathers, husbands, sons, and brothers, that there was nought to fear for, them, and that should a brutal soldiery take possession of their city, there yet remained a protection against the foe, viz., nerve to plant the steel deep in the heart of the dastard who should dare to outrage or oppress them. Carriages, with the fairest and loveliest of the city, were rolling on towards the depôt to bid a passionate farewell to departing friends, and when the train moved off with the mass of human freight, it was amidst tears, blessings, and sobs. But hope yet remained, and the citizens of New Orleans believed their city still secure, as forts Jackson and *Phillip had not fallen. Alas! on the morning of the next day the Federal fleet turned the point and came in sight of the city.

The Confederate troops were still busy in the evacuation, and the streets were thronged with all descriptions of vehicles, laden with every article of warfare. Mounted officers were galloping to and fro, in a state of the greatest excitement, and the streets were crowded with persons, who were laden with provisions plundered

from the public stores, while others, more patriotic, were
busy in destroying property which would prove of value
to the enemy, and huge loads of cotton were seen
rumbling along on the way to the levee.

When the Federal fleet made its appearance, it was
amidst the smoke of burning cotton, and the stifling
odour of the sugar and bacon consigned to the flames.
Vast columns of flame rose in the air, and vied with the
sunlight, and sublimely grand became the scene, when
the torch was set to the steam-boats, ships, and gun-
boats which were in the river, and they were sent
floating down the stream into the midst of the enemy's
fleet, threatening destruction to it.   In the sacrifice was
included the celebrated iron-clad frigate the "Mississippi,"
which was accounted the most important naval structure
the Confederate Government had yet undertaken. Fifteen
thousand bales were consumed, the value of which was
estimated at a million and a-half of dollars.   The specie
of the banks, to the amount of twelve or fifteen millions,
was removed from the city, and placed in concealment
as well as all the stores and moveable property of the
Confederate States.   Thus when the Federal Commander took possession of the city, a few days afterwards,
it was to find it deserted, and in place of the royal
monarch " King Cotton," whom he had expected to grace
his triumphal entrance, he found only the smoking
funeral pyre of this Sardanapolis.   Throughout the city
deeds of heroism were being enacted, and in Carrollton
the cannon were spiked by Mrs. Brown and her maid,
while the delicate hands of the former were swollen and
bleeding from her patriotic effort to prevent the guns
being of use to the enemy. New Orleans should remem-

ber this fair lady and her spirited conduct. Beautiful and delicate, you would scarcely suppose her possessed of such nerve—to gaze upon her when her beautiful dreamy eyes were in repose. Her husband had left with his command, and she remained to do what she could for the cause of her country.

The city was now under the jurisdiction of Mayor Monroe, and *nobly, gallantly,* did he perform his part in this trying hour. To the demand from Flag Officer Farragut to the Mayor, that all the flags should be hauled down that were flying from the various public buildings in the city, the latter replied, that the citizens of New Orleans yielded to physical force alone, and that they maintained their allegiance to the Confederate States. On the 26th of April, however, a force landed from the sloop-of-war " Pensacola " lying opposite Esplanade Street, and hoisted a United States flag upon the Mint. The excitement was intense, and this was the moment in which an act was done, that in a few days after added one more martyr to the list of Confederates. In that crowd stood one in whose eyes flashed indignant fire, and with whom to think was to act, when, mounting to the dome, he tore the emblem of oppression from the staff, and descending with it, he was joined by others, who trailed it through the dust of the streets, until it was soiled and in rags.

Flag-Officer Farragut, exasperated beyond all bounds, determined to spare no mortification to a city, whose only protection was now in its civil officers. The State flag still floated from the City Hall, an emblem of State sovereignty, nothing more, yet it was required that this should be lowered by the citizens.

Again the fair and lovely women of New Orleans proved their claims to an immortal wreath of glory, when the proudest and wealthiest of them signed a memorial, praying the Common Council to protect at least the emblem of their State sovereignty from insult. The copy of the memorial I place before you :—

" This petition was drawn up and signed by some fifty to sixty names before it was known that the Mayor and Council had decided upon their reply to Captain Farragut's ultimatum :

" To the Honourable the Mayor and Common Council of the city of New Orleans :—

" The petition of the wives, the daughters, the mothers and the sisters of your constituents :—

" Understanding that Flag-Officer Farragut, commanding the naval squadron now threatening the city, has given notice to the authorities to haul down the Louisiana State flag from the City Hall, and to make a formal act of surrender of the city of New Orleans, with the alternative of removing the women and children within forty-eight hours, we do pray your Honour and your honourable body to refuse to surrender the city, or to haul down the flag, which is the emblem of the sovereignty of Louisiana, promising you our countenance and support."

On the 28th of April Flag-Officer Farragut addressed his ultimatum to the Mayor, and threatening a bombardment of the city, and notification to remove the women and children within forty-eight hours.

I place these, too, before you, not, kind reader, to

weary you with useless detail, but to prove the worth
of one who held within his hand the fair fame of the
Crescent City, and though his was a delicate and responsible duty, he proved his claims to the eternal gratitude
of all by his dignified, resolute, and heroic conduct :—

"U. S. Flag-ship "Hartford,"
"At Anchor off the city of New Orleans,
"April 28th, 1862.

" To his Honour the Mayor and City Council of the city
of New Orleans :—

"Your communication of the 26th instant has been
received, together with that of the City Council.

"I deeply regret to see, both by their contents, and
the continued display of the flag of Louisiana on the
court-house, a determination on the part of the city
authorities not to haul it down. Moreover, when my
officers and men were sent on shore to communicate
with the authorities, and to hoist the United States flag
on the Custom House, with the strictest order not to
use their arms unless assailed, they were insulted in the
grossest manner, and the flag which had been hoisted
by my orders on the Mint, was pulled down and dragged
through the streets.

"All of which go to show that the fire of this fleet
may be drawn upon the city at any moment, and in
such an event the levee would in all probability be cut
by the shells, and an amount of distress ensue to the
innocent population, which I have heretofore endeavoured to assure you that I desired by all means
to avoid. The election is therefore with you. But

it becomes my duty to notify you to remove the women and children from the city within forty-eight hours, if *I have rightly understood your determination.*

"Very respectfully your obedient servant,

"(Signed)   D. G. FARRAGUT,

"Flag-Officer, Western Gulf Blockading

"Squadron."

The Mayor replied verbally to the communication, by saying he would call the Council together, and send a communication to the Flag-Officer to-morrow morning.

After the reception of Captain Farragut's communication, the Mayor convened the City Council, which met at 2 o'clock in joint session.

HOME DEPARTMENT.

Action of the City Authorities.

The Mayor's message to the Common Council; Action of that Body; Mayor's Reply to Commodore Farragut's Renewed Demand; His Letter Announcing the Surrender of the Forts.

The following is the Mayor's message to the Council, accompanying Flag-Officer's communication, received yesterday:—

"Mayoralty of New Orleans.

"City Hall, April 28th, 1862.

"Gentlemen of the Common Council,

"I herewith transmit to you a communication from Flag-Officer Farragut, commanding the United States' fleet now lying in front of this city. I have informed the officer bearing the communication that I would lay it before you, and return such answer as the city authorities might deem proper to be made.

"In the meantime, permit me to suggest that Flag-Officer Farragut appears to have misunderstood the City of New Orleans. He has been distinctly informed that, at this moment, the city has no power to impede the exercise of such acts of forcible authority as the Commander of the United States' naval forces may choose to exercise; and that, therefore, no resistance could be offered to the occupation of the city by the United States' forces. If it is deemed necessary to remove the flag now floating from this building, or to raise United States' flags on others, the power which threatens the destruction of our city is certainly capable of performing those acts. New Orleans is not now a military post; there is no military commander within its limits; it is like an unoccupied fortress, of which an assailant may at any moment take possession. But I do not believe that the constituency represented by you or by me embraces one loyal citizen who would be willing to incur the odium of tearing down the symbol representing the State authority to which New Orleans owes her municipal existence. I am deeply sensible of the distress which would be brought upon our community by a consummation of the inhuman threats of the United States' commander; but I cannot conceive that those who so recently declared themselves to be animated by a Christian spirit, and by a regard for the rights of private property, would venture to incur for themselves and the government they represent, the universal execration of the civilized world, by attempting to achieve, through a

wanton destruction of life and property, that which they
can accomplish without bloodshed, and without a resort
to those hostile measures which the law of nations
condemns and execrates, when employed upon the
defenceless women and children of an unresisting city.

"Very respectfully,

"JOHN T. MONROE, Mayor."

The following is the resolution of the City Council,
after receiving the Mayor's message :—

Resolved—"That the views communicated by his
Honour the Mayor to the Common Council, respecting
the answer which it behoves the City of New Orleans
to return to the ultimatum of Flag-Officer Farragut,
meet the unreserved approbation of this Council, and
embody their own views and sentiments, and the Mayor
is therefore respectfully requested to act accordingly.

"S. P. DE LABARRE, President, pro tem.,

" of Board of Aldermen.

" J. MAGIONI, President Board Assistant

"Alderman.

"Approved April 28th, 1862,

"JOHN T. MONROE, Mayor.

"A true copy,

"M. A. BAKER, Secretary to Mayor."

The following is the Mayor's reply to the communication of Flag-Officer Farragut, received yesterday :—

"City Hall, New Orleans, April 29th, 1862.

" To Flag-Officer D. C. Farragut,

" U. S. Flag-Ship 'Hartford.'

" Sir,—Your communication is the first intimation

I ever had that it was by 'your strict orders' that the United States' flag was attempted to be hoisted upon certain of our public edifices, by officers sent on shore to communicate with the authorities. The officers who approached me, in your name, disclosed no such order, and intimated no such design on your part; nor could I have for a moment entertained the remotest suspicion that they could have been invested with such powers to enter on such an errand, while the negotiation for a surrender between you and the city authorities were still pending. The interference of any one, under your command, as long as these negotiations were not brought to a close, could not be viewed by me otherwise than as a flagrant violation of those courtesies, if not the absolute rights, which prevail between belligerents under such circumstances. My views and my sentiments, with reference to such conduct, remain unchanged.

"You now renew the demand made in your former communication, and you insist on their being complied with, unconditionally, under a threat of bombardment, within forty-eight hours; and you notify me to remove the women and children from the city, that they may be protected from your shells.

"Sir, you cannot but know that there is no possible exit from this city for a population which still exceeds in number one hundred and forty thousand, and you must, therefore, be aware of the utter inanity of such a notification. Our women and children cannot escape from your shells, if it be your pleasure to murder them on a mere question of etiquette; but, if they could, there are but few among them who would consent to

S

desert their families and their homes, and the graves of their relatives, in so awful a moment; they would bravely stand the sight of your shells rolling over the bones of those who were once dear to them, and would deem that they died not ingloriously by the side of the tombs erected by their piety to the memory of departed relatives.

" You are not satisfied with the peaceable possession of an undefended city, opposing no resistance to your guns, because of its bearing its doom with some manliness and dignity; and you wish to humble and disgrace us by the performance of an act against which our nature rebels.   This satisfaction you cannot expect to obtain at our hands.

" We will stand your bombardment, unarmed and undefended as we are.   The civilized world will consign to indelible infamy the heart that will conceive the deed and the hand that will dare to consummate it.

"Respectfully,
" JOHN T. MONROE, Mayor."

The following letter was received by the Mayor this morning from Flag-Officer Farragut :—

" U.S. Flag-ship 'Hartford,'
" At anchor off the City of New Orleans.
"April 29th, 1862.

" To His Honour the Mayor and City Council
of the City of Orleans.

"Gentlemen,—The Forts St. Phillip and Jackson having surrendered, and all the military defences of the city being either capitulated or abandoned, you are required, as the sole representative of any supposed authority in the city, to haul down and suppress every ensign and symbol of government, whether State or Confederate, except that of the United States. I am now about to raise the flag of the United States upon the Custom House, and you will see that it is respected with all the civil power of the city.

"I have the honour to be, very respectfully, your obedient servant,

"D. G. FARRAGUT,

"Flag-Officer, Western Gulf, Blockading
Squadron."

Correspondence between the Mayor and Captain Farragut:—

The following letters conclude the correspondence which has been going on for several days between the U.S. Flag-Officer and the Mayor of this city. It will be seen from the letter of Captain Farragut that he seeks to vindicate himself from the conclusion that he intended to threaten the city in a certain event. We would further add, in justification of the construction placed by the Mayor and the people, and we may say of the foreign Consuls, on Flag-Officer Farragut's letter, that when Commander Bell delivered the last letter to the Mayor the following conversation occurred:—

Mayor Monroe—"As I consider this a threat to bombard the city, and as it is a matter about which the notice should be clear and specific, I desire to know when the forty-eight hours began to run?"

Commander Bell—"It begins from the time you receive this notice."

The Mayor then drew his watch, and showing it to Commander Bell, said, "Then you see it is fifteen minutes past twelve o'clock."

The Commander recognised the correctness of the time, and made some remarks, which were understood by all present to convey distinctly the threat, that if the flag was not hauled down in forty-eight hours, the city would be shelled.

The letters below were laid before the Council by the Mayor, but the Council did not see any necessity for any action on them:—

"Mayoralty of New Orleans,
"City Hall, May 1st, 1862.

"To the Common Council in Joint Session.

"Gentlemen,—I herewith lay before you a copy of a communication received yesterday from Flag-Officer Farragut. You will observe that the note intimates a misinterpretation on the part of the city authorities of Flag-Officer Farragut's previous communication. I venture to say, gentlemen, that no reasoning mind can fail to place on the note of Monday, the 28th instant, the interpretation attached to it by the people of this city. The notification to remove our women and children within forty-eight hours, in case we adhered to our resolution not to haul down our flag, can be construed in no other way than as a threat to bombard the city. The meaning was plain, not only to us, but to the Consuls of the foreign nations residing here. But in so clear a case argument is superfluous.

" Flag-Officer Farragut informs us that, in consequence of the offensive nature of our answer to his threat, he declines further communication with us, and shall, on the arrival of General Butler, hand the city over to his charge. He certainly should be conscious that the city of New Orleans sought no communication with him or his forces, and that the cessation of intercourse, while it depended entirely on his will, could not fail to be quite as agreeable to us as to him.

" It would add still further to our gratification should General Butler find it equally unpleasant to hold communication with the city.

" Respectfully,

(Signed)   " JOHN T. MONROE, Mayor."

'· U. S. Flag-ship 'Hartford,'

"At Anchor off the City of New Orleans,

" April 30th, 1862.'

" To His Honour the Mayor and City Council of New Orleans.

" Gentlemen,—I informed you in my communication of 28th of April, that your determination, as I understood it, was not to haul down the flag of Louisiana on the City Hall, and that my officers and men were treated with insult and rudeness when they landed, even with a flag of truce, to communicate with the authorities, &c., and that if such was to be the determined course of the people, the fire of the vessels might at any moment be drawn upon the city.

" This you have thought proper to construe into a determination on my part to murder your women and children, and made your letter so offensive that it will terminate our intercourse, and so soon as General Butler arrives with his force, I shall turn over the charge of the city to him, and resume my naval duties.

"Very respectfully, your obedient servant,

"(Signed)   D. G. FARRAGUT.

"Flag-Officer, Western Gulf, Blockading Squadron."

Thus he forced the insolent foe to perform this act of insult, and reluctantly Flag-Officer Farragut consented to send his own forces to take down the flag. At noon appeared a force of about two hundred armed marines, and a number of sailors, dragging two brass howitzers, and the officer in command mounting to the dome of the building, removed the flag of the State, in sight of an immense crowd, who stood viewing this act with a solemn and sad regard. The stillness was awful of that vast assembly, and the tears bedewed the cheeks of stern men, as well as fair maidens. The scene of humiliation was over, and as the crowd dispersed for their homes, the silent grasp of the hand spoke volumes, and told of the agony of heart with which they left the spot. An incident of the time is well deserving of record. .

A prominent citizen—one of the city fathers—passing the residence of one of our most patriotic and warmhearted women, not a thousand miles from the City Hall, and seeing the ladies of the house on the front steps, saluted them, and entered into conversation respecting the events of the hour. He remarked upon the demand of Commodore Farragut to haul down our flag from the City Hall, and said that if even the Mayor and Council came to the determination to yield, there was no *man* to be found willing to perform the humiliating and craven act. He then, by way of banter, said to one of the ladies :—

"Won't you relieve us from the difficulty, and go up to the roof and take the flag down?"

To which she replied, "*Yes, I will go up, but will take a hammer with me, and nail the flag to the flag-staff.*"

We wish it were possible to transfer to paper the spirit and manner of the utterance of this noble and fearless woman. The expression of her feelings was worthy of her—worthy of the cause, and a fit representation of the sentiment which animated both sexes. In this moment of excitement, the most shameful and outrageous scandals were being circulated, and without grounds or satisfactory evidence. Generals Lovell and Duncan, though they had done all that men could do to defend forts Jackson and St. Phillip, were by the ignorant, rash, and inconsiderate, pronounced "traitors." General Lovell acted upon the advice of the Mayor and City Council, and General Duncan only surrendered when the soldiers threatened to fire upon their own officers, and spiked their guns. He had no other resource than to haul down his flag, and when on his return he made his address to the citizens of New Orleans, he wept like a child. But even for the poor worn out, weary soldiers there is some excuse for this conduct, as they had been exposed for many days to the furious and terrible fire of the bombardment, having been in water to their waists during the whole time. One company, however, refused to join the rest of the garrison in this act of mutiny, and in letters of gold let their names shine for ever, the "St. Mary's Cannoniers."

The Mayor thanked General Duncan, in the name of the citizens, for his gallant conduct, and the Hon. Pierre Soulé was called upon to express to General Duncan the sentiments of the people, and that he would be held in everlasting remembrance for his gallant conduct. This scene was void of formality, and had no display or useless parade.   In the hearts of all honest individuals Generals Lovell and Duncan were awarded their proper praise and merited admiration.

An article appearing about this time, General Lovell presumed it referred to him, and accordingly responded. Both are worthy of perusal, and I place them before you.

"Fallen but not Disgraced.

" Let us not be humiliated.   New Orleans has borne herself in this great struggle as became the renown of her people.   She has fought, singly and alone, with her own resources, and those of a small State, with less than half a million of population, the naval and military power of a great nation of twenty millions of people, and with vast military resources.   She has kept that hostile nation at bay for more than twelve months.   She has only yielded now to an overwhelming power.   Her only protection, the forts below the city, have held out for ten days against a hostile squadron, carrying over three hundred guns, including mortars of unusual calibre, and against a land and naval force of many thousands. It was only when the small garrisons of these forts were worn out and exhausted by the constant toil and sleeplessness of an uninterrupted bombardment of ten days that they succumbed. When the United States' squadron succeeded stealthily in passing the forts, they were met by a small and weak squadron of gunboats, which grappled their huge ships, and fought until they were sunk or blown up. The success of the hostile squadron in passing the forts left the city at their mercy. The surface of the Mississippi, now at its highest stage, gave their four large frigates, carrying over one hundred large guns, and their ten smaller ships, bearing as many more, complete range of our streets and houses. It was folly long to resist such a power. Our troops had left the city. There only remained the foreign brigades, the non-combatants, the women and children. The demeanour of these was noble and heroic beyond all example.

When on a point of etiquette to them, but a point of honour to us, the city was menaced with a bombardment, there was no panic, no hesitation, no fear. Awful as the consequences would have been in such a city, with no place to retreat save the swamps, already submerged, the people cheerfully awaited the fate with which they were threatened. If the men had dared to yield the point of honour, the women would have scourged them from the city; but there was no yielding. The civil authorities were worthy of the people. No flag was lowered by them, none hoisted but that which the enemy alone could by his physical force raise. The invader met no friend, no ally, no sympathizer among us; the people presented their breasts to his guns and bayonets, in a solid phalanx.

Thus far, we can honestly say that, except in the

inconsistent, unauthorised, and cruel demand of the commanding officer of the fleet relative to the State flag, and, in the event of refusal, the menace to bombard the city, the enemy has borne himself with dignity and propriety. The terms yielded to the gallant garrison of our forts were honourable. The officers retired on their parole with their side-arms. The highest tributes were paid by the enemy to the heroism of the defence.

The United States' flag waves over the city. It is the flag of the conqueror. Its presence has made doubly dear the standard which it has displaced. That will be embalmed in the hearts and memories of this people.

This sad fate has come upon our city from no fault of our people and authorities. Louisiana was left alone to defend this great city. The forts were prepared, armed and defended exclusively by the troops of this State; the river by hastily constructed gunboats, manned by our own volunteers. The Government at Richmond gave us little aid, and, indeed, embarrassed us by the aid which it attempted to give. The defences would have been stronger and more formidable if a Confederate naval officer had never had command in our river. The lack of energy and earnestness on the part of the agents of the Confederate Government deprived us of the most powerful of our resources for defence. Indeed, had not our resources been drained for the defences of other and far less important portions of the Confederacy, Louisiana would have had ample means for the maintenance of her own integrity; but we had already nearly exhausted our military resources to protect distant sections of our Confederacy.

There is another source of consolation to us. All

the great cities of the world have been subjected to the humiliation which we are now passing through. Paris, Vienna, Moscow, London, Madrid, Antwerp, and all the great capitals of Europe, have in their turn been occupied by hostile armies. So, too, in our own country, Boston, New York, Philadelphia, Washington, Charleston, and Savannah, have had to succumb to invaders. There is no disgrace or dishonour in this. The only disgrace and dishonour that can come to us will be when we surrender the convictions of our minds, the loyalty of our hearts, and the duties of our conscience. The physical victory has been won by the invader; it is for us to see that the moral victory is ours.

GENERAL LOVELL.

We publish below a letter from General Lovell, which presents a clear and satisfactory vindication of his course in the defence of this city. The statements of General Lovell, we believe, are fully sustained by the facts. In vindication of ourselves for the allusion to which the General takes exception, we beg to say that he never was in the contemplation of the writer in reference to lack of energy and earnestness on the part of the agents of the Confederate Government. We believe, on the contrary, that General Lovell, so far from being obnoxious to the charge of a lack of earnestness and energy, accomplished with the resources placed at his command, results of a character which have excited general surprise and admiration. There were other parties who were in our view in the allusion to which the General takes exception, who did not prove equal to the occasion.

We would further add, that in the several allusions
to the evacuation of the city by General Lovell, we do
not think it was intended by any sober-thinking person
to convey any censure or any doubt as to the propriety
of General Lovell's conduct in withdrawing his troops
from the city after the fortifications had been forced by
the enemy.   Left with only an infantry force, General
Lovell remained in the city after the enemy's fleet had
anchored in its port.   He was willing and ready to
share the fate of the city; but it was evident that he
was not only impotent for defence, but the enemy, with
his command of the river, would have had it in his
power to reduce the city to starvation, by cutting off all
communication with the interior.   Besides, the continu-
ation of the troops in the city would have exposed it to
a bombardment, in which the enemy would have been
justified by the laws of war, a garrisoned town being
always subject to such a fate.   If General Lovell had
had five or ten times the infantry force which he really
had, he could not have made any adequate defence
against the enemy's powerful fleet. His retirement was,
therefore, not only an act of sound policy and wisdom,
but one of absolute necessity for the salvation of the
city from the most terrible disaster, as well as for the
security of the army, which General Lovell has saved to
lead to other fields, where their valour may be made
available for the maintenance and defence of our cause.

"New Orleans, April 29th, 1862.
" To Judge Walker.
"Dear Sir.—In the 'Evening Delta,' in an article
headed 'Fallen but not Disgraced,' this expression

occurs :—'The lack of energy and earnestness on the part of the agents of the Confederate Government,' &c.

"This includes me in its sweep, and I think unjustly. When I came here, but a few short months since, I found the State completely defenceless; its ports blockaded, and its young men gone to other parts of the Confederacy in the army. Without anything but what was created, every inlet was put in a position to offer a protracted and gallant defence. Forts were armed, powder and munitions of every description were made, and a gallant body of troops organized and drilled. Guns were cast and materials of all kinds extemporized by incessant labour and activity. The river, at the forts, was twice bridged by obstructions which would have resisted anything but the formidable rush of the great Mississippi in its swollen wrath.

"My troops, at the call of their country, rushed to Corinth, and the deeds of the Louisiana regiments on the 6th and 7th of April, indicated their courage and their training. Our founderies were beginning to turn out heavy guns of the best quality; and a newly-erected arsenal furnished us with various implements of war. All this has been done since October, besides preparing sixteen vessels for river defence, eight of which are now defending the upper river, and eight have been destroyed in the vain attempt to keep back the enemy's fleet of war vessels below. This has been done with no host of generals and staff-officers of experience to assist. Almost alone, with but few exceptions, I have worked day and night for more than five months to defend this great city. The responsibility of its fall is not due to any want of 'energy or earnestness' on my part.

In a short time more I should have had guns enough, and men enough, to defend the numerous approaches on that element on which the enemy is so pre-eminently powerful; and I, therefore, beg that you will do me the justice to say to the people of New Orleans, that I did all that one man could do to preserve them from an insolent and powerful foe.

"When their fleets passed all our batteries, I withdrew my infantry forces beyond the city limits, in order to permit the people of New Orleans to decide whether they would subject their wives, their children, and property to bombardment in the endeavour to maintain their freedom intact; and returned to the city to-day to learn their decision, and to offer myself and my command to stand by them to the last moment, in case they should decide to undergo a bombardment. I know that there are many gentlemen here who will bear me witness that all that is here set forth, and much more, has been done to avert this sad disaster. An examination of my letter and order books and telegraphic despatches, will show that no stone has been left unturned by me to save New Orleans from this humiliation; and I feel well convinced that a few short weeks would have rendered the position impregnable. All I ask is simple justice, and nothing more. In conclusion I will add, that terrible as the blow has been, I am neither disheartened nor in despair. This war of independence is not yet fought out. Our ancestors struggled on against the massive power of Great Britain, when Boston, New York, Philadelphia, Charleston, and Savannah were all in possession of the enemy, and gained their liberty.

"It is a moral and physical impossibility that we can be conquered. Let us but be true to ourselves and our cause—never tiring, never despairing—but rising, Actæon-like, with renewed vigour from every fall, and we shall yet be rewarded with success. Above all, we should not crush down the spirit and the energies of those who are using all the faculties, mental and physical, that God has given them, by making light of their labours, because, with limited means and under adverse circumstances, they have not been successful in resisting at all points a great, wealthy, and powerful enemy, with all the appliances of modern warfare, both military and naval, in great abundance at his control. We have never yet seen such dark days as those which environed George Washington at Valley Forge; and should such be our lot, I trust that the same spirit will animate us to work out the same successful results.

"Respectfully your obedient servant,

"M. LOVELL,

"Major-General, C.S.A."

Could such sentiments exist in the heart of a traitor? I answer, No!

The brigade of foreign residents, under command of General Paul Juge, deserve lasting gratitude for the efficiency displayed in maintaining peace and order in the city, during the confusion and trouble incident to the appearance of the United States' fleet in the port. And now little remains to be said. The city was taken possession of by General B. F. Butler, and as his troops marched into the city, they found how great was the mistake that Union sentiments existed in New Orleans,

and well they know that Union feelings could not be
masked by the darkened visages which met their gaze
at every step, and the fearful scowls, and muttered
curses of the few men who gathered around to witness
their entrance, left them no hope for establishing, on
anything like a firm basis, Federal government in
Louisiana.

General Butler established himself at the St. Charles
Hotel, which, on the arrival of the Federals, was by the
Southerners vacated, and the Yankees were thus left
to occupy it.   General Butler, as well as several officers
of the Federal army, were accompanied by their wives,
but unfortunately for those ladies they were regarded
in quite a different light by the citizens of New Orleans,
and thus subjected to the most cruel suspicions; the
commanding general's own wife was regarded as a
courtezan, and in a few days after her arrival, was
called upon by two women of infamous character, who
represented themselves as the wives of Confederate
officers.   A longer stay, and greater knowledge of the
Southern women, proved to General Butler and his
staff, that none save a courtezan, and one of the most
reckless character, would have dared to countenance or
recognize them or their wives.   They were thus forced
to seek society amongst their kind; and the Southern
man or woman base enough to stretch forth the hand
of recognition to them, was stamped with the brand of
infamy, and their *names* remembered for that day in
which the traitor shall be judged.

No kind glance, no word of welcome met the eye,
or fell upon the ear, and the lone sentinel paced the
streets of the silent and fallen city, with a vision ever

before his eyes of a gleaming stiletto, and muffled form, for they knew not at what moment they might fall victims to the suppressed, but burning hatred of the citizens. Tremblingly the pickets marched to their duty on the outskirts of the city, as with blanched cheeks they each day heard of the guerilla bands and their daring deeds. Within the city military rule was now established, and soon "The Reign of Terror" was inaugurated, which has given to future ages even more material than its sister period in France. General Butler won the title of Robespierre, and many other tender soubriquets, which will appear in their proper places. Officers and men paraded the streets daily, investigating matters, to them of great importance, and houses were searched throughout for Confederate arms, flags, tents, clothing, and money. A party for the above purpose landed from one of the enemy's ships above Carrollton, and proceeding to the abandoned fortifications inspected them, and tore up a small Confederate flag which they found flying over the works. Returning down the Levee, the officers met a family of ladies and children, accompanied by their coloured servant. The Federals, addressing themselves first to the ladies, expressed a hope that the presence of the fleet was not a cause of fear to them. We will relate, verbatim, the conversation that ensued :—

Mrs. B.: "That sensation, Sir, is unknown to us here."

Officer: "Madame, may I ask you if there is any Union sentiment here?"

Mrs. B.: "None, Sir, that I am aware of; certainly none among the ladies."

T

Officer: "Then we may take it for granted that there is none among either sex, as the ladies generally go with the gentlemen in political questions?"

Mrs. B.: "I am confident, Sir, your inference as to the entire absence of any Union sentiments is correct. As to the ladies following the gentlemen in political questions, I beg you to understand that, however it may be in your section, the ladies here advocate that only which is just and honourable."

Officer: (Turning his attention to one of the servants) "Well, Sis, can you tell me if all the troops have left yet?"

Nancy being for a moment quiet, the lady said: "Nancy, why don't you answer your brother?"

Nancy: (With great indignation) "Don't you call me Sis again. I don't want no Yankee for a bruder."

The whole Federal party passed on without another word. This was the reception they met with on every side, and Mrs. Brown proved herself as spirited in her converse with the foe, as she did when spiking the guns. Then long live such women, and may the foe, when he comes in his insolent pride, ever meet with the scorn of all true women. We will now close the veil upon this scene, and introduce you, reader, to spectacles of interest which will never fade from memory, though they be lost to vision.

CHAPTER XVII.

"Our earth as it rolls through the regions of space,
 Wears always two faces, the dark side and sunny;
And poor human life runs the same sort of race,
 Being sad, on one side,—on the other side funny.

"For our parts, though gravity's good for the soul,
 Such a fancy have we for the side that there's fun on,
We'd rather, with Sydney, south-west take a 'stroll,'
 Than *coach* it north-east with his Lordship of Lunnun."

"And in her air
There was a something which bespoke command,
As one who was a lady in the land."

"But faith, fanatic faith, once wedded fast
To some dear falsehood, hugs it to the last."

THE fall of New Orleans, though a most dreadful blow
to the Confederacy, in no manner decided the fate
of the war, and the victories of the brave troops in the
battles around Richmond gave them renewed hopes for
the future. The Confederates needed something to
awaken them from the lethargy into which they had
fallen, through their long and almost constant success.
Like a storm this broke upon them after their empyream
repose, and now those men who had been even cari-
catured in their own journals in the following spicy

tone, threw off their habits of indolence, and on
the battle field, it were difficult indeed to recognise
in the tanned and resolute soldier a resemblance to
the portrait below, which was indeed life-like in every
feature, when the clarion notes first burst upon the
land.

The Drill of the Lapstone Rangers.—This body of
citizen soldiery, composed of the best blood of the
land, has grown into a regiment, and has so organised
in advance to meet the requirements of the new law
which goes into effect on the 15th, that Colonel Sole,
commanding the regiment, assures us that the regiment embraces in its ranks none but gentlemen; and
Colonel Sole being a reliable gentleman himself, we
repose the greatest confidence in his statement. He
has presented us with a revised copy of Hardee, designed for the exclusive government of the Lapstone
Rangers, which certainly goes to show that the regi-
mental orders, the drill exercises, and the manual
generally, were gotten up expressly for the government
of gentlemen.

Colonel Sole always publishes the order for battalion
drill on the second page of a morning paper—headed
notice—and in the following courteous style :—

" Gentlemen of the Lapstone Rangers,

" If in perfect accordance with the economy of your
digestive code, I have the honour to invite you to ride
down town to your respective armouries, as soon after
dinner as you may deem it prudent, to-morrow, to par-
ticipate in a portion of the exercises incident to battalion

drill. *Provided* the weather be not threatening or inclement.

"I have the honour, gentlemen, to be,
"yours, very truly,
"CRISPIN SOLE,
"Colonel Commanding Lapstone Rangers."

Supposing, of course, the invitation harmonises with "digestive code," the different companies composing the regiment of Lapstone Rangers appear, according to card, upon the field used for drill, Colonel Sole, after saluting the vast number of ladies who are gathered on the field, and replacing his white handkerchief, turns to the regiment, draws his sword, and opens—

"Gentlemen,—If any gentleman in the battalion has in his mouth a cigar that is not quite smoked, I have the honour to inform him that the hour has arrived when he can throw it away with impunity, if he chooses to do so."

Upon this courteously delivered piece of military information, sundry gentlemen proceed to suck sundry cigar stumps, preparatory to the whiff that will consign these stumps to the usual position of "old sojors."

Whereupon Colonel Sole draws his sword, lifts off his hat, throws his eyes to the left, then to the right, wreathes his military lips into a bland smile, and says, "Gentlemen of the Battalion —I desire to state, to insinuate, with due sense of the courteous relations existing between the members of this regiment and your humble Colonel, that if perfectly agreeable to you, you will place yourselves in the attitude of attention."

The gentlemen thus courteously appealed to, of course respond, with the exception of one or two of the men who are deeply absorbed in an argument with their Captain and 1st Lieutenant upon the most improved method of tanning hides without the use of bark. They too, however, take their proper position in line, and the Colonel, after acknowledging the fact, proceeds—

"Gentlemen,—You will do me the favour to shoulder arms—if you please."

The arms are duly shouldered in gentlemanly style. The Colonel now goes on—

"Gentlemen,—Alexander wept for a second world to conquer, Solomon sighed for the wings of a dove, but neither of them, could they have realised their desires, would have been happier than your Colonel would be if you, by the right of companies, would change your position to the rear into column. In order to accomplish this very important manœuvre, gentlemen, I will beg that each company will face to the right. Now do me the kindness to march?"

The request is complied with to the extreme satisfaction of the Colonel and the delight of the ladies. The applause of the latter is gracefully acknowledged by Colonel Sole, who gallops away to the right of the line, and then gallops back again. After satisfying himself that the line is dressed to suit those in it, he continues—

"Gentlemen,—It would probably be more to your convenience and ease—and I assure you it would meet with the entire approbation of your Colonel—were you to come to an 'order arms.'"

Of course, the regiment comes to an "order arms." Whereupon Colonel Sole says:—

" Gentlemen,—Your Colonel, ever mindful of the fact that the human frame, after the performance of arduous duties, should indulge in reasonable repose, you are invited to assume the position usually assumed by soldiers when the order is given to 'rest.' It now devolves upon Major Strap to see that every gentleman in the ranks who is suffering from fatigue is supplied with refreshments."

A reasonable time having elapsed for rest, the Colonel respectfully insinuates, in an extremely delicate manner, that the gentlemen should resume the attitude of a corps in attention. The Colonel then states :—

" Gentlemen,—You would place me under lasting obligations if you would kindly consent to shoulder arms."

The regiment courteously complied.

" Gentlemen,—Would you now honour your Colonel and please the ladies by showing them the perfect regularity with which you can support arms."

The regiment kindly honoured the Colonel and pleased the ladies by executing the order.

Colonel Sole, highly delighted, put his white handkerchief into his pocket, and relieved himself thus :—

" Gentlemen,—There is one more manoeuvre which I desire executed, provided it meets with your approval. Gentlemen,—If you are not too much fatigued (I will not ask you to shoulder arms), gladden the heart of your commanding officer and yield to the request he will now make of you. Gentlemen,—I beg that you will now form a column upon the company which has the deserved honour of being the first—that is, if the front had not been changed—and I hope the gentlemen who command the different companies will hire people to see that wheeling distance is observed."

This is a movement which belongs especially to the regiment of Lapstone Rangers, and is executed in superior style. Whereupon Colonel Sole, in the pride of his heart and the full satisfaction of the afternoon's performance, addresses the regiment :—

" Gentlemen,—The country is safe. I have the honour to congratulate you, gentlemen, upon the punctuality of your attendance, the precision of your movements, and the military bearing which every gentleman exhibits. Gentlemen, you will now take the first street you come to without the formality of forming into line and sending the commissioned gentlemen to the front and centre. Gentlemen,—If you should find it inconvenient to take the first street you come to, please take any street or streets convenient to you. And you would consult your own interests and future welfare if you would select those thoroughfares in which the mud is less than two feet deep. Gentlemen,—Hoping to meet you again upon the occasion of our next drill, I have the honour to wish you a very good evening."

The Lapstone Rangers, it is almost unnecessary to state, form the very upper leather of society. Awl the chivalry of the parish, not connected with other regiments, may be found in its ranks; and should they wax wroth, and have to foot it to the borders of the land, the bristles will be taken from some of the Yanks sure. Colonel Sole assures us that the Feds *may* hammer other portions of our reserve corps, but when they come to the regiment of Lapstone Rangers, the latter will welt them till they are thinned out like shoe thread, and are compelled to peg out at last.

This likeness bears a strong resemblance to those who filled the volunteer ranks in New Orleans, and their sybarite customs could not be laid aside until the stern experience of camp life made them feel that to the patriot Lacedemonian fare and the "black broth" of Sparta is sufficient luxury.

The above picture was not overdrawn, and though it only referred to the working men of Southern cities, who, not like the opulent planter, in whom this indolence was by nature, became inoculated with this truly tropical spirit. But this scene was too bright to be lasting, and it wanted some shadow to relieve the dazzling hues, whose glow and voluptuous richness were but the true harbinger of storm and devastation. We were not sorry thus to see the sinews of the South strung to the war-pitch, as much was to be dreaded from the national languor which the last blow felled by the Federals dissipated for ever. The spirit which actuated the South was not that of fanaticism, which in its mad orgies kindles the torch of intolerance, and in its insane fury threatens destruction to all, save those who join in its diabolical rites. The fanaticism of the North has plotted the death of the Goddess of Liberty, and though she still struggles to shun the fate which the world knows awaits her, Fanaticism has pronounced her sentence, and she must die.

Then let the South take warning, and give no encouragement to the stranger—let them extend no welcome, and let their hearts close upon this demon, whose kiss is poison, whose embrace is deadly, whose triumph would

banish God from creation, and convert creation into chaos.
It plotted the massacre of St. Bartholomew, and organised
the Reign of Terror. It set up the Inquisition in Spain,
and in France worshipped Reason in the form of a
courtezan, and chose a madman for its priest, a fitting
representative of its hellish ceremonies. It was Abolition fanaticism, which appeared *sans toilette*, and in its
most hideous deformity in its last character before the
world, which elicited the compliment, "*Nothing civilizes
them*" from the London "Times," and pronounces the
Northern people "neither amenable to courtesy nor
misfortune" and now to quote a criticism on this remark,
I will beg, dear reader, your kind attention :—

> "The barbarism of the North,
> Nothing civilizes them."

It is held by some writers on the philosophy of history,
that civilisation is not the result of gradual development,
but is an essential condition—that it is not an incident
to progress, but an inherent principle ; that it cannot
be superadded where it is not already an indwelling
quality, appertaining to the thoughts and sentiments,
and manifesting itself in the manners and institutions of
a people. History has proved, as far as history can
prove anything, the utter incapacity of certain races to
acquire a genuine and intrinsic civilisation. No amount
of white-washing can place the African on the same
social platform with the civilised European. No tempta-
tions of commerce, of comfort, of security, can localise
the nomadic Arabs and Tartars. No laws, no treaties,
no threats, no promises, can overcome the ferine propensities of the North American aborigine. We have had

good historical grounds for regarding these races as uncivilised and uncivilisable. But what are we to say to the bold assertion of the London "Times," that the Yankee race belongs to the same category? Will the glorious land of universal Sham consent to see its claims to superior civilisation thus contumeliously spurned? Will the famous authors of liqueous nutmegs, and the similitudes of hams that are perfectly innocent of pork, peaceably bear to have those eminent tokens of march of mind and culmination of art insultingly overlooked by the leading organ of English opinion? We pause breathless for an answer. Meantime let us note more particularly the proposition of the London "Times."

That journal (as may be seen in its article published in another column), while speaking of the battle of Manasses—of the vulgar bravado of the Lincoln press that preceded it, the rout and disaster that attended it; the monstrous mendacity and brutal sentiments of the same press, that followed it—remarks that, judged by these and like indications, the Northern people "are amenable neither to courtesy nor misfortune. Nothing civilises them." Strange, indeed, must such language sound to an English public, which had been so long schooled in the belief that if there was any civilisation in the States lying between the St. Lawrence and the Rio Grande, the true and only well assured seat of it existed in what was known as the Northern section. All the rest—Seward and Sumner, Beecher and Stowe Cheever and Helper had told them, and their press, with small exception, with indolent complacency, had parroted the canting accusation—was blighted with the "black

curse of slavery." The text of the last and longest of
Sumner's senatorial philippics was "The barbarism of
slavery." The South, he maintained, was maculate
with all manner of vice and crime, and barbaric to the
core by reason of slavery, and it was the rightful and
bounden mission of the North, immaculate, saintly, and
pre-eminently enlightened and progressive, to broad-
cast the seeds of genuine civilisation to the moral
wilderness of the slaveholding States. Now, what is
Mr. Sumner to think? What are his constituency
at Boston, that "hub of creation," that "Athens of
America," to think? What are the great war party of
the North to think? What are the pen-and-ink warriors
of the Northern war press to think? What is the
whole Abolition and Lincoln capoodle of them to think,
when told by the principal journalistic representative of
the English public, whose sympathies they have so
assiduously courted, and so confidently counted on, that,
taken upon evidence of their own making, upon their
avowed acts and public professions, they are uncivilised,
and incapable of civilisation? The language of the
London "Times," to which we refer, is doubtless to be
construed, with some allowance for an exaggeration of
bitter sarcasm. But the words contain a cruel sting,
which no qualification of that kind can remove. It is
the sting of truth—of truth as inexorable as death, as
remorseless as the grave. Allowing for all excess of
badinage, for all extravagance of ridicule, the general
accusation against our vaunting enemies at the North
remains, that in their arrogation of superior civilisation,
in their assumption of moral and intellectual supremacy
over their Southern neighbours, they were practising a

stupendous cheat upon the world, and that now, when war, with its vicissitudes and excitements, reveals them in the nakedness of their nature, in all the coarseness of their bad propensities, they are found to be "amenable neither to courtesy nor misfortune," that, in fact, "nothing civilises them." Even so. The Abolition fanaticism of the North is only another name for barbarism. Slavery is an occasion, not the cause of its manifestation. The Union is the symbol of cohesion employed by the leaders of barbarous hosts thirsting for rapine and slaughter, not the intelligible object of the war which is waged upon the South. If there were no cry of slavery, no cry of Union, there would have been some other cry, which would have meant the same thing. Substantially the same issue would have been forced upon us under any disposition of events. It is a proverbial impossibility to manufacture a "silk purse out of a sow's ear." With the "Times," so we exclaim, "Nothing civilises them," and not till New Orleans fell did these savages prove their claim to ancestry with the Aborigines—and full scope was now given by their chief B. F. B. (which being translated means brute, fiend, butcher), whose acts of brutality, military domination, and insult, causing the universal poverty and beggary of millions, and the triumph of the vilest individuals in the community, and abasement of the honest and industrious, together with the outlawry of slaves (with whom on his arrival in New Orleans he professed to have no sympathy) the destruction in this region of agriculture and commerce, and the emigration of some of the wealthiest and most thriving citizens.

But the soldiers of the Confederacy left for other

fields, where they could meet the foe on equal terms, and none remained save those who had families dependent on them, and were incapable of efficient military duty. But those who remained proved themselves as patriotic perhaps as those upon the field, in their noble resistance to the Federal authority. On the arrival of the Federals, every one who could conveniently leave the city did so at once, and amongst the number Judge de Breuil, leaving his sister and Miss de Villerie to follow at leisure.

As the fleet came slowly up the river, passing "Rosale Plantation," one of the sentinels on board the "Pensicola" remarked, "Is not that a Confederate flag which I see floating from the turret of yonder mansion?"

"By heavens, it is!" exclaimed one and all.

"And methinks a lady is standing with her arms around the staff."

"Fire a volley at it," remarked the commander, "and blow the woman and flag into h—ll!"

A thundering sound was heard, and, when the smoke cleared away, the flag which a few moments before had streamed out so defiantly was now no longer to be seen, and those who looked through the telescope could perceive that much damage was done to the building, and, from the seeming confusion amongst the persons on the plantation, that it was more than probable the captain's order had been obeyed.

And now turn we to Rosale. Miss de Villerie, on learning the approach of the fleet, had gone up into a turret of the building, and taking with her the Confederate flag, resolved to die beneath its folds. Standing out on the small balcony in front of the turret, she placed the staff firmly in one corner, and, clasping her arms around it, she stood awaiting the penalty of her rash course. Thus, when the shot struck one, it struck both; and when Madame de Breuil and her terrified servants sought Miss de Villerie, it was to find her wounded and bleeding beneath the folds of the "Southern Flag," whose every fold was saturated with the blood of this intrepid girl.

"Let me die here!" she murmured, as they sought to restore and to remove her. "Oh! let me die beneath the folds of our own true banner. I ask no greater glory than to share a like fate to those who have fallen beneath it!"

"This is an act of madness, dear Natalie," murmured Madame de Breuil, as she washed the blood from her wounds, and endeavoured to staunch it ere the physician would arrive.

On the arrival of Dr. S——, he pronounced her wounds not dangerous, and, administering an opiate, left her, with the injunctions to Madame de Breuil that all exciting news should be kept from her, and no one should visit her until she was entirely well.

With a constitution such as hers she was soon able to dispense with all services of the disciple of Esculapius, and her first resolve was to leave the city, or rather her home, which was now within the Federal lines. Ordering her carriage one morning, she drove, unaccompanied, to the St. Charles Hotel, and, sending her card to, General B. F. Butler, requested an interview, as she desired to obtain passports to go into the Confederacy. She was shown into the reception-room, and soon afterwards the General entered. Bowing to Miss de Villerie, who rose upon his entrance, he said, " Madame, can I serve you? "

" Yes, Sir," she answered, " if you are so disposed. I wish to obtain a couple of passports to go into the Confederacy, and trust you will have the kindness to grant them."

" I am granting no passports at present, but in a few days I shall be happy to oblige you, or that is, as soon as Vicksburg shall be in our possession, which is momentarily expected."

" Am I to wait, General," she replied, " until Vicksburg falls, for a passport? "

" I can grant none until that event."

" Then," she responded, " I may as well take a farewell to my hopes of getting one, for I am convinced you will not be troubled soon for them, as Vicksburg is regarded as an impregnable fortress."

" I believe, Madame, that Forts Jackson and St. Phillip were also so deemed, but they were by our fleet regarded as but toy fortifications."

" Rather formidable toys, I should judge, that kept at bay your fleet for four months, *and when you did make* the attack, held out seven days against all the engines of destruction that your imagination could devise."

" Truly, this is the case, Madame; yet you must acknowledge your fleet is but a burlesque when compared to that of the Federal."

" Most assuredly, Sir, and so much the more credit our officers and men deserve for combatting the giant of which you boast. Yes, Sir, I admit your superiority over us in a *naval point*, but to us belongs the victor's wreath *on land, where physical force proves the warrior's claim to praise,* and where, I believe, *our* soldiers have ever proved themselves the most entitled to eulogy."

" You cannot claim much glory for them in the last engagement, and the traitor Lovell at their head was the most contemptible of all."

" Spare General Lovell, and do not term him *traitor,* for that is our name for him, *if he deserves it of either;* but remember him gratefully, for if he be a traitor you are indebted to him, and others of the same sort, for your present victory."

" We are indebted to none save our own valour, Madame, which has placed us in possession of this city, and which will soon open the Mississippi River, which has been so long closed from Western commerce, and thus place within my power the means to assist your starving population."

" I was not aware, General Butler, that our population were in this condition before, and feel assured it must have been *since your* arrival, as thus all communication has been cut off from whence supplies heretofore were sent to New Orleans."

" No, Madame; when I arrived here I found them in a starving state, and it is not even the poor that have sought me for assistance, but I have had your wealthy men, *slave-owners,* to come and plead to me on their knees for bread for their families and food for their slaves."

" Permit me, Sir, then, to say to you that you have been most terribly imposed upon, if this be the case, as I can assure you there is no man, no real Southerner and slave-owner in the South, base enough for such an

U

action. There may be persons who have represented themselves as such, but *they were neither Southerners or slave-owners.* It were impossible that any one could have been in such a state of extreme distress, and in so short a time after your entrance, as before you came there was an abundance of provisions, and such a thing as a mendicant in our streets was unknown. Never, Sir, never, was there less pauperism known in the South (where it at all times exists less than in any part of the world) than since the war commenced, for our State Government provided against the wants of the families of her soldiers, and even in the country, in the different parishes, so much is allowed to each family, say $20 to the wife, and $5 to each child, until it amounts to $50, and then it ceases. Besides this, provision is given them by the surrounding planters, and thus, you perceive, Sir, our poor are properly cared for. No, Sir, you may be assured there are none now in the city vile enough to take the oath, to save their property or obtain provision."

"Madame, will you be so kind as to name some of those you imagine so loyal, and I will send for them this moment and prove to you that *they will take the oath, and in your presence?*"

"Doubtless, Sir, as a man would deliver his purse to a highwayman. I could name many to you, Sir, that not even *such a threat* could intimidate, but I have no desire to compromise my friends."

"I should imagine that your confidence in the spirit of your people was somewhat lessened since their inglorious flight, leaving only the ladies and children to defend the city."

"They could not, General, have left it under better protection, women are no mean adversaries, as has been proved, more than once, both in the field and in the Chamber of Council. Do not presume, however, that *we* regard the exit of our troops from the city as you do. What would you have the handful of men do? Remain and subject the city to a bombardment (which was threatened by Farragut) and perhaps perish with the women and children, with no means left them to defend it?"

"There was no reason," he answered, "for the flight of these men, nor the destruction of property, and as for a bombardment it was never threatened."

"Pardon me, General Butler, if I tell you that I am not dull of comprehension, and I do not know what other interpretation could have been put upon the words of Commander Farragut, when he ordered that the women and children should be re-moved *within forty-eight hours.* Or if it be, General, that this is not the case, and if you pretend to have taken our city by any other means than by your fleet, which frowned upon us threatening destruction every moment, *though your soldiers feared to land,* I say that no *personal* valour was displayed, and that if you wish to put your soldiers and our own to the test, just signify to General Lovell that you will meet him at Camp Moore, out of range of your gun-boats, and that a physical combat will decide the right of conquest, and you will find, Sir, that though you may outnumber him in men he will give you as nice a thrashing as was administered at Bull Run, and Manasses."

"Your soldiers certainly know how to fight," he

rejoined, "but pray tell me who are your men of the South? As for the North has she not given to America all the inventive genius, and has she not produced the ship-builders, and manufacturers, as well as constructed your railroads, and dug your canals, in fact been the great lever which raised her to her present gigantic height amongst the nations of the globe, while the South, what has she done ? "

" If you will allow me, Sir, I will tell you who our men of the South are first; secondly, what they have done; and thirdly, what they intend doing. To begin. History, I presume, will inform you that the South gave to you many Presidents and Statesmen, and ruled the Cabinet at Washington long enough at least that you might have *felt* who the South was. Secondly, the Southern people being mostly proprietors of estates, they had no necessity for trying their inventive genius in any manner, but left *such work* for their more needy neighbours, who were generally well paid for their services, as often in exchange for a hogshead of sugar, or a bale of cotton, they would manage to smuggle in a wooden ham into the hogshead of pork, which was sent for the consumption of the Negroes, which even they could not be forced nor tempted to believe was genuine, as they knew it came from the land of universal sham, and harshly as the Southerners treat their slaves they would not insist upon their partaking of this fare so kindly sent them from their sympathisers. Lastly, the Southerners, aroused from their slumbers of Oriental repose, *have sworn to burst their bonds and extermi-nate their enemies, or be exterminated.* This, Sir, is what the South has done, and what she intends doing."

"My dear Madame, what can the South do in the lilliputian struggle with the Federal giant? Tell me, of what is your army composed?"

"A dwarf in earlier days slew the giant, and we would consider it no miracle now. *Who* are our troops? *What* are they, did you ask? I, Sir, will tell you. They are the flower of the land, and men that were most of them nursed in the lap of luxury, and this is why they fight so well, for history tells us that the patricians have been better soldiers than the plebians. They do not shrink from suffering, and already have given proof of their ability as warriors, orators, statesmen, and authors. Amongst the first named we place the immortal Washington, amongst the second, *their names are too numerous to mention.* Can you now deny our claims?"

"Granting all this, Madame, you cannot deny the great superiority of intelligence of the masses of the North compared with the South, and, for instance, I can point out to you in one company (which he named) alone twenty-five graduates of Harvard College."

"Twenty-five graduates of Harvard College," she scornfully replied, "I can point out to you, General, one company of the Parish of West Feliciana, in which there is scarce an exception in it, and those who compose it are graduates of the first colleges, either in the North, South, or of Europe. They are each and everyone worth at least some four or five hundred thousand dollars, and thus you will perceive they were not educated, like most of your Northern young men, *with the view* of making their way in the world by their talents—therefore I cannot admit a superiority of intellect. Probably, had the youth of the North the same inducements towards idleness and ignorance, they would prove less worthy than our Southerners."

"I am well aware," he responded, "of your vast wealth, but, Madam, when we look at all this we must consider that it is the poor slave who works for it, and that it is his hands that fill your purses and provide these luxuries, and that no personal endeavour on your part have ever placed one penny in your pockets. As for me," he added, "I would prefer to earn my bread by the sweat of my brow."

"General, as we have broached this subject, what, presume you, must your soldiers have thought on arriving in New Orleans, to find the negroes promenading in the square and streets, dressed in broad-cloth, and some in silks and satins, carrying gold watches in their pockets, and looking better, and living better, than their poor families at home, whom they had left there in poverty to fight for the negro, and to loosen their bonds of slavery. *What were your sentiments?*"

"Oh, my dear Madame, as for me, I have ceased to be astonished at anything; and I must assure you that *I am no Abolitionist, have never been one, nor have I any sympathy in this cause; I came here to fight for the Union, to restore order, and to feed your starving people.*"

"Well, kind sir, I would advise you to begin at home in the latter work of charity, for if the poor of the North have enough to eat and drink *now*, it is more than they ever had *before*. They should pray for a continuance of the war; and the Abolitionists of the North should first begin their work of enfranchisement in New

York and Philadelphia, where the free negroes are the most God-forsaken wretches on earth, and where the chains of filth and poverty bind the millions of black and white stronger than any manacles forged from iron. Go to the Five Points of New York and glance at the miserable hovels on the shore of the Bay of Brooklyn, and tell me then if you can find a negro in the whole South who would change his quarters with the poor white slave of your cities? You made use, Sir, of the remark, 'I would prefer to earn my bread by the sweat of my brow.' This, Sir, may be a pleasant enough *theory* seated, as you are, in a cool apartment of the St. Charles, in the most delightful part of the city, and with ices to drink every hour, and when inclination prompts a promenade, seat yourself in an equipage; but if you would like the *practice* for a few moments, I would advise you to enter a cotton-field and begin your day of labour by pulling off your coat and exposing yourself to the sun's rays, and then take the cotton-bag in your hand, cull a few of the beautiful white blossoms that look so delicate, or take the hoe (if earlier in the season) and turn the soil up, even lightly, for a few hours, *and then give me your idea of 'earning your own bread.' Theory,* most usually, is pleasant—*practice,* seldom so."

" I must say, notwithstanding all this, Madame, that the life of a Southern man reflects little credit upon the Creator, and leaves him without aim or object, save the pursuit of pleasure."

" Yet, Sir, they place yearly in the hands of the Northerners the profits of the planters' crops, and Northern shopkeepers and the landlords of the hotels in your various watering-places have generally reaped a golden harvest from the pockets of the Southerners, who, as soon as spring, arrived—like all geese prepared to be plucked."

"Yes, as you say," he answered, "they spent their money recklessly, and, after a grand dash and flourish, usually handed over a draft on their merchants, and returned to their homes satisfied, I believe, with having made a display."

Miss de Villerie was about to reply, but at this point a lady made her appearance at the door of the apartment, and said, addressing the General, "Before you go out I wish to see you."

The General rose, and bowing, said, "I will attend you soon."

Then the lady withdrew. She was ladylike and graceful in appearance, and Miss de Villerie being anxious to learn who it could be, remarked, "I was not aware there were ladies in the hotel now; I presumed they had all left the day of the arrival of the fleet."

"My wife, Madam," he replied; " and thus you will perceive I have come prepared to stay."

"We are all liable, Sir, to grievous disappointment in this world, and this may prove your greatest."

"Well, when I leave New Orleans I will leave it what it was, viz.—the home of the alligator."

"Thank you, courteous Sir, for your compliment; do you pretend to say you found nothing here but alligators? Do I look much like that amphibious creature?"

"Excuse me," he laughingly responded, " I meant in its original state; and when I do leave, I shall leave the d——l to take it (pardon the expression, I pray you," he added); a prophecy which was fulfilled to the letter.

"You are pardoned, Sir, for the hasty expression, and be as indulgent, I pray you, with me when I say to you that had you been in New Orleans the day on which your soldiers landed and marched up the streets, you would have presumed his Satanic majesty had already arrived with all his imps; and I assure you, Sir, we never wish to see anything bearing a stronger resemblance to him than the Yankees."

"Well, Madam, I own they might have done worse than we did; for instance, we have a right to take the feather beds from under the people even, and it would only be considered just according to the rules of warfare."

"I assure you you are quite welcome to all the feather-beds you find; but fortunately we don't use them, spring mattresses are in vogue here; and now, General, I presume that I must leave without a pass, as you need not have the slightest hopes of placing Vicksburg within your lines."

"We shall see, madam; and should you feel disposed to take the oath and return here within two weeks, I will provide you with a passport."

"Bidding you good morning, General, I will state that I should not value nor accept a passport purchased at such a price," and thus saying she bowed low to the commander, who accompanied her to the door.

Entering her carriage, she drove to the office of the provost marshal, and there obtaining passports, for which she paid two dollars in silver, she proceeded to the City Hall, and had them signed by General G. F.

Shapley (who for his courtesy towards the ladies of New Orleans will long be remembered), and once more seating herself in her equipage, drove to Rosale.

In a few days, the latter plantation was deserted by all the white inmates, and Miss de Villerie had gone to figure in other scenes. General Butler soon established his head-quarters at the Custom House, and the orders for confiscation and arrest began. He took possession of the residence of General D. F. Twiggs (the latter having left immediately on the arrival of the fleet), and also seized all the silver and articles of value he could find in the house, as well as the jewels of Mrs. Myer (the daughter of General Twiggs), but returned the latter by request of Dr. N. Mercer. Ascertaining, through the domestics, that General Twiggs had left his swords in the keeping of the Florence family, as also some silver, he sent an order to the family to give them up, which they refused to do, asserting that General Twiggs had presented those articles to Miss Florence, but this was considered as a mere subterfuge, and General Butler took them without further ceremony.

He forbade all display of Confederate badges, emblems, or other rebel demonstrations. Yet in the face of threats, and with Ship Island and Fort Jackson as the penalty, there were those reckless enough to sport the colours, and to meet, face to face, the Union officers and soldiers without a tremor for the consequences. Amongst the number famous for such conduct was Mrs. Phillips (formerly of Washington) and her daughters. They had suffered in Washington at the commencement of the war, and Mrs. Phillips at that time was arrested on the charge of an intention to illuminate her mansion after the victory of Bull's Run. Her treatment then should have taught her a lesson, as also that of Mrs. Greenhow and others. The latter's ride, where she acted as chief of the fair band of female prisoners in the old Capital Prison, though a most amusing incident of prison-life, scarce repaid her for her suffering during her captivity. But I cannot say that I advocate such a course. It but exasperates the enemy, while it benefits the cause in no way. The only course to be pursued in such circumstances is one of quiet dignity. I feel that all ladies of pride will agree with me in saying I would not care to sport my flag where it was simply tolerated, and could only feel at ease in wearing my colours where they floated triumphant. It was the mistaken zeal of some well-meaning, but rash and thoughtless persons, that created bitter sentiments and unjust acts to spring up and originate in the minds of the many, that a proper self-respect and guarded manner would have avoided. Before the city was invested, all acts of heroism were to be admired, but once it had fallen, the only course should have been a silent, cautious, and resolute endeavour to bear the chains in cold disdain, until the moment should arrive when they might cast aside their shackles and walk forth free. But it would be useless to advise the almost frenzied citizens of New Orleans; and often when the commanding general was driving with all the state of office in his equipage, followed by twelve armed cavalry, he would see a Confederate fan flirted before him, or perhaps catch the glimpse of a head with a Confederate rosette, as it hastily withdrew from a window on his approach.

In vain were menaces of vengeance ; the Confederate emblems were everywhere seen, and sported even by the French, British, and Spanish officers. The Spanish man-of-war generally was crowded during the evening ; and the commander, who was a most splendid performer on the piano, generally regaled the assemblies with Confederate music during the intervals of the dance ; and the summer evenings passed off gaily in this manner, for those who remained in the city.

Though Lincoln's emancipation proclamation had not been published, the negroes arrived in vast numbers every day in the city, as they heard their deliverers were come, and soon the plantations in the vicinity of New Orleans were depopulated, not through any will of their own, but by the violence of the Yankee soldiery they were forced to leave their comfortable quarters, and take lodgings at the Custom House, where, being closely confined and treated to rations from the refuse of the soldiers, they became sick, and daily the remains of those who died were borne off in waggons to the commons, were a hole was dug in the damp earth, into which their bodies were rudely pitched and left to decay. Hundreds in this manner died and were buried; and when, half-starved and almost mad, they, in their moments of recreation, wandered through the streets with no kind glance to meet theirs, sadly they sighed for their comfortable cabins, and the green bright fields, where the breath of heaven fanned their cheeks, when the day's labour was ended. Gladly would they have returned, but alas ! the spot once so dear to them was deserted, and the masters' or mistresses' kind smile would greet them never again.

Do we blame you, ye misguided beings, for what ye *were* and *are?* No. Our hearts bleed for you, victims that you are to the lying hypocrisy that led you from all that could render your lives pleasant; and ten thousand curses rest upon your murderers, who tore you from the arms of repose and happiness, only that they might see your bones bleaching upon the earth.

"Vengeance is mine saith the Lord." Ay! with blood shall blood be paid. Not alone were they tempted to leave their homes, ay, forced, but they were advised, like the Israelites of old, to "spoil the Egyptians," and daily were heard of ladies who were left without a garment, or one article of dress or jewellery—the most valuable articles were stolen, and the *receivers were the officers* and soldiers of the *United States Army and Navy*. All that could not be confiscated was purloined, and no redress could be had for any grievance whatever.

General Butler at first did not countenance this conduct on the part of the slaves, but General Phelps did, and the former, when the proclamation was issued, became as violent an Abolitionist as the latter, notwithstanding his asserting to Miss de Villerie that he sympathized in no way with the negroes, and his public address to the authorities in Washington, where he ends by quoting from Lord Chatham's celebrated address :—
"I will never consent to so vile an act, and if ye wish to adopt this course, you must find some other instrument to carry out your intentions, for I will never be used as such."

Is it not a pity that the beauty of the concluding remark should be marred for ever by after deeds, and is it not to be regretted that a speech which fills the mind with ideas of a lofty and elevated being should, when compared in contrast to his other and later expressions, leave only the impression that the nobleness of feeling was only borrowed for the occasion, and the address but penned in order to make use of a portion of the eloquence and elegant sentiment of Chatham's when speaking of the employing of Indians against the colonies?

In vain do we attire ourselves in character; if the mask be not raised before the end of the pageant, it must fall from the face at its close, and when morning dawns we appear in our own garb. Once the mask dropped from General Butler's face he did not seek to conceal aught further, and we must admire his boldness and the entire indifference with which he regarded public opinion. The first men of New Orleans and its vicinity were arraigned before this absolute monarch, and for the most trifling offences were sent to Fort Jackson. Mayor Monroe, Dr. Stone, and others of celebrity, were imprisoned there, and now the clergy trembled for their safety, though many of them positively refused to pray for the President of the United States, and were threatened with torture in consequence.

One fact is here worthy of record, and this is, that the Reverend Father Mullen, of St. Patrick's Cathedral, resisted to the last all threats of the General's, and when called before the Commander said, in response to his menace of Fort Jackson, "Sir, I do not fear you in the least; and were you to dare to interfere with me, you would find your ranks of soldiery quickly thinned, as more than two-thirds of your army is composed of *Irish Catholics, and with them their God and Religion is first, and then their country; so touch me at your peril!*"

General Butler, feeling the force as well as truth of the remark, made no further threat, but insisted on the prayer for the Confederacy being dispensed with, to which Father Mullen consented, and on the next Sunday made the following remarks:—"My Beloved Brethren, there are some here to-day who have listened to my voice of instruction from infancy to womanhood and manhood, and others who have but just entered the fold of which I am the shepherd. We have passed through various changes of life, and yet we never dreamed the hour would arrive when the invader would silence our tongues, or close our ears to the dictates of conscience; but it has come, the invader is at our doors, and now we can only pray in silence for that which is dearest and nearest. Beloved Brethren, *I have taught you how to pray, and what to pray, and now do your duty! ! !*"

Comment is unnecessary. On another occasion he was requested by General Butler to officiate at the burial of an officer, and, to the inquiry of whether he would do so or not, he replied, "Most assuredly, with a great deal of pleasure; *it will afford me happiness to bury the whole army!*"

Officers attended the various churches, not from motives of piety, but to act as spies upon the ministers. The places of worship were for a time deserted almost, as the inhabitants refused to bow at the altars of the same God with their cruel and heartless persecutors. But the Houses of God were not long ere they were once again filled with the sad worshippers, who, even in their desolate woe, prayed for their enemies, that they might become changed in heart, and true followers of Him whose last injunction was, "Love ye one another."

CHAPTER XVIII.

"She gave the thirsty, water.
  And dressed the bleeding wound,
And gentle prayer she uttered
  For those who sighed around.

"She cast a look of anguish
  On dying and on dead, ‘
Her lap she made the pillow
  For those who groaned and bled.

"And when the dying soldier
  For one bright gleam did pray,
He blessed this gentle being,
  As his spirit passed away."

ONCE arrived in the Confederacy, Miss de Villerie sought to aid the cause of her people in contributing towards the support of the soldiers, and her first act was at Crystal Springs, Copiah County, Mississippi. Madame de Breuil and herself, on entering Rebeldom, proposed remaining at the first village which would promise any degree of comfort, until they should be joined by Judge de Breuil, who had gone to Richmond. Learning that Crystal Springs was a quiet, beautifully-situated retreat, and free from soldiery, they determined to await the Judge there, and, accordingly, they engaged rooms at a cleanly-looking mansion in view of the railroad, and

X

which gloried in the poetic and floral name of "The May House." The proprietress of this establishment, a Mrs. May, was a lady of about sixty years of age, a thrifty, hard-working dame of the olden time, and one who had constantly "many irons in the fire," as keeping boarders was not her sole means of subsistence, but together with keeping a loom, and sewing for the soldiers, she seemed to coin money. Hers was such a face "as would a home-spun dress adorn," and Miss de Villerie did not refuse to enter the weaving-room where the old lady invited her. After watching for some moments the manner in which the rosy, good-looking rustic lass (a niece of the proprietress) dashed the shuttle to and fro, she sat down at the loom and commenced weaving with even more celerity than the rustic maid. The old lady was quite charmed at the "city gal's" condescension, and vowed she'd make "Elie" (her lubberly bumpkin son, whose name was Elijah) set up to her; "for," she ended, "arter all, when it kums to the pint, I believe the town gals is just as *rashanal* as the country wuns, and it all depends upon their fotchen up."

After having weaved a quarter of a yard, which the old lady pronounced a "nashun site evener than Jemima's," Miss de Villerie was desired to walk out and see the gyardin (garden), and afterwards the chief beauties of each plant, ornamental and useful, were dis-cussed; the old lady pointed out a beautiful hedge of the Cayenne pepper, saying, "I alliz liked um, and them's purty to look at, and mazen healthy, and I'se tried to get a contract from the Government for furnishin the soldiers with bottles of pepper sarss, which would save a heap of sickness 'mongst 'um, but I couldn't git um to do it, and I wan't gwine to make the vinegar and raise the pepper for nothin, so if they want sarss they may pay for it."

Next Miss de Villerie was shown the process of smoking beef, which in the language of *those who understand it* is termed "jerked." The latter, though delightful to the taste *(to those who have strength to masticate it)*, threatens momentarily to demonstrate the definition of its name. Miss de Villerie was next invited to ride with the old lady in a search through the country after homespun, which she intended purchasing to speculate upon, and forthwith they started in a nice little buggy, with one horse, which the dame herself drove.

As they passed through the country, Mrs. May explained to our heroine each object of interest, and drove to the beautiful and truly crystal *spring* from which the village derives its name. In the midst of a lovely pine forest, and at the base of charming hills, it gushes forth, and invites the weary traveller to a drink from its mossy brink.

Miss de Villerie, getting out of the buggy, drew near to the well of nature, and plucking a leaf from a small tree which grew near, formed it into a cup, and dipping it into the water, regaled herself with a draught of pure Adam's ale. After this they re-entered the buggy, and drove to each and every cottage for miles around, and then returned to the May House, when Miss de Villerie recounted her adventures to Madame de Breuil, and dwelt upon the extreme poverty of what is termed the "piney woods" people, and their extreme filth, and almost brute ignorance, concluding her account of them by saying that more intelligence, and more marks of

civilisation might be found amongst the wildest and
most roving tribes of the desert.   But like all countries
where great and intelligent men have existed, there
may also be found their opposites.   Ireland, amidst all
her poverty, has produced some of the greatest lumi-
naries of the world, and in her firmament has sparkled
some of the greatest constellations of the British realm.
Charonea, in Greece, gave to the world one of its greatest historians, and Plutarch is an example of where the
mire produced a gem.   Mississippi produced many
brilliant men, and Kentucky a Jeff Davis, with many
others whose intelligence more than compensate us for
the ignorance of her masses.   However partial we may
be to Mississippi, for having given birth to illustrious
statesmen, we cannot forgive her treatment of Confederate soldiers, nor can we forget that on the retreat
of the army from Tupelo they (the soldiers) were
*charged by the patriotic inhabitants twenty-five cents for a
canteen of water, and ten cents for a glass !*   Think of this,
Mississippians, and ye who boast of your deeds of
patriotism.   " By their works ye shall know them," and
thus do we judge you.   Coming generations shall point
with the finger of scorn to this fact in history, and speak
in trumpet-tones of the self-sacrificing spirit of those
who ministered to the weary soldiers for *filthy lucre*.
In sorrow do we trace the words which record your avari-
ciousness, but *truth* alone we write, and therefore " *let the
galled jade wince*."   Long years after ye are gathered
home, and when even the little mounds that mark your
resting place lie level with the earth around it, these
deeds will be your only mausoleum, to remind us that ye
existed, and more huge this memorial shall be of ye

than the pyramids of Egypt; but ye have erected it yourselves, and it is neither of stone, silver, nor gold, neither of iron nor brass, but of *pinchbeck*, emblematic of your narrow hearts. Sad is it that it should rain "alike on the just and the unjust," and though there certainly were more than "ten just," we could not spare like Him, the rest. Miss de Villerie, who in her own State had witnessed naught but the most ardent endeavours to add to the happiness and comfort of the soldiers, saw with feelings of surprise and indignation their treatment at every place in this State. Famished soldiers ordered on a hasty movement to some point, and having no time for waiting to cook rations, would beg even for a crust of cold bread wherever they stopped, and were invariably refused. Becoming desperate at times, they would scale walls, leap fences, and break down gates to steal a few vegetables, such as turnips or onions, which they would eat raw. Occasionally a soldier more bold than the rest would shoot a chicken, or a turkey, and for this offence be severely punished by the officer in command, whose well-filled stomach left him no room for sympathy with the starving soldiers. On all occasions the officers fared well, as wherever they went the best was at their disposal, but RANK was treated not MERIT.

Miss de Villerie had just returned from Jackson, where she had been for some months, and was now established again at Crystal Springs. One morning towards the close of October Mrs. May, the proprietress, who has already been presented to the reader, came into Miss de Villerie's room, and, seating herself, remarked, "Dr. R—— has jist *bin* to see me, and to ax me to take into my house a sick soldier, but you knows yourself, Miss Villery, I hasn't any room."

"Then, my dear Madame," exclaimed Miss de Villerie, "I trust you will not refuse to take him on this account, as Madame de Breuil and myself will consent to occupy the same chamber, that you may give place to him. I assure you, I would much prefer yielding all claims to comfort, than one of those men should be deprived who has fallen ill for my sake and for yours."

"Wall," replied the old lady, whose features were seemingly carved out of stone, "I'll see him, and, if he ain't too sick, I'll have him fotched over, for he's lying now in the depôt, and they talk 'bout takin him to the hospital at Magnolia," and so saying she left the room, and donning her sun-bonnet, left the house.

In a few moments she returned, and said, "I'm not gwine to take him, for he's most dead anyhow ; *and, besides, he ain't got any money,* and I'm too old to have the trouble of him, and ther's plenty folks in the neighbourhood sides me."

This was quite true, and so thought Miss de Villerie ; but she replied, "My good Madame, it should be no reason that, because others act unkindly and uncharitably, we should follow their example ; by no means, and I would much prefer your taking this man, as his being so ill is a greater call upon our charity. I beg you will do this, and I will endeavour to make him as little trouble as possible to yourself and servants, by waiting on him myself; and, if money be the object with you, I will pay you."

"No, money hain't the reason," the old dame responded "but I don't like sick folks in the house."

"Mrs. May," said our heroine, "did I understand you to say that this man is in the depôt?"

"Yes, and it's orful cold too thar, and it's jist bloin a perfect harricane out doors. I'm sorry, but, Miss Villery, I can't take him."

Miss de Villerie arose, and, remarking to Madame de Breuil that she would go and see what she could do for him, and at the same time she took a couple of letters for the mail, as she wished this to serve as an excuse for going to the depôt, the post-office being at this place, and, owing to the absence of most of the gentlemen, the ladies now crowded the depôt.

Entering the depôt, Miss de Villerie deposited her letters in the box, and then, casting a glance around the room, where several of the villagers were assembled, she perceived the sick man lying on a hard bench, and seemingly near dying. From his emaciated form, sunken cheeks, and hollow eyes, even the careless observer would know that he could not live many hours, and that the flickering light of life was about being extinguished for ever. Seated in the same room were the cold heartless beings who had refused him shelter, and talking, laughing, smoking, and chewing, they sat there, viewing with stolid indifference a fellow-creature's suffering and last hours.

Miss de Villerie, who was exasperated almost beyond bounds at the brutal conduct of these men, turned towards the most respectable in appearance of the group, and asked, in a clear and imperative voice, "Is this the man you intend sending to the Magnolia Hospital?"

"Yes, Madame," responded the gentleman addressed.

"What, *this* man?" she said; "why he does not

seem scarcely to have life in him, and how do you imagine he will be able to make such a trip? Is there no person in Crystal Springs that will give him shelter until he is able to travel? To send him now, in his weak state, and in such cold weather, will be murder. May I ask how came he here?"

The dying man turned upon her his languid eyes, and opening them to their fullest extent, as it were, to gaze in wonder at this being who dared speak in his defence, said, "Lady, they would not have treated me so if I had had money; but," he added, "I did have a little, about $160, which my captain keeps for me, but now it is too late, it would not do me much good if I even had it."

"Money!" exclaimed our heroine; "what do you want with money? *Should not every man's money be the soldiers' money*, who have gone forth to defend their homes from the enemy, who spill their heart's blood for their country's safety, and expose themselves to all kinds of danger for the public defence? Money, indeed, my poor man; *you are entitled to every man's money, and none save brutes could refuse you.* Protecting these people and their property has brought you to this, and while such lazy louts as are here assembled have been lolling on downy couches, eating and drinking of the best, you, poor man, were lying on the cold, damp earth, with your musket clasped close, even in your sleep, to your breast, that you might be ready for the foe at any moment; and now," she said, turning to those around her, "what must you think of yourselves, in a village of plenty, where no troops are quartered, that you refuse even to grant this man, *this soldier*, a roof to shield him from the inclement weather, and a bed whereon to die? To term you savages and Hottentots would be to pay you a high compliment. I am houseless myself, or I would take you, my poor man," she said, addressing him. "I have already proffered my room, if the person with whom I am boarding will take you, and, if there is any one to give you shelter, I will pay them."

"Are you a Mississippian?" inquired the person first addressed by Miss de Villerie.

"Mississippian!" she almost thundered out, "*Mississippian!* Oh! no, Sir. I would scorn the name; and if I had been so unfortunate as to have been born here, I would, after *this example of their patriotism*, and generous, high-souled, and charitable conduct, disown for ever all knowledge of such a State."

Miss de Villerie left the room, and soon after returning to the depôt with some brandy and port-wine for the invalid, found that the people, brought to a sense of their duty by her bold and stern remarks, had lifted him on a mattress and taken him to the hotel on the opposite side of the rail-road, then placing him in bed, in the most comfortable room in the house, they sought by their attention to efface the unfavourable impression, and to gain a charitable reputation. Alas! the cloven foot had been displayed, and no arrangement of the drapery around the form of the hideous figure could disguise or erase the vision of its *natural* deformity. However, Miss de Villerie was delighted to think her conduct had been the means of even gaining for one human being repose in the last sad moments of his pilgrimage here, and proceeding to the hotel, she placed brandy, port wine, and tea in the hands of the proprietor of the house, to be used for the patient, and then made a search through the village for some one who would sell her a chicken at any price, to make soup for the invalid. She was fortunate enough to meet with a German woman who was kind enough to let her have one for 50 cents (at this time a most reasonable price) and paying her for it, had it sent to the May House, where she had a soup prepared, and took it herself to Stubbs' Hotel, where the sick man was quartered. Alas! it was almost too late for attentions, and he was too weak to eat the chicken, but sipped a few mouthfuls of soup from the spoon, which Miss de Villerie held to his lips.

After remaining with him until late that night, Miss de Villerie returned to her hotel, at the same time extracting a promise from several men that they would remain for the rest of the night, and administer the medicine which the physician had ordered for him.

Returning early the next morning, Miss de Villerie *found the medicine on the mantel-piece, the room deserted,* and the poor soldier evidently dying fast. She had said and done all she could; her vocabulary of invectives was exhausted the day previous, so, seating herself by the bedside, after she had wet his parched lips with brandy and water, she took the soldier's hand in her own, and while the tears hung upon her fringed lids, endeavoured to discover his name and family, that she might apprise them of his death.

The day previous, he could speak distinctly, but now it was with difficulty she could make out what he said. At last she learned all that was necessary, his name, place of residence, and his mother's address, and also that he was the son of a widow—whose husband was an Episcopalian minister in Tennessee. Miss de Villerie stayed with him until dinner hour; when, returning with Madame de Breuil (who had offered to watch the poor man during the next night), they found that his spirit had fled from the coldness and sorrow of earth to its home in Heaven, where, we trust, that in the glory and happiness there he is amply repaid for his suffering here below.

The tears fell fast over the form of the poor soldier; *and I will do the town of Crystal Springs the justice to say that it did wash the body, and give it a clean shirt, as well as bestow a few feet of earth on the edge of the public road (land belonging to the government), and—to their honour be it said for ever—they did bury him.*

" *Tennesseeans, remember your debt to Mississippians, you owe them one day's lodging for a soldier, and the price of six feet of public earth. I, Natalie de Villerie, am witness to it,*" said our heroine, as she sadly walked into the house from the gallery where she had remained gazing at the waggon which contained all that was mortal of a widow's hope.

That night, Miss de Villerie seated herself to pen a letter to the bereaved mother, and she endeavoured to send balm for the wound which she knew the information would inflict, by stating the *kind* treatment her son had received in his last hours; and though she felt she was doing a foul injustice to the human race by slandering the inhabitants of Crystal Springs so greatly as to call them *kind*, Miss de Villerie did state that *her son had received every attention in the power* of the people of

Crystal Springs. At the same time she enclosed a lock of his hair, which she caused to be cut off, reserving another in case the first letter should not reach its destination ; his canteen was the only souvenir of him that she could obtain, and she sent this to the express office at Vicksburg, to be forwarded to his mother, but was told there was no express farther than to Okolona.

In a few weeks she received a response from the mother, a beautiful and grateful epistle, penned by the family physician, and in heart-inspired tones it breathed of gratitude.

But now that we have broached this subject, we must not forget to give to the public the name of the chief actor in this scene. The young man whose melancholy end we have just recorded, was on his way on board the cars, with his company, to Camp Moore. The train being very much crowded, and having stopped for a few moments at this station, he got out to walk about, and when the whistle sounded, and the cars started, he endeavoured to get on again, but was pushed off by the crowd, and left behind.

Wandering around the village, he was met by a man living in the neighbourhood, who, though not the representative of a Southern planter, was a very rich person, and owned a number of slaves. He lived in the vicinity of the village, and was considered the wealthiest person in the neighbourhood. This day he happened to be in town, and meeting with the soldier, asked him to accompany him home in his buggy, and remain until he got well, which invitation the poor fellow gladly and thankfully accepted.

In a few days after his arrival, Mr. Robinson (for

such is the person's name) went off to some place, most probably to Jackson, where he intended remaining some days. Mrs. Robinson, finding the man was becoming worse instead of better, and considering him very troublesome, determined to send for the village doctor, with the view of obtaining an order for his removal to the hospital. She having accomplished this, on a cold and blustering day in October, the man was told by Mrs. Robinson that she had ordered the buggy, and that the driver would take him to the depôt, whence he could go to the Magnolia Hospital. The poor man arose from his bed, the picture of death, and started out into the cold air, *less cold than the heart that turned him forth.* Two days after, God released him from his pain, and we trust He may forgive the unkindness of those into whose hands he fell.

Had this woman been a person who had never been a mother there might possibly be an excuse for such conduct, but in one who had herself lost a son a few months before on the battle-field, and who was told that it was not certain *where* or *how* he died, it cannot be overlooked. Lost to all feeling must that mother be who can gaze upon the sufferings, in any form, of the child of another and not feel that perhaps *her own* may yet be in the same condition, *and need a friend.* Base, beyond conception, are those who can view the necessities and miseries of their fellow-beings and not seek to relieve them. But " Vengeance is mine, saith the Lord, I will repay." The soldier was buried on the evening of the last day of October, 1862, and the next day Miss de Villerie, according to the custom in New Orleans on All Saints' Day, gathered a few blossoms and, accompanied by a young lady of the village, strewed them over the grave of the humble dead.   Seven other soldiers were sleeping beneath the brown hillocks, and Miss de Villerie was alike thoughtful of them as she strewed the blossoms around.   Kneeling at the head of each grave, she breathed a fervent prayer to the One who alone can give either celestial or terrestial peace, and transcendently beautiful was the tableau, as with hands clasped, and eyes raised to heaven, she knelt in holy prayer.   The last rays of the setting sun, as it glinted through the autumn foliage, fell upon her; and it seemed to enfold her in its last embrace, and to cast a halo around her which nought save a celestial being could wear.   She arose from her knees as the last rays of the sunlight died in the West, and, as she turned to leave the spot, she raised her hand, and making the sign of the cross in the air above the eight sleeping forms, thus consecrated their resting-place, and departed for home.

Judge de Breuil arrived at Crystal Springs a few weeks after, and Madame de Breuil and Miss de Villerie left *without regret* the village which, possessing all the natural characteristics of beautiful scenery, will be always engraven on her memory as the most frightful of all spots on earth, from the unpleasant circumstances above-mentioned.

Miss de Villerie, on arriving in the capital, joined at once the association for contributing towards the wants of the soldiers, and in her dress of Confederate grey she might be seen every morning at the rooms of the various societies, aiding with money and counsel to the utmost of her power.   Miss de Villerie was charmed with the patriotic spirit of the ladies of Richmond and Virginia generally, and, in her letter to her friends in New Orleans, spoke of their conduct in the most glowing terms. And well the maidens of Virginia deserved her admiration, for more faithfully than the vestals of Rome did they tend the sacred fire of patriotism, and kept it blazing brightly amidst the dim clouds of war. South Carolina's women are also worthy of undying praise, and many a wearied soldier will long remember the bright faces and willing hands of those he met at the " Soldiers' Rests " (established by the side of the railroad, tended by ladies and their servants), and the generous attention received there.

The scene presented on the arrival of the different trains at the various stations were interesting to the beholders, as, laden with provisions, the ladies flocked towards the cars bearing abundance of fruit and delicacies, as well as the more substantial articles of diet —viz., bread, and meats cooked in every manner, made doubly delicious by being bestowed by the fair and lovely women of the South. On every hand they administered aid to the weary soldiers, and in filling canteens with water and milk, and in distributing loaves of bread, these ladies would stand for hours seemingly unwearied, smiling and speaking words of encouragement and good counsel to the rough and stern-looking soldiers, who, in their dusty attire, formed a strong contrast to the lovely women and girls by whom they were served. Much lighter felt the knapsack of the trudging infantry man as he turned from one of these "Rests," and stouter grew his heart when he felt he was not fighting uncared-for, and that kind hearts and gentle hands were ready to nurse him should disease lay low his form or render him unfit for service.

Willingly, devotedly, worked the women of the South for the promotion of the Confederate cause, and day and night in untiring labour were their fair hands employed in knitting, sewing, and mending for the army, and the most expensive articles of dress were sacrificed to provide comfortable apparel. Elegant India shawls were cut up and made shirts of, while silk, satin, and merino dresses were sacrificed in the same manner. Carpets were dispensed with in every mansion, and when army blankets became scarce, these were formed into blankets for the soldiers. Everything that could be found about the homes and in the apartments of the rich, were bestowed at once upon the public altar for the use of the country as soon as its value was known to the possessor. Few were the cases in which those who could bestow refused, and when such were met with, and the avaricious being who refused was known, the Government, like a sensible mother, said to the base and ignoble child, " Your brothers and sisters have divided their portion with you, and now I shall force you (since fair means have proven ineffectual) to share with them," and accordingly she acted.

How proud, how gratified, must those persons be who generously came forward when the tocsin first sounded and placed their all at stake for the country ! How happy they must feel to think they did not wait, like many others, to have it all swept from them, and by the foe; and who, in their ruined state, are now left to wander homeless, without the *thanks* or eulogy those *will* ever receive who spring to the assistance of their treasury at the first cry of alarm! In vain those selfish individuals looked forward to peace, and in vain they counted their rich herds and flocks, hoping that the storm of war would pass over their heads, and leave them possessed of their treasure. "All is vanity," saith the preacher, and these beings proved the truth of the proverb. *Sans remorse*, we have seen the torch applied to hundreds—ay, thousands, of cotton-bales which were heaped in the gin-houses of these national thieves, and with delight we witnessed the ruin of those miserable narrow-minded specimens of the human race, that were ever ready, for avarice' sake, to plant the poignard in the heart of patriotism. Yes, I have seen these "Gods of their idolatry cast to the earth."

> "And the widows of Ashur were loud in their wail,
> And the idols were broke in the temple of Baal."

Not less, kind reader, were the widowers; and when the moment shall dawn wherein our country shall have properly chastised these worshippers of false gods, let us hope that they will view, with different ideas, their former misguided actions, and in the freedom of their country kneel with us in the worship of the true *God*, and of liberty.

CHAPTER XIX.

"What is it that you would impart to me?
If it be aught toward the general good,
Set honor in one eye, and death in the other,
And I will look on both indifferently:
For let the gods so speed me, as I love
The name of honour more than I fear death."

"Let the galled jade wince."

"Madam, are you willing to undertake this business?" said General J——, to a lady who ;had just entered his tent, escorted there by one of the General's staff officers.

"Most assuredly, General," she replied! "Do I look like one that would fear the consequences, if resolved upon an act?"

"Then, Madam, I feel I can safely entrust you with this despatch," he said, as he handed to her a folded paper, "and trust to hear of your successful entrance into L——, and your safe exit once your mission be ended. Please give strict attention, Madam, to directions in regard to delivery. On entering L——, go at once to the —— House, and once there, attire yourself in gray, when you will enter the drawing-room, and seat yourself immediately in front of the door, holding in your hand a book, and to appearance be reading attentively. There will enter a person dressed in citizen's clothing, who will at once advance and call you by name, and address you in the familiar style of an old acquaintance. He will wear a slouched felt hat, and over his left eyebrow you will perceive a deep scar. You will deliver to him, without delay, the paper; and now, dear Madam, this accomplished, I shall hope for the pleasure of meeting you again."

The lady arose, and bowing to the General, was escorted to her carriage, and was soon on her way to L——.

On arriving in L——, she drove as directed to the —— House. She soon procured a room, and entering made a hasty toilette, and descended to the drawing-room. There she sat for hours, and looked and looked in vain for the person to whom she was to deliver the despatches. She knew not at what moment she would be arrested, and probably searched, as she had been suspected on a former visit to the place as a spy. She at last (when day commenced to close, and he had not made his appearance) resolved to retire to her chamber, feeling fatigued and annoyed. Once in her apartment, she began to think of some means of secreting the despatch, as she feared keeping it about her person. In her fear no place seemed safe, and after thinking of several modes of concealing it, decided on placing it under the carpet. She was just in the act of stooping down to raise the carpet, when a rap at the door startled her, and the blood rushed from her heart in terror. She unlocked her door, however, and to her amazement she received from the waiter the card of a *Federal officer*. Though it was one whom she had some acquaintance with, and who had done her several acts of kindness in his official capacity, she knew not at this moment to what cause she should attribute his visit. In her confusion she knew not what to do with the paper, fearing that should she leave it in the room, it might be found there (should they have it searched during her absence); having no time to conceal it with any certainty of safety, and presuming that at the very moment, probably, she would not have it ready to deliver when the person would call; resolving, however, to dare the worst, she placed it in her pocket, and proceeded to the drawing-room.

The cordial manner of the officer soon placed her at ease. A few moments passed in agreeable converse, when Colonel D——, said,

"With your permission, I shall be most happy to present to you my friends General G——d and Major N——n."

With a feeling of uneasiness Miss C—— consented, saying "I shall be most happy," when excusing himself, he withdrew, and returned in a few moments with two gentlemen, whom he introduced to her.

She conversed for an hour or more quite affably, and then being asked to sing and play, arose, and seated herself at the piano, thus placing her back towards the door. She struck the chords nervously, and was so excited she could scarcely command her voice to sing. She had not been long thus, however, when the door opened, and turning to see who had entered, she beheld the person to whom the despatch was to be delivered. Recognizing her at once, he came forward, saying,—

"I am pleased to see you again, Miss C——; when I left you about three hours since, I went to my aunts, and informed them of your arrival; they will be down to see you in the morning."

Surprised at his cool manner, she said, "I shall be pleased to see your aunt and Cousin Mattie."

"May I request you to continue your musical entertainment of your friends," he rejoined; "do not permit my entrance to interrupt your performance," and leaning on the piano, he said, "By-the-way have you written, or rather copied those words of 'Lorena,' which you promised me this morning?"

Taking the hint, she replied, as she drew forth the despatch, and threw it on the piano, "Yes Charles, I scribbled them off this morning. I doubt if you can read them, but I assure you you may make the most of this copy, as I dislike of all things copying."

Taking up the paper, he said, with nonchalance, as he placed it in his vest-pocket, "Thanks, many thanks," and after waiting some fifteen minutes, said, "I have an engagement with a party of gentlemen, and if you will excuse me, will go and keep it, and return in one hour hence."

"*Au revoir*, then," she answered; "but remember, if later than an hour hence, you will not find me in the parlour, and I shall ask you to excuse my receiving you until to-morrow."

"I shall return in an hour," and bowing to the gentlemen, he left the room.

Feeling free now that the despatch was out of her possession, she soon excused herself on the plea of fatigue to the officers, and left the room, after having summoned a servant, in the presence of the officers, to whom she said,—

"You will say to a gentleman who will ask for me this evening, that I am quite indisposed, and will see him in the morning."

Once alone in her apartment, and the paper no longer in her possession, she breathed a sigh of relief, and sought her couch to seek repose, for the first time since she had undertaken the mission. Of course, *friend Charles* did not return, and it is more than probable these patriots had met for the first and last time on this side of the grave.

Miss C—— determined she would not leave the city with a less important object than she entered, so remained several days, until learning that the bridge between the Federal and Confederate lines had been destroyed, to prevent an attack on the city, which it was rumoured was contemplated by General M—— that night, she resolved to *cross the lines*, and thus give warning to the Confederates.

She sought her friend, the Federal officer, and stated that it was absolutely necessary she should reach home in two days, and implored him to obtain her a pass.

"Are you aware, Miss C——, that there is no exit in the direction you wish to go, the bridge having been destroyed?"

"I am aware of that, Colonel D——. Only obtain a pass for me to leave, I will find the means to cross the bridge."

"Why, my dear lady, nought remains save the beams, the flooring has been removed ; and surely you would not venture upon the beams without further support."

"Obtain the pass, Colonel, and you will see whether I will or not."

"Then be it as you desire, fair lady," and, leaving the apartment, soon returned with the desired pass.

"Thanks, Colonel, thanks; I value this pass more than my life."

Miss C—— left the city in a few hours, *led over the beams of the bridge by a Federal soldier!* By this fearless act she saved the destruction of General M—— and his whole force.

On arriving in the Confederacy, she at once proceeded to the head-quarters of General J——. It is needless to say that he received her kindly, and once again placed in her hands despatches. These were of much greater importance than the former, and were to be borne several hundred miles. They were written upon two small slips of paper. One of these slips of paper she rolled tightly, and placed in the top of a quill tooth-pick; the other she folded and placed conveniently, that, at a moment's warning, she might place it in her mouth. She had many miles to travel, and, seating herself in a rude conveyance, a carry-all (on the style of an army ambulance), she started upon her hazardous expedition. Her driver was a negro man, and, with some degree of doubt, she had resolved to go with him. They drove all the first day through a lonely plain, and at night stopped at a plantation. Early on the next morning they began their journey, and late in the evening came upon the head-quarters of General R——, situated on the river R——; and some twenty miles beyond this point it was necessary she should cross the river, and this would place her within the Federal lines. As she stopped in front of the tent (or rather as the conveyance stopped) she bade the negro to summon a soldier, and ask him to request the General to step to the carriage (we will thus dignify it), that a lady wished to speak with him. A soldier advancing, he and the driver entered the General's tent, and in a few moments re-appeared with the General, who walked at once up to the carriage, and, politely bowing to Miss C——, re-marked, " Madame, can I serve you?"

" You can, Sir, if you desire."

" In what manner, Madame ? "

" I wish to cross the river some twenty miles distant from here, and to enter the Federal lines. Will you be so kind as to furnish me with a pass?"

" Most assuredly *not*, Madame. I would not permit at this moment a colonel of our army to do so. I regret it, Madame ; but I cannot comply with your request."

" *You will let me pass*, General," she said, smiling, as, stooping down, she drew off her shoe, " *and in less than ten minutes.*"

" Not if I know myself," he rejoined.

Raising the shoe, she handed it to him, at the same time saying, " General, does this article look *imperative*, commanding, authoritative, or anything in that style ?"

He answered her, though his risibles were much affected, " Madame, there was a time in my life that the sight of a *slipper* might awe me, but I am past that age."

" Not yet, General," she said; " you are still under dominion of sole leather."

Pressing the heel of the shoe, the sole flew apart,

and therein lay a small strip of paper, which, taking out of its bed, she handed to the General.

He glanced at it, and said, "I have nothing further to say, Madame. You shall have a pass."

In less than ten minutes it was in her possession, and she was on her way. It became quite dark as she reached the river, and in a dense swamp, with the rain pouring in torrents, she was forced to abandon further travel. Imagine the scene, gentle ladies, in your quiet homes. Out in a lonely marsh, the rain falling, thunder rolling, lightning flashing, the terrified birds screaming in the midnight air, with venomous reptiles around you, and a burly negro, dark as Erebus, as your sole companion. Imagine yourselves thus, and seated back in the corner of a dilapidated vehicle, with your hand grasping a revolver, and your thumb upon the trigger, not daring to close your eyes ; the negro a stranger to you, and fearing lest he should prove less gentle or merciful than the elements. If you have, dear ladies, imagination to picture this to yourselves, you can form some idea of what one of your own sex suffered in her character of Confederate emissary.

The negro *was true to his trust,* and in this act might have put to the blush many a free man, with fair face, but with a *black* heart. Here was *beauty, youth,* and *money,* all within the negro's reach ; yet, like "an honest man, the noblest work of God," he laid him down to rest, with the warring elements as his lullaby, and when morning's roseate stole upon the world once more, he arose, and they proceeded on their journey. God bless you, noble man ! You are a bright example of the " genus homo." Yes, erring, sinful man ! As

you read this does it not *strike home*? Ponder upon it,
ye who have injured the brightest beings! Ponder
upon it, ye who have had charge of the youthful
maiden, and have destroyed her! Ponder upon it,
ye who have blighted homes, and sent the gray-haired
sire to his grave with a broken heart! Ponder upon
it, ye who have ruthlessly torn from her home the
young and fair, and have then cast her from you to
sink in the mire of destitution and disgrace! Yes, go
think of it, and compare your heart with that of this
dark son of Afric, and ask yourselves whose crown
should be the brightest in that home to which we are
all passing, slowly but surely, and where He who sees
all hearts shall judge. There, indeed, will appear distinction, not of *skin*, but *soul*. Oh! could we but
remove the silver veil, so dazzling, from the faces of
some we deem so fair, would not we, indeed, find revealed the loathsome visage of a Mokenna?

Miss C—— soon arrived at the point from which she
would be forced to continue her journey alone, as the
negro could not venture further. She bade adieu to
her faithful attendant, and after having purchased a
mule and a buggy, seated herself in it, and was soon on
the other side of the river, on what is termed neutral
ground—being within Federal authority at one time
and Confederate at other, as well as being infested with
guerilla bands, making it dangerous for any one to
venture within the limits.

On the side to which Miss C—— crossed, ran a road,
in a direct line of a mile and a half, through a dense
swamp, bordered with oak and cypress, whose sombre
forms were rendered still more so by the Spanish moss

which drooped in festoons from the boughs; the under-brush was impenetrable, while weeds and coarse marshy plants grew in profusion ; the decaying trunks of trees formed asylums for the serpents which the traveller might observe trailing across the road, or coiling them-selves around the huge bodies of giant lords of the forest.

Miss C—— shuddered as she entered upon this scene, but felt that if it were only these reptiles to fear she could brave them undaunted; she grew faint as she thought of the human eyes that might be staring upon her, whose glance was more deadly than the serpents'. She summoned all her courage, and rising in her seat, struck the mule with the hickory-rod (in lieu of a whip), and plying it well, she almost flew past this mile of horrors, and soon entered upon a less dangerous part of the country.

Warm, weary, and soiled with dust and mud, she arrived in the suburbs of M——, and at the station where a train every half-hour conveyed the passengers into the city. She was just about congratulating her-self upon the success of her journey, when, in front of the depôt in M——, two officers stepped up to the train, and just as she was descending from the car, one of them accosted her, saying, " Miss C——, I presume ? "

" Yes, Sir."

" I regret exceedingly, then, that I am under the painful orders to arrest you."

The passengers becoming quite excited at this, an old lady ran forward, and placing her arms around Miss C——, said, " Oh, dear, what have you done, young lady ? I trust you have not been guilty of any crime."

Miss C—— answered in dignified tones, "Pray do not be alarmed, dear madame, I have committed no crime, nor have I offended in any manner against the ten commandments; permit this gentleman to perform his duty. I am quite ready," she said, " to accompany you, Sir, and may I ask upon what charge I am arrested ? "

" I regret to state I am not fully informed, but think it is simply on suspicion as a *spy*. We will go to the ladies' waiting room of the depôt, madame, where I will leave you in the charge of a couple of soldiers, until such time as I can summon some ladies to search you."

She bowed, and withdrawing from the crowd they were soon in the apartment mentioned. Calling a couple of soldiers, he said, " You will guard this lady until my return, and do not for a moment. withdraw your eyes from her; pardon me, lady, such is their duty ; " and taking up her cabasse, he said, "I will keep this safe for you, and hope, for your own sake, you may prove innocent of any charge against you."

Miss C——, now left alone with her guards, proceeded to scan their appearance. Their faces were ruddy and smiling, and bespoke them honest plain fellows. She entered into conversation with them at once, and turned the subject upon home and friends. She could perceive their eyes fill as they spoke of loved ones there, and, knowing she had not a moment's time to spare, said, when she felt their hearts were filled with tender memories, "Just see that great boy in front of the door imposing on that little urchin—is it not shameful?" They turned, as quick as a flash of lightning the tooth-pick was in the grate by which they were standing; and when they turned their eyes upon her, she was quietly poking the fire.

One despatch still remained, and what to do with it she knew not—to destroy both she could not bear the thought of it, and after undergoing so many difficulties in reaching this point. Time was flying, their eyes were upon her, and she could not, dare not, place her hand in her pocket, to pull out her purse (in which the other despatch lay) and open it before them. She glanced at every object, did everything to divert their attention, and at last saw an old fruiterer passing the door. She turned to the soldiers, and said, " I am very thirsty, and hungry as well, would you not let me have some apples ? You, do not object to my purchasing, do you ? "

" Certainly not, lady."

" Then call the man ; " at the same time drawing forth her purse and emptying the contents into the palm of her hand.

Miss C—— paid for the apples, and saying " Help yourselves, my good men," returned the money to her purse, keeping the despatch in her hand. Peeling an apple, she cut a small piece, and placed it with the despatch in her mouth ; and, laughing at the time, pretended she was quite choked, and coughed violently, thus finding an excuse to place her finger in her mouth, and arranged the despatch between her cheek and gum. She now felt *safe*; and it was with an air of indifference she viewed the return of the officer, in a few minutes after, and the *ladies*, with whom he entered.

The officer left the females to perform the work, and withdrew. Miss C—— stood viewing them contemptuously, as they undressed her, and searched each article of clothing—ripping open hems, letting out tucks, and tearing away the linings of her garments. Satisfied with this, they next proceeded to take down and comb out her hair, apologizing for this last act, Miss C—— not even condescending to acknowledge it.   She was quite determined they should do their work alone, and stood quite nonchalant as they undressed and re-arranged her toilet.   When finished, her national-paid *femme des chambres*, left the room mortified, not even having claimed the perquisites of the office.

The officer now entered, and said, "Madam, you are quite at liberty, and I will take pleasure in placing my carriage at your disposal to proceed to the hotel."

Miss C—— thanking him, accepted his polite offer, and was soon in her apartment at *the* hotel.   *One* despatch reached its destination, when she returned once again into the Confederacy.

Miss C—— was untiring in her efforts to promote the interests of her country, and Louisiana and Tennessee are as much indebted to her as Virginia to Miss Belle Boyd (the present Mrs. Hardinge).   The latter's career, though more brilliant and dashing, is not more praise-worthy.   Miss Clayton and Miss B—— were kindred spirits.   The former was to General T—— in Louisiana what Miss Boyd was to Stonewall Jackson in Virginia. Both risked life and liberty for the Southern cause. Miss Boyd's patriotism gushed forth like the mountain torrent; Miss Clayton's, like a hidden spring in the desert—each alike destined to empty in the sea of glory.

CHAPTER XX.

"He is bending his brow o'er some plan
For the hospital service ; wise, skilful, humane.
The officer standing beside him is fain
To refer to the angel-solicitous care
Of the sisters of charity ; one he declares
To be known thro' the camp as a seraph of grace,
He has seen, all have seen her, indeed, in each place
Where suffering is seen, silent, active—the
⠀⠀⠀Sœur ————
Sœur ———— how do you call her ?

⠀⠀⠀⠀⠀⠀⠀⠀⠀⠀"Ay, truly of her
I have heard much ! the General, musing, replied ;
And we owe her already (unless rumour lies)
The lives of not few of our bravest. You mean—
Ay, how do you call her ?————the Sœur Seraphine.
(Is it not so ?) I rarely forget names once heard,
Yes, the Sœur Seraphine. Her I meant."

⠀⠀⠀⠀⠀⠀⠀⠀⠀⠀⠀"On my word
I have much wish'd to see her, something more than
The grace of an angel. I mean an acute, human mind,
Ingenious, constructive, intelligent. Find,
And, if possible, let her come to me. We shall,
I think, aid each other."

TOWARDS one of the hospitals in Richmond was borne
a litter, upon which a wounded Federal officer was
lying. No groan escaped him, though his pallid face
bespoke intense suffering. His brow, over which his
dark brown hair swept, was bathed in blood.

"This way, if you please," said a lady, as they entered the door of the hospital. "You may place this gentleman in Sœur Secessia's Ward, all the others are thronged, at any rate she has the best accommodation for him, and I think he may be put in her own room, as she is absent at the lower hospital, where she will be "for a week yet."

They gently bore the litter towards the room, as directed, and entering they placed him upon the pure white couch.. The lady sent an attendant to summon the surgeon, and placed bands and lint convenient for his use when he should arrive. The surgeon soon entered, and prepared to examine the wounds. Anxiously the lady awaited to learn his opinion, and when he whispered softly, "Poor young gentleman, his race is almost run; not many hours ere Death shall claim him," she clasped her hands, and bowing her head, prayed for his soul's rest in that clime where no evil cometh, and her tears fell fast for those to whom he should return no more.

"You will please summon Sœur Secessia to attend this patient," the Doctor said; "she is a fitting nurse, and well prepared to prepare one for such a journey as he is soon to enter upon."

"I am sorry to say she is at the upper hospital, Doctor, but if you will call and say to her as much, she will, I know, return here at once. She felt that the invalids at the other hospital were neglected, and went there to remain a week; but I am certain she will not refuse to return here if requested by you to do so."

"I will speak with her, then," he said, and bowing, left the apartment.

Sœur Secessia was the favourite nurse amongst all

the invalids of the various hospitals which she in turn attended. Like a new star, she beamed in the clouded firmament of the sick and suffering. She was welcome everywhere, and in her floating black serge garb, and religieuse cap, she glided through the chamber, tending the sick, speaking words of hope and comfort to the sorrowful, praying with the despairing, kneeling beside the couch of the dying, and placing wreaths on the brow of the dead. The small apartment which was allotted to her was now occupied by the wounded Federal officer. The couch upon which she sometimes reclined when overpowered by fatigue, was simple in its style, and covered with snowy dimity, spoke of purity. The room was devoid of all luxury, as a hermit's cell. One large window descending to the floor, was curtained with the same material as the couch. Graceful wreaths of woodbine and wild yellow jessamine looped back the drapery from the casement, permitting balmy breezes to float through the room. A crucifix twined with garlands of sweet briar and honeysuckle, was suspended over the mantelshelf, while two vases filled with myrtle and orange blossoms, completed the ornamental part. Three cane-seat chairs and a lavabo, and you have a list of the furniture.

The officer lay in this chamber, seemingly unconscious, nor did he move even when the door softly opened, and a form glided to his bedside. His face was covered, and turned from her, but one of his hands lay outside. Taking it in her own she felt the pulse, and then summoning a domestic, ordered a basin of ice-water and lavender. Turning up the cuffs of her habit, she prepared to bathe his temples, and softly drew the

z

cover from the face, when the officer, opening his eyes, turned them upon her. She cast her eyes down, as he rested his gaze searchingly on her face, and she said, quietly,

"Pardon me, Sir, I should not have disturbed you, but I was only going to lave your brow."

"*Can it be?*" he faintly murmured, "or am I but dreaming, and yet it is the voice."

Sœur Secessia raised her eyes, and they rested full upon his face. She grew pale, and wildly crying, "Clarence, Clarence," she threw herself on her knees beside the couch, saying, "At last we have met. Oh, God, that it should be thus ordained."

The wounded officer, with all the energy of an almost dying struggle, raised himself, and bending over the side of the couch, clasped his arms around the kneeling form, as he said,

"Yes, darling Natalie, we have met, and *I* to release you from your promise in a few short hours; tell me, oh tell me, ere I die, that in heart you have been true to me, and reveal the reason for this strange apparel."

While sobs choked the utterance, she answered,

"Clarence, beloved, when I had strength to sacrifice you on the altar of my country, I needed not so great a struggle to renounce the world. *You* were my world. Without, all was as a fearful night. I donned this garb that none should love me more; that voice of man should never breathe to me of love again. They are but worn for the period in which I attend here. I did not vow to wear them. Say, tell me, was not this love?"

She had said this through her tears, and with

unnatural composure, but then came such a sudden and agonised change over his features, that her calmness forsook her, and rising she said, as she kissed his pale brow, —

"I thought not of this, dreamed not of this, even in the sombre shadow clinging around the hour of meeting. Oh, Clarence, Clarence, would to God it were but a dream!"

He caught her to his heart and impressed a kiss on her brow, while the hot tears (which physical pain had failed to draw forth) fell upon her burning cheek. "Natalie," he said, "I wish to see thee as in the olden time. Cast aside this cap, dearest, in this last parting hour."

She threw off the religieuse hood, and her hair thus unconfined fell in sweeping tresses around her, like a sombre pall. She knelt beside him, and bowed her head upon his throbbing bosom. The excitement caused by this scene brought on a hemorrhage, and feeling something cold dripping upon her, she glanced up, and found his life-blood streaming over her dark hair. She sprang to her feet, uttering a cry of despair, to summon assistance, but he held her firmly, and, as a smile of ineffable happiness wreathed his lips, said, "Let us be alone, Natalie; it is meet we should thus part, and may He who parts us, hear my prayer, and grant that we shall at last meet where there shall be no more griefs, trials, or separations; and may God for ever guide, guard, and bless thee. We were each true unto the cause we espoused—true also unto each other. I am happy, dearest, though soon to enter another country, dear alike unto both. God has granted my orisons, I am passing from earth as I would, darling, clasped in your arms, with heart to heart and hand in hand. Weep not, dearest, I shall soon rest calmly, but what shall comfort *thee*—what shall fill the void of everlasting absence when I leave to return no more, and when I shall have entered the chambers of death's dreary mansion ?"

"Say not—say no !—no !—no ! Clarence. Clarence, say not death ! live for my sake, though not *for* me ! My vow was made to the dead not to wed with thee, as thou wert the foe of my country. I made the vow, but my heart was still thine ; promise to live—add not—add not the pang of death to my already crucified heart —it is broken, and is only now cemented (like a ruined vase) by ties of *duty* and of *honour*—then, Clarence, pray with me to Him to give thee life. I have borne much, suffered much, and my worn frame only remains like a casket from which the jewel has departed."

"Natalie, for thy sake I will. Cease, pray do not sob so."

"Oh! Clarence, Clarence, thou knowest not all I have suffered—the anguish caused by the vow to which I was impelled by an imperious conscience, and which I must hold sacred, as it was sworn to the dead and registered in heaven, by death alone to be absolved."

"Thou wilt be mine above, darling," he answered ; we were not destined for each other here."

She kissed his pale brow, and twining her arms around him, said, " Yes, thine indeed above."

Silence, like a shadow, rested for a moment, and then folding her to his heart, he murmured, " Farewell, press closer to my heart, its last struggle will soon be over. Natalie, good-bye—do not weep ; it is thus I would depart. Stay, do not leave, I wish none near save thee, dearest. Kiss me, love; thy kisses are laden with balm from the flowers of thine own bright land. I feel now that the cause of thy country is that of TRUTH, RIGHT and JUSTICE; and may the God of battles give to thee and thy cause success and victory. Nay, do not grieve; I am passing away tranquilly to the goal of the human race. God has granted my prayer, to die beside thee—then—do not weep when I am gone—I only ask thee to sometimes remember me, and to visit the spot where I shall be reposing, and then, love, think of me as one whose spirit will ever linger near thee."

"Clarence, Clarence, do not speak thus—oh! I could have borne exile from you through life, did I know you still *lived*—I could have seen you another's without pain—I could have loved you had you not one spark of affection for me—I would have sacrificed all to you—could bear all but to see you die." She wrung her hands wildly, and then madly clasped him to her heart with a cry of intense agony, saying imploringly, "Stay with me, Clarence, or pray that God may permit us to enter upon this unknown shore together. I cannot bear to think of your entering upon the labyrinthian passage to the world of shades alone."

"Natalie, beloved, all is light beyond—I see its glories beaming even now—I hear the music from the world afar stealing upon mine ear; but the breezes are chilling me, dearest, they are cold and damp—the dews are already on my brow, I feel them, love—do not, love —stay—I shall soon breathe freely, and I would speak with thee to the last. Think of me, love, at twilight's hour; remember me when autumn's winds are sighing

and decking my grave with nature's mosaic gems;
forget me not by moonlight—pray for me at starlight;
by streamlets and fountains let my memory dwell with
thee—in every scene of beauty and repose—yet let it
not sit with thee as a shadow.   I would have thee
cherish the memory of our love; but let it not come as
clouds o'er another's happiness.   I grow weary—my
eyes seem closing—I grow faint—I am going home—
adieu—beloved Nat——" His lips closed with a seraphic smile and the sentence was finished in another
world.

One heart-rending shriek burst upon the startled
inmates of the hospital, and the surgeon entered the
apartment with an officer of high rank.   The two stood
in speechless amazement gazing upon the scene, while
the room was filling with the frightened convalescents,
attendants, and servants.   Seated upon the couch,
pressing in her arms the rigid corpse of her lover, her
long raven tresses (clotted with his life-blood), streaming
around her, her dress of black serge stained with gore,
and her dark eyes staring upon his marble face.   The
surgeon was first to approach her, and, as he did so, she
clasped the form of her lover more tightly, saying,
" You shall not take him from me, in death at least he's
mine."

The officer now approached, and, with the surgeon,
disengaged her hold, when she fell in their arms fainting.
The officer regarded her features attentively for some
moments, and said slowly to himself, as he placed her
in charge of the female attendants, "I feel it is the
same, yet how changed.   Who can this Sœur Secessia be?   it is plain her habit was but donned for a

purpose. I almost feel assured I am correct in my surmise."

Soon the story rang through the city, and Sœur Secessia was borne to the mansion of Mrs. General L—, where she received every attention. The shock, it was supposed, was such that she could not speedily recover from. The Federal officer, Major Clarence Belden, was interred with the honour due to his rank, and the small chamber, where he breathed his last in the embrace of Miss Natalie de Villerie, was closed by order of the Commanding General, made sacred to his memory, and only permitted to be entered by Sœur Secessia (as she was now known). Nought was removed, the flowers withered in their vases, the woodbine and jessamine wreaths decayed and scattered their petals and leaves upon the floor, the alpine-hued dimity changed to amber-tint, and silence hung its mournful pall around SŒUR SECESSIA'S CELL.

CHAPTER XXI.

" Why should this man
So mock us with the semblance of our kind ?
Moor ! Moor ! thou dost too daringly provoke,
In thy bold cruelty, th' all-judging One,
Who visits for such things !   Hast thou no sense
Of thy frail nature ?   'Twill be taught thee yet ;
And darkly shall the anguish of my soul,
Darkly and heavily, pour itself on thine,
When thou shalt cry for mercy from the dust,
And be denied ! "

AMONGST the first plantations that were seized were
those of Mr. Milleudon, one termed the Milleudon, and
the other the Estelle.   The atrocities committed on
these places by both the Federal soldiery and the
negroes are beyond description.   I will, however, endeavour to give an account of some of the scenes which
transpired.

It was in the month of October, '62, that Colonel
Thomas and Captain Lynes, of Co. I, 98th Vermont,
were sent to take possession of the plantations just
mentioned, belonging to Mr. Milleudon.   Captain Lynes
informed Mr. M—— that his plantations were in possession of the United States Government, and that they
would take off the crop.   Mr. M—— went immediately to
New Orleans, and, having consulted some of his friends,

was advised to call on General Butler, which he did at once, and was told by the General that he would make inquiry in regard to the affair. Mr. M——, after having left General Butler, called upon the General's brother, Colonel Butler, to endeavour to make some arrangement for the sale of his crop, but, failing to come to satisfactory terms, he entered into a bargain with a Mr. Benjamin F. Smith, the latter agreeing to protect the plantations and take off the crops.

Colonel Butler, or rather General Butler, hearing of this arrangement, sent a company of coloured soldiers to the plantations to take possession. When Mr. Milleudon returned to his home he found that his negroes had been tampered with, and that they were completely demoralized. The overseer complained repeatedly of the insubordination of the slaves, and of one especially, called Freeman. Mr. Milleudon summoned Freeman before him, and rebuked him for his impudence to the overseer, and threatened him with chastisement, when the negro actually attacked his master, and, a scuffle ensuing, they both fell to the ground. By some most fortunate chance, Mr. M—— obtained possession of his revolver, which, the negro perceiving, relinquished his hold and fled.

· Mr. M—— then returned to the city, and the first thing he heard from his plantation was that the negro Freeman had seized an axe, and incited the slaves to revolt, and had made an attack on the overseer, who was obliged to fly to his house for safety. The negroes then surrounded the house, into which they fired several shots. The overseer, being armed, returned their fire bravely, until, wounded and exhausted, he sank upon the floor. The negroes then determined to set fire to the building, observing which, the overseer endeavoured to creep out at the back door, and by this means to make his escape; but he was observed, pursued by the negroes, overtaken, and hewed to pieces.

Freeman, having been the ringleader, was arrested, with one or two others, and taken to the city for trial, and are still in gaol (or were up to February 1, '64) awaiting sentence.

General Butler had arrested, some few weeks after his arrival, the man who had torn down the flag from the Mint, and he was placed in confinement until the month of August, when, after a trial, he was sentenced to be hanged. Up to the moment of the verdict being given there were but few cognizant of the name of this man, which has been traced in blood upon the escutcheon of the Confederacy. But as soon as the fate which awaited him was known, the name of Mumford was pronounced and blazoned forth by Northern journals as that of a traitor, and by the Southern as that of a martyr.

In vain were petitions of mercy drawn up and signed by the most prominent citizens, in vain did Mrs. Butler plead upon her knees for his life. The fiat of this stern monarch had gone forth, and would not be recalled; Mumford must die, and meet the penalty of his daring. Not even when the scaffold was erected did the people believe that Butler would dare out this act of worse than Haynau atrocity. But they little knew the man until he had proved, by his countless acts of despotism, his claim to be classed amongst those whom Shakespeare has pourtrayed so faithfully in the lines :—

> " But man, proud man,
> Drest in a little brief authority ;
> Most ignorant of what he's most assured ;
> His glossy essence—like an angry ape,
> Plays such fantastic tricks before high heaven,
> As make the angels weep."

On a bright and beautiful morning the sun rose for the last time to meet the gaze of the condemned prisoner, and its glorious rays illumined the cell whose portals would only open to usher him into the arms of death. Bravely, manfully, heroically, he met his doom! Tried and condemned to death, and such a death! How would he have rushed to meet it on the battle-field in Freedom's strife, in any form save this most vile and most degrading one. To the last moment he was profferred life, if he would forswear his allegiance to the Confederacy ; but no, he spurned the proffer at such a price, saying death had no terrors for him, and with un-blanched cheek, upon the verge of eternity, bade them do their duty, and to finish their work of cruelty and infamy. One more act—the rope was drawn, a soul was ushered into the presence of its Creator—Butler stood before the world an assassin and a murderer—while the "dew-fall of a nation's tears" consecrated the spot where Mumford, the martyr, fell a victim to fanatic hate.

After large confiscations of property and beggaring thousands, General Butler prepared to leave New Orleans, having been recalled by his President, Mr. Lincoln. Prior to his departure he made the following address to his soldiers:—

" Head Quarters, Department of the Gulf,
"New Orleans, Dec. 15, 1862.
" General Orders, No. 106.

" Soldiers of the Army of the Gulf!

"Relieved from further duties in this department, by direction of the President, under date of November 9th, 1862, I take leave of you by this final order, it being impossible to visit your scattered outposts, covering hundreds of miles of the frontier of a larger territory than some of the kingdoms of Europe. I greet you, my brave comrades, and say Farewell! This word—endeared, as you are, by community of privations, hardships, dangers, victories, successes, military and civil— is the only sorrowful thought I have. You have deserved well of your country. Without a murmur you sustained an encampment on a sand-bar, so desolate that banishment to it, with every care and comfort possible, has been the most dreaded punishment inflicted upon your bitterest and most insulting enemies. You had so few means of transportation that but a handful could advance to compel submission by the queen city of the rebellion, whilst others waded breast deep in the marshes which surround St. Philip, and forced the surrender of a fort deemed impregnable to land attack by the most skilful engineers of your country and her enemy. At your occupation, order, law, quiet and peace sprang to this city, filled with the bravos of all nations, where, for a score of years, during the profoundest peace, human life was scarcely safe at noonday. By your discipline you illustrated the best traits of the American soldier, and enchained the admiration of those who came to scoff. Landing with a

military chest containing but seventy-five dollars from
the hoards of a rebel government, you have given to
your country's treasury nearly a half a million of dollars,
and so supplied yourselves with the needs of your services that your expedition has cost your government
less by *four-fifths than any other.* You have fed the
starving poor, the wives and children of your enemies,
so converting enemies into friends that they have sent
their representatives to your Congress by a vote greater
than your entire numbers from districts in which, when
you entered, you were tauntingly told that there was
' no one to raise your flag.' By your practical philanthropy you have won the confidence of the ' oppressed
race' and the slave. Hailing you as deliverers, they are
ready to aid you as willing servants, faithful labourers,
or, using the tactics taught them by our enemies, to
fight with you in the field. By steady attention to the
laws of health you have stayed the pestilence, and,
humble instruments in the hands of God, you have
demonstrated the necessity that His creatures should
obey his laws; and, reaping His blessing in this most
unhealthy climate, you have preserved your ranks
fuller than those of any other battalions of the same
length of service. You have met double numbers of
the enemy, and defeated him in the open field; but I
need not further enlarge upon this topic. You were
sent here to do that. I commend you to your Commander. You are worthy of his love. Farewell, my
comrades! Again farewell!

" BENJAMIN F. BUTLER,

" Major General Commanding."

To one who had exerted himself so assiduously in his various efforts to please the ladies, it was deemed but just that they should present him a testimonial of their appreciation, and they, I believe, endeavoured to embrace within their remarks all that tender regard which each and all felt for him ; and it was with beating hearts they drained their goblets to the following toast the moment his departure was signalised :—

THE LADIES OF NEW ORLEANS' FAREWELL TO GEN. BUTLER.

" We fill this cup to one made up
　Of beastliness alone,
The caitiff of his dastard crew,
　The seeming paragon
Who had a coward heart bestowed,
　And brutal instincts given,
In fiendish mirth then spawned on earth
　To shame the God of heaven.

His every tone is murder's own,
　Like those unhallowed birds
Who feed on corpses, and the lie
　Dwells ever in his word.
His very face a living curse
　To mankind's lofty state,
Marked with the stain of branded Cain,
　None knew him but to hate.

Fair woman's fame he makes his game,
　On children wreaks his spite,
A tyrant 'mid his bayonets,
　He never dared a fight.
Think you a mother's holy smile
　E'er beamed for him ?   Ah ! no ;
The jackall nursed the whelps accursed
　Humanity's worst foe.

On every hand in every land
The scoundrel is despised ;
In Butler's name the foulest wrongs
And crimes are all comprised.
'Twill be the sign of infamy
Unto time's utmost verge ;
Ages unborn will tell in scorn
Of him as mankind's scourge.

We filled this cup to one made up
Of beastliness alone,
The caitiff of his Yankee crew,
The lauded paragon.
Farewell ! and if in hell there dwells
A demon such as thou,
Then, Satan, yield the sceptre up,
Thy mission's over now.

New Orleans, December 20th.''

CHAPTER XXII.

"O Conspiracy !
Sham'st thou to show thy dangerous brow by night,
When evils are most free ? O ! then by day,
Where wilt thou find a cavern dark enough
To mask thy monstrous visage ? Seek none, Conspiracy,
Hide it in smiles and affability."

WE all know how, in the communities in which we live, that there are many facts bearing upon the habits and character of public men, which in no way appear in the journals; and invariably there is an under-current of action and of interest, which, if known, would satisfactorily explain an inexplicable political combination, which the world at large never knows. But as the actors die, and the causes of reserve cease to exist, so truth is laid bare, and a future generation finds nothing concealed. The riddle is thus solved.

It is almost impossible correctly to analyse the various causes, influences, and motives which, have stirred up the fearful strife. It is hard, indeed, to fancy any one, however earnest, however loyal in his connections, and however deep his feelings, contemplating beforehand this four years' contest, with its misery, its bloodshed, its hundreds of thousands of victims, its myriads of happy homes devastated, the anguish it has caused, the innocence it has polluted. Who could find in his heart reasons to justify such a holocaust? But events grow from events, and a small matter is often the commencement of great things.

The first inflammatory signal of civil war was flung upon the winds in Kansas, and with every breeze from the North it increased, until its burning breath has consumed all kindly feeling between North and South, and trodden out every brotherly sentiment. Who cast this brand amidst us? Who sounded the clarion note that started the fears, the passions, the furies which have their haunt amidst the multitude? Who guided on the ship of state to this fearful pass—this strait between Scylla and Charybdis? Who, for all this mischief that has accrued to us in fact, and still guiltier design, is responsible? Who, but the Black Republicans? They broke in upon the peace of our country, and filled it with bayonets, angry blood, desperate broils, confusion, and wrong. The Catalines of America wrought this work of turbulence and sedition, and with torch-light processions and riotous songs are now slowly, but surely, bearing the corpse of the Union to its interment.

Yes, these conspirators left no means untried· to advance their schemes; and a press, venal and un-scrupulous, backed them by its pestilential influence, and in its task of devotion to the cause, paled its almost ineffectual fires before the fulminations of brimstone, which issued from the pulpits of the Beechers and the Brownlows. Ministers of the gospel, with a voca-tion only for cant and slander, thundered their anathemas against the Southern people; and fibrous old maids, secure of self-approbation and trusting to notoriety, as a *dernier resort*, set up their hue and cry, and went to raising subscriptions for the purchase of Bibles, to be sent to their barbaric brethren of the South. The gaol-birds were loosed even, to fill the ranks; and Billy Wilson and Ellsworth were placed in command of men whom, to use the expression of their own commanders, it was necessary to place six feet apart, when in line of march, to prevent their picking each others' pockets. These were the braves sent to subdue the "rebellion." These were the men sent into the heart of a lovely land to ravage and lay waste all before them; these were the men our unprotected women had to face, and these were the dastards that applied the torch to the dwellings of our gallant absent soldiers, and left our women and children without a shelter from the summer's gale or winter's storm.

Yes, in Alexandria, the citizens, after the town was laid in ashes, had to shelter themselves under the boughs of the trees; and a Mrs. Texhada (whose husband had been a wealthy man, and a Louisiana State senator, ere the war), when heard of last, was seated in a go-cart, with her six little children, and with rope reins attached to a mule, was driving to General Banks' head-quarters, to beg rations for herself and little ones, while the ruins of her once happy home was still vivid in her memory.

Such scenes are common to the view of our people; and the agitators of the North are exulting, though they pretend to be overwhelmed with despair and grief. Nero-like, they now sit upon their tower, fiddling over the conflagration of their country, and singing pæans of triumph over the success of their vile project.

" Sing hey ! sing ho ! for the royal death,
That scatters a host with a single breath,
That opens the prison to spoil the palace,
And rids honest necks from the hangman's malice ;
Here's a health to the plague ! let the mighty ones dread.
The poor never lived 'till the wealthy were dead ;
A health to the plague ! may she ever as now,
Loose the rogue from his chain and the nun from her vow,
To the jailor a sword, to the captive a key,
Hurrah for earth's curse, 'tis a blessing to me ! "

Yes, it is now four years since the first sound of
strife awoke the world from slumber, and startled the
echoes in our mountains, hills, and valleys. It is now
four years since the turbulent passions of man broke
loose his shackles of virtuous restraint, and wooed the
demon intolerance. It is now four years since the mad
fanaticism of our Northern brethren cast the firebrand
of desolation into the midst of our Southern homes, and
left in the charred ruins their lasting testimonial of
fiendish hate. Yes, four years of deadly contest has
passed into the ocean of time, and its billows now roll
over friend and foe alike.

Where are now the misguided beings, on the one
hand, who rushed to battle for filthy lucre? Where are
now the valiant heroes, on the other, who fought for
country and their firesides? Echo answers, " Where?"
Gone for ever from ʼamongst us, and both alike to be
judged by Him who giveth victory to the just.
Thousands have fallen, and yet the struggle is no
nearer closing; and on the altars of Mars and Bellona
hecatombs of victims have been offered, while sanguine
streams are purling through our forests, whose source is
the hearts of Northern hirelings and Southern chivalry.

2 A 2

Even in death their blood refuses to mingle, and
that of the Southerners, · like the Gulf Stream, winds
clearly on, distinct from the darker waves around it,
which flow from springs of rancour and jealousy.

The breach which has been made by crafty politicians,
whose only aim was (and is) pecuniary interest, cannot
now be closed by coercive measures ; and they care not
so long as the Goddess of Liberty dispenses her golden
favours, or rather now her *emerald* gifts, for the fickle
Goddess Fortune, tired of weighing out her gold and
silver, has chosen to measure her gifts in a lighter substance, and thus she rewards her chosen by several
yards of tissue paper, which, at a short distance, might
be taken for the Hibernian flag, if it did not bear the portraits of *demons* instead of *saints*.   The wily politicians, in
the present instance displayed their diplomacy, as the
colour was given to the shin-plasters in compliment to
the sons of the Green Isle whom they expected to rally
around the Stars and Stripes, as in former days, and
whom they deemed could feel themselves repaid for loss
of blood, life, or limb, by gazing upon their wages paid
them *in their own colours*.   The Winifield Scott style
of compliment was paid the troops, and the "rich Irish
brogue," and the "sweet German accent," were made
the "Faughaballach" to many a battle field of the Union.
Yes, the poor deluded victims of foreign birth, by the
cunning of Yankee eloquence and Yankee trickery, were
marched out and placed foremost in the ranks, that
should death await *any*, the foreigners should be the first
to meet it.   The places of honour were bestowed upon
them, not from love, but because they felt by so doing
they secured their own safety.

Will you not learn wisdom from the past? Will you still madly rush on death and suffering, when you know the award which awaits your generous conduct? Have you not heard already of Know-nothingism—of the many isms, which ere the war sprang up in the North, had for their aim the depriving of foreigners of any of the rights of citizenship? Are you blind to the treachery of former conduct? The Janus-faced people of the North still lure you on, and her army proves to-day that you still remain deaf to every entreaty. It is said to be a belief in Africa, that people can be destroyed or withered up, not by curses but by praises. I feel assured that the Northerners have adopted this style for the annihilation of all who come within their influence. The South was beginning to feel the workings of the charm, when the "fetich" was procured which broke the spell.

CHAPTER XXIII.

" It is hard to act a part long—for where Truth is not at the
bottom, Nature will always be endeavouring to return, and will peep
out and betray herself one time or other."—*Tillotson.*

I WILL now direct your attention to other scenes. You
will please accompany me in fancy to New Orleans, the
theatre of those scenes. General Banks was now
stationed here, and he entered upon his duties with
seemingly a disposition to efface by gentle treatment
the evil impression left upon the minds of the people
by the despotic rule of General Butler. General Banks
bore an air of mildness and suavity towards all who
approached him, while his promises of protection, assistance, and influence were lavished on every side. The
dictatorial style of his predecessor was not adopted by
him, and in driving out for an airing, he could scarce be
recognised from the plainest citizen. But the inhabitants of New Orleans soon discovered this habit of humility was but the sheep's clothing to conceal the wolf,
and he had not been long in the city ere he might have
heard, had he listened attentively, the same compliment
paid him as the tyrant of Syracuse received. Thus
it runs:—" One day a tyrant of old Syracuse overheard
a woman praying to the gods to prolong his life. He
demanded of her what he had ever done for her, that
she prayed thus. Frightened into sincerity, she said,
' You have done nothing for me, but the tyrant that
reigned before your predecessor, oppressed the people

so that we prayed for his death. When he died, the tyrant that succeeded him was worse than he had been. We prayed for his death, and the gods have sent you. Taught by the past, I see that each change of tyrants increases the common misery. Hell itself may find some even worse than you. So I pray for your life.'"

General Banks' principal achievement in the South was the capture of Port Hudson, General Grant having the entire honour of the surrender of Vicksburg. Both these places were strongly garrisoned, but poorly victualled ; after suffering innumerable, hardships at Port Hudson, its commander, General Gardiner, surrendered, and was sent with the famished prisoners to New Orleans. There is no eulogistic expression of sufficient strength to give an idea of the esteem in which General Gardiner, the modern Massena, was and is held. On his arrival in New Orleans, he was sought by high and low, and the Federal officers were each day galled at the attentions which the noble captive received, who, as he promenaded the streets during his hours of liberty, clad in his sober garb of gray, was surrounded by bevies of ladies, each desirous of the honour of his acquaintance, as his gallant and self-sacrificing conduct had won their undying gratitude and admiration.

General Banks stationed at Port Hudson several coloured regiments, under command of General Andrews. Port Hudson had been fortified by the Confederates, after the attack, and though the fortification was but hastily constructed, it could have withstood a siege of any length had it been well supplied with provisions. General Banks, after the laurels won at Port Hudson, deemed it best to rest from his labours for awhile, and enjoy the effulgence of the sun of glory which radiated from his past conquests. His was now a life of ease and luxury; driving to the office on a fine morning, after a late breakfast, such as the most fastidious disciple of Epicurus would feel content to partake of; residing in a confiscated mansion, with the servants and equipage of the former owner at his disposal, and treating his staff and honoured guests to sumptuous entertainments, which the unfortunate Confederates were forced to pay for. The next acts of this "most potent, grave, and reverend seignior" were his banishment of those who refused to take the oath, and his victory over the female sex on the occasion of the departure of husbands, sons, and brothers for the "Land of Dixie." Banks is immortalised in the graphic description given of his troops, by the fair poetess Eugenie in her poem of " Le Bataille des mouchoirs," which I place before you.

LE BATAILLE DES MOUCHOIRS.

The Greatest Victory of the War.

Fought Friday, February 20th, 1863.

" Of all the battles, modern or old,
  By poet sung or historian told ;
  Of all the routs that ever were seen
  From the days of Saladin to Marshal Tureme ;
  Or all the victories late—yet won,
  From Waterloo's field to that of Buller Run ;
  All, all must hide their fading light,
  In the radiant glow of the handkerchief figh ;
  And a pæan of joy must thrill the land,
  When they hear the deeds of Banks's band.

'Twas on the Levee, where the tide
Of Father Mississippi flows ;
Our gallant lads their country's pride,
Won this great victory o'er her foes.
Four hundred rebels were to leave
That morning for Secessia's shades,
When down there came (you'd scarce believe)
A troop of children, wives and maids,
To wave farewell, to bid God speed,
To shed for them the parting tear,
To waft them kisses as the meed
Of praise, to soldiers' hearts most dear.
They came in hundreds—thousands lined
The streets, the roofs, the shipping too,
Their ribbons dancing in the wind,
Their bright eyes flashing love's adieu.

'Twas then to danger *we* awoke,
But nobly faced the unarmed throng,
And beat them back with hearty stroke,
Till reinforcements came along.
We waited long ; our aching sight
Was strained in eager, anxious gaze—
At last we saw the bayonets bright
Flash in the sunlight's welcome rays ;
The cannon's dull and heavy roll,
Fell greeting on our gladdened ear—
Then fired each eye, then glowed each soul,
For well we knew the strife was near.

Charge ! rang the cry, and on we dashed
Upon our female foes,
As seas, in stormy fury lashed,
Where'er the tempest blows.
Like chaff their parasols went down,
As on our gallants rushed,
And many a bonnet, robe and gown,
Was torn to shreds or crushed.
Though well we plied the bayonet,
Still some our efforts braved,
Defiant both of blow and threat,
Their handkerchiefs still waved.

Thick grew the fight, loud rolled the din—
When "Charge!" rang out again,
And then the cannon thundered in,
And scoured o'er the plain.
Down 'neath the unpitying iron heels
Of horses, children sank,
While through the crowd the cannon wheels
Mowed roads on either flank.
One startled shriek, one hollow groan,
One headlong rush and then—
Huzzah! the field was all our own,
For *we* were Banks's men.

That night, released from all our toils,
Our danger past and gone,
We gladly gathered up the spoils
Our chivalry had won.
Five hundred 'kerchiefs we had snatched
From rebel ladies' hands,
Ten parasols, two shoes (not matched),
Some ribbons, belts, and bands,
And other things that I forgot;
But then you'll find them all,—
As trophies in that hallowed spot—
The cradle ——— Faneuil Hall!

And long on Massachusets' shore,
Or on green mountain's side,
Or where Long Islands' breakers roar,
And by the Hudsons' tide,
In times to come, when lamps are lit,
As fires brightly blaze,
While round the knees of heroes sit
The young of happier days,
Who listen to their storied deeds,
To them sublimely grand,
Then glory shall award its meed
Of praise to Banks's band,
And fame proclaim that they alone
(In triumph's loudest note)
May wear henceforth for valour shown
A woman's petticoat!"

Mrs. Banks, after this great conquest of her lord's, felt that she was losing the opportunity of getting into first class society, which she felt assured she had only to go South to enter. Thus one fine morning she arrived in the city, much to the delight of the Federal ladies, who had been awaiting her entrance into New Orleans as the signal for the season of gaiety, which they knew would follow. They were not disappointed. After Mrs. Banks had received several calls from her Union friends, she gave a *fête*, to which all who had called upon her were invited, *as well as those who had not.* Rumour says it was a most gorgeous affair: the incense or perfume which floated through the extensive *salons* was most delightful and agreeable to the sympathisers of the sable race, and an odour only patronised by Republicans or Abolitionists; it is distilled in Boston, in the largest quantities, and is called "L'eau d'Afrique," or essence of Africa. Mrs. Banks was attired in a blue silk dress, with an overdress of point lace, with diamonds adorning ears, neck, and arms. She exhibited the elegant taste of being the *best dressed at her own reception*, thus introducing to the ladies of the South a new code of etiquette.

Mrs. Banks's next effort to become the leader of the 'ton' was in getting up tableaux representations at the Opera House, in Bourbon Street. She personated the North, while several Federal ladies were surrounding the pedestal on which she stood, and kneeling in supplication to her, the latter representing the Southern States. Think of it women of the South, kneeling to the North, and that represented· in the person of a MASSACHUSETS FACTORY GIRL !

By a strange coincidence, on the *very* day of the

night in which this farce was enacted, General Banks
was defeated on Red River, and sent flying pursued a
second time by General Taylor, leaving all his stores
behind for the Confederates, who have a particular fondness for General Banks, as he is said and known to be
the best Quartermaster the Confederacy can boast of;
he invariably leaves them an abundance of provisions,
clothing, arms, and ammunition.   General Banks's fickle
master at Washington was about to send him for this
last defeat, to join that procession of fallen Generals
who have long since passed into the gulf of oblivion,
but whose shades yet wander sadly on the shores.   The
banner of their country, the faithless "Stars and Stripes,"
now waves over their successors, who in their turn,
too, must join the ranks of those phantoms of illustrious
men, who have not died, but only "gone before," to meet
contempt and shame as the reward of their valour.
The " Stars and Stripes" is a beautiful standard, and was
given up with regret by many.   The poem introduced
will display the cause of its being renounced for its
noble substitute the glorious STARS and BARS.

STARS AND STRIPES.

" O ! there was a time, but 'twas long ago,
    In the days of my childhood's years,
 Ere the North had evoked this cloud of woe
    With its tempests of blood and tears—
 When I loved to look on the stars and stripes,
    On that banner waving so free,
 O'er the hills and vales of a happy land,
    And o'er many a rolling sea.

" But that day has passed—and the land is changed,
    And that flag's a degraded flag ;

Aye, that banner is nothing now to me
  But a soiled and a worthless rag.
It is fann'd by the frenzied breath of hate,
  It is borne by cowards and knaves ;
In my heart I loathe such a flag as that,
  And the cause over which it waves.

" Aye, I loved it once, with a childish pride,
  When I read on the scroll of fame
Of the victories won beneath its folds,
  As it flashed like an Oriflamme.
But *now* I can see it with cold contempt
  As *our* battle fields have seen,
Torn, faded, and trampled down in the dust,
  In the hands of the base and mean.

" Yes, I loved it once, I despise it now,
  'Tis the ensign of fraud and wrong ;
And here in the presence of God and man,
  I recant each word of that song !
Aye, that childish song, when with childhood's trust
  I believed the North to be true,
Nor dreamed it would seek, in its soulless lust,
  To defile the land to its rue.

" I sang of that banner an artless song,
  Such as ignorant childhood sings ;
'Twas childish, I know, ' but now I'm a man,
  I have put away childish things.'
And I say to the reckless, heartless crew,
  Who insanely rave at the North,
That your 'Union ' is *dead*, its requiem said,
  And what is its *prestige* worth ?

Worth ? Scarcely the dust in which it is laid,
  Slain, slain by your murderous hands !
And its tomb, enwreathed by the stars and stripes,
  In the field ' Aceldama ' stands.
I've finished my song—'tis my manhood's lay,
  Not the chant of the foolish child ;
The banner I worshipp'd in boyhood's day,
  Is sullied, degraded, defiled!"

CHAPTER XXIV.

" Thy sails, my friend, are to me the clouds of the morning ; thy ships the light of heaven, and thou thyself a pillar of fire that beams on the world by night.—*Ossian.*

RECLINING on a pile of cushions on the deck of a blockade-runner might be seen a beautiful lady, apparelled in deep mourning. The bark was steadily advancing through the dense fog, and anxiously she watched through her ivory lorgnette the course of the vessel as it glided out of the harbour of M—— and pursued its perilous way through the vapour and invisible guns of the enemy's ships. The few passengers calmly and almost breathlessly awaited the moment when they should arrive in the open sea, and thus have space to spread their canvas and to dare the foe. No fear was exhibited in the countenance of either passengers or crew, but a determination to meet the foe man to man, hand to hand, should they encounter them.

On flew the fairy craft, like a frightened bird o'er the waves. First poising on a mountain billow, then sinking, seemingly, the next minute, to rise to the surface. Several hours passed thus in suspense, and then safely the bark was afloat on the deep. One long, loud, cheer for Jeff. Davis and the Southern Confederacy, and then the "Bonny Blue Flag" was sung in stirring tones.

The passengers and crew, when this was ended, sought amusement to while away the time.

The morning of the sixth day had dawned upon the voyagers, and they were just entering the *salon* from their respective state rooms when they were startled by a voice crying out, " The Alabama ! the Alabama !" In a moment all were on deck, and straining their eyes for a glimpse of the fast approaching noted privateer. Just in front, and grimly frowning upon the little bark, loomed the dreadful " demon of the deep." Guns protruded from the port-holes, and the stern-looking crew seemed armed to the teeth.

All was excitement on board the blockade-runner. and everyone was anxious to catch a view of Commander Semmes as he stood upon the bow of the vessel.

The lady whom I mentioned as dressed in mourning, said to the Captain, as the vessel drew near the Alabama, " Sir, may I ask if we are to have the pleasure of meeting Captain Semmes *en personne*, or does he condescend to board us ?"

" I think it is not his custom, lady, to leave his own vessel, though we cannot answer for his movements."

" Oh, I should so like to meet him," she said, " and I may never have such another opportunity ; would he think it unladylike if I should go over in the small boat? Oh ! if I could but grasp his hand, and say to him how his valorous conduct is appreciated, and how the Southern people long for the moment wherein they shall bear him in triumph through their cities. Pray, Captain, permit me to enter the boat ; I would dare death to feel that I had but clasped his hand !"

" Certainly, lady," the old weather-beaten Captain

replied; "I will await you here until you get your hat."

She disappeared, and in a moment returned, when she was placed in the dancing boat, and was soon beside the "Alabama." Commander Semmes was not a little surprised to see this lady mounting the side of the vessel, and stood politely awaiting her. The moment she placed her feet upon the deck she advanced frankly towards the Captain, saying—

"Fame, Sir, has already presented you to me, and I will take the liberty of introducing to you (in the person of myself) Miss Louise Laval, who has overstepped, perhaps, the boundary of propriety in her desire to *see* and *hear* Captain Semmes."

"Thanks," replied the "pirate" Captain, as he clasped both her hands within his own, while the blushes tinged his bronzed face; "thanks, dear lady, I am scarce able to reply to so complimentary a' speech. I will say, however, that I am gratified for the kind expressions you have honoured me in using, and would further state, you need have no fear as to the propriety of the act, as you are amongst gentlemen, and those, I feel, who appreciate your conduct, and who, if necessary, would be prepared to chastise any who might impugn your motives."

"Most gallant Captain! accept my most profound acknowledgments. I have only met the reception I anticipated at the hands of yourself and brave companions, but come, Captain, I wish you to show me over your vessel, and to point out each gun yourself— would that I could assist in sweeping from off the ocean the fleet of our grim foe. Yours, Captain, is an enviable position." Captain Semmes smiled, and, accompanied by several officers, he showed her over the vessel.

She examined the works minutely, and said, as she turned to go on deck, "Oh! how glorious and transcendent must be the feeling when after a combat with the enemy, when victory has crowned your arms, you exclaim, as you furl your sails contentedly, 'Alabama' (*Here we rest*)."

They had reached the side of the ship, and Miss Laval raised her hands to her neck, and, unclasping a necklace of exquisite pearls, said as she took the Captain's hand within her own, " Permit me, Captain Semmes, in the name of all my sex, to place upon your brow this little offering, suggestive of the crown of more unfading gems with which your brow is decked in the image of yourself, which every loyal man and woman of the South wear enshrined within their hearts."

Captain Semmes bowed; she placed it over his brow; he then, smiling, took it off, and, kissing it, said, " I have met the enemy many times, Miss Laval, and met them to defeat them, but I have never had, I confess, so surprising, and yet so embarrassing, an adventure on land or sea as the present. I accept your gift in your own name and that of the lovely sex which, in yourself, is so well represented, trusting that the purity of my course, devoid of self interest, will prove me worthy of this offering."

" Farewell, Captain, we may never meet again. Had I never met you I could not be a less ardent admirer than this brief personal acquaintance has made me. Farewell, Captain, once again; such men as Davis,

Semmes, Lee, Jackson, and Beauregard need not the 'painted flourish' of mine or anyone's 'praise.'"

He handed her into the boat, and the "Alabama" and blockade-runner were soon parted on life's wide sea, perhaps never to meet again; but we will follow our little bark, for it bears within its bosom much that is precious.

Miss Laval promenaded the deck late on the evening of the morning of her interview with Captain Semmes, and when the stars peeped forth she was still wrapped in her shawl and Nubia, gazing upon the sea and sky, and soliloquising thus—"I am a wanderer and alone; what should I care for if not for my country? I gaze upon the past, and down its solemn aisles I see the forms of loved ones draped in habiliments of woe, and gloom shrouds their once happy homes. I am lost in immeasurable darkness, the torch of patriotism alone lights my course or cheers the solitary—— Heavens!" she exclaimed, as a cannot-shot burst across the bows of the vessel.

In a moment the startled passengers were on deck, and, though the Captain knew he must surrender, he steadily kept on his course through a perfect river of fire; on flew the pursued and pursuer, and with intense excitement gazed Miss Laval; at last one appalling burst boomed across the waters, and when the smoke cleared away the blockade-runner was seen in a dismantled and sinking state, with the crew and passengers seemingly collected, awaiting their doom. Not a word was spoken; not a cry for mercy arose upon the air, not a voice to cry "Save or we perish."

Miss Laval drew forth a small Confederate flag, which had been concealed beneath the folds of her attire, and, raising it on high, said, "Beneath this emblem none need fear death!"

The waters gathered around the little barque, the pursuing ship was soon beside them, and, though the pursuers sprang on board, they could not rescue all that determined band. The boats were, ready, and vainly the foe sought to persuade them to board their vessel; they coolly stood amid the rush of waters, with defiance gleaming in their eyes and scorn upon their lips.

"My dear lady, place yourself under my protection," said a Federal officer, as he approached Miss Laval; "You have not a moment to lose."

"Away!" she answered; "I scorn the succour afforded by an enemy, I will die beside my friends."

"Madam, pardon me, I shall not permit you to thus perish." Seizing her gently around the waist, he bore her per force to the side of the vessel and lowered her into the arms of the men, who awaited to receive any who might seek the boats.

He returned to seek out others, and was with his companions near perishing with the resolute crew of the blockade runner. The few females were saved, but the men preferred death to languishing in Federal dungeons. Down like a flash almost sank the Confederate steamer, while the few whom the mercy of the enemy saved were borne to the victorious vessel.

Miss Laval bore with her the banneret, and closely she pressed it to her heart, as she left the wrecked vessel and its inmates in their watery couch.

"Sir," she said, "I cannot thank you for my life; for I have suffered death in seeing my friends engulphed."

He bowed, and politely ushered her into the cabin, where she was most comfortably provided for.

The Captain soon entered, and addressing the group of ladies who stood weeping and wringing their hands, said, " Dear ladies, permit me to say how sincerely I regret the fortune of war which has placed both yourselves and me in so painful a position. I shall, however, do all I can to mitigate your troubles, and will send you to your various homes at the earliest convenience, or land you at any port you may wish to enter."

Miss Laval being the only one who could command her voice, said,

" If you will but send us to Havre, you will be acting in accordance with the desire of one and all."

" You shall, ladies, be sent upon the first vessel bound for Havre, and in the meantime I will exert myself, as well as all my officers, to make you comfortable."

He kept his word. The ladies were placed upon a vessel, and not many days elapsed, ere the following note was received by a Confederate Commissioner:—

" Paris, Rue Chaussée d'Antin.

Sir,—I send by the bearer of this note a package ; it contains a black Irish poplin dress. You will doubtless deem this a strange gift, yet if you will rip the seams you will discover that the cord is valuable, and only manufactured in ' Richmond on the James,' and used for tying up Government documents. The buttons are large, and if uncovered will ' a tale unfold.' Should you find it serve you, retain it as a model, but if you should

design any improvement on the style, I will take pleasure
in bearing a specimen of your model for Gabrielles to
Richmond, which I may safely have patented.

"Hoping for an early response,

"I am, respectfully,

(Signed) "LOUISE LAVAL."

It is needless to state the Commissioner's surprise,
when on taking out the cord it proved to be despatches
on diplomatised paper, and rolled as cord and covered
as such. The buttons each bore *one word*, and when
placed all together, formed quite a long despatch. In
wonder the Commissioner gazed upon this dress—at
the wit which could have conceived this plan of
artifice. Miss Laval had worn this dress, changing
neither night or day during the voyage. She feigned
her desire to perish, and had the Federal officer known
that in his arms was held a contraband parcel, he would
doubtless have left it on board the wreck.

In a few days Miss Laval was again attired in the
black Irish poplin gabrielle, and on her way to Richmond, where I will introduce you to her in an interview
with the noble President, Jefferson Davis.

The room in which Miss Lavall sat awaiting the
President, was furnished with Cretan simplicity. No
glare of sunlight illumined gilding or fresco, but papers,
books, maps, and designs were scattered over the plain
tables, " étagères," &c., which filled the room. Miss
Laval was gazing intently on a portrait, when a step fell
upon her ear. She turned, and met the kindly beaming
but worn face of the President, who said, as he warmly
grasped her hand,

"Welcome! thrice welcome to these halls once again ; their echoes, Miss Laval, can never be awakened by truer voice than thine."

"Thanks" she answered, smiling; "feeling the sincerity, and being conscious myself of the truth of your speech, I will not accuse you of gallantry. Yes, I am true to my country. I feel there can be no doubt of this, with my weak ability true as yourself. The mind, the power, the vast erudition of the President is greater, but his energy is not superior to Miss Laval's. I have returned after a successful mission to Europe, and now I stand ready and willing to serve my country or its ruler, should either choose to honour me again. Would, Sir, that I had eloquence sufficient to utter the *just eulogies* which everywhere in Europe I have heard lavished upon my country and its wise and renowned President. Would that I could have borne these foreign, priceless gems of rich and rare value in a proper casket to present you; but they come to you not the less pure in a Confederate case of rude workmanship, but honest and firm setting. The sleepless nights, the long, long weary hours by day that you have spent in planning, reasoning, counselling, are each numbered in golden sheen upon the record of Fame."

"Lady, I am gratified for your generous appreciation, and feel that I am indebted to many from your report of my character abroad. I serve my country and her people, however, with no desire or expectation of reward, yet I must say it is refreshing to feel that our motives are understood, and that such men as Lee and Jackson have, as warriors and men, entitled themselves to rank amongst those whom Fisher Ames would call great, when he says, "The most substantial glory of a country is in its virtuous great men; its prosperity will depend on its docility to learn from their example; that nation is fated to ignominy and servitude for which such men have lived in vain. Power may be seized by a nation that is yet barbarous, and wealth may be enjoyed by one that it finds or renders sordid. The one is the gift and sport of accident, and the other is the gift and sport of power. Both are mutable, and have passed away without leaving behind them any other memorial than ruins that offend taste, and traditions that baffle conjecture." Good and noble actions, lady, strike an everlasting root, and leave perennial blossoms on the grave. Man should not consider self; our men have been regardless of their lives, their fortunes, their all, in the great endeavour to promote the interest of their country. I have much to be thankful for, Miss Laval, for if success has thus far crowned my efforts, I owe much of it to Messrs. Benjamin Stephens, Yancey, and such like, on the one hand; while in the field, Lee, Beauregard, Jackson, Hardee, Taylor, Stewart, and others too numerous for mention, have made the sword finish all the pen or tongue was incapable of executing."

"Had we, Sir, a less sage President," Miss Laval replied, "I fear we would, ere this, have had a disgraceful compromise, which I feel assured will never be listened to by you."

"Not for a moment, lady, trust me. We have sacrificed too many of our best and bravest; we have been called to witness the devastation of our homes; we have felt the sting of their vile pens where they have presumed to caricature our ragged and worn troops. These are people who would turn to ridicule such men as Marion and his suffering host, and would point the finger of scorn at a George Washington, if mounted upon a "Rosinante." But let them laugh, so much the more credit to us, and shame to them, if we can still say, in the face of want of every kind, and starvation, 'Come on; we defy you!'"

"I am glad to hear you speak thus; I knew I was not deceived in my ideas of your intentions, and may God grant thee and thy countrymen heart and nerve to bide the issue. Honoured representative of my country, thou art faithful and firm."

They clasped hands and parted, Miss Laval to enter again upon her path of duty, the President to return to the affairs of the nation, where I shall drop the curtain upon him, not again to be drawn aside until gentle Peace shall part it, and display our noble President in the jewelled niche of Glory, wearing his well-merited wreath of laurel, and receiving the homage of a grateful people for his exalted virtues and public service.

CHAPTER XXV.

THE heart-rending scenes which have taken place in the Valley of the Shenandoah by command of General Sherman, have so far outshone in diabolical intent all other actions of earlier date, and so greatly out-Butler'd Butler, that my brain can scarcely conceive the reality of them, and it is with feelings of horror I even place them before the world, through the medium of such letters and articles as this chapter will embrace. If Butler was outlawed, Sherman should be doubly so.. Butler confiscated, and even may have placed the proceeds in his own purse, but he never adopted the wholesale style of individual destruction as did Sherman. The following letter is one of the many worthy of record, which was penned by "A Daughter of a Revolutionary Hero" to General Hunter, U.S.A.

(From the RICHMOND EXAMINER.)
"Shepherdstown, Va., July 20.
" General Hunter,
" Yesterday your underling, Captain Martindale, of the First New York Veteran Cavalry, executed your infamous order, and burned my house. You have had the satisfaction, ere this, of receiving from him the information that your orders were fulfilled to the letter,

the dwelling and every outbuilding, seven in number, with their contents, being burned. I, therefore, a helpless woman, whom you have cruelly wronged, address you, a Major-General of the United States Army, and demand why this was done ?

" What was my offence ?

"My husband was absent, an exile. He has never been a politician, or in any way engaged in the struggle now going on—his age preventing it. This fact, David Strother, your chief of staff, could have told you. The house was built by my father, a revolutionary soldier, who served the whole seven years for your independence. There was I born; there the sacred dead repose; it was my house and my home; and there has your niece, who lived among us during this horrid war, up to the present moment, met with every kindness and hospitality at my hands.

"Was it for this that you turned me, my young daughter, and little son out upon the world without a shelter? or was it because my husband is the grandson of the revolutionary patriot, and of the noblest of Christian warriors, the greatest of generals, Robert E. Lee? Heaven's blessings be upon his head for ever! You and your government have failed to conquer, subdue, or match him; and disappointed rage and malice find vent upon the helpless and inoffensive.

" Hyena-like, you have torn my heart to pieces, for all hallowed memories clustered around that homestead; and, demon-like, you have done it without even the pretext of revenge—for I never saw or harmed you. Your office is not to lead, like a brave man and soldier, your men to fight in the ranks of war, but your work has been to

separate yourself from danger, and, with your incendiary
band, steal unawares upon helpless women and children,
to insult and destroy. Two fair homes did you, yesterday, ruthlessly lay in ashes, giving not a moment's
warning to the startled inmates of your wicked purpose ; turning mothers and children out of doors ; your
very name execrated by your own men, for the cruel
work you gave them to do.

"In the case of Mr. A. R. Boteler, both father and
mother were far away. Any heart but that of Captain
Martindale (and yours) would have been touched by
that little circle, comprising a widowed daughter, just
risen from her bed of illness, her three little fatherless
babies, the eldest not five years old, and her heroic
sister. I repeat that any man would have been touched
at that sight but Captain Martindale ; one might as
well hope to find mercy and feeling in the heart of a
wolf, bent on its prey of young lambs, as to search for
such qualities in his bosom. You have chosen well
your man for such deeds ; doubtless you will promote
him.

"A colonel of the Federal army has stated that you
deprived forty of your officers of their commands because
they refused to carry out your malignant mischief. All
honour to their names for this, at least. They are men ;
they have human hearts, and blush for such a commander.

"I ask, who that does not wish infamy and disgrace
attached to him for ever, would serve under you?
Your name will stand on history's page as the hunter of
weak women and innocent children ; the hunter to
destroy defenceless villages and refined and beautiful

homes; to torture afresh the agonized hearts of suffering widows; the hunter of Africa's poor sons and daughters, to lure them on to ruin and death of soul and body; the hunter with the relentless heart of a wild beast, the face of a fiend, and the form of a man. Oh, earth! behold the monster.

"Can I say 'God forgive you?' No prayer can be offered for you. Were it possible for human lips to raise your name heavenward, angels would thrust the foul thing back again, and demons claim their own. The curses of thousands, the scorn of the manly and upright, and the hatred of the true and honourable will follow you and yours through all time, and brand your name—infamy! infamy!!

"Again I demand why you have burned my house? Answer, as you must answer before the Searcher of all hearts, why have you added this cruel wicked deed to your many crimes?"

We glance at another paper, and, behold, another bitter maddening wail is upon our ear, from one who, in all her anguish, pours forth her soul's agony in flowing poesy. Read it; your blood will chill as the wild rhythm gushes from that lacerated heart.

"THIS IS A TIME TO DANCE."

[From the "Chattanooga Rebel."]

" Let hypocrite " or "puritan"
Dethrone fair Pleasure if they can.
What if our friends are dying now ?
And every drop of kindred blood
Has ceased its living course to flow,
And joined the dark and clotted flood ?
Still fill it up, the sparkling cup, and let us sup,

A draught to-night, of nectar bright, with crimson light
Whate'er may chance, to-night we dance, 'neath pleasure's glance.

" For what to us is stiffened clay
     If pleasure holds her joyous sway,
     Or what are tears or mourner's groan,
          If still to sweet and mirthful sound
     Our laughing queen sits on her throne
          To see the dancers circle round ?
Still fill it up, the sparkling cup, &c.

" Our sisters danced in olden time
     Like us to music's merry chime ;
     Of gay ' glee girls' we've often read,
          Who waited till the death of day,
     Then to the battlefield they sped,
          And danced until the morning gray.
Then fill it up, the sparkling cup, &c.

" Like them we'll dance, this is the time,
     When dying groans make sweetest chime,
     Then fill the cup with crimson gore,
          Fresh from the flooded battle-ground.
     I never drank a draught before
          That half so sweet as *blood* I found.
Then fill it up, the sparkling cup, &c.

" I hear a glad and joyous sound,
     Come deep and far from under ground,
     Far our loud call of mirth's been heard,
          By every fiend in hell's expanse
     And all its darkest depths are stirred,
          To give us music for the dance.
Then fill it up, the sparkling cup, &c.

" Come want, and death, and rapine come !
     As partners come to youth and bloom,
     Grim Want, you closed my mother's eyes,
          And Death, you laid my brother low,
     Rapine, my home in ashes lies,
          But still come on, the dance is slow.
Then fill it up, the sparkling cup, &c.

" We've left the hall and battlefield,
 We've danced till every head has reeled,
 But still we circle round and round,
   Nor stop, for ' 'tis a time to dance.'
 But see that *chasm* in the ground !
 And see the *bluelights* upward glance !
I hear a sound, deep under ground, a fiendish sound :
The demons come, yes, every one, our dance begun,
Will *never* end, and *hell* we'll spend in bow and bend,
Our cup's mixed up, a fiery cup with blood mixed up."

Then again we glance at a journal; it is not our
own; but read what it says also. How calmly this
fiend writes, how smoothly his pen glides over bloody
battle-fields, devastation, ruin, and death !—

" SECESSIA FEMININA.

" The faces that look down from the windows of
this valley have, in many instances, a strange and fasci-
nating beauty. Between them and one who glances up
that glamor, so fatal to Phyrsis, rises to cheat the senses,
and inform the heart with the most persuasive lie.
There is no tenderness in these faces. Their charm is
far different from that known to Northern courtiers; it
is a steel-cold languor, to witness which is chilling to
the soul. One who commences speech with these
damsels finds himself wondering what sort of beings
have arisen in this soil, in place of the children of Eve.
Here are smiles, and courtesy, and refinement ; but, oh !
how very like a cymbal is the hollow something in the
sound of all. These women have suffered. War is
nearer their hearths than to ours. It is a sterner thing
by far. Their hearts are in it, buried, some of them, in
graves that thicken every day upon the soil.

"Along this valley, in which, from the Potomac to Staunton, there is no law nor safety, the scourge of battle is a monthly episode. All the horror, all the sacrifice of war, knocks at the door of every mansion on the way. Property and life are things of chance.

"People make few plans for the future. To-morrow may shatter them for ever. Marriage is little thought of; all marriageable men are under arms, and marriageable women let them go with little murmur. There is no use in murmuring. War is the one great passion to which both sexes are alike devoted, and for which both are ready to make any sacrifice. These women seem to have tacitly accepted the fact that, until the war is over, courtship is a mockery that had better not be thought of.

" The maiden who says good-bye to her lover makes up her mind for the worst that can befall. Death is the rival of love; and death, nine times out of ten, is conqueror. Is it strange, then, that we who seek for tenderness in the hearts of these women must seek deep? Wrong as is the cause, it has a more wide-spread, and a bitterer, deeper devotion among the masses in this region than has ours. One of the most beautiful of any women in the valley, who visited the North before the war, and was a belle at several watering-places during the summer months, refused last week to take the hand of an old friend, in Federal uniform, who presented himself at her door.

" I have heard no less than half-a-dozen damsels say, in a tone of perfect calmness, that they had rather have every friend they had die, and die themselves, than have the South submit to a restoration with those whom they esteem to be its enemies. I believe they meant what they said, and would abide by it to the letter. Such women as these are influential enemies, and it will be said by many that they deserve all the insult and harm they have received in return for their enmity. I do not think so, and, far as I am from defending their devotion to a cause wicked in its inception, I cannot refrain from as much wonder as admiration of the few among the many in the valley who preserve a like devotion to the sacred cause of the Union.

"One incident will always be grateful and thrilling in the memory of this army. While the troops were passing through Winchester, on their return, three young and accomplished ladies, wearing the colours of our flag upon their breasts, and waving the same banner borne by the marching regiments, stood in front of a single dwelling, smiling welcome. To the officers who stopped to greet them they expressed a heartfelt joy at the presence of our soldiers, and to those officers they bade farewell with trembling voices, and eyes swimming in regretful tears."

See, here is another paper; look at it also; it is from my own loved State, dear reader, and, bidding adieu to Sherman and his associate band of thieving, murdering outlaws, we will just read this letter, whose caption promises much for the Confederacy in the event of the supposed extermination of her male heroes:—

A PROVOST-MARSHAL BEARDED BY A GIRL OF SEVENTEEN.

Bayon des Allemands, October 20, 1863.

" O ! whither hast thou led me, Egypt (nigger), see
How I convey my shame out of thine eyes

By looking back on what I have left behind,
'Stroy'd in dishonour."
Antony and Cleopatra, Act iii. Sc. ix.

"Mr. Editor,—What have we come to? Has this cruel and unnatural war scattered away manly feelings? Has it destroyed that courtesy and those delicate attentions towards ladies for which our country was once so justly famed? It would seem, indeed, that our instincts were changed, and that our sense of propriety had worn itself out.

" The tale I will now tell does not seem to appertain to an order of things apparently possible in the nineteenth century, and yet I vouch that it is not taken from the history of the Goths, Vandals, or Saracens. The whole is modern history; not that of the middle ages, but of yesterday. The hero is an officer of volunteers, a captain, a provost-marshal, and not one of Attila, Totila, or Tamerlane's savage hordes. The heroine is a pretty girl of seventeen, of French descent, a sweet, a lovely Creole.

" There you have, Mr. Editor, the ' dramatis personæ.' Reader, blush, not through modesty; there is no love in my story, and it will not end in a marriage, I am sure ; for some one must blush through shame when he looks back on what 'he has left behind,' ' 'stroy'd in dishonour.'

" In Napoleonville, a pretty village on Bayon Lafourche, Louisiana, on the 9th of October, as the rich sun of the South was descending behind the tall cypresses, in the year of our Lord one thousand eight hundred and sixty-three, and in the full face of the nineteenth century, a man, an officer of the United

2 c

States Volunteers, drove in his buggy to a gate opening into a flower garden, stretched before a mansion with some pretension to taste, comfort, and even elegance. Whilst the man secures his horse near the gate, watch him; he is fretting; he looks all-sorts; his step, his mien, tell of his designs of anger. He comes in all the grandeur of his wrath—he, the representative of an almighty power—to exercise retributive justice. On the piazza you may see a young lady, reading. Mr. Editor, I will introduce her to you—'Miss Leontia Bordis.' . She rose to receive, with a courtesy, the man who approached the house.

"'Miss Bordis, I suppose?'

"'Yes, Sir,' she replied.

"'You have here a coloured girl?'

"'Yes, Sir,' she returned. 'You are Capt. Rudgard, I presume?'

"'I am Captain Rudgard,' said he, advancing towards her, with a threat in his looks and in the gesture of his hands. 'Go for that girl,' continued he, pointing to the door.

"'The masters of this house, Sir, receive no one's orders; they are not your servants.'

"However, as this Miss Leontia had heard of the man's temper and character, she directed her younger sister to call Julienne, the servant girl.

"'Go yourself, I command you; do you understand me?'

"'No, Sir, never!' was the reply.

"The servant had now come, when the Captain commenced speaking to her in English, of which Julienne did not understand one word.

" ' *Sis*, you will come with me ? '

" The girl shakes her head, rolls her eyes, grins; she does not understand. Then with emphasis, 'Miss, you shall interpret for me.'

" 'Never!' she replied.

" Having lost all hope of subduing that noble spirit, he turned to the younger sister with a peremptory order to repeat faithfully to the servant all he would tell her, and to return her answers to him.

" 'Ondine,' said Leontia, 'not a word, sister, speak not a word.'

" She had scarcely finished, when that man—if I can call him a man—sprang towards Leontia, and, seizing her by the shoulders, tried to throw her down. He did not succeed in the attempt, but he pushed her against the wall. A second time he made an effort to throw her, when she, taking hold of his long beard, fell upon his breast. She clung to that beard with all the desperate energy of an offended female. There were present at that hideous scuffle Leontia's venerable grandmother and little Ondine; her mother is in the grave, her father was not at home—he is far away, *he will come*.

" The maddened provost, now bearded, seized her wrists, tearing her skin with his nails, shaking her whole frame with all his power, while she, having become frantic with pain, convulsed with indignation, clings to his whiskers and beard, tearing both away. Her efforts to protect herself have enraged him; *with his nails he digs in her flesh;* but she cannot be overcome. So far *the little rebel* has won the field!

" When bloody tragedy ceases, then commences

ludicrous comedy. There is no flag of truce sent from one belligerent to the other; they are still face to face, but panting, bleeding, choked with pain and madness, in the presence of the witnesses whom his roaring, the cries of the children, and the loud supplication of the grandmother have caused to assemble. The Captain asks for quarter; he proposes terms to her who is nearly fainting, but whose indomitable courage bears up against the weakness of her sex.

"He capitulates, 'Please, miss, let my beard go!' She at first says nothing, but continues to hold on firmly. 'If I let your arms go will you let my beard go?'

"'Yes,' she answers.

"'Well, then let my beard go.'

"'No, let my arms free first.'

"Then he released her. He can look on what he has left behind, "'stroy'd in dishonour," scattered on the floor, and hanging to those delicate fingers which an iron will has made terrible; he maddens at the sight; it is a whole wreck of his manhood around him. But he dares not return to the charge; there stands before him that pretty girl of seventeen, with her large beautiful black eyes, her dark tresses, her delicate features of the deepest crimson. All her blood seems to have rushed to her heart to make it stout, and to her face, returning to render her more lovely. There she stands, mute, bidding defiance.

"'Say,' exclaims the man, the Captain, the Provost-Marshal. 'Say that hereafter you will behave like a lady!'

"'I have always been a lady. I was born one.'

"Again Mr. Editor, the man, sprung upon her, scratching and bruising her; but he bethought himself of his beard before she had time to recommence hostilities. It was well; it was in good time that he drew back his fangs. At that moment he remembers that he is Provost-Marshal, and he says, 'I arrest you, Miss; you are my prisoner; you shall follow me.'

" 'No, Sir, I shall not follow you.'

" 'If you do not, I will send for my guard and take you in my arms.' Good heavens! such a girl in the arms of such a man! 'By force I will put you in my buggy.'

" Leontia pauses, she trembles, her breast heaves with fear; with a sigh, in a low tone of voice, she says, ' I will go.'

" 'To-night you shall stay in prison, to-morrow you shall be sent to New Orleans.' And then, coming nearer to her and holding a handful of that hair which had been his beard, he piteously said, ' What must I do with it ?'

" 'Give it to me,' she replied; 'I will take proper care of it.'

" He does not answer, but carefully puts it in his pocket. It will be produced in court; a witness—an undeniable proof of guilt when he sits in judgment against her.

" Whilst she puts on her gloves, before leaving the house, he whispers to her, ' I shall make it impossible for you, when you are in New Orleans, to——' she heard no more, his words are low, inaudible, incomprehensible sounds, falling upon the ears of one, whom her present emotions made insensible to all except to pain, and her dread of the future.

"They leave; Leontia's grandmother has obtained permission to accompany her child; they reach the Court-house. The Provost-Marshal sends for Mr. D. Leblanc to be a protection to his captive—perhaps this means to be her security against further attempts on his beard; for, taking in both hands what he had already bestowed in his pockets—'See two handfuls.' He sits looking gloomily on what had been ''stroy'd in dishonour.' After telling his own version of the facts he orders that Leontia should spend the night in prison; but Mr. Leblanc prays so hard, begs so earnestly, supplicates with so much humility, that he consents, at last, that she should stay for the night in Mr. Leblanc's house, with a Provost-Marshal's guard keeping the watch.

"Early in the morning Leontia and her friends appeared at the Court-house. Mr. Leblanc has sent for Mr. Gentil, a friend of the Bordis family. The Captain Provost-Marshal sits calm and composed on the judge's chair, in the quadruple capacity of plaintiff, prosecuting attorney, witness—the evidence in his pocket—and judge, to mete out justice. Hear! hear! he spake first of Julienne, the servant-girl, stating that she had been cruelly treated by Miss Bordis. To this statement Leontia gave an indignant denial. There was contempt enough in her curved lip to crush an ordinary man, but not enough for a captain of volunteers; there was a flash of indignation in her eyes—erect, she was beautifully scornful. The judge dropped the nigger, and his beard was the next charge. Some has been saved, it is true; he has it in his pocket; but there is no salve that will remedy the evil. From the judge's hands it cannot be replanted on the judge's face. Whereas this cannot be done, the court condemns the accused, found guilty of tearing a provost-marshal's beard, to take forthwith the oath of allegiance to the United States Constitution—a reparation, an atonement, due to the majesty of the law. On the fulfilling of this infliction the accused shall be set at liberty.

" Miss Leontia, who, like most of the pretty girls of seventeen, seems to be made up of such components as self-will, self-dignity, with a little of reckless stubbornness, replies in the negative to the judge's injunction. ' No,' she says ; ' I will never take the oath of allegiance.'

" ' Something must be done. Take her to the next room, and prevail upon her to take the oath,' says the judge. Officious friends expostulate with her; her grandmother cries ; they all beg her to yield.

" ' No,' she repeats ; ' I will never take that oath.'

" ' Then write to the judge a letter of apology.'

" She writes; it is not a letter of apology ; it is refused. She writes another ; it is also refused, and both are sent back. She will write no more. It is for the judge to extricate himself from the difficulty the best way he can ; the girl demurs, and stays all proceedings towards an adjustment. Another effort is made; she yields at last, and sends her ultimatum—' I consider myself French ; I will consent to take the oath of neutrality.'

" ' That will do,' says the judge, ' provided I regain possession of one of those letters I refused to receive.'

" The letter is given to him; he administers the oath of neutrality to Miss Leontia Bordis, who returns to her home with her grandmother and her friends.

"Girls of the World! nine cheers for Leontia! Men of all nations! nine groans for the Captain Provost-Marshal.   "MODERN HISTORY."

From scenes like the first of this chapter—painful, and like the last—farcical, I will now, dear reader, turn and beg your perusal of the letter which will conclude this recital, which, in its false prophecy, reminds us of the oft-repeated " On to Richmond;" but its sentiment finds an echo in all Southern hearts, teeming as it does with hope, confidence in God, and firm intention to conquer or to die.

" Address to the Citizens of New Orleans,

"Executive Office, Shreveport, La.,
January 30, 1864.

" To the Citizens of New Orleans,—

"I greet you as the Governor of Louisiana. Your trials and your troubles are well known, and your patriotic conduct fully appreciated by the Executive of your State. Do not be despondent! Do not despair; but rather let the fires of patriotism burn brightly at every fireside; for in a few short months you shall be free. You have been despoiled and robbed, and basely insulted. Every indignity that a brutal, unprincipled, and a vindictive foe could invent, has been heaped upon you. Bear your persecutions as did your fathers before you, and nerve your hearts for the coming hour. Our people are flocking to the army in every direction, and when the spring campaign opens, half a million of gallant Confederate soldiers will strike for liberty and independence.

"Citizens of New Orleans,—Be true to yourselves, and your State will be true to you. Spurn all propositions for compromises of any kind. Spit upon the insulting proposal for a bastard State Government. Keep your own counsels. Do your duty and bide your time. You shall be free! The hated tyrants who lord it over you now, who daily insult you without remorse, and rob you without shame—these accursed villains, this crew of thieves and murderers, will yet receive their reward.

"Ladies of New Orleans,—God Almighty bless you and sustain you in all your trials; may Heaven guard you and protect you! 'When spring-time comes,' gentle ladies, you will see the 'Grey Coats' again, and then you shall welcome back to New Orleans the sons and daughters of Louisiana. You are the treasures of the earth. Oh! be not weary in well doing. Cheer up the desponding. Be kind to our prisoners who are languishing in the wretched cells of the enemy. You will receive the undying gratitude of your country, and in heaven above you will be crowned among the angels of the living God.

"(Signed)   "HENRY W. ALLEN,
"Governor of the State of Louisiana."

CHAPTER XXVI.

While sacred music floats upon the air,
  The mournful cortège wends its way along
Through myrtle groves, while feathered warblers waking
  Blend with the chant their melancholy song.

The grove is reached ! the last sad notes are over,
  The requiem fades upon the morning air !
They strew bright blossoms on the earth above her,
  And leave her, while they breathe a silent prayer.
No cypress tree above her couch is waving,
  But palm and date trees shade her lonely grave,
While glancing sunbeams, and the bright stars shining,
  Keep quiet vigil by the amber wave.

" Be just and fear not."

AGAIN we turn to New Orleans to witness a mournful
spectacle, one in its solemnity, sublimely grand.   The
bells are pealing the funeral knell of one of Louisiana's
fairest and best beloved daughters, and we behold in
front of her residence, corner of Rampart and Esplanade
Streets, the sympathising multitude, who have assembled
from humble cottages and stately homes to catch a
glimpse of the coffin, in which the mortal remains of
Marguerite Caroline Deslonde, wife of General G. T.
Beauregard, are enshrined.   Hushed and respectful
stand the vast multitude.   A stifled sob arises at intervals, but breaks softly on the rock of despotism, which

it struggles against. The voice of the petty tyrant has proclaimed that she may be borne to her last resting place, in the parish of Saint John Baptist, "provided there be no demonstration." The procession of priests in their robes, with Bishop Odin at the head; the array of youth and age; the sad regard that each face wears, the silent tear coursing down the cheek; the flower-covered streets which lead from her mansion to where the steamer lay; the almost audible beating of hearts as the burial casket comes in view of the multitude on its bed of lilies, roses, and orange blossoms; the bowed heads of the awe-inspired thousands; the whispered prayer of the vast throng—*is demonstration*, such as no tyrant can suppress, and beyond the power of language to pourtray. Only sixty persons are allowed to act as escort to the body, and Marguerite Caroline Deslonde, the honoured, noble wife of G. T. Beauregard, is soon borne down the river to the plantation, where, after an imposing service, she is left in quiet peace, alike uncon-scious of homage or of insult.

General Banks would scarcely have granted the request, to convey her body to the plantation, nor would he have placed his own steamer, the "Nebraska," at the disposal of her family, had not the organ through which he breathes his true sentiments, betrayed his inhuman and indelicate feelings, when it published the following brutal announcement of Mrs. Beauregard's death :—

" The morning papers announce the death of the wife of G. T. Beauregard. She died at her residence, on Esplanade Street, on the evening of the 2nd instant. This woman has, we learn, been in poor health for the past two or three years, and has required, what has been denied her, the care and attention of the man who gave her his word at the altar to cherish and protect her. He also swore at one time to support the constitution of the United States. He does not hold his oath in very high estimation, as we find him not only plotting for the destruction of his country, but deserting his invalid wife for years together, and leaving her dependant upon others for those acts of kindness and support that should be given by a husband. We know very little of the life or character of the deceased, further than that she was an invalid, neglected by her sworn protector, and left by him under the powerful protection of the flag whose glory he is devoting his puny energies to sully. But when he is called to his final account, he will have the mortification of knowing that the lustre of the Stars and Stripes is all the brighter, and his betrayed country the more powerful, for the treason of himself and co-conspirators."

The intense excitement caused by this article filled General Banks's soul with dread, and in order, after a fashion, to make some show of manliness, he permitted a public funeral. This was poor atonement for the base insult, and the scowl which rested upon the brow of Southerners, as they read "this woman," told of a deeper thrust of the poignard of outrage than the *famous article No. 28, of General-Butler-notoriety, which only pointed to "women styling themselves ladies," and whose conduct in the public thoroughfares deserved reproach.* "*This woman*" was applied to a lady, born and bred such. One whose position during her whole life was exalted, and whose career from the cradle to the grave was one of virtue and unparalleled excellence. Not content with casting a slur upon the dead, he has presumed in this article to asperse the character of the noble Beauregard, whose attachment to his wife is well known. Yes, in the silent face of the dead has this vile loathsome wretch dared to utter falsehood. General Banks did not even require his mouthpiece to apologise.

How different did General Butler act, when upon his arrival in New Orleans, he heard that Mrs. Beauregard was ill. He sent for Mr. Sauvé, and said to him, "I learn that Mrs. Beauregard is quite ill—not expected to live; if this be the case, and she desires an interview with her husband, he may enter the city unmolested, *I shall not see it*."

It was said that General Beauregard *did* visit Mrs. Beauregard, but *I* can only vouch for the conduct of General Butler, as related by an intimate friend of General Beauregard.

General Butler again evinced charitable feeling upon an occasion which it may not be inappropriate to mention here. I had been staying some few weeks at the Ursuline Convent, and it was during the dearth of provisions (flour especially), when Generals Butler and Shepley monopolised the purchase and sale. One of the nuns (the Mother Assistant) said to me,

"From what I have heard you say regarding your interviews with Generals Butler and Shepley, they may allow us, at your request, to purchase flour, for if they do not we shall have to discharge our scholars, retaining only our orphans, whom we are forced to keep. We cannot get provisions, and are nearly out."

I told her that I would do so, and when I went into

the city visited General Butler, for the purpose of asking a pass to enter the Confederacy.

I was received most courteously, but was refused the pass unless I would take the oath of allegiance to the United States, which I refused most positively to do. Upon rising to leave, I mentioned briefly my conversation with the Mother Assistant of the Ursuline Convent.

" When did this occur, Miss?" he said.

I responded, "Last week."

" Then present my compliments to the Superior, and say to her, that if she will make out a list of what provisions she requires, I will fill it with pleasure *with* or *without money*."

I forthwith bore the message, and was told by Sister St. Michel that they had that day been fortunate enough to make a purchase at auction of all they would need for some time.

I wrote the General a note of thanks, in the name of the ladies, saying that they would be most happy to accept his proffer should a dearth occur again. I write this from my *personal experience*, and to prove to the world that there is a difference between " *to seem* " and " *to be*."

I was detained in New Orleans after its occupation, for five months, and though I was granted every favour which I condescended to ask of either Generals Butler or Shepley, I was thus put to many inconveniences, but at last made my escape, with a pass *penned by General Butler himself*, for a Miss " Jane Florence," which he gave to a lady who had taken the oath for a person whom he deemed her *protégé*, as the individual led him to suppose. The lady who procured it for me was an entire stranger to me, but having heard I was anxious to leave the city, volunteered to obtain a pass, which I told her could not be done if my own name were given, so she merely reversed my pro and cognomen, and succeeded in deceiving the General. General Butler did many acts while in New Orleans, for which he has just claims on the regard of some of the first families; in fact the *élite* of the city in many instances wrote him letters, in which were expressed the most unbounded admiration and esteem.

Mrs. Slocum of New Orleans, wound up her epistle of grateful acknowledgments (for his protection of her property) by a sentence which speaks volumes for Butler, while it reflects no credit upon her as a Confederate and Southerner, whose son was *then* in the Confederate States Army. She concluded, " Your magnanimity can only be equalled by the cowardice of the men of New Orleans."

" I have a plain, unvarnished
Tale delivered ; " receive it or
Reject it, as you like.

CHAPTER XXVII.

"A strange woman, truly—not young ; yet her face,
Wan and worn as it was, bore about it the trace
Of a beauty time could not ruin.   For the whole
Quiet cheek, youth's lost bloom left transparent, the soul
Seem'd to fill with its own light, like some sunny fountain
Everlastingly fed from far off in the mountain,
That pours, in a garden deserted, its streams,
And all the more lovely for loneliness seems.
So that watching that face, you would scarce pause to guess
The years which its calm careworn lines might express,
Feeling only what suffering with these must have past,
To have perfected there so much sweetness at last."

Loud boomed the cannon, shrill sounded fife and drum,
and gaily rang the stirring music of the various bands
throughout the city of Richmond, on the morning of
the ———, while the patriotic citizens were seen
hurrying to and fro in holiday costume; and regiments
of worn soldiers were drawn up in front of the President's mansion, whose doors, windows, and gates were
garlanded with bright blossoms from wood and glen,
and floating ribbons fluttered in the breeze; and though
war was at their threshold, they veiled the vision for
this day, and even danced with mirth and song, when
assembled in the *Grey Mansion* to do honour to one

whose name and fame had cast a lustre upon the Confederate arms. General Beaumont, a French gentleman of distinction, had gallantly fought, side by side, with the renowned General Lee; and, grateful for his service, the people of Richmond had determined to present him and his brave troops with a testimonial of their regard in the form of a flag, made by the fairest women of the South.

Miss de Villerie was chosen to present the colours; and in military style, in front of the President's mansion, and in presence of the entire population, Miss de Villerie, at the appointed hour, escorted by a corps of ladies, attired in grey, and mounted, like herself, on magnificent steeds, and wearing the military ¸chapeau, proceeded to the place of rendezvous.

Arrayed in thread-bare uniforms, and mounted upon war-worn steeds, awaited the generals and military men, and when Miss de Villerie appeared, a cheer of enthusiastic greeting arose and rent the air; an avenue at the same time opening through the dense throng to admit the cavalcade. General Beaumont was seated beside the President, in an open landau, drawn by four magnificent grey chargers. Miss de Villerie, joined by General S—— (who bore the banner), advanced towards the equipage and stopped immediately in front, a burst of applause startling the echoes of city, hill, and dale. When silence reigned, she spoke in clear tones; addressing a few appropriate remarks to the General, expressive of the appreciation of the Southern people for his services, so nobly, gallantly rendered, and placing her hand upon the flag-staff, she said, in conclusion, "Accept this tribute of a bleeding nation's esteem, hallowed as

2 D

its folds are by the tears of mothers, wives, and sisters, and consecrated to the cause of *Truth* and *Justice*."

She ceased, and General Beaumont replied in a few brief sentences, gracefully delivered; the band struck *La Marseillaise;*—the crowd dispersed,—and de Miss Villerie, with her escort, proceeded to the President's mansion, where music, dance, and harmony reigned until a late hour.

Miss de Villerie passed through this scene in dreamy abstractedness; her pale cheek, from which the roses had long since fled, bespeaking suffering such as only those who have seen their brightest highest hopes perish, and have witnessed the entombing even of their best and firmest trust, can feel. She passed amidst the crowd regardless of the praise which rang from the lips of gay cavaliers around her. In this brilliant assembly she was *with*, not *of* them, and her eye seemed to follow—

> " Her heart, and that was far away,
> Where a rude *grave by James River lay.*"

CHAPTER XXVIII.

" 'T is not that—but, alas !—but I cannot conceal
That I have not forgotten the past—but I feel
That I cannot accept all these gifts on your part,—
Rank, wealth, love, esteem—in return for a heart,
Which is only a ruin ! "
        With words warm and wild,
" Tho' a ruin it be, trust me yet to rebuild
And restore," the Duke cried ; " tho' ruin it be,
Since so dear is that ruin, ah ! yield it to me."

ON the morning after the day on which the above scene
was enacted Miss De Villerie sat alone in her boudoir.
Reader, when first she was presented to your notice, it
was in the zenith of her beauty and bloom; when the
star of hope shone bright in mid-heaven, and sur·
rounded by friends tried and faithful—she stood the
peerless queen of the Crescent city, and the fair representative of its Creole maidens. A brief period of years
has passed since then, but a century of woe has rolled
over her soul, and her raven tresses, besprinkled by
Care's argent threads, bespeak a tale of mental anguish,
and shadow forth a ruin such as Father Time could not
have paralleled. She now sits arrayed in cloud-like
India muslin morning-dress, richly trimmed in Valen-
ciennes lace, and the misty floating folds of her dress are

confined to her slender waist by a sash of lilac ribbon, a
few sprigs of lilies of the valley worn in the side of her
hair, which is combed in a Grecian knot low on her
neck, complete her simple yet elegant toilette. She was
seated beside a small table on which rested three miniatures and a lock of nut-brown hair; she had placed the
latter to her lips when a gentle rap at the door of the
apartment caused her to drop the hair into the case of
the miniature and say, "*Entrez.*"

Her servant, Victorine, who remained faithful to her
amidst every change, entered with a card, which she
handed to her mistress.

"Ah! General Beaumont," she said, "ask him to
enter, and place these (pointing to the miniatures) in
my jewel-casket."

General Beaumont entering, gracefully, the compliments of the morning were exchanged, when the General,
politely alluding to the event of the day previous, said,
" Miss De Villerie, yesterday, to me, was indeed a day of
triumph, and of happy recollections never to be forgotten!
Not that I received your country's homage and witnessed
its gratitude, but because God should have so ordained it
that the offering should be made by Natalie De Villerie,
the only being I ever loved;" at the same time throwing
off the light wig and whiskers he stood before Miss De
Villerie's astonished gaze the veritable Count Beauharnais, he continued, "Natalie, do you not know me? Do
you not feel me at last worthy of your love? I who have
so long, so ardently hoped and prayed for this moment
when your country would have acknowledged me
worthy its lovely daughter. Speak, Natalie; tell me
I have not loved in vain."

Miss De Villerie trembled with emotion at this *dénouement*, she clasped her hands to her forehead as it were to shut out some vision; gradually her head sunk upon her breast—he approached her, she waived him off, but he knelt before her, saying, "forgive me, Natalie, if my expressions of a feeling which overpowers me pain you. I know your heart and read its story long ago, and none, save love pure as mine, could have worshipped you, even when you held the cold lifeless form of another pressed to your heart, and prayed for your happiness while you kissed another's lips. Natalie, nought but love, enduring as Time could have recognised under the various forms and disguises of Miss Clayton, Sœur Secessia, and Miss Laval, the beautiful Natalie De Villerie. I have traced you everywhere; I have followed on faithfully; I know your suffering, I respect it; but, Natalie, endeavour to forget, and trust to my love for future happiness."

She answered through her tears, "Happiness, Count! Alas, there is none for me in this world. My heart is in the grave. I speak thus, as you seem to know all. I never loved but once—can never love again. You ask me to be yours; would you care to wed with one between whose love and yours would hang a funeral pall? Would you wish to place the firm foundation of such a structure as love has reared in your noble heart upon a quagmire in which it would sink to rise no more? Do you desire to place golden drapery on the windows of a ruin where the mildew of cold and damp shall gather? No! no! I cannot consent to a deed of sacrilege."

"Natalie, I will not urge the matter, nor say more

at present. You have termed your heart a ruin, it is, nevertheless, dear to me. I will rebuild its broken arches, I will on the adamantine base of my own rear again its fallen columns of beauty, and on the pinnacle of this edifice inscribe my motto, '*Nil desperandum.*' Farewell." Respectfully he raised her hand, and pressing it to his lips arose and left the apartment.

Again the tide of bitter memories rose and fell, and once again she was called upon for a sacrifice. The morning passed away in tears and reflection, and when evening fell she wrote thus :—

" Count Beauharnais,—If the gratitude and esteem of one whose love dwells with the dead are deemed a sufficient recompense for your long and faithful service to my country, and your unwavering devotion to me, I consent to be yours; trusting that if I cannot be happy myself, I shall thus render happy one who is worthy of a purer and more profound affection than I can ever give him.

" Give me but until the end of this unhappy strife, and by that time, perhaps, the feeling which now seems perjury to the dead will have somewhat lessened, and I shall be more fit to vow fealty as your bride, and more strengthened in the idea of the duty I owe towards the living as well as the dead. The heart, withered and crushed, could never be revived by a less noble or ardent love than that of a Beauharnais; *this name alone* is worthy the heart's first offering, which, alas ! it is not mine to yield.

" Farewell ! Rest content with my promise; if God

so ordains it, it will be fulfilled. Until then we are, before the world and to each other, but as friends.

"NATALIE DE VILLERIE."

Reader, I feel you would fain know more. Would that I might rise the dim veil of futurity, and take your hand in mine, and, pressing it to my lips, say farewell to her and thee, as I pointed to a happy home, environed by all which is bright and beautiful.

> " Shut out by Alpine hills from the rude world,
> Near a clear lake, margined by fruits of gold
> And whispering myrtles ; glassing softest skies,
> As cloudless, save with rare and roseate shadows,
> As *we* would have *her* fate ! "

ROSALE PLANTATION.

1865.

> " The steed is vanish'd from the stall ;
> No serf is seen in Hassan's hall ;
> The lonely spider's thin grey pall
> Waves slowly widening o'er the wall :
> The bat builds in his harem bower,
> And in the fortress of his power,
> The owl usurps the beacon-tower ;
> The wild dog howls o'er the fountain's brim
> With baffled thirst, and famine grim ;
> For the stream has shrunk from its marble bed,
> Where the weeds and the desolate dust are spread."

The once beautifully cultivated fields are overgrown with nettles, and the fences are torn down ; the slaves are no longer to be heard by the traveller, at morn or at eve, singing their songs of merry, innocent glee ; the charred ruins of their once pretty cottages are seen, and the cattle even are no more heard, nor tinkling bells of sheep greet the ear, while within all speaks of ruin

and decay. The shrubs are withered and uncared for,
the parterres are weed-grown, and reptiles lurk beneath;
now and then a shattered marble rises amidst the rank
grass and brambles, to speak of some spent shell aimed
at an imaginary guerilla; the places where statues once
stood are now but the resting-place of the couchant invader on sentinel duty; the fountains are fissured and
broken, and their once clear streams are now a sanguine
hue; the birds, even, have flown to sunnier scenes, and
warble their strains amidst gayer foliage; the chateau
is in a state of dilapidation, and the mournful winds
sweep through its open casements, wailing for the dead
and absent; the floor is strewn with pieces of marble of
exquisite workmanship, while the fresco work of walls
and ceilings is covered with ruin, and insects are creeping over all; the bat flaps his dark wings in the upper
chambers; and the dove alone remains to moan in piteous
strains o'er DESOLATION'S TABLEAUX!!!

REPLY

To the Addresses of

Messrs. Hiestand and Horner (Union),

Appearing before the public for the first time, as the press feared arrest, suppression, and imprisonment, should they publish it.

CONCLUSION.

" There was a little man, and he had a little soul,
   And he said, ' Little Soul, let us try, try, try,
     Whether it's within our reach
     To make up a little speech
   Just between little you, and little I, I, I,
   Just between little you and little I ! '

" Away then cheek by jowl,
   Little Man and little Soul
     Went and spoke their little speech to a tittle, tittle, tittle,
   And the world all declare
   That this priggish little pair
     Never yet in all their lives look'd so little, little, little,
     Never yet in all their lives looked so little."

THE vaunted liberty of an American press has been long the theme upon which all nations have dwelt with praise, and their admiration has been unbounded, at the privilege which they have heretofore imagined all free citizens of our far-famed country possessed, namely, liberty to think, speak, and write as each and every one felt inclined.

I will now lay before the eyes of the civilized world a case in point, and prove this impression false. In the month of November, 1863, I was called upon by a gentleman, and asked by him if I had seen the last "Era," to which I replied in the negative; he went on to state its contents, and remarked that it was teeming with interesting matter, and that he would send it to me; stating that I might probably find the speeches of Messrs. Hiestand and Horner worthy a perusal, as they seemed devoted exclusively to the abuse of my sex, and the ridiculing of "old men," who were so indiscreet as to venture upon any subjects in their presence, save the most common-place remarks.

The same evening I received the paper, and found the address to be of the same style as those delivered some months previously by the same gentlemen, and which, strange to state, I had in my possession (not being retained for their rhetorical beauty, but their absurd remarks and inelegant language); and I will now lay them both before the public, with the regret that, like Herastratus, who burned the Temple of Diana at Ephesus, for the purpose of having his name immortalized, the author will gain notoriety by even ignoble means.

On reading the article, I was fired with indignation, and, seizing my pen, wrote hastily a reponse, which I took to the office of one of the leading journals, for publication; but, after retaining it three days, the editor, who desired to publish it, returned it, with the note which you will also find herein. It speaks for itself. I then, *en personne*, asked several editors to publish it, saying that *I in no way feared the* consequences; but though all were solicitous to have it published, each in turn returned it, saying that they feared their offices would be closed by the authorities, and that the greatest difficulty would be that it would never be believed a woman had written it.

But forced to abandon the idea of publishing it, I resolved to place it before the public in this form, and trust that the " Ladies of New Orleans " may not deem their defence as arrived too late. Heaven bless them ! they need none ; but like the little rivulet that though small its offering, it forms a part of the many waters which go to make up the vast ocean, I like it, have contributed one ripple more to the surface of that sea of eulogy, on which the Southern women must ever float triumphant above the malignity and envy of their enemies. With an apology for digression, and quoting Byron, I will place the subject before you.

I must own,
If I have any fault, it is digression,
Leaving my people to proceed alone,
While I soliloquize beyond expression ;
But these are my addresses from the throne,
Which put off business to the ensuing session :
Forgetting each omission is a loss to
The world, not quite so great as Ariosto.

SHAM STATE GOVERNMENT.

" The traitors in New Orleans, who have shifted their allegiance with the same facility that they do their

garments, have held a meeting to precipitate the forma-
tion of a civil government for the State. It does not
appear whether they have been disturbed by any qualms
of conscience concerning the legality of their military
government, or whether they are itching for a share of
power.   It is most likely, since the prominent actors in
the proceedings are lawyers, that the distribution of
the judicial posts, and the desire to open others by the
appointment of a Supreme Court, have been the incen-
tives.   This suggestion derives some plausibility from
the fact that a meeting of those lawyers who dena-
tionalized and degraded themselves by taking the oath,
was recently held to request General Shipley, the
" Military Governor of Louisiana," to appoint a Supreme
Court, or to fill the vacancies in it, Judge Buchanan
having qualified himself for infamy by retracting his
oath of loyalty to the Confederacy, and swearing
another to the United States, with a promptitude that
entitles him to their highest consideration.

We have before us the "Era" of the 15th March,
from which it appears that Dr. Riddell presided at the
meeting of the Union Association to which we have
alluded, and Hiestand was the principal speaker.   The
report proceeds :—

Judge Hiestand took up the question as to the
expediency of organizing a provisional State Government.   He remarked that "at the present critical period
it were far better to raise armies than to make constitutions.   There is no civil government in Louisiana.
Our escutcheon bears an eagle, with the olive branch
in one hand and the thunderbolt in the other.   Until the
rebellion is quelled we should dispense only thunder-

bolts; then make constitutions. I appeal to this assemblage to know if there are not thousands of 'loyal' traitors in New Orleans to-night—men who have taken the oath of allegiance? I ask if there are not men holding high positions in this city to-day who are traitors? The truth must be told, and I am not afraid to tell it. Why do we never see here the faces of our city officials? Their very silence is damning to them. The women of New Orleans yet insult loyal men by the rebel badge in their bonnets, two red roses with a white one in the centre. Our national constitution is strong enough to protect us. Civil government is impracticable in the face of these military operations.

"Mr. President, take away these Federal bayonets and I doubt if you or I would live twenty-four hours, simply because, through all these dark days of rebellion, we have been true to the old flag. Are you aware that on the pine trees across the lake, there is posted a black list containing the names of those who would be instantly sacrificed should New Orleans be retaken? The South has rebelled against progress and the laws of God Almighty. I sleep more soundly at night, because I know I am protected by Federal bayonets. To me, almost a refugee from all I hold dear, the absence of military protection at present would be a degradation worse than damnation itself. Inaugurate civil government and you will give the cotton barons of Caronnelet Street the exclusive control of our liberties. For God's sake, let us do nothing to hazard the lives of our soldiers or ourselves."

It is gratifying to perceive that the perjured miscreants have some foretaste and conception of the doom which certainly awaits them when the day of righteous vengeance shall come.

Mr. Horner and Colonel Field seem not to be so nervous. They insist on a re-establishment of civil government. Hiestand was appointed a judge by Shepley. Horner and Field are out in the cold.

Mr. Horner said the speaker had entirely failed to convince him of the truth of his statements. Our flag is the emblem of progress, not of regress. The great cause of the rebellion has passed away from this section of Louisiana, and all the powers of hell cannot revive it. Every State is guaranteed a republican form of government. We want the reign of bayonets to continue no longer than is absolutely necessary. I am in favour of civil government here. Let us take advantage of the presence of the military to inaugurate it. I have confidence in the integrity and honesty of the masses.

Colonel Field said he could not agree with the doctrines of the first speaker. Have not members of Congress been admitted from Louisiana? Is not civil law in force here? Does not the Governor, as also his judges and justices, administer civil law? Does military law conflict with the exercise of civil right? It was always a principle of our government that the military was subservient to the civil power. I believe in the motto of Senator Davis "Fight, pay, or emigrate." Do you suppose any but a loyal man could be elected to a responsible position here? And yet one of the chief arguments against the establishment of a provisional government is that it would fall into the hands of disloyal men.

Mr. Rozier followed, favouring the scheme, and Madison Day " closed the debate by hoping the rebellion would be crushed before measures were taken to inaugurate civil government," when the further consideration of the question was postponed until the next meeting.

Can any punishment be too rigorous for men who dip their hands so deep in treason? Some commiseration can be felt, and perhaps some excuse made for those who, timid by nature and threatened by starvation to their families, have incurred the guilt of forswearing their country, but the participators in this meeting and others of like principles are bearing a willing allegiance to the enemy. When New Orleans shall again come under our rule they will attempt to justify their conduct on the plea of obligation to obey the authorities, who had the military means to enforce their orders. If our people accept the plea as sufficient they are made of different material than we now believe.

It appears that the traitors propose to fill the various civil offices, governor, judges, legislature, &c. Such proceedings can of course lay no claim to legality, but if the enemy shall control sufficient territory to prevent our election next fall of one-half of the legislature, where will the power of making laws reside? Will it be suspended? Some persons ridicule the argument of Chief Justice Verrick by which he attempts to prove that a majority of those elected within our lines will constitute a constitutional legislature. We do not venture an opinion on the subject. We leave it to lawyers to discuss and judges to decide,

2 E

but if the contrary doctrine be correct, and one-half of the legislature fail of an election by the presence of Federal bayonets, the State will have lost one of the most important attributes of her sovereignty, viz., her legislative function.   Our jocose picture of a heated canvass for the Chief Justiceship, which extorted the judge's argument, will have served to set on foot an investigation of this curious question.

UNION ASSOCIATION.

Meeting at the Lyceum Hall.

Speeches of C. W. Horner, Esq., and Judge Hiestand.

There was another grand gathering of the friends of the Union at Lyceum Hall last night, and, although the weather was rather unpropitious, the attendance on the part of the ladies was very large—showing the deep interest our fair friends take in the Union cause.

. The meeting was presided over by Dr. Schuppert, and Mr. Chadwick acted as secretary.   The president announced that Mr. Horner and Judge Hiestand had been invited to address the Association, and Mr. H. immediately took the stand, and was greeted with a round of applause.

He thanked the audience for their kind welcome on his return.   He came back to them confirmed in the convictions with which he left them—that this rebellion would finally be crushed.   He left New Orleans in the latter part of June, at a time when the clouds of defeat had darkened o'er the land, and the friends of the Union were despondent, if not despairing.   The city was excited to an intense degree.   Hooker had fought the battle of Chancellorsville, and some twelve or fifteen thousand of our fellow-countrymen lay killed or wounded on the bloody field. So much for Hooker! Grant had commenced his campaign in Mississippi, and was besieging the boasted Gibraltar of the rebels. The Confederates were threatening New Orleans, and had all the means at their disposal to make good their threats. Such was the condition of our army when he left the city for the North. Treason was the common conversation in the streets and saloons, and the spiteful "she adders" spit and spluttered more venomously than ever. Arriving at New York, he found the same state of affairs. The Unionists were sad and gloomy; the Copperheads were jubilant, and our friends gave up all as lost. "The game is up," they said, "our money is worthless, our armies are defeated, our leaders outgeneraled;" and hearing them talk, he almost imagined himself back again on Canal Street, standing by the statute of the noble Clay—the great champion of the Union, whose hand of fellowship is always stretched out, not across the way, directing you to "get your shirts at Moody's," but towards the North, as it ever was during his lifetime—he imagined himself standing there and listening to the foul treason of our New Orleans secessionists, for he found the Copperheadism of New York even more bitterly disunion than was the secessionism of New Orleans.

He returned, however, and all was changed. The grand battle of Gettysburg had been fought, crowning the Union arms with a glorious and complete victory. Lee had been hurled back to Virginia in a terrible defeat—discomfited, overwhelmed, and pelted by the

merciless elements. Grant had taken the impregnable
fortress of Vicksburg, and the cowering and starving
garrison had been forced to humble itself before the
Stars and Stripes. And Banks, at Port Hudson, had
re-enacted the same glorious drama, and inscribed his
own, and the names of the heroic army he commanded,
upon the roll of those names who have deserved so well
of their country. He returned to find no indications of
joy in the eyes of the secession ladies, they were as
meek as lambs, and their tongues had lost the accustomed sting. With the traitors all was gloom,
while joy reigned in the heart of each friend of the
Union. It was a glorious change, and had been
wrought by the prowess of our gallant armies on many
a bloody field.

A few days after he got home, he met a very old
and wealthy citizen, who has devoted all his energies
in life to making money, and who had formerly published a newspaper called the "National Advocate," a
Secession sheet, that for the sake of the few picayunes
that it wrung from the hands of its Secession supporters,
was wont to issue an extra every fifteen minutes, containing the most encouraging news of the rebel cause
that could be gathered from the four quarters of the
Confederacy. This old man asked him if he had read
his *brochure*, entitled " The Birth, Life, and Death of the
' National Advocate.' " He replied that he had not, but
since then he has read it, and he found that the old
gentlemen was right in the view he had taken of the
condition of affairs in this State, and of the necessities
of the times, for he therein puts forth the very doctrine
for which we are contending. He is sound in his prin-

ciples, and to prove that he is, the speaker then read
the following extract from the pamphlet alluded to:—

"By the new census, Louisiana is entitled to five
members. Let them be elected on a general ticket,
to be voted for by every white loyal citizen who
has resided in the State a required period; and at the
proper time, let there be a convention to form a new
constitution, providing for an immediate or ultimate
emancipation of slaves."

Napoleon had said that he more dreaded three newspapers than a hundred thousand bayonets; and since he
had been gone from the city three newspapers had
sprung into existence—three loyal papers, advocating
the principles of liberty and free speech—a fact which
shows that freedom of the press and of speech exist
here.

He spoke in terms of commendation of the coloured
schools, and was glad to see the little children of a
down-trodden race receiving the benefits of an education. He hoped these institutions would flourish and
prosper, and that they might prove the germ of a higher
and brighter civilization. It was an indication of the
progress of the times.

He had met a rank Secessionist a few days since,
who seemed to forget his former rancorous feelings, and
had entered into conversation with him. This man expressed an unwillingness to speak on the politics of the
times; but was very anxious about getting rid of
martial law, that the civil authorities should be rein-
stated, and the government of Louisiana be set in
motion once more in the old way; and he asked his
opinion as to the feasibility of adopting some measure

to bring about such a state of affairs. "Sir," said I, "we will never get rid of martial law till we get rid of African slavery. Never can we sever the destinies of Louisiana from the North-west, so long as that grand chain, that perpetual bond of union, the Mississippi, continues to roll her mighty flood down to the great gulf below."

With calm resignation the Roman father of old, bound in chains, awaited the coming of his sons to release him. With equal patience will Louisiana, bound by the chains of slavery, wait, and never accept relief, except at the hands of her own noble sons; and the day is not far distant when they will come in their strength, and strike off her shackles, and she will rise in the grandeur of her newly-acquired liberty, redeemed, regenerated, and disenthralled.

He visited Boston while in the North, and paid his devotions to Liberty at the shrine erected on Bunker Hill. He remembered, too, that this monument commemorated a defeat. It was the first great battle for American liberty, and it was the first defeat. And from this first field of our first struggle for liberty his thoughts turned to the battle-stained plains of Manassas. The coincidence was striking. There, too, had the armies of freedom met defeat in their first encounter; and after we had washed out by our blood all record of our sinful temporizing with foul treason, and had achieved the victory in this second war of independence, by crushing out black rebellion, he wanted to see a monument twice as high as that of Bunker Hill erected upon the plains of Manassas, upon which shall be engraved the words, in letters of gold, "One God, one nation, one people, and one freedom." "Liberty, justice, and truth, now and for ever."

The splendid effort of Mr. Horner, to which we have failed to do justice by this hasty sketch, was received with delight by the audience.

Judge Hiestand was next introduced. As he was slightly indisposed, he feared that he would not be able to entertain or interest his auditors, but his apology was unnecessary, for he made an excellent and powerful speech. We have only room for some of the most important parts this morning, but shall endeavour to give it more in full in our next issue.

He told of his trip to the North—how, like the devout Mahomedan, he had made a pilgrimage to the Meccas of America, to renew his faith and his patriotism, by bowing where our fathers bled for freedom in the early days of the Republic. He had also visited the seat of government, that he might learn from the lips of the President himself the policy he intended to pursue, both with regard to the emancipation proclamation and the return of Louisiana to the Union. In company with Mr. Horner and another citizen of Louisiana he called upon Mr. Lincoln. It was the belief of some in this city that the President would recede from the proclamation freeing the slaves, and he was desirous of being satisfied upon that point. Mr. Lincoln expressed much anxiety that Louisiana should, as soon as it could be consistently done, range herself in line with the other loyal States of the Union; "but at the same time," he remarked, "the loyal people of Louisiana are themselves the best judges as to the moment when such a movement shall become practicable."

In regard to the question of receding from the proclamation, during the conversation on the subject the
President said:—"It is dangerous for a man to say
what he will not do, for thrice did Peter deny his Lord;
but, if I know myself, while I occupy the Presidential
chair, not one jot or tittle of that proclamation shall be
withdrawn."

The interview with the President was in every way
satisfactory.

In New York, Judge Hiestand could not but contrast the universal prosperity of all classes; so marked
was the difference in every respect from the state of
affairs at home, even in the most peaceful times, that he
was convinced there never had been any prosperity in
the South, except that of a privileged class, and the only
way to make our State prosperous is to imitate those
great States of the North, and cast loose from that
crushing incubus which weighs down our energies and
destroys our wealth and power—African slavery.

He spoke of the almost universal determination of
the North to persist in this war till the rebellion was
crushed. He had met with but few who held any other
opinion or desire. As for himself, he wished that he
could stand in the centre of the Confederacy and proclaim the only grounds upon which this struggle can be
brought to a close. He would tell them, "Lay down
your arms, depart from the country, or die!" Twenty
millions will not surrender up their liberties, or be
dictated to by these rebels. They may meet with
reverses, may suffer defeats; but in the end the cause
of justice and humanity will prevail, the rebellion *will
be* crushed, and the Southern States will take their place

once more among the glorious stars that shine with eternal brightness in the American constellation.

In the North he was approached by many with the question : " What are you going to do with the negroes? They are lazy, thievish, and, when freed from the power of their masters, will not work, and what can you do with them?"

He replied : " We will put them in a position to take care of themselves, and then, if they don't do it, why let them go down as other worthless races have done, and let their places be filled by others who will work. We will release them from their chains, and give them liberty to act for themselves. Give them a trial ere we condemn them."

He wished it particularly to be understood that he was no negro worshipper, nor had he ever had any scruples about the morality of slavery ; but the question is, shall we sacrifice that institution or sacrifice our country—the free institutions bequeathed to us by our fathers. Forbid it, Heaven ! He would rather see the earth open and swallow up the entire Confederacy, himself included, than that the rebellion should succeed and such a fate overtake the Republic, which is now the only hope of freedom in the world. The people of the United States are playing for no small stake. He could calculate to a fraction the value of the vast wealth and resources of the country, but he could not calculate the value of that inestimable privilege the freeman enjoys of sitting beneath his own vine and fig tree with none to make him afraid, as he plucks his grapes and figs in peace and freedom. God Almighty never intended that so great a creation should be so lightly destroyed.

He has seen many negroes in New York who were industrious, worked faithfully, were honest and trustworthy, and when he asked those who seemed so deeply concerned about what we would do with the negroes, how they managed to get along with that class of their population, the answer was, " Oh, they are educated.' Well, our negroes are also educated—educated to work, and there is no reason why in their altered condition they should not become as honest and industrious as the same race has proved in the North. He did not wish to be understood as holding the opinion that the negroes can be at once brought into a condition to fully enjoy all the privileges of freedom. It was difficult to elevate a race from absolute slavery to a high state of civilisation immediately, but that was no reason why a commencement should not be made. It is a great political question we have to solve. What shall we do with the 4,000,000 of human beings that have been released from slavery—but that is a secondary matter to the grand object of putting down the rebellion. Let all our energies be directed to the accomplishment of that great task; let us get rid of that first, and then we shall find a way to get rid of the negro question.

In closing, he would take occasion to express his heartfelt satisfaction at the manner in which he was received wherever he went, in the East and in the West. He was warmly and cordially welcomed by his brethren in the great cause of the Union everywhere he went, and could not but feel gratified with the many proofs of friendship that had been exhibited towards him by the supporters of the Union in the loyal States; and when the proper time comes none will rejoice more than he to see Louisiana the first to range herself by their side in the glorious cause of Union and liberty.

He retired from the stand amid loud plaudits of his auditors, and the meeting was adjourned.

Previous to the adjournment Dr. Dostie announced that Colonel A. P. Field and Rufus Waples, Esq., would address the Association on next Saturday evening.

" Messrs. Horner and Hiestand,

" I have read with mingled feelings of disgust and contempt your stump-orator-like address delivered before the audience which assembled at the Lyceum Hall on Saturday evening last. I have always been under the impression that persons who go abroad to see the world, or in other words make a tour, generally return more cultivated and refined; what your claims to the above may have been ere your *extensive* tour I am unable to state, but judging from the feeble, nay, abortive efforts made in your orations of 31st ultimo to find words to convey your ideas, I should say your tour was not like that of ' the dove who flies over the earth and rests upon the beautiful only,' but, like the buzzard, you alighted on nought save *filthy* carrion, and having become impregnated with the stench, you now seek to ' *spit* and *splutter*' it over your hearers, who must have felt themselves degraded, be their politics what they may, at the presumption of individuals so little gifted by nature, as well as education, in advancing such remarks as the extracts teem with. But as your genius seldom soars above the ' *roses* ' in a lady's bonnet, or, at the farthest, the top of ' Moody's signboard,' which board must forcibly remind you of the stained garments of deceit, malice, and treachery in which you walk daily habited. I was not surprised at the spoutings of bad English and *slang*, only suited to the haunts where the dark sons of Africa 'most do congregate.'—A fit orator indeed for the SABLE RACE.

"Though I looked, and looked in vain, for that *high stand* (Hiestand) of rhetoric which I had expected to find *you had assumed*, I found only the sting of the Horner (t) throughout. The next thing to be considered is the entire absence of the bump of reverence in your cranium (which, if you ever possessed it, was certainly by some accident 'stove in'), when you are so lost to everything like veneration as to facetiously dub the gentleman referred to of the National Advocate '*The Old Man.*' Of course we recognize the person thus irreverently alluded to as Jacob Barker, Esq., whose character as a *loyal citizen* you would fain asperse by your *vile* insinuations of Secessionism. Has the *learned* gentleman ever read the history of his country, or does he presume any one else has? Is he aware that the gentleman whom he thus *dares* to tamper with, and hold up to public ridicule, is styled by all who are acquainted with the dark struggle of 1812 – 14, '*The Preserver of the Union?*' Is the *honourable* speaker aware that this 'OLD MAN' furnished the means to carry on the war which led to our final independence, and by his herculean efforts cast into the then empty United States treasury the sum of over *five millions* of dollars, and came gallantly to the rescue of the sinking ship of state when others held tight their purse-strings? Is the very urbane gentleman acquainted with the antecedents of this *old man*, and of the fact of his having 'exhausted all his means and energies' years agone to *preserve* this GLORIOUS UNION, of which all can talk and babble, but few have had the honour of framing? Is he cognizant of these facts? If not I am happy to be able to inform him, but probably *history* can do so more lucidly. 'The great champion of the noble Union,' whom you have termed Henry Clay, was the intimate friend of this '*old man*,' as well as others, many others, too numerous to mention, upon whose brow Fame's laurel wreath has rested. I am fully aware that, in all revolutions, the scum of society rises to the surface for a brief while, but I trust, like all fermentations of a *sappy* nature, it may soon be skimmed off by the *ladle* of *good sense* and *discrimination*. There are some characters which, like the sun, are too effulgent to gaze upon, and pain the vision until, like the sun, they are in eclipse; does the *courteous* and *kind* speaker wish to cast over Jacob Barker, Esq., an eclipse, that his brightness may not be so painful to him? If so he will find himself unsuccessful in his attempts, as the halo of glory which beams upon this '*old man's*' brow will but increase in radience as he nears the shore of eternity. There may be individuals forgetful or ignorant of his worth, but so long as the 'Stars and Stripes' shall wave shall the name of Jacob Barker be dear to every true Unionist. What has excited your animosity against this gentleman is, I presume, his having espoused the cause of the LADIES OF NEW ORLEANS, and his having endeavoured to place them before those in command in the proper light, as well as to discern prejudice. For this act he should have been lauded, instead of being traduced and made the mark for poisoned shafts; and I believe that his remarks *did* find an echo in the heart of every honest

gentleman, be they Unionist or Secessionist. What
must your opinion of yourself be, or what imagine you
must *the public* think of an individual so lost to all claims
to manhood as to employ his *eloquence* (ye gods forgive
for this misnomer!) and pen in the *noble abuse of women?*
Surely you are but a burlesque man, not the elevated,
high-souled being formed to the image and likeness of
God? Truly, there is nought of the Don Quixote in
you. What, presume you, must ·your mother think of
you? I am sure if she were possessed of any of the
principles of a lady she would, if living, blush to acknowledge you, and if dead, *her very ashes would turn a sanguine hue* at the scurrilous vituperations used against her
sex. But, alas! we generally judge the tree by its fruit;
and I pity from my heart a son whose ungentlemanly
conduct has caused me to cast reflection upon the mother.
Have not the ladies of New Orleans been sufficiently
humiliated in seeing their beautiful city in the possession
of strangers? and have they not suffered enough of
anguish in being deprived of all that life holds dear, viz.,
the presence of husbands, fathers, sons, and brothers,
parted never to meet again on earth? If they choose
to wear a few blossoms twined from *memory's* wreath,
(even be they *red*, *white* and *red*), should this be cause
for such *wholesale abuse?* Are ladies whose presence you
would not *dare* to enter to calmly submit to such insolence, because you deem yourself protected by a *row of*
bayonets? (Judge H——, I believe, is the one who
objected so strongly to the *military government* being dispensed with, as he considered *himself safe* only when
behind a rampart of steel.) Forbid it, Heaven! I am
a lady, and as such pronounce you CONTEMPTIBLE

POLTROONS.   If there be any females who are so devoid
of the respect and homage that is due to their sex as to
endorse anything you have said or may say, I would
suggest to them to weave a chaplet of *spotless unfading
mushrooms for the brow of this modern Cicero and
Demosthenes.*

"N.B.—Will the very erudite speaker be so kind as
to inform us where the Meccas of America are geo-
graphically situated, or whom he deems the Mahomets
of the Western world, as he so generously and gratuit-
ously informs us of the situation of the '*gulf below?*'
But possibly we were mistaken as to the point to which
the gentleman would fain direct our attention, and that
it is not the Gulf of Mexico to which he refers, but the
fiery gulf of which we read in Scripture, towards which,
in my mind's eye, I see him rapidly approaching in the
steam-frigate 'Self-Importance,' whose figure-head is a
'SHE ADDER.'"*

"———— Office,

"Miss F. J. O'Connor.

"I am very sorry I cannot have the pleasure of publishing the communication, but *I'm over-ruled*.   Indeed,
I find it is considered a much more dangerous document
than I can regard it, so much so, that parties who have
hitherto printed similar effusions, now refuse to do this.
'Order,' you are aware, 'reigns in Warsaw,' and with it
a very successful system of espionage, one begotten in
fear, and pursued in the interest of the first law of
nature—self-preservation.   The Unionists would band
together, and hunt down, like a pack of bloodhounds,
the author and publisher of such a writing.   To my

* The name given to females by General Butler.

own knowledge they have done such things already, and the military authorities were compelled to sustain them, and to punish by heavy fine the authors of some pasquinades on Doske and others. Even the distributors of them were also fined. Believe me, you are giving those creatures an undue importance when you consider their ' bad eminence.' ·

> " So do not honour him so much
> To prick thy finger, though to wound his heart ;
> What valour were it, when a cur doth grin,
> For one to thrust his hand between his teeth,
> When he might spurn him with his foot away."

"Your obedient servant."

*. *. *****

PRINTED BY HARRISON AND SONS, ST. MARTIN'S LANE.

www.ingramcontent.com/pod-product-compliance
Lightning Source LLC
Chambersburg PA
CBHW030948110726
47900CB00004B/1179